THE DEATH CHAMBER

Also by Sarah Rayne

SPIDER LIGHT
ROOTS OF EVIL
A DARK DIVIDING
TOWER OF SILENCE

Visit www.sarahrayne.co.uk

THE DEATH CHAMBER

Sarah Rayne

SIMON & SCHUSTER

LONDON • NEW YORK • TORONTO • SYDNEY

First published in Great Britain by Simon & Schuster UK Ltd, 2008
A CBS COMPANY

Copyright © Sarah Rayne, 2008

Simon & Schuster UK Ltd
Africa House
64–78 Kingsway
London WC2B 6AH

Simon & Schuster Australia
Sydney

A CIP catalogue record for this book is available from the British Library

ISBN: 978-0-7394-9685-5

Typeset by Rowland Phototypesetting Ltd, Bury St Edmunds, Suffolk
Printed and bound in Great Britain by CPI Mackays

AUTHOR'S ACKNOWLEDGEMENTS

Research for this book has necessarily been very varied. However, I do wish to record my thanks to the following people, who very generously helped me to establish the accuracy of certain facts.

Mr G. Hendry, Governor of Shrewsbury Prison.
Bev Baker, Collections Manager, Galleries of Justice Museum, Nottingham.
Tony Duggan, for valuable assistance with miscellaneous research.
Stewart McLaughlin, whose book, *Execution Suite*, has been of great help.

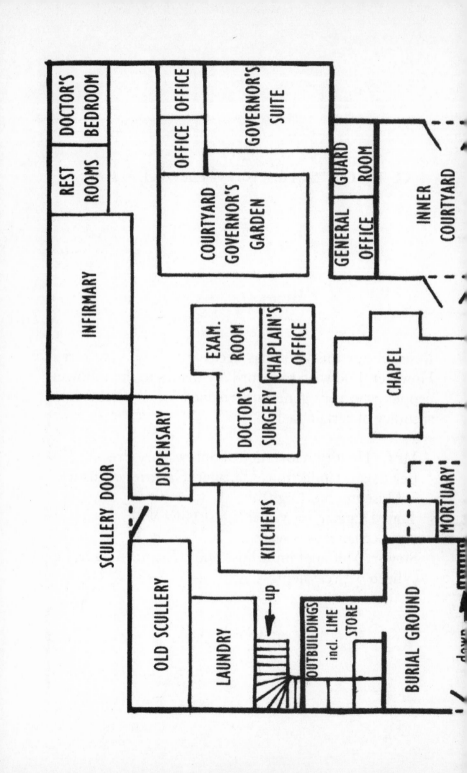

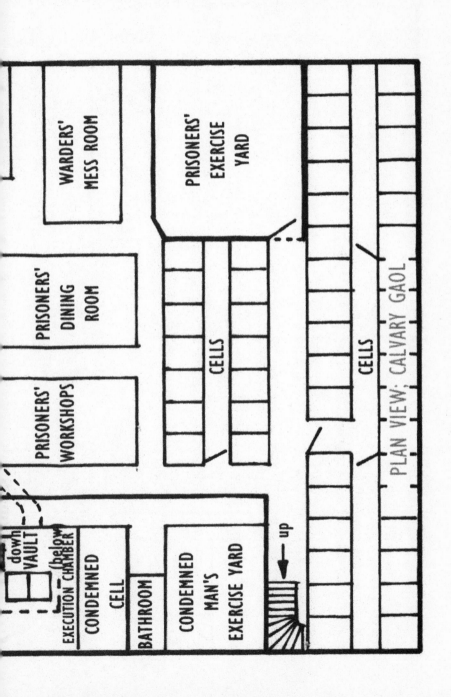

PLAN VIEW; CALVARY GAOL

WARDERS' MESS ROOM

PRISONERS' EXERCISE YARD

PRISONERS' DINING ROOM

PRISONERS' WORKSHOPS

CELLS

CELLS

CELLS

down VAULT
(below)
EXECUTION CHAMBER
CONDEMNED CELL
BATHROOM
CONDEMNED MAN'S EXERCISE YARD

up

CHAPTER ONE

Georgina read the letter a second time – and then a third – because it was so extraordinary there was a strong possibility she had misunderstood it. The heading was impressive. In ornate lettering, it announced itself as being, 'The Caradoc Society for the pursuit of knowledge of psychic phenomena and the paranormal. Founded 1917.'

15 October 20—

Dear Miss Grey

I am asked by the trustees of the Caradoc Society to enquire if you might be able to help us with the disposal of the Society's assets.

This was the first astonishing statement, although to someone who had spent the last ten days trying to count up the damage wrought by a cheating business partner, the word 'assets' struck an optimistic note. The fact that the business partner had not only absconded with most of the money but had taken David with her was not making Georgina's task any easier.

The writer of the letter went on to explain, with careful politeness, that it had recently been decided to bring the Society and its activities to an end. Georgina thought the wording suggested this was a decision taken voluntarily, which was cheering to someone who had just been made abruptly and comprehensively broke.

As you will know, the generous bequest in 1940 from your great-grandfather, Dr Walter Kane, enabled the Society to buy its present headquarters – Caradoc House. Unfortunately the house must now be sold and the greater part of the proceeds used to pay off our debts. However, we are told there should be a little money left over, and the Society's solicitor believes that any credit balance can legally be passed to Dr Kane's descendants. The Society's bankers also feel this to be reasonable.

However, just to strengthen this decision, it would be helpful if you, and any other direct descendants of Dr Kane could provide family papers – perhaps letters written by Dr Kane around the time he created the Trust. We have a few documents which came to us on his death, which we shall, of course, pass on to you.

I look forward to hearing from you, and if you felt you could travel to Thornbeck to bring any appropriate papers to us, we would be very pleased to see you. The King's Head has quite pleasant accommodation, or we have a tiny flatlet in Caradoc

House itself which in the past we have used for visiting speakers. You would be most welcome to make use of that as our guest.

Yours sincerely
Vincent N. Meade
Secretary to Caradoc Society

Clearly Vincent N. Meade assumed Georgina knew all about great-grandfather Walter Kane's bequest, but this was the first she had heard of it. She did not really know much about Walter at all, except that he had been a prison doctor in Cumbria in the 1930s and had apparently abandoned his wife and small daughter to live abroad. A bequest to a society dedicated to psychic research was intriguingly at odds with the image of a prison doctor.

Georgina had no clear idea what kind of evidence would substantiate her claim to any leftover moneys from the Thornbeck set up: ordinary proof of identity would surely be enough on its own. But the possession of letters from or to Walter might be a useful addition, in the way that correspondence about paintings or porcelain were useful in creating a provenance. It was just possible there might be something in the bundle of family photographs which had been stored in the attic since Georgina's parents died nearly ten years ago. She pulled on an old tracksuit and skewered her hair on top of her head with a clip before climbing up there. It was cramped and awkward in the attic and stiflingly hot. It was unexpectedly good to realize there was no likelihood of David coming in and making disparaging remarks: 'Goodness, George, you *have* made a fright of yourself, haven't you?' or frowning at dispossessed spiders that had scuttled angrily down into the flat.

There weren't any photos of Walter in the suitcase, which was annoying because Georgina was getting interested in him and would have liked to know what he had looked like. Had he had the family grey eyes and lightish brown hair?

There were several tattered medical articles – none of which had been written by Walter – and some faded postcards sent from unidentifiable people and places, but these would not be the kind of thing Vincent N. or the Caradoc Society solicitor wanted. Was there anything else? She picked out a handwritten letter dated September 1940, and felt a wholly illogical thump of pleasurable anticipation at seeing the words in graceful handwriting, 'My dear Walter' at the head.

The letter had a Thornbeck address, and was signed by Lewis Caradoc.

I am glad to know you are still safe. Up here, we are managing to dodge the bombing, in fact we are very free of raids, although I cannot dissuade my wife from making her regular visits to London. Even after so many years she is still searching for people to replace that infamous pair of tricksters in Finchley, but I never question her activities, just as she never questions mine. Are you smiling that narrow-eyed smile as you read that, my dear Walter?

My very warmest regards to you, my dear boy. Try to remain safe if you can – after all we went through together I should be devastated to lose you.

4

I was very interested to hear you have invited a young nurse to dinner on your forthcoming leave – are you going to succumb to romance at last? I hope so, and I look forward to hearing more. The Berkeley Grill was as good as ever the last time I was there, but if you do decide on the Hungaria, mention my name to Luigi, and I'm sure he will find you a decent table.

Georgina rather liked the sound of Lewis Caradoc who had been known at the Berkeley Grill and the Hungaria and had made that dry remark about his activities not being questioned by his wife. Who had the Finchley tricksters been? And had it been her own great-grandmother Walter had been taking to dinner? The dates would be about right.

She thought she would telephone Vincent N. Meade to explain about this letter, and ask if it would be of use. It was a pity it did not provide any clues about why Walter had left money to psychic research, though. Might there be answers in Thornbeck itself? If Georgina went there, would she find them? More to the point, could she afford to go there?

'Just about,' said Georgina's accountant, who was trying to tow her out of this financial crisis, 'but you're running dangerously low.'

'I know.'

'What about this place?' She cast a sharp professional eye over the small Chelsea shop, the lease of which had cost Georgina everything she owned and a bit more besides because freeholders in London demanded your life blood like Dracula, if not your soul, as a down payment like Faust. 'From the look of it you won't be able to afford to keep it on by yourself.'

'I know.'

'How long has the lease actually got to run? . . . *How* long? Oh dear. You'd better try to sub-let. And there's the stock.' This was said with a glance at the fabric swatches, books of wallpaper patterns, and the narrow shop window with the careful display of chairs covered in William Morris patterned material and silky waterfalls of fabric. Georgina and the perfidious partner had tried to be thrifty over the buying in of fabrics and papers, but it had been necessary to have bales of material for curtains and sofa coverings on hand, and to have a few choice pieces of furniture to set colours and materials against as well.

'You'll probably have to sell what you can,' said the accountant, having taken in the nearly Chippendale chairs, the little Regency table and a few other things. Some pieces had been bought quite cheaply in street markets, but the sort of clients Georgina and her partner had been targeting knew the difference between Christie's and the Portobello Road, so the showroom furniture had had to be good. 'You'll only get a fraction of what you originally paid, anyway.'

'I know.'

'George, I wish you'd stop saying you know and think what you're going to do next.'

'I know exactly what I'm going to do next,' said Georgina. 'I'm going to drive up to Thornbeck to find out about my great-grandfather's peculiar bequest to this Caradoc Society.'

'Is there likely to be any money in it?'

'Well, that's not why I'm going, but if I'm lucky I might get next month's rent out of it.'

'Where will you stay in Thornbeck?'

'At Caradoc House. The local pub's a bit booked up. Vincent Meade says a television company's in Thornbeck – they're assessing whether to use an old prison in some programme that focuses on unusual buildings. C.R. Ingram's researching the possibility.'

'That sounds rather fun,' said the accountant. 'Is it the C.R. Ingram who writes those books about ancient cultures and the human psyche and the power of the imagination and whatnot?'

'I think so. I don't expect there's more than one C.R. Ingram.'

'He's quite eminent,' said the accountant. 'I saw that TV documentary he did last year about the empty reassurances of religion. He followed it up with a book.'

'*Talismans of the Mind*,' said Georgina. 'I didn't read it, but I saw the programme.'

'Didn't the Archbishop of Canterbury condemn it, or the Pope issue a proclamation or something?'

'I don't think it got as far as that,' said Georgina. 'One or two vicars might have objected.'

'Still, he's probably worth meeting if you can engineer it, although personally I wouldn't trust a man who goes by his initials.'

'I wouldn't trust any man at all,' said Georgina, and went to phone estate agents about sub-letting the shop and after that to look out road maps for the journey to Cumbria.

*

The drive to Thornbeck took longer than Georgina expected, but she did not mind because it almost felt as if she was leaving the tangled mess of faithless lovers and failed business ventures behind, and entering a different world altogether. By the time she got onto the north-bound M6, she was thinking how good it was not to have David with her unfavourably comparing her car with newer, faster ones on the road and looking out for hotels and restaurants with Egon Ronay stars where they could have lunch. Remembering this Georgina took a perverse pleasure in pulling into a service station near Coventry, and buying ham rolls and fruit which she ate in the car.

By the time she left the motorway it was growing dark. The roads were becoming steeper and mountains reared up on the horizon; they were bleakly mono-chrome in the failing light and slightly menacing, but Georgina thought them beautiful. You could plan an entire room in those colours; rather minimalist it would have to be. Soft grey walls, with inset oblongs of cream ... velvety sofas in that really deep charcoal that was not quite black but much darker than grey ... modern, matt black pottery ... She remembered with a fresh stab of bitterness that the days of planning beautiful rooms were temporarily on hold.

The further north she went, the more the place names began to have the cadences of Old England, and even of Middle Earth. Ambleside and Ravenglass; Thirlspot and Drigg; Grizedale Forest. This was all unexpectedly restful.

She skirted Wast Water, which was the loneliest, most broodingly sullen stretch of water she had ever seen, and thought that if the car broke down out here she would be marooned. Probably she would become one of the many ghosts that lurked here, and people of the future would refer sombrely to an early twenty-first-century traveller who had vanished one late-autumn day. 'No one knew where she came from,' they might say, 'and no one ever knew what happened to her, but on moonless nights her shade can occasionally be seen, wringing its hands . . .'

This image cheered Georgina up so much that she drove all the way round Wast Water singing the famous feminist anthem, 'I Will Survive' with discordant defiance, after which, in deference to the surroundings, she went on to 'River Deep, Mountain High'. At least David was not there to wince, make sarcastic comments and pointedly switch on the radio.

She reached a set of crossroads, and pulled onto the side of the road to check the map. Straight across, sharp right, and then it was about six miles to Thornbeck, which was the merest fleck on the map. Good. She had just taken the right turn, when she saw the weather-beaten signpost with its worn lettering pointing down a narrow lane leading away from the main road. It was the kind of lane that was so narrow you might easily miss it altogether, but Georgina did not miss it. She slowed down to study it.

TO CALVARY it said, and underneath, in smaller, faded letters, were the words, TWO MILES, and a tiny arrow pointing the way.

Calvary. It was not precisely a place name you would expect to see on a signpost in the heart of this quintessentially English countryside in the twenty-first century, but it was a deeply evocative word. You had only to see it written or hear it spoken aloud, and you instantly saw the image of the hill in Jerusalem, and the stark rearing silhouette of the crucifixion. It did not matter if you had not travelled any further east than the Norfolk Broads, or if you had spent your life in a remote Tibetan valley and never been within hailing distance of a Christian church; it was an image that everyone, regardless of beliefs or disbeliefs, recognized.

Georgina recognized these images as well as anyone, but for her the word also conjured fragments of memories handed down within her family. 'Your great-grandfather was a doctor . . .' 'He worked in a prison – Calvary Gaol in Cumbria, where they took condemned men to be executed . . .'

So down that lonely looking lane was Calvary. Had Walter lived there – had he been entitled to prison quarters – or had he had a house somewhere nearby? Georgina wished all over again that she knew more about him. It was somehow unfair of him not to have left any memories behind, although it made him rather a good ancestor because it made him mysterious.

Georgina thought the landscape would have looked much the same in Walter's time. He must have known this road; he must have travelled along it dozens of times and turned down the narrow lane. Am I going to do that now? thought Georgina, still staring up at the sign.

She put the car into gear and drove on to Thornbeck, leaving Calvary and its disturbing echoes firmly behind her.

October 1938

Walter Kane almost missed the signpost to Calvary Gaol, but he saw it at the last minute and swung the car sharply across the road and into the narrow lane.

It had been quite a long drive to Thornbeck, but it had been fun because he was still enjoying the novelty of owning a car. It had been an extravagant purchase – if his mother had been alive, she would have been deeply shocked. A very imprudent thing to have done, she would have said. The action of a spendthrift. Oh Walter, how could you be so feckless? It had always been tacitly understood that when Walter reached twenty-one and inherited his father's money outright, it would be sensibly invested. To provide a little income, his mother said; that's what you want, Walter, because you won't make a lot of money from doctoring: don't expect that you will.

Walter had not said he did not want to make money from being a doctor, and he had not said he did not want his father's money, either. On his twenty-first birthday he had deposited it in a bank, vowing he would have to be in very dire financial straits indeed before he touched it, but he had relented sufficiently to draw out enough to buy the car – a dogged little Austin Seven. It was not really so very spendthrift of him: if he was offered this Calvary appointment a car would be very useful in such a remote place.

No. Let's be honest about one thing if about nothing else, he thought. The car is because I don't want any comparisons between this journey and the one my father took along this road over twenty years ago. I want to arrive at Calvary as my own master, in command of my own life, and I don't want any ghosts travelling with me.

But the ghosts were with him anyway and, as he drove along the narrow road towards the prison, he found himself thinking that the landscape could not have changed very much since 1917. There might have been fewer houses then, although the farmhouse across the fields would have existed – to an untrained eye it looked Elizabethan. I don't suppose you'd have seen it, though, said Walter to the memory of his father. You wouldn't have seen the lanes or the hedgerows either. Oh damn, in another minute I'll be conjuring up a reproachful spectre from the past, like something out of *Hamlet*, doomed to walk the night, forbidden to tell the secrets of the prison-house. That would be just like my father, as well, because from all accounts he was fond of dramatic gestures.

But there were no such things as ghosts and if this particular prison-house did have secrets it could keep them locked inside its walls, because he did not want to know what they were. He would not think about them. He would think instead that his appointment with the board of prison governors was for three o'clock, and if he did not drive a bit faster he would be late. He had no intention of being late, or of doing anything that might jeopardize his chances of getting this job. He wondered if there would be a house to go with it. It had not been mentioned in the correspondence, but perhaps they would discuss it during the interview.

He rounded a curve in the lane, and there, looking down from a gentle slope of the English countryside, was Calvary. The place of execution set on the hill.

CHAPTER TWO

'It's one of the original murderers' prisons,' said Chad Ingram, studying the photographs spread out on the table in the King's Head coffee room. 'It's two hundred years old and brimful of memories, and its execution shed must be absolutely boiling with despair, terror and hatred.'

The youngest member of Chad Ingram's team, who was a final-year student on loan from Harvard University, and who was bowled over by England in general and by Dr Ingram's glossy British courtesy in particular, studied the photographs with absorption and said it was a sinister-looking place.

'It does look quite sinister but I think that's partly because it's built on the top of that sloping ground,' said Chad. 'It makes it seem as if it's staring down at everything.'

'I don't suppose you want my opinion,' said the third member of the team.

'But you think it's a waste of time being here,' said Chad, smiling.

'Oh God, the ultimate nightmare – a boss who reads minds. But yes, I do think it's a waste of time,' said Drusilla. 'Calvary's much too well known. You'll never get objective reactions to it.'

The Harvard student considered Drusilla's statement and then diffidently supported it. His name, to his end-less annoyance, was Phineas Farrell, although luckily most people settled for calling him Phin. He said, 'See, what we're trying to do is prove whether or not buildings might have the imprint of their pasts, or if people just react to what they already know, right?'

'Quite right, Phin. That's why we're avoiding places like the Tower of London or Glamis Castle.'

'Family monsters and beheaded queens,' said Drusilla. 'Too predictable for words. Unless, of course you want to send your viewers to sleep.'

'But Calvary will almost fall into the same category as those two,' said Phin, who had secretly been hoping Dr Ingram's project would take in the Tower and Glamis but would not now have admitted this to save his life. 'People mightn't know the actual history of Calvary, but unless they're – uh – Martians or some-thing they'd know what happened inside a condemned cell.'

'I'd have to agree with Phin on that,' said Drusilla. 'People will be halfway to seeing ghosts before you so much as switch on a tape recorder. Actually, Chad, I'm surprised you got permission to film.'

'The government's trying to sell the entire building,' said Chad. 'I think they're hoping a TV programme will help – it sounded as if they were having a bit of difficulty getting a buyer.'

'I'm not surprised,' said Drusilla at once. 'There isn't, actually, a great deal you can do with a defunct gaol, is there?'

'There must be all kinds of things. You could, um, convert it to something, or you could just mow it down and rebuild on the site.'

'It's a Grade II listed building,' said Chad.

'Oh, I see.'

'And they think getting it on TV will help them to flog it? Phooey,' said Drusilla. 'But listen, if they pay me enough to retire to the Bahamas I'll wait for a moonless night and burn the place down so they can claim on the insurance. Phin, you can help me, it'll add some excitement to your life.'

Phin, who felt he was having more than enough excitement in his life as it was but who was beginning to understand British irony, said gravely that he would carry the matches.

'Before you get involved in your arson plot, could we hear what you've unearthed about Calvary, Phin?'

Phin put on his glasses and reached for his notes. He had taken a great deal of care over his research, and had smoothed his cowlick of hair into place for this meeting so as to look serious and scholarly – he hated the way it tumbled down when he got enthusiastic over things. Drusilla said it made him look like an eager yak, but Phin had tried having it cut before he left home and his father had told him he looked like a convict. Phin would rather look like a yak than a convict, so he had let it grow.

He read his notes aloud. Calvary Gaol had been built

in 1790, and was credited with an average of eight hangings a year. 'That sounds kind of a high figure because it's quite a small gaol, but in its day it served a wide area. And it's not so high when you compare it with Newgate or Tyburn. It dealt with a lot more than eight executions in the early years, but then they stopped hanging people for sheep stealing or poaching, or for . . .' He frowned, then said, 'This one's a little flaky, but it seems that it used to be a capital offence to lie in wait for victims with the aim of disabling their tongues or slitting their noses.' The other two appeared to accept this without comment and Phin supposed the British were used to the eccentricities of their laws. 'And then from around the early 1800s the death sentence was often commuted to transportation so the figures go right down. Calvary still gets an impressive total, though.'

He turned a page, losing his place in the process, and Drusilla said, 'The suspense is killing me.'

'Anyhow, overall it's had about eight hundred executions.'

'I knew it would be some frightfully grisly quantity.'

'Was the execution shed in use all the way through?' asked Chad. 'Or did they trundle one of those scaffold carts out and prop it against the wall for the occasion?'

'They built an entire death block right at the start, and they used the same execution chamber all the way back from 1790,' said Phin, thankful he had anticipated this question and had the answer ready.

'Oh, wonderful. Two hundred years of concentrated despair in one place. We'll all be positively wallowing in melancholy and *Weltschmerz* by the time we get the cameras in.'

'Did you pick up any individual cases?' asked Chad, ignoring this. 'Neville Fremlin was executed at Calvary, wasn't he?'

'Wait a bit and I'll find ... Yes. Neville Fremlin, hanged in October 1938.'

'Oh well, then I rest my case,' said Drusilla. 'I shouldn't think there's anyone in existence – except possibly your Martians, Phin – who hasn't heard of Neville Fremlin, even seventy or so years on. Even I've heard of him.'

'The press of the day called him the Silver-Tongued Murderer,' said Chad thoughtfully. 'All his victims were women, weren't they? But Fremlin's secondary to our project. You might almost call him a bonus.'

'Whatever you call him, he reinforces my point,' said Drusilla. 'Fremlin was one of the better-known murderers of the twentieth century, which means that the place where he was hanged is nearly as famous. Anyone we put in there will know its history. It wouldn't be a clean slate.'

'I know it won't,' said Chad. 'That's why we're going to use someone who won't know Calvary's history.'

'Wouldn't that be kind of difficult?' asked Phin.

'Only if he really has got a Martian lined up and I wouldn't put it past him.'

Chad leaned forward, his face alight with enthusiasm, and Phin stared at him and thought Dr Ingram must be at least forty but when he became keen on a thing – like he was keen now – he looked at least fifteen years younger and you felt as if a magnet had suddenly sparked into life.

'An uninfluenced subject isn't so difficult,' he was

saying. 'And it wouldn't need to be a Martian, either. There's a colleague of mine – his name's Jude Stratton, and . . . Yes, Drusilla? D'you know Jude?'

'I know of him,' said Drusilla, who had looked up at the sound of the name. 'He was a freelance journalist, wasn't he? Foreign affairs mostly. He used to do a lot of stuff for documentaries and programmes like *Newsnight*.'

'Yes, but two years ago he turned to full-time writing.'

'You mean after he was in the bomb blast in the Middle East.'

'Yes,' said Chad, looking at her very levelly. 'I did mean that.'

'The blast blinded him,' said Drusilla slowly. 'Permanently. I remember the news reports.' She looked at Chad. 'Have I got this right? You're going to put a blind man into Calvary without telling him where he is – and see how it affects him? Watch his reactions to the atmosphere of the place?'

'And then make a television programme from it?' said Phin.

'That's exactly what I'm going to do,' said Chad. 'Jude Stratton is going to spend a night in Calvary's execution shed without knowing where he is.'

'You can't do it,' said Drusilla, and from her tone Phin realized that for once she had forgotten about being languid. 'I know you're my boss, and I know I'm not always entirely respectful—'

'You're hardly ever respectful.'

'But you simply can't do it. It's – it's inhumane.'

'It's not,' said Chad. 'I've already talked to Jude – he's intrigued and curious and he'll do it. He'll be a good subject, as well – he's certainly got his fair share of imagination, but he's also extremely analytical. I'm driving back to London tonight to collect him. I'll stay at his flat overnight and, traffic permitting, we'll be back here late tomorrow afternoon. We'll make the experiment tomorrow evening.'

'You'll never manage the practicalities,' said Drusilla. 'He'll realize where he is.'

'He won't know precisely. He'll probably get the sense of travelling north, but that'll be all.'

'At the very least he'll pick up regional accents and know which part of the country he's in.'

'I don't know that it matters if he does. But we can minimize that risk. If he doesn't come into the bar he won't hear many people. I'll arrange for him to have a meal in his room, and we'll drive him to Calvary about nine. He says he'll bring a Walkman or an MP3 player, and listen to Mozart as we go in. That way he won't get any clues until he's where we want him. Did you get the keys, Drusilla?'

'Yes, the solicitor – what's his name? Huxley Small – left them at reception. I picked them up and got cornered by that man from the Caradoc Society at the same time.'

'Vincent Meade,' said Phin. 'He's very eager to help us.'

'I don't know about eager, I thought he was bloody pushy,' said Drusilla. 'He's already written an intro script for us – he pressed it into my hand and closed my fingers over it.'

'Have you looked at it? Is it any good?'

'Flowery,' said Drusilla. 'In fact he's rather flowery

himself. I have to admit he knows quite a bit about Calvary, though.'

'Then he might be useful at some point.' Chad stood up. 'If I'm going to get to London by tonight I'd better set off. Phin, I'd suggest you came with me – there'd be room at Jude's flat for you and you'd be perfectly welcome – but I don't think there'd be room for you in the car.'

'Because of the equipment?' Phin was by now used to the jumble of cameras and recording machines which usually littered Dr Ingram's car. It made for an uncomfortable journey but at least it took your mind off Dr Ingram's driving which was just about the worst Phin had ever encountered.

Chad grinned. 'No, not equipment. Jude's bringing a few bottles of wine with him and some caviar and smoked salmon. He says if he's taking part in one of my wild experiments he'll do so in civilized comfort.'

Phin thought it would take a certain amount of style to walk into an unknown building you could not see, suspecting there was something sinister about it but listening to Mozart as you went and eating caviar while you camped out. He was starting to look forward to meeting Jude Stratton.

Jude Stratton had tided his flat in readiness for Chad Ingram's visit, doing so in the impatient, but organized way which had become a habit over the last two years. The necessary enforcement of routines and systems had not come naturally to him, and there were still times when, in bitter fury against the stifling black wall perpetually before his eyes, he flung things about, not caring where they landed or what they hit. The specialist nurse who had tried to teach him the ways of the blind – the little practical tricks designed to make life easier – had said severely that this was simply a waste of time and energy; since he insisted on continuing to live on his own, at some point he would have to pick up whatever he had thrown, and if he broke a mirror or a window he would very likely walk into the splintered glass in bare feet and end up in hospital.

Jude had not cared and had said so. But in the end he started to adopt the ways he had been taught, although there were still too many times when anger got the better of him. He supposed those times would get fewer, and he even supposed he might one day become used to being blind, although he would never be resigned.

Chad Ingram's project had intrigued him, although he had proposed it in terms so guarded Jude had said that if it turned out to be a plot to overthrow the House of Windsor or infiltrate the White House, he could count him out. 'And if it involves reality television, I'd rather have the insurrection.'

'It's not reality television and it's not insurrection,' Chad had said. 'It's completely seemly and perfectly proper. I just want you to spend a few hours in a building – a building you'll never have entered before – and see what emotions get dredged up. I can't tell you what it is, or even where it is, because that might give you a clue.'

The chances were that it would be a follow-on from one of Chad's recent projects – that television documentary he had done about the spurious safety net of religion – *Talismans of the Mind*. It had been vividly presented and the subjects covered controversial and it had caught the public's imagination. On the strength of the programme a publisher brought out a book which had gone straight into the bestseller lists.

If Jude had been a betting man he would have put money on there being some kind of ghost legend in Chad's latest venture. He thought that was all right; he thought he would not be fazed by other people's ghosts; it was his own ghosts he could not handle. The ghosts of all those journeys with the camera crews and the interpreters to the war-torn zones of the Middle East, none of them really knowing what they might have to face, most of them frightened but managing to hide the fear under flippancy. And then that last trip, when the bomb had gone off near the Syrian border and the world had exploded in a searing display of sky rockets and comets. When the sky rockets had died away, there had been the appalling realization that there was nothing in front of his eyes but a smothering darkness.

Still, after the coping with the ravages of rose-red cities with biblical names and histories older than time, and pretending to dodge bombs as if they were no more troublesome than mosquitoes, spending a few hours in a haunted house would be a stroll in the park. So Jude had agreed to Chad's request, remarking that he had never thought he would find himself taking part in one of Chad's bizarre experiments.

'It's very lucrative bizarre-ness, especially if the programme gets made. I'll even put you on the strength for expenses.'

'Can you afford me?'

'Can anyone afford you?' said Chad, and on that note had rung off.

Jude had enjoyed the conversation and he would enjoy being with Chad again. He packed a suitcase, identifying clothes by the small squares of fabric sewn into the hems. This was one of the many things he had been taught, and it was one of the many things he had initially resisted. Who cared what you wore? he had said angrily, but the nurse had said people did care and he did not want to find he had put on a dinner jacket to go shopping in the supermarket or worn an anorak on a hot dinner date.

'Some chance of dinner dates, hot or otherwise,' Jude had said, beating down the stab of regret for Fenella who had ended their relationship, employing her own brand of hurtful flippancy. ('Really, Jude, darling, can you see me toting a lover with a white stick and dark glasses, now honestly, *can* you? In any case, we were never even within hailing distance of the sickness and health stuff, were we?') He had pretended to agree and not to care, but Fenella's behaviour had hurt.

He closed the case, feeling for the lock, and closed his mind to the past at the same time. He had already found that the only way to cope was by not looking back.

October 1938

Walter Kane knew there were times when the only way to cope was by not looking back into the past.

He was not sure, however, if this was going to be possible at Thornbeck. The governing board of Calvary might not know who he was, but Sir Lewis Caradoc certainly would. Walter had not been able to decide if that would be awkward. Still, Caradoc's letter had been friendly and courteous, although Walter already knew this was an extremely courteous man.

'If you could arrange to arrive in Thornbeck at around midday,' Caradoc had written, 'it would be my pleasure to give you lunch at my house. As you are probably aware it's some years since I held the post of Calvary's governor, but I still take an interest in it and the present board are kind enough to consult me on administrative decisions. For that reason, if for no other, I should very much like to meet you.'

Walter, understanding that the lunch was probably an informal preliminary interview, had written back to accept, and Sir Lewis had sent directions on how to find his house. It was a slight surprise when he turned out to live in the old farmhouse Walter had admired from the road.

'Were you thinking I've chosen to remain in Calvary's shadow?' said Sir Lewis, welcoming him, and Walter, who had not expected quite such perception or direct-ness, said, 'Yes, I was thinking that. It's a beautiful house, though.'

'It is, isn't it? Parts of it are Tudor. It's much too beautiful for a discussion about the judicial killing of murderers, but we'd better discuss it anyway.'

It was slightly disconcerting to take a seat in the mellow, low-ceilinged room, and know that the man facing him across the table had lived most of his life among convicted killers. Caradoc must be sixty at least but he had the energy of a man far younger, and his eyes were dark and intelligent. There was no one else present; Walter tried to remember if there was a Lady Caradoc and could not.

'Hanging's an ugly business, Dr Kane,' said Sir Lewis. 'I make no apology for talking about it while we eat, by the way: if you get this job that kind of ugliness will be part of your life.'

'I understand that. And I'm aware that hanging's an ugly process.'

'It's squalid and raw.' Caradoc studied Walter for a moment. 'And,' he said softly, 'whatever your private beliefs, hanging a man is a distressing business.'

They looked at one another. Then Walter said, 'You're thinking of my father, aren't you, sir?'

'Ah. So you do know what happened to him,' said Caradoc. 'I wasn't sure whether you did.'

'I do know.'

'You can't have been more than seven when he died. Hardly old enough to have understood.'

'I didn't understand,' said Walter. 'Not then, not properly. But later on I did.'

'Did you know I was Calvary's governor at the time?' said Sir Lewis.

'Yes.' No need to delve into that memory of over twenty years ago: a younger Sir Lewis seated behind a desk and Walter's mother seated opposite him, her face hidden by a thick veil but the tear marks nonetheless visible.

'Say goodbye to your father, Walter . . .' That was what she had said as they were taken down the long passages with the cold stone floors. For a moment, he could see his own seven-year-old self, frightened and bewildered, not understanding why he had been brought into a place of clanging doors and turning locks, and of people looking at him with pity.

'Say goodbye, Walter, that's what we're here for.'

'Yes,' said Walter at last. 'I did know you were at Calvary then.'

'I thought you must.' Sir Lewis frowned and then said, 'Dr Kane, you're young to be a prison doctor, but your qualifications are very good indeed and I think the board will look favourably on your application. There's no reason why any of them should connect you with your father. You've changed your name – it's only a slight change, but it's remarkable how different Kane sounds from O'Kane. And it's not for me to grill you about your work, but there is one question I'd like to ask.'

'Yes?'

'Was it because of your father – because of what he did and because of what happened to him – that you decided to study medicine and applied for the post here?'

'It was partly because of my father, sir. It made me want to – to make lives more bearable for people facing death, or facing a life sentence. There's still a dignity owing to them, no matter what they might have done.' He frowned. 'That sounds a bit high-minded and grand, but it's what I feel.'

'I understand. Your mother's dead, I think?'

'Yes.' There was no need to elaborate; to tell Caradoc that she had died of a broken heart and because she could not face the world any longer. Walter said, 'I would very much like to have this appointment, Sir Lewis.'

The smile came again. 'I would very much like you to have it as well, Walter,' said Lewis Caradoc.

'He's very young, of course,' said Edgar Higneth, Calvary's governor. 'I had hoped for an older man. More experienced. More able to deal with the really difficult ones. But the other applicants were quite impossible.' He mimed the lifting of a glass. 'One drank, the other was clearly inept. And you can't have either in a prison of this nature, as you know, Sir Lewis.'

'I think Kane will deal with Calvary's inmates very well,' said Lewis. 'He's serious about his work and he's completely honest. They'll see that and they'll respect it.'

'Yes. Very well, I'll back your decision,' said Higneth. He paused, and then said, 'It looks as if Kane will have a baptism of fire. You've read the newspapers, I take it?'

'The Knaresborough case? Neville Fremlin? Yes, certainly, I have. There doesn't seem to be much doubt about his guilt.'

'I don't think there's any doubt at all,' said Higneth. 'Five women killed for sure – two stabbed through the base of the skull and two probably strangled. The fifth was too badly decomposed for them to establish how she died. The bodies were all buried in Becks Forest a few miles outside Knaresborough.'

'And one other possible victim, wasn't there?' said Lewis.

'Yes, except they haven't found her body. They're bringing Fremlin here tomorrow, so I shouldn't wonder if the newspaper reporters don't flock here as well. Still, it'll be over by this time next month.'

Extract from Talismans of the Mind *by C. R. Ingram.*

It's undeniable that down the centuries, men and women have ceaselessly sought for reassurances to ward off the darknesses of death – charms, spells, formulae.

Sometimes the charms have been elaborate and cere-monious – Druidic rituals or the breaking of bread and wine before an altar – and sometimes they have been macabre, as in the theft of the hand of a hanged murderer.

Answers have been sought in strange places – a round table in a darkened room with a group of grief-stricken people groping for a hand-holding assurance that death is not the end. There have even been men and women who have sought enlightenment within the death cells of the world's prison-houses – the despair-soaked rooms where the remaining minutes of a life ticked away like tiny hammer blows, all the way to the stroke of eight . . .

CHAPTER THREE

Thornbeck, when Georgina reached it, was one of those nice little market towns with which this part of England is sprinkled. It was tucked into the foothills of an un-assuming mountain which the local map disclosed as being Mount Torven. There was a clean-looking main street with bow-fronted shops and a couple of large chain stores specializing in walking boots and camping and climbing equipment. There were also three white-fronted, bow-windowed pubs advertising bar food. None of it was aggressively touristy and at half past five in the afternoon the place was modestly busy with people clambering onto buses or negotiating cars out of parking areas. After the lemming-like migration of London's rush hour this was restful.

Caradoc House was on the outskirts of this subdued activity. Georgina, following Vincent Meade's directions, was not quite sure what she had expected of a place that had been built or purchased with Walter's bequest, and she had whiled away the drearier parts of the journey by considering the possibilities. In the event, it turned out to be a medium-sized grey-stone house that might originally have belonged to a modestly prosperous businessman, and it was situated on a steep winding little street near to a rather attractive square. Mount Torven reared up behind it. Even on the brightest of summer days the rooms at the back would not get very much light, but if you lived here you probably would not mind because the surroundings were so gorgeous. Georgina liked the house. It faced straight onto the road, but she managed to park at the side, and then walked around to the front. A square brass plate proclaimed it as, 'The registered headquarters of the Caradoc Society, formed for the pursuit of knowledge of psychic phenomena and the paranormal. Founded in 1917 by Sir Lewis Caradoc.'

The Caradoc Society might be winding itself down but it appeared to be doing so in a civilized and gentle-manly manner. The door was painted a glossy green, the brass door-knocker was polished. As Georgina reached for the knocker a curtain in one of the downstairs windows twitched, and then the door was opened by a man who was presumably Vincent N. Meade. He was older than he had sounded on the phone – at least sixty and probably a bit more – and well-built in a rather soft, flabby fashion. He wore a dark red velvet jacket, (*velvet* at half past five in the afternoon?), with a pale pink shirt and a flowing cravat knotted at the neck. Georgina's inner eye placed him in a sugary pink room furnished with puffy white sofas and tasselled satin cushions.

Vincent Meade was apparently charmed to meet

Georgina – actually Walter Kane's great-granddaughter, my word, this was a historic day in the Society's annals. His large soft hands enfolded Georgina's, and she had to repress the urge to snatch them away from him.

They were all so pleased she had agreed to make the journey, said Vincent, especially at this time of year, so dreary the autumn he always thought, and no doubt she led a very busy life. And was this the only suitcase she had brought? Then he would carry it upstairs for her there and then – no, he insisted; there were two flights of stairs, and the second one was quite steep. To someone who had had three years of David's equality ('You can manage your own cases, can't you, George? Yes, thought you could,'), this modest chivalry was agreeable.

The flat was on the second floor, and consisted of an L-shaped room with easy chairs and a coffee table in the larger half, and sink, cooker and fridge in the shorter half. There was a narrow bedroom with a divan and wall cupboards, and a minuscule shower room and loo opening directly off it. It was all perfectly clean and comfortable, although it had the characterless look of a hotel bedroom and Georgina itched to bring the marvellous purple hillside colours into the house, and to put strong green ferns in copper pots to contrast with the white walls and beige carpet.

'I think you'll find it all right here, Miss Grey,' said Vincent, setting the case down. 'It's very small, but we always hope it's acceptable to our visitors.'

'It's fine,' said Georgina. 'I'll be very comfortable.'

'There's milk and bread in the kitchen, and the bed's made up. There's a radio but no television I'm afraid, on account of being almost smack up against the foothills of

Torven, as you might say. It's only a small mountain, well, the purists would say it's not really a mountain at all – not *high* enough, you see – but whether it's a mountain or a molehill the TV signal's virtually non-existent.'

'I believe I'd rather have Torven than television anyway,' said Georgina, glancing through the window at the sweeping scenery. Even on a dark October evening the would-be mountain was a spectacular, velvety sweep of purple and cobalt blue. She would leave the curtains open tonight so she could watch the light changing on Torven's slopes.

'Would you really? Now I'll just bring you up a cup of tea – no, it's no trouble at all, I had the kettle on in readiness for your arrival. I won't be a minute.'

He bumbled happily away, and while he was gone Georgina unpacked the few things she had brought with her, hanging her jacket in the wardrobe where it rattled emptily.

The tea, when it came, was in china cups with lemon as well as milk, and biscuits arranged on a paper doily.

'The Society's solicitor is expecting us at his office tomorrow morning,' said Vincent busily pouring out the tea. 'He'll see the letters you've brought with you, and there are a few of your great-grandfather's papers that he'll probably hand over at the same time. Ten o'clock. That won't be too early after your long drive today?'

'No, of course not.' Georgina was conscious of a twist of pleasurable anticipation. Papers that had been Walter's. Perhaps letters or photographs . . . She had not realized how much she had been looking forward to reaching back and taking hold of a hand out of the past.

She asked Vincent if he had been secretary of the Trust for long.

'I have held the post for forty-one years,' said Vincent, with a sad brave smile. 'I came to Thornbeck as a young man of twenty-one, and the Society has been a major part of my life since that day – I have written a great many articles and pamphlets about our work. It's very sad for me to see it all ending – and seeing this house sold as well. It was bought with the Kane bequest in 1940, you know.'

'Well, no, I didn't. I don't actually know very much about any of it,' said Georgina. 'I do know my great-grandfather worked at Calvary Gaol in the 1930s, but other than that—'

'Ah, Calvary,' said Vincent, infusing his voice with a kind of affectionate sadness. 'Calvary, Miss Grey—'

'Georgina.'

'Calvary, Georgina, has been almost as much a part of my life as this Society. Who knows what happened inside those grim walls in the past?'

He does like to ham it up, thought Georgina. I wonder if I ought to point out that his cravat is trailing in his tea cup? But Vincent, seeing she had finished her cup of tea, said she would be wanting to unpack and have a rest after the journey. In fact, whatever must she think of him, keeping her talking. It was just that when he began talking about the Society – his life's work, it had been – he feared he could be a sad bore on the subject.

It had not occurred to Georgina that anyone outside the pages of Jane Austen used 'sad' in quite that context any longer. She said it must have been absorbing work and she would look forward to hearing more about it.

'Well, if you're *sure* you'll be all right here?' said Vincent, finally getting up to take his leave.

'Quite sure. You've been very kind. I'll see you in the morning,' said Georgina firmly, in case he felt obliged to ask her out to dinner.

But he did not. He only said, 'I usually arrive here about half past nine. Oh, this is a key to the main street door in case you want to have a little look round the town later on, or walk along to the King's Head for a meal. But there's eggs and cheese in the fridge, and some tins of soup in the cupboard.'

Georgina listened to him going down the stairs and out through the main door, and then peered out of the window to watch him walk along the street. There he went – he was re-knotting the cravat as he walked along and glancing in shop windows at his reflection. Still, vanity was not the greatest of the sins. She watched him for a moment and then was annoyed with herself for falling victim to the curtain-twitching syndrome.

It was half past six. She would have a shower and walk along to the King's Head for a meal because she was blowed if she was going to spend the whole evening on her own, particularly since she kept imagining David and the ex-business partner watching her, and saying, 'Oh, *poorest* George, all on her own in that depressing room for the whole evening, eating tinned soup and bread and cheese.'

The room was not depressing at all, and Georgina did not in the least mind bread and cheese, but she would still take herself out to dinner.

*

Vincent had debated whether to ask Georgina Grey, this great-granddaughter of Walter Kane's out to dinner. The idea of walking into the King's Head with her was appealing – a number of the locals were sure to be there and everyone knew Vincent of course, so his appearance would cause a bit of a stir. My word, people would say, there's Vincent Meade with a lady. Life in the old dog yet, eh?

But there were two drawbacks to this plan. One was that Miss Grey was younger than Vincent had been expecting – probably around twenty-six or seven – and he did not want those admiring looks to turn into sniggers about ageing gentlemen making fools of themselves with young girls. He was, in fact, ageing gracefully – he fancied he was becoming quite distinguished of late and these days he dressed rather jauntily which helped – and the idea that he might make a fool of himself with any young girl was ridiculous. Still, people could be unkind and jealous.

The other drawback to inviting Miss Grey to dinner was the presence of the television people who were at the King's Head looking into the possibility of a programme about the area. People had said it was to be about unusual buildings in England's north-west and quirky pockets of Britain's countryside, and hearing this, Vincent had at once realized his own local knowledge might be very useful. He had assembled some details about Calvary – nothing dangerous, nothing that might draw them to that part of Calvary's history Vincent needed to keep hidden. Facts such as how it had been built in the 1790s, originally as a place to hold prisoners before trial or awaiting execution, but how, after an Act of Parliament in the mid-1800s, the distinction between Gaol and House of Correction had been abolished, and Calvary had consequently housed quite a lot of men serving life sentences. And little bits of local gossip and legend, so it was not too dry. Such as how the old turnkey's room was reputed to be haunted by a Victorian gaoler who had operated the old Newgate system of forcing prisoners to pay for quite basic services.

It had turned out to be rather a snappy little piece, but then he had always had a knack with words. Mother often used to say so. 'I don't know why you don't do something with your writing, Vincent,' she would say. 'All those compositions you did at school.'

It would be very gratifying if the TV people used his article, although he would insist on a proper credit. "Our thanks are due to Vincent N. Meade who gave so generously of his time and knowledge during the making of this programme." Something on those lines would look well.

He had given the article to the female assistant – Drusilla somebody she was called – and she had said they would be extremely interested in reading it, and yes, certainly he should give her his phone number so they could contact him. Vincent thought they would have studied it properly by now, which meant they might be looking to talk to him. So he would go along to the King's Head later, but he would go alone so as to be free if they wanted him. His appearance in the bar would not be thought strange: he sometimes looked in for a glass of sherry of an evening. He rather thought they kept the sherry especially for him and he visualized the barman saying to the landlord, 'Goodness me, we must order another bottle or two of Mr Meade's sherry this week: it won't do to run out of that.'

In any case, Miss Grey – Georgina – had indicated that she wanted to spend the evening on her own. Probably she was tired after the long drive; ladies never had as much stamina as men. Vincent's mother often used to say so. 'Poor fragile creatures that we are,' she would say, lying back in her chair, smiling as everyone ran around waiting on her. Vincent had been one of the people who had waited on her most often, but he had never minded.

Girls today were nothing like Vincent's mother. They were brisk and efficient like Georgina Grey seemed to be, and they were casual about long drives to unfamiliar places and about dining with strange men. Vincent's mother, if she was alive, would not have cared for that – not ladylike, she would have said – and she would not have approved of Georgina. One of these flippant modern girls, she would have called her. Hard. And what is it she does for a living? Oh, an interior designer? Well, she may call it that if she wishes, but a wallpaper shop with a curtain-making service is my guess. I shan't be impressed by *that*, thank you very much.

Vincent would not be impressed by it either. He was glad, though, that he had mentioned his work for the Society to Georgina and the articles he had written about its work – not boasting, just mentioning the fact *en passant* as you might say. He was also glad he had worn the velvet jacket for the meeting; it had cost a shocking amount of money but he fancied it gave him a slightly Bohemian look. The cravat was a recent touch; Vincent had been rather pleased with it so it had been annoying, when he got home, to find that the fringe had inadvertently trailed itself in the teapot. He would try soaking it in a solution of lemon juice; his mother had sworn by lemon juice for getting rid of tea stains.

Mother would not have wanted him to ask Georgina Grey out to dinner. Not a suitable thing to have done, she would have said – there are standards that have to be upheld, Vincent. Standards are very important, you must never forget that.

CHAPTER FOUR

October 1938

'Standards are important,' said Edgar Higneth to Walter on the day Neville Fremlin was brought to Calvary. 'When I took over as governor here I was determined to follow as many of Sir Lewis Caradoc's standards as I could.' He paused, and then said, 'Fremlin is a cold-blooded killer – he's murdered five women for their money. But he has only three weeks of life left to him – two weeks and five days now – and we have to treat him with as much humanity as possible.'

Walter said he understood this.

'I'm sorry you'll have an execution to deal with so soon after your arrival,' said Higneth. 'It might have been months – a year or more – before one happened. But it can't be helped. You'll be required to attend the hanging, of course, and to pronounce death. I'll make sure you meet Mr Pierrepoint beforehand.'

'Pierrepoint? Oh, the executioner.'

'Yes. He and his assistant will spend the night here before the execution.' Higneth glanced at the thin-faced young man seated in his office and wished Dr Kane was not so extremely young. Twenty-seven? Twenty-eight?

Choosing his words with care, he said, 'Dr Kane, there are often certain unpleasant aspects to a hanging. Men – and women – faced with the gallows suffer the extremes of terror. Sometimes they fight and we have to restrain them. If they faint they have to be strapped to a chair on the gallows itself. Sometimes they're physically sick or their bowels turn to water.' Higneth knew he should be hardened to the squalid side of human nature after being Calvary's governor for more than ten years but he was not. Although he knew the men who passed through his hands were killers, he had never got used to seeing them led to their deaths.

Kane said, 'Mr Higneth, I'm perfectly used to the involuntary reactions of the human body in its death throes. I trained at Bart's Hospital which is close to one of the poorest parts of London, so I'm entirely accustomed to the rougher sorts of men and women as well.'

'Fremlin isn't rough,' said Higneth at once. 'The papers called him the Silver-Tongued Murderer, and having talked to him this morning I'm bound to agree with them. He's extremely charming, highly intelligent and very widely read, and, frankly, I find it difficult to think of him as a man who has killed five women—'

He broke off, and Walter said, 'But there's no doubt about his guilt, is there?'

'None whatsoever. They'd been suspicious of him for some time. In the end they caught him actually in the act of burying his last victim – the inspector in charge of the case was beside himself that they hadn't been in time to save that woman's life, but they hadn't. All the corpses they eventually found were naked – he'd burned all the clothes – obviously thinking the victims wouldn't be identified. But they did identify them, of course – two of them at any rate.'

'They traced the dental records, didn't they?' said Walter. 'They use that quite a lot for identification these days. I remember thinking it was odd that Fremlin went to all that trouble – burying them in that remote forest outside Knaresborough, burning their clothes and all the rest of it – but that he hadn't thought of dental identification. As a chemist, you'd think he'd be aware of something like that.'

'They always miss something.' Higneth paused, because what he had to say next would not be easy. 'You'll be seeing Fremlin sometime today?'

'Yes. I've set aside half an hour each afternoon and evening.' This was part of Walter's duties, and he hoped there would be ways of smoothing out what was left of the condemned prisoners' lives. How he did that would depend a great deal on the individual, but for Fremlin he had prepared a laudanum-based sedative which would help the man sleep. He thought that explaining the sedative's compounds to this former chemist might create a tenuous link of friendship.

'Yes, good,' said Higneth when Walter explained this. 'But see now, the Yorkshire police have asked me—' Dammit, this was an impossible position for a man to be put in! Higneth abandoned the sideways approach, and said bluntly, 'They want to find out about the girl whose body was never found.'

'Yes?'

'She lived in the Knaresborough area and she vanished at the start of Fremlin's killings. The police couldn't add her name to the charges, because they never found any evidence that he killed her. But she's known to have frequented his chemist's shop – there was a little section for hand lotions and scented soaps and fancy notepaper and so on – and they believe Fremlin killed her.'

'Giving him the round half dozen,' said Walter thoughtfully.

'Yes. She was only eighteen or nineteen, and quite sheltered. She came from a prosperous middle-class home – Fremlin would have seen that at once – and she would have been ideal prey for him.'

'But even if he killed her, there wouldn't have been any way he could have got at any money, would there?' said Walter. 'Weren't most of the victims older ladies? Lonely widows?'

'They were, but this girl – her name was Elizabeth Molland – was wearing jewellery when she disappeared,' said Higneth. 'Quite valuable stuff, apparently. Necklace, earrings, bracelet. She had been to a big formal reception with her parents – some kind of musical society. That was just the kind of hunting ground Fremlin liked, of course, although it was never established if he had actually been present. Elizabeth vanished at the end of the evening; you know how confused it can be at those affairs – people milling in and out of cloakrooms, collecting wraps, waiting for cabs. When her parents realized she had gone they called the police, but the girl was never found.'

'And then Fremlin was arrested for the other murders in the same area,' said Walter.

'Yes. The Mollands followed the trial closely hoping for some clue, but there was nothing. They want to know the truth about what happened to their daughter.'

'Even if the truth is that Fremlin killed her?'

'Yes. That may sound strange but I can only liken it to the telegrams that used to be delivered to families in the war. "Missing, believed killed", that was the wording used. People who were sent those telegrams always said that not knowing was the worst part – that they would rather have a clean grief to cope with. You're too young to remember the war, of course, but—'

'Sir, are you trying to ask me if I'll question Fremlin about this girl, this Elizabeth Molland? In the hope that he'll – what? Confess?'

'Yes,' said Higneth thankful to have it in the open. 'Not question precisely, but probe a little. The inspector in charge of the case has made a private request to me that we do all we can to find out.'

'Why me?' said Walter. 'Why not you?'

'It's unlikely Fremlin will talk to me,' said Higneth. 'Although I shall try, of course. But he'll see me as an authority figure – an enemy, even, and he'll close down.'

'What about the chaplain?'

'The chaplain,' said Higneth sourly, 'feels it would not be right for him to quiz a man under sentence of death, or to make use of any subterfuge. In any case, he will apparently feel obliged to regard anything Fremlin tells him as under the seal of the confessional.'

'Fremlin's not a Catholic, is he?' said Walter.

'No, but the chaplain considers the same rules apply. Dr Kane, if you do this you must be very careful.'

'Yes, of course.'

Higneth made an impatient gesture. 'I don't mean physically. I mean during conversations with him. He's a clever devil and extremely charming. He'll assess your weak spots and make use of them. He'll find out about you – who you are, what your hopes and ambitions are, details about your family. He'll slide under your skin and you won't even realize he's doing it. That's how he'll have got the confidence of all those women, and charm's a thing that works on men as well as females, Dr Kane. So you must be very wary of giving away any information about yourself.'

'Would he use information to get sympathy?'

'He might try coaxing you into some kind of mad escape plan,' said Higneth. 'It wouldn't succeed – he'll be well guarded – but that mightn't stop him trying. And if he decides he can't charm you into helping him, he might try blackmailing you.'

'Surely he wouldn't do that.'

'He's got three weeks to live,' said Higneth drily. 'He's got nothing to lose.'

Walter considered for a moment. 'I won't force anything with Fremlin,' he said at last. 'And I won't use subterfuge.'

'But you will do it?'

'Yes, I will. I'll talk to him.'

November 1917

'Talk to him, Walter,' his mother had said on that long-ago day. 'Tell him what you're going to do with your life.'

'Will he want to know?' The small Walter had not

really understood what this was all about – he did not understand why his father had to be in this place or why they were going to see him like this – but he did not like to ask questions. His mother had been crying and he had never seen her cry before, so he would have promised her anything in the world. He had said, yes, he would tell about what he wanted to do when he was grown-up, and when finally they sat in the terrible room he had done as she had asked. The room had a smell to it that his seven-year-old self had not recognized, but which his grown-up self later knew for human despair and misery. The dark-haired man seated at the table had not seemed to care about it or even, thought Walter, to notice. It was difficult to think of him as his father because Walter did not really know him – he was always away fighting people it seemed.

But he explained about wanting to be a doctor when he grew up, so he could make people better.

'That's a very praiseworthy ambition, Walter.'

Walter had not known what praiseworthy meant nor what an ambition was, but his father seemed pleased, which was good.

'There'll be some money,' he said, looking at Walter's mother. 'You understand that, don't you? More than enough money to pay for his training – university – whatever he ends up wanting.'

At the mention of money Walter's mother had glanced at the other two people in the room, which Walter knew was because you did not talk about private things in front of strangers. The two people were stand- ing just inside the door, not speaking and not looking at anything; one was quite a young man with skin like lumpy porridge and little squinty eyes like a pig, but the other was a lady, with fair hair and a face that slanted upwards like one of the pictures in *Peter Pan*, which was Walter's most favourite book in the world. He had not expected to find a naughty fairy like Tinkerbell in this bad-smelling place, and he had wanted to go on looking at her. He had not done so because it was rude to stare at people.

'It's all right,' said Walter's father. 'They hear everything I say. These two – or two like them are with me all the time.' He paused, and then said softly, 'It's to make sure I don't die too early. Death watch, they call it.'

At this, Walter's mother pressed her handkerchief to her lips as if she might be sick which worried Walter greatly. She said, 'The money – I don't want the money. Every time I used it I should see the drowned faces of all those young men you betrayed.'

'That's being melodramatic. See now—'

'It's the money they gave you for what you did, isn't it?'

There was a pause then he said, 'It is not,' but Walter knew from his voice his father was lying.

Walter's mother knew as well. She said, 'It's tainted. I'd rather give it away.'

'Then give it to Walter. Let it help him when he needs it – sometime in the future.' He made an impatient gesture, and said, 'I never wanted paying, you know. I believed in what I did – I thought I was serving a cause.' A brief shrug. 'All wrong, of course. I was angry with the British – you never saw what they did in Ireland, did you? And we had a dream – Irish Independence.' He frowned, and then said, 'Remember, Walter, that it's a marvellous thing to have a dream, an ideal. But you have to make sure it's the right dream.'

'Yes, sir,' mumbled Walter, who had no idea what they were talking about but was trying to store the words in his mind. He thought one day he might understand; so it was important to remember as much as he could.

'I had the wrong dream, you see. Dying in a war – for a cause you believe in – that's romantic. It's very nearly noble. But if it turns to hatred, that's a bad thing.

'The Easter Rising was meant to achieve so much. But it achieved nothing except failure. Dublin fell, and they executed the rebels in Kilmainham Gaol . . . De Valera's in gaol, and the sovereignty they promised Ireland isn't likely to happen – remember I said that, will you? We all expected to die,' he said. 'Patrick Pearse, Michael Collins and all the rest. Everyone who signed the Proclamation of an Irish Republic knew there was about a thousand to one chance of surviving.' He blinked, and then seemed to realize where he was. 'But I never expected to die like this, in a squalid death cell, counting the hours away until the day after tomorrow.' A look passed between them at that point; as if, Walter thought, they had clasped their hands together. 'You know it will happen the day after tomorrow?'

'Yes. Sir Lewis Caradoc told me.'

'Eight o'clock,' said Walter's father. 'I understand they're always punctual. They've got extra guards on, I think.'

'In case you fight to get free?' It came out on another of the stifled sobs.

'I shan't fight my love. But they're worried in case a rescue's tried.'

SARAH RAYNE

'Will it be?'

'I don't think so. No. You mustn't even think it.' He looked back at Walter. 'Walter, there's a piece of writing I want you to have. Part of a poem. You won't understand it now, but one day – perhaps when you're that doctor you'd like to be and you're helping to make people better – then you will understand it.' He held a sheet of paper up for the two people at the door to see, and the mischievous-fairy lady nodded, and he said, 'Thank you, Belinda,' and gave it to Walter.

Walter was not sure if he was meant to read it at once, and when he looked at the words, he did not think he could manage them anyway. He looked at his mother in sudden panic, but then his father said, very softly, 'Walter, this is what it says.

> Know that we fools, now with the foolish dead,
> Died not for flag, nor King, nor Emperor,
> But for a dream, born in a herdsman's shed,
> And for the secret Scripture of the poor.

'It's a poem written by an Irishman called Tom Kettle. I know you don't understand it now, but one day I think you might. So when you're a bit older I'd like you to read it sometimes and think about me. Will you do that, Walter? For me? Because I'm about to die for a dream, you see.'

'Yes,' said Walter. Not really knowing what he was promising. 'Yes, I promise.'

'Nicholas, they are looking after you, aren't they? They are being kind to you?'

'I have no complaints,' he said, and smiled. 'Although

48

there's a doctor here who stares at me as if he'd like to collect my soul. It's not worth the collecting, of course.' He glanced at the warders, and then reached for her hand and held it tightly. In a totally different voice, he said, 'Pray for me when eight o'clock chimes the day after tomorrow. Will you?'

'Yes. There's no chance of—'

'A reprieve? A rescue? No chance at all.'

After they got home – two long train journeys, the carriages stuffy and crowded with bad-tempered people – Walter had his supper, and went to bed as usual.

All through the next day he thought about the dreadful room and the man in it, and he pored over the writing on the paper trying to make out the words. He thought about the woman with the slanty face and tilting-up eyes, as well. Belinda, that had been her name. It was a very suitable name for her, and he was glad she was there with his father in the sad room. Once or twice he thought about the doctor who had wanted to collect souls. You surely could not collect a soul, could you?

On the second morning his mother came into his bedroom very early – it was barely half past six and a thin grey light trickled in through the curtains; it was only then that he remembered this was the day after tomorrow.

He had a mug of milk and some bread and honey, and they walked quietly along the street to the little church where they went each Sunday morning and which smelled of the stuff the vicar put on his chest every winter.

'It's not your father's Church,' said his mother. 'Not

exactly, because he's Catholic. But it's my Church and it's where I want to be now. There's no one about,' she said, pushing the door open and peering inside. 'That's very good, because no one must know any of this. You understand that, don't you, Walter? You must never tell anyone where we were two days ago. In any case, we're going to live somewhere else soon, and we won't be called O'Kane any longer, just Kane.'

'Won't that cost a great lot of money?'

'We have some money,' said Walter's mother, but she shuddered as she said this and Walter remembered what she had said about the drowned faces in the money. He thought he would make sure not to look at the money too closely in case the poor drowned faces swam up out of it like dead fish.

But he was intrigued by the thought of going to live somewhere else and of changing his name, and he thought about it while they knelt down in the pew they always had on Sundays. His mother read bits from her Bible, and then she read the writing on Walter's piece of paper. Walter listened, not speaking, because you had to be very quiet in church. He supposed that one day he would understand the words about dying not for a king but for a dream.

He was so absorbed in thinking about all these things, that he did not hear the church clock begin to chime eight.

Extract from Talismans of the Mind *by C. R. Ingram*

During the First World War, telegrams were sent to inform relatives that their sons, husbands, brothers, were 'Missing, believed killed'. They were grim, soulless little pieces of paper but, given the circumstances and the technology of the times, it's difficult to know how else the information could have been conveyed.

And so, from the complex emotions of not knowing whether their loved ones were alive or dead, a whole new culture of spiritualism grew up – a culture of table-turners and mediums offering to contact the spirits of the dead young men; of automatic writing and Ouija boards. Letters of the alphabet arranged in a ring with fingers on a glass tumbler to pick the letters out so a message was spelt out, often to the accompaniment of accusing voices claiming that somebody had pushed the tumbler. Was it you who pushed it, Arthur? Certainly not, says Arthur indignantly, even though he did in fact push the tumbler. But to be fair to him, it was because he is weary of his poor wife's grief and of his own grief as well, and if there can be a message from their boy who died on the Somme perhaps the family can find some peace at last.

'J', says the tumbler squeaking decisively across the table top, and there's a gasp from the darkness. A female voice, pitiful with hope, whispers, 'Is that you, John?' or 'James?' or 'Joseph?' And, oh yes, of course, it *is* John or James or Joseph. Such a useful letter to choose: J, the start of so many good English names.

Don't worry about me, ma, spells the message laboriously; it's all peace and love and sunshine up here, and Baby Jack who died of the cholera when he was a mite, sends his best, and grandma says hello . . . Oh, and remind pa to make a contribution as you go out – there's a box in the hall . . .

Within that culture grew a subterranean culture of

its own – that of avaricious charlatans, manipulators and what were once called thimble-riggers, all of them hell-bent on exploiting the bereaved.

One such pair of fraudsters were Bartlam and Violette Partridge, who began their table-turning evenings towards the end of 1916. Bartlam and Violette ('Call me Vita, love, most people do.'), operated from a house in North London: a narrow, unremarkable three-storey house, the kind of house that people passed without a second glance. It's no longer there, that house, and no photographs have survived, but in 1915 Bartlam bought it for the princely sum of £356, so it must have been a very smart residence indeed.

Precise facts about this infamous duo are difficult to establish, but there are some clues. A series of sharply written articles in the *Finchley Recorder*, apparently by a journalist who attended several seances, has provided remarkable first-hand accounts of their exploits. This series of articles has been of immense help in the research for these chapters. The newspaper itself has long since closed down, and as it has not been possible to trace the journalist in question, acknowledgement is here grate-fully recorded to the writer, whoever he – or she – may have been.

In addition to the newspaper articles, a few letters exist – letters written by grateful 'clients' to Bart and Vita. There are bank statements as well, from which it appears that the predatory Bartlam had epicurean tastes, although he was careful to order two gradings of sherry, one at £104 the dozen bottles, the other at a meagre £54 the dozen. Vita was apparently devoted to the flowing velvet and chiffon tea-gowns of the era, although several entries for items of ladies' corsetry (discreet and firm, with whalebone supports for the bosom), suggest that while she purported to cavort with the ethereal denizens of the Great Beyond, her own proportions were earthly rather than ethereal. Vita, to put it politely must have been a majestically built lady. There are also several accounts from, 'purveyors of genuine French perfume', itemizing, 'Scent of Evening Violets, large flagon, one guinea,' and, 'Bath salts, 3/6d'.

For two years this vulpine pair drew their victims into the narrow North London house, the rigidly corseted Vita exuding the fragrance of evening violets, Bartlam perhaps offering their guests a glass of the cheap sherry.

They were a motley crew, the victims who came to this house, and the only thing they had in common was their ability – and their willingness – to subscribe generously to the Partridge Cause.

CHAPTER FIVE

Vincent Meade escorted Georgina to the solicitor's office just before ten o'clock. Georgina would have preferred to go by herself, but Vincent appeared to think it part of his duties. This morning he was wearing a dignified pinstripe suit with a pale green silk shirt and a flower in his buttonhole. Of course, thought Georgina, secretly entertained, this is a business meeting, so one puts on a formal suit, but there still has to be the touch of flamboyance.

The solicitor's name was Mr Huxley Small, and there was no nonsense about flowers or silk shirts with him. He was probably approaching seventy, and wore a plain dark suit with old-fashioned shoes. Georgina liked his office, which was also old-fashioned, with mahogany woodwork and a desk with an inset leather skiver, although a computer and fax machine supplied touches of modernity.

They were given cups of coffee while Mr Small read

the letter from Lewis Caradoc to Walter Kane. He made several notes, and then said the letter was very useful – it confirmed the link between Miss Grey and Dr Kane. They had not needed much confirmation but it was as well to have something. It had, however, been an easy enough matter of finding and then following the birth certificate of Walter Kane's daughter.

'That was your grandmother, of course, Miss Grey. But she was born in the early 1940s, and that was a time of confusion. Register offices were bombed, and marriage and birth certificates were destroyed and information incorrectly remembered afterwards. We had to be sure we had followed the right trail, so to speak.'

'Yes, of course. Was Lewis Caradoc local? Or did the Society just take him as a patron or something?'

'My dear Miss Grey—' began Mr Small, looking up, startled.

'Sir Lewis was governor of Calvary Gaol for many years,' said Vincent so quickly that Georgina suspected he spoke more out of a desire to show off his knowledge than to explain Lewis Caradoc's identity to her.

'Oh, I see. I didn't realize.'

'When Dr Kane came to Thornbeck, Sir Lewis had, of course, been retired for many years,' said Mr Small. 'But it's known that he still played quite an active part in the administration.'

'Sort of consultant,' said Georgina.

'I don't suppose they called it that, but yes, it would be something on those lines.' Mr Small studied the letter again. 'Entirely suitable,' he said. 'I can't see that there'll be a problem about passing any credit balance to you, Miss Grey. I'm afraid it isn't likely to be a very large sum, though, the Society has been running at a loss for a good many years and the bank have a substantial call on the sale.' Georgina supposed this was a polite way of saying the house had been mortgaged at some stage.

'The Caradoc Society is bankrupt and bereft, you see,' said Vincent mournfully. 'There's no longer the interest in psychic research – at least not at such a purely local level. People no longer make donations or subscribe to the membership magazine or come to lectures. It's all very tragic. The passing of the Society will leave a great void in my life.'

'How sad,' said Georgina helplessly.

'I've made out a receipt for Sir Lewis's letter,' said Mr Small, briskly, as if he found Vincent's display of sentiment embarrassing. 'And I'll make sure you have the original back as soon as possible. Would you like me to get it photocopied while you're here?'

Georgina explained she had already taken a copy, which Mr Small said was very efficient of her.

'These are the papers which belonged to Dr Kane, and which were sent to the Society after his death in the early 1960s. I believe,' said Mr Small, handing Georgina two deed boxes marked *Kane*, 'that he had been living in Switzerland for some years. These papers are of no help to me, so I don't see why you shouldn't have them right away. We could do with the room, to be honest. They're somewhat disorganized, I'm afraid.' His tone suggested that disorganized papers were no more than might be expected from someone who had chosen to live in Switzerland. 'However, you will know more about it all than we do.'

'I don't think I shall,' said Georgina, taking the boxes, and resisting the temptation to open them there and then. 'My parents died when I was in my teens and what family there was got sort of fragmented. Are there any photographs, do you know? I don't even know what Walter looked like. Or my great-grandmother.'

'As far as I remember there aren't any photographs of anyone,' said Mr Small, and Vincent looked up.

'I didn't know you had looked at the contents,' he said, and Georgina heard the slight petulance in his tone as if he were thinking, They might have let me in on that. Poor old Vincent with his jaunty buttonhole and his natty suit.

'Certainly I inspected the contents.' Mr Small was plainly shocked that anyone might think otherwise. 'I did so as soon as the parcel came to us from Switzerland. We had no idea what it might contain.'

Georgina wondered if he had suspected Walter of squirrelling away state secrets or blueprints for world war three. But to smooth over the faint ruffle of annoyance, she said, 'I don't actually know a great deal about my family. There aren't even any aunts or cousins.'

'Oh, how sad,' said Vincent, at once switching from petulance to sympathy and Georgina, who had been about to say blithely that what you had never had you never missed, changed her mind.

When they got up to go, Mr Small said, 'We are really very glad to have traced you, Miss Grey. Dr Kane doesn't seem to have thought about the possibility of this house – the house his money bought – ever being sold. There was nothing in the Trust about the disposal of it if the Society should cease to exist.'

He's quite a nice old boy after all, thought Georgina. He'd like me to have some of Walter's dosh.

'So the only other option,' said Mr Small, 'was to place any credit in a specially created bank account, and appoint someone to administer it – to deal with income tax due on the accrued interest and so on.'

'Or look for a society with similar aims,' said Vincent, a bit too eagerly.

'Yes, but that would have taken time,' said Mr Small repressively. 'And since I am looking to retire I didn't feel I could take on that kind of task, even if there were to be a fee involved, which practically speaking there would not.'

So after all, it came down to money. Georgina supposed most things did.

'The house is presently being valued prior to being offered for sale,' said Huxley Small. 'We will keep you fully informed of progress, of course.'

'Thank you very much.'

Vincent accompanied Georgina back to Caradoc House, carrying the boxes for her and bringing them up the stairs to the flat.

'I'll stay for a while and help you sort the stuff out, shall I? Huxley Small said everything was a bit haphazard, and two heads are better than one with these things I always think.'

'Please don't bother,' said Georgina at once. 'I'll manage perfectly well.'

'It wouldn't be any bother.'

Georgina said firmly, 'I wouldn't dream of putting you to the trouble. Truly, I'll be fine. In fact, I think I might walk along to the King's Head and have an early lunch, then come back and spend the afternoon and the evening working.' She had enjoyed the bar meal she had had the previous evening; she had wondered if Walter had been in the habit of coming here; if he had sat in the inglenook with a drink and talked to the local people. Vincent was looking so crestfallen, she felt obliged to say, 'I'll let you know how I get on, if you'd be interested.'

'I would indeed. Come down to my room at any time. Any time at all. This is my home telephone number. I'm only a few minutes' walk from here.'

Georgina waited until he had gone, and then locked the door leading out to the landing. This was probably a bit over the top; he was just inquisitive, which was perfectly natural. But it was somehow disturbing to remember that he had a key to this house and her rooms.

It was just on eleven o'clock, and as Vincent had already pointed out the little flat had tinned soup and bread and cheese. She would forage in the cupboards for lunch when she felt like it or go to the pub, but for the moment she was far more interested in making the acquaintance of her great-grandfather.

As Vincent left Georgina and went down to what he thought of as his own little domain, he felt extremely worried.

The deed boxes. The square ordinary metal boxes that Huxley Small had handed over to Georgina Grey and that contained papers – documents – sent to the Society on Walter Kane's death. What were those papers and those documents? What might Walter Kane have written in medical reports and records during his life?

And how many of those reports might have survived, and have found their way into those deed boxes? Anything could be in there, *anything* . . .

Vincent realized he was clenching his fists so tightly his nails were digging into his palms. He forced his hands to uncurl, and took several deep, calming breaths.

But feeling calmer was not going to make the problem go away. It was starting to look as if he might have to formulate some kind of plan about all this, which was irritating when he had been expecting to enjoy the presence of Chad Ingram and the television people in Thornbeck.

Jude Stratton had not expected to particularly enjoy the journey to wherever Chad Ingram was taking him, because these days he hated all journeys. Being guided into a car – 'Mind your head, no a bit lower – can you find the seat belt – or p'raps I'd better fasten it for you, had I?' – and then the painstaking descriptions of the views through the car windows: he bitterly hated those. Who the hell cared if it was a glorious spring day with daffodils when you would never be able to see daffodils or spring sunshine for yourself again?

The worst thing of all was hurtling along a road with no idea where you were or what the traffic might be doing. If the driver broke the journey there was the guiding hand again, this time into the coffee bar or the restaurant, and then into the men's loo afterwards. 'The taps are just there, and the hand dryer is on your left . . .' He knew it was ungracious and disagreeable of him to feel like this when people were trying to be kind, but ungracious and disagreeable was how he felt.

There had been times during the past two years when Jude would have traded his soul to be back in the days when he and the camera crew had rattled across war-torn landscapes in one of the terrifyingly erratic jeeps they used to hire. Jude would be writing the reports as they went, trusting to heaven or hell they would get back to the base to send them; the camera crew would be cursing because the terrain was too uneven for filming, the interpreter would be looking out for likely people to interview along the way . . . There had been a great many times during those journeys when they had known they might be the target of a sniper or that a bomb might explode in their path at any minute, because their luck would not last for ever. But they had gone on anyway. Until the day when the luck had run out, and the bomb had exploded, and two of the camera crew had been killed and Jude had been blinded.

But when it came to this journey, Chad merely said, 'I expect you'd prefer to sit in the front, wouldn't you?' opened the car door and left Jude to find his own way in, and grapple with the seat belt by himself. Then he said, 'Are you set to go? The journey's a good five hours, although once we're clear of London quite a lot of it's motorway. I thought we'd stop off for some lunch about halfway, and we'll probably reach the destination about five. Is that all right with you?'

'Fine.'

'I usually have a tape on while I'm driving,' said Chad, and Jude felt the movement as he reached forward to slot a cassette into the tape deck.

'That suits me. I shan't have to listen to the other drivers sounding their horns when you cut them up. I suppose you still drive as badly as ever.' He listened for Chad's reaction to this, and was absurdly pleased when he picked up a ruffle of amusement. This sensing of other people's responses and emotions was not something he could do with everyone and it really only worked if it was someone with whom he was properly in tune, but he was getting better at it. He was sufficiently pleased at picking up Chad's amusement to say, 'I won't probe for clues about the destination because that might spoil your experiment, but I already think we're travelling north.'

'Why do you say that? Magnetic pull of the north pole or something?'

'No, the timing' said Jude. 'If we drove for five hours due south or east we'd end up in the English Channel or the North Sea.'

'Holmes, my dear fellow, you never cease to amaze me. But how d'you know we aren't going due west? Into Cornwall or Devon.'

'We might be, but I don't think so. I don't care where we're going, anyway. It's just a pity five hours isn't long enough to take us into Scotland.'

'Why the sudden yearning for Scotland?'

'Single malt, dear boy. I may be blind, but I can still drink you under the table.'

'And have done so on several occasions. We'll put it to the test when this is over,' said Chad. 'I liked your new flat, by the way.'

'Mortgaged up to the hilt,' said Jude carelessly, but he was pleased because finding and buying the lease of the big airy flat in Little Venice had been difficult, and then furnishing it without knowing what he was buying or how the rooms looked, had been bitterly frustrating. 'I've only been there for three months but it costs the absolute earth, in fact I suspect the bailiffs are already gathering, and— God Almighty! what's just thundered past?'

'A juggernaut.'

'Are you sure that's all it was? It felt more like the four horsemen of the apocalypse, or at the very least a herd of Valkyries. Listen, would you mind not playing hopscotch with pantechnicons? I don't much care if you prang your car, but there're six bottles of wine on the back seat, to say nothing of two jars of caviar, and I'd like them all to arrive intact.'

At first sight, the deed boxes with their printed legend of *Kane* on the lid did not appear to contain anything of very much interest. Georgina, curled up on the floor, meticulously sifting papers, thought that Walter, rather than becoming clearer, seemed to be getting more obscure.

There was some correspondence about a house he had bought in the early 1950s a few miles outside Lucerne; most of this was in German, but Georgina managed to make out a few phrases of what appeared to be the Swiss equivalent of an estate agent's advertisement, from which it seemed that the house had been attractive and had lovely views and lush gardens. This could probably be taken with a pinch of salt, and stripped of estate agent's language it might just as easily have been a poky cowshed or directly under a ski-lift mechanism.

His daughter, Georgina's grandmother, did not seem to be mentioned anywhere. Why? Was it simply that nothing about her had found its way into the boxes?

63

But after a time a faint pattern did start to emerge. Walter had apparently left Calvary at the beginning of 1940 – there was a note from someone called Edgar Higneth, written from there in March 1940, saying, 'We are missing you greatly, but our loss is the army's gain.' So Walter must have offered his services to the medical corps shortly after the outbreak of the Second World War, which suggested he had cared more about helping the living than about psychic research, at that stage of his life at any rate.

There were medical journals – Georgina wondered if these might be of any interest to medical schools – and a couple of postcards, apparently from prison staff, one of them asking Walter if the army made him wear woolly bedsocks, or whether he had found a better way of keeping warm at night, haha, and one or two scrappy notes from people Georgina thought must have been prisoners. 'Wishing you well, and thanks for everything, Dr Kane,' said one.

There were seed catalogues in English and German, and a couple of brochures for sales of antique furniture in London and also in Lucerne. The dates tallied with the purchase of the Swiss house, so it looked as if Walter had been stocking his garden and also his rooms. Georgina had a sudden strong wish to see the house he had bought and the things he had put into it.

But other than the indication that Walter had liked good furniture and presumably been able to afford it, there was nothing that opened up his life. He was as much of a mystery as ever.

Extract from Talismans of the Mind, *by C. R. Ingram*

It is likely that even without the spectacular unmasking that finally took place amid such tragic and bizarre circumstances, Bartlam and Violette Partridge would not have flourished very far into the nineteen twenties. To some extent, most of us are products of our own era, and these two were classic products of theirs.

The details of their unmasking are reasonably well documented, but what happened to their clients? To ladies such as the one who wrote the letter reproduced below? Did they seek out other vultures who would fasten onto their sensibilities, their griefs and their bank balances? The authenticity of this letter cannot be verified, nor has it been possible to trace the full name of the sender, since she only signs her Christian name. But it does give a few more details about the machinations in the house in North London.

November 1917

My dear Bartlam and Violette

I must begin by thanking you for last evening's Meeting. For the first time since the news of his death in France, I felt my beloved boy close to me again, and the manifestation we saw as we sat around the table was a truly moving experience. It was unmistakably him, and I see now that you were right to counsel me to be patient: to wait until I had attended three or four Meetings, and until the three of us and the other friends in the Circle, knew one another better. How true it is that those of us who seek to go beyond this life must be properly attuned.

My husband makes no objection to my attending your Meetings, and I shall do all I can to persuade him to accompany me in the near future, although he is, of course, extremely busy.

You referred to some degree of financial embarrassment when last we met. Between such friends as we have become I should not like to think that lack of funds might hinder your work. Vita, my dear, you have been such a sympathetic friend and such a willing listener to my memories of my dear boy, that I hope you will not find it tactless of me to send you the enclosed bank draft. Please do accept it in the spirit in which it is sent, and use it in whatever way will best benefit your work.

Until our next Meeting,
I am your very dear friend and admirer
Clara

There is no means of knowing how much money the trusting Clara sent or how it was used, although it's likely that Bartlam's wine merchants benefited quite heftily.

There is no means of knowing, either, how Clara coped with the removal of Bartlam and Violette Partridge from her world.

CHAPTER SIX

Georgina had intended to spend all day immersed in Walter's world, but by midday her head was starting to ache from poring over faded writing and tattered receipts that were of no interest to even the most avid researcher. She would have an hour's break – some fresh air and modern-day reality.

The King's Head provided exactly the right note of modern reality. It also served very substantial bar lunches; Georgina's plate came heaped with crisp fresh salad and several thick slices of home-cured ham. She took it to a table in the little dining alcove, along with a copy of *Talismans of the Mind*, which she had bought on the drive here, and which she was reading out of curiosity and also out of vague deference to the proximity of C. R. Ingram. She was enjoying the book; she propped it up on her table while she ate because she always felt a bit self-conscious about being on her own in a pub.

The tables were fairly close together and the King's Head was quite crowded. Georgina was not listening to anyone else's conversation, but it was difficult to avoid hearing the discussion at an adjoining table, where a girl of around her own age and a young earnest-looking boy with a flop of brown hair and glasses, were eating lasagne.

'If you want to know the truth,' said the girl, who had long fair hair and a languid voice, 'I'm actually finding Neville Fremlin deeply interesting – I've turned up a fair bit of stuff about him already. As a matter of fact, I think there's something very nearly sexy about villainy on that scale.'

'I think you're winding me up,' said the boy in an American accent.

'You're not sure if I am though, are you?' said the girl. 'Listen, I know we didn't set out to focus on Fremlin, but Chad's getting seriously interested in him. I bet he'd look at the budget to see if we could do a spin-off. Or extend what we've got into a two-parter. I tell you what, let's rough something out anyway.'

'I admit Fremlin's turning out to be kind of interesting.'

'He is, isn't he? He must have had terrific sex appeal to lure those females into his murderous den. But how did he behave in ordinary life? That's what I find most interesting. Everyone focuses on the killing parts of murderers' lives, but what were they like for the rest of the time?'

The American boy appeared to think for a moment, then said carefully, 'When the enterprising burglar's not a-burgling/When the cut-throat isn't occupied in crime.'

'Oh God, now, you're quoting something at me.'

'Gilbert and Sullivan.'

'You're so highbrow, Phin, I don't know how you can stand yourself.'

'*The Pirates of Penzance* isn't highbrow—' said Phin hotly.

'It is to me. But I suppose you just *lerve* English light opera.'

'My father has the complete works of Gilbert and Sullivan and I think they're just the wittiest . . . Anyhow, you were the one talking about villains not engaged in villainy.'

'It is an interesting angle though, isn't it? Was Fremlin the average, run-of-the-mill pharmacist, measuring out pills and potions, and whatnot? "Our newest line in face creams, moddom, and did you want something for the weekend, sir?" Sorry, Phin, that's an old English expression, you probably wouldn't know what I mean – But presumably Neville Fremlin didn't spend his entire time murdering gullible females and then burying their naked bodies to avoid getting caught. He'd have a living to make between times, wouldn't he?'

'I thought he murdered his victims for their money. Why would he need to work at all?'

'P'raps he just liked killing people. Or maybe they didn't have as much money as he thought. Or he liked a really glitzy life and used the money up very fast.'

'Or,' said Phin and Georgina received the impression that he made a mental pounce, 'he needed the chemist's shop as a bait for the victims. Like, uh, a spider's parlour for the fly to walk into.'

'It kills me to say it, but that's actually very shrewd of

you. In any case he'd have had bills to pay, wouldn't he? Electricity and income tax. Even a mortgage.'

'Would Fremlin have had a mortgage?' Phin sounded doubtful.

'He might have done. And he wouldn't give murdering as his occupation when he applied. He'd say chemist, which is very respectable indeed. I'll bet he'd have been looked on as a very safe thing for a loan. "Come into the office, Mr Fremlin, sign here and there's your cheque." It'd all make a good angle for a programme, wouldn't it?'

'An ordinary day in the life of a murderer,' said Phin, thoughtfully.

'Yes. I'll tell you what else we could do, Phin, we could check who was working in Calvary when Fremlin was executed. We can find out who the hangman was easily enough, but how about others? There'd have been a prison chaplain and a doctor, wouldn't there?'

'That might be a really good angle. It's not so very far back, either.'

'Nineteen thirty-eight. I should have thought that was pre-history to a child of your tender years.'

I'll have to say something to them, thought Georgina, and before she could worry about whether they would think she was intruding, she moved to their table, and said, a bit diffidently, 'I hope you don't think I'm butting in, but I couldn't help hearing what you said about people who worked at Calvary. Uh – I'm Georgina Grey and my great-grandfather was the prison doctor there in the thirties. His name was Walter Kane. I'm in Thornbeck for a few days to sort out some of his old papers.'

Far from thinking she was intruding, they welcomed

her enthusiastically. The girl, whose name was Drusilla, invited her to sit down and despatched the American boy who was called Phin Farrell, to the bar to buy her a drink. Drusilla explained about the television programme.

'We're sort of the advance party – research and preliminary material.'

'Except we're starting to think there's more than one programme in all this,' said Phin.

'Yes, and if your great-grandfather really did attend Neville Fremlin's execution . . .'

'I should think it's a good possibility,' said Georgina. 'The dates fit.'

'Well then, if you do find anything that mentions Calvary, and if you felt like giving us permission to use it . . .'

'As far as I'm concerned,' said Georgina, 'you're welcome to Walter's entire history. All I know about him is that he was Calvary's doctor in the years leading up to the Second World War, and that he lived abroad afterwards.'

'It's the Calvary years we're after,' said Phin. 'Nothing – uh – private, of course.'

Georgina said she didn't think there was anything private. 'Or if there is, I haven't found it yet. How long are you staying in Thornbeck? Because if you want to come up to Caradoc House sometime, you can see what there is. So far I've only found mostly medical papers, but there's a second box of stuff I haven't looked at yet. That might yield something more interesting.'

'We'll take you up on that offer,' said Drusilla at once. 'Can we bring Chad? Dr Ingram? He absolutely loves primary source material.'

'Yes, of course.' Georgina did not say she would be intrigued to meet Chad Ingram. 'If you think it'll be worth it. When would you like to come?'

They looked at one another. 'Would Friday be all right?' said Drusilla.

'Yes, certainly. Would you . . .' Georgina hesitated, and then said, 'Would lunchtime suit you? I expect you've got a lot to do, so I could put out some salad and cheese or something and you could eat while you look at everything.'

'We'd like that,' said Drusilla at once. 'Thank you very much.'

She likes to give the appearance of finding life too boring for words, thought Georgina. But she's genuinely keen on her job. And Phin is like an eager puppy. They're nice, both of them.

She said, 'I'll expect you any time after midday.'

They exchanged mobile phone numbers in case of any last-minute change of plan, and Georgina went back to Caradoc House pleased to have made this small, friendly contact.

October 1938

As Walter prepared for his first meeting with Neville Fremlin he felt tremors of nervous apprehension, and as he walked along Calvary's corridors, the gaolers unlocking gates and doors as he went, the ghost of his seven-year-old self walked with him. The gaolers on that morning had studiously avoided looking either at him or his mother and, at a brief word from Sir Lewis Caradoc, they had unlocked the doors. For years afterwards one of Walter's childhood nightmares had been the sound of keys being turned in locks.

He could still remember the female gaoler who had been on duty in his father's cell. She had had a pixie face, and his father had called her Belinda.

It was important that Fremlin did not pick up his nervousness. Fremlin must regard him as sympathetic but detached. Walter reminded himself that he was no longer a fearful seven-year-old; he was a qualified doctor and the health of everyone in Calvary was his responsibility. It was not his father who was waiting for him in the condemned cell, it was a stranger – a man who was not going to the gallows for a belief and a cause, but for the deaths of five women. And he, Walter, had been charged with finding out if that five might be six. He had no idea, yet, how he would go about this, but he had given his word to Edgar Higneth that he would try.

The warders were waiting for him. They would not remain in the cell during his visit – doctors and clergymen were allowed the small privilege of complete privacy with any condemned prisoner – but they would be just outside the door. Walter did not know their names because he was still getting to know the staff here, but he nodded his thanks as they opened the door and stood back to allow him to go in. As the door closed behind him, he heard the sound of a match striking, and then the faint scent of a cigarette. They were snatching a crafty smoke. But he was not paying attention to them; his whole attention was focused on the man seated at the table.

The first thing to strike him was that Neville Fremlin was considerably older than he had been expecting –

probably nearer fifty than forty. He was seated at the table and turned his head to look at the visitor, exactly as Walter's father had turned his head on that long-ago morning. For a moment the ghosts of the past crowded suffocatingly in, then Fremlin stood up, the ghosts receded and Walter took the chair on the other side of the table.

'Good morning, Mr Fremlin. I'm Dr Kane – Walter Kane. I'll be visiting you a couple of times a day.'

'I know who you are, Dr Kane. Edgar Higneth told me you would be coming along. I believe we aren't permitted to shake hands, so you'll have to take that courtesy for granted. I'm glad to see you, although I could wish our surroundings were less austere.'

He had a rather soft voice, and his eyes, which were dark and intelligent, studied Walter with interest. He's not in the least frightening, thought Walter, in fact he's very nearly ordinary. He said, 'Is there anything you would like? Anything that might make the days a bit easier for you?'

'A few dancing girls, perhaps? A case of good Beaujolais?' The words came out deadpan, but then he smiled and Walter saw at once that he was not at all ordinary. If he had smiled like that at his victims it was no wonder they had let themselves be cheated out of their life savings or their jewellery.

But he said, lightly, 'We can't manage either of those, I'm afraid. The best we can offer is prison-strength cocoa. But I can stir a mild sedative into it if that would help you to sleep.'

'But it'll be a case of "sleep perchance to dream", won't it?' said Fremlin. 'And there's the rub, of course.

But it's considerate of you to offer and I'll take you up on it. You're very young to be a doctor, aren't you?'

The sudden switch of subject and the direct question disconcerted Walter, but he remembered Edgar Higneth's warnings, and said, 'I promise you I'm fully qualified.'

'I'm sure you are. A tough training though, isn't it? My own was quite tough, but full-blown medicine is a rigorous road.'

Walter was determined not to be thrown off balance. He said, 'Yes, it was tough, but I got through it. Did you enjoy pharmacy? There's a good deal of studying to be done for that, isn't there?' Mentally, he crossed his fingers, hoping this might lead to Fremlin talking about his crimes.

If Fremlin saw through the ruse, he gave no indication, but only said, 'Yes, a great deal, but I enjoyed it.' He sent Walter the sudden blinding smile again. 'Dr Kane, you mentioned helping the days along for me.'

'Yes?'

'Books,' said Fremlin. 'Could you get me books?'

'I don't see why not. Exactly what would you . . .'

'Something light. H. G. Wells, maybe. He has a wonderful sense of irony. And perhaps some plays. I saw Noel Coward's *Hay Fever* some years ago; I should like to read that and imagine myself in a London theatre for a first night again.' His voice was suddenly warm. 'Always such an occasion, a first night. One wore black tie, of course,' said the man who had stabbed and strangled five women before burying their bodies in a forest. 'There were drinks at the interval, and often a little supper afterwards.'

'With friends? A lady?'

'Sometimes. These things are always more enjoyable in the company of a friend.' The dark eyes flickered, and Walter had the impression of a shutter being closed. Damn, I've pushed him too far. 'And,' said Fremlin, 'could you get some poetry for me as well?'

'I expect so. Any particular poet? Byron? Wordsworth?'

'Either of those two. And Wilfred Owen, perhaps. Not Oscar Wilde. There might be a certain amount of style in walking to the gallows reading Byron's poems,' said Neville Fremlin thoughtfully, 'but I'm damned if I'll do so with "The Ballad of Reading Gaol". But then of course,' he said looking at Walter, 'I daresay I'm damned anyway.'

'There's supposed to be some comfort in repentance,' said Walter a bit awkwardly.

'The payment of a debt? So the padre keeps telling me.'

'The trial must have been a great ordeal,' said Walter, choosing his words with care. 'Waiting for the verdict – and then hearing the sentence pronounced.'

'I expected the verdict. I expected the sentence, as well.'

'The newspapers said you were perfectly calm throughout.'

'Yes, I believe I was. It's supposed to be one of the obligations of a gentleman,' said Fremlin, but he said it with such irony that Walter found himself exchanging an appreciative smile with the man before he realized it.

'Even so, one of the reports said you hardly seemed to notice the crowds.' It was a fair bet that some of the victims' families would have been in court on that last day, and Walter thought this might be a way of getting Fremlin to open up about Elizabeth Molland.

'It was quite crowded now I think back. But I wasn't playing to the gallery, at least not consciously. Most of the watchers were probably direct descendants of people who used to attend public hangings,' said Fremlin. 'All those crones who sat knitting at the foot of the guillotine and the Victorian ballad sellers who made up songs at Tyburn. They won't make up ballads about me, I don't suppose, but if they do they'll have enough material to work with.'

'The Silver-Tongued Murderer and his five victims?'

This time there was definitely a reaction. Fremlin looked at Walter very hard for a moment. But he only said, 'It makes for a good title, doesn't it? But I shouldn't think there'd be many dance bands who'd want to play it. Thank you for offering to get the books for me, Dr Kane. That's something I very much appreciate.'

'I suppose I have to be convinced of his guilt,' said Walter to Lewis Caradoc three nights later. 'A jury found him guilty and a judge pronounced the death sentence.'

'Juries aren't infallible,' said Lewis Caradoc. 'More wine?'

'Thank you, sir, yes please.' Walter waited for the wine to be poured, and Lewis Caradoc thought that one of the nice things about this young man was his politeness. It was impossible to imagine him being discourteous in any situation. He's the son I haven't got, thought Lewis sadly, or perhaps he's the son I lost . . .

But this was not a thought to dwell on, and this informal dinner at his house was intended to be half friendly, half professional, so he said, 'You're not seriously doubting Fremlin's guilt, are you?'

'Not really,' said Walter. 'I suppose it's natural to wonder a bit though, isn't it? Or does it all become just part of the routine after a time?'

'I never found it did,' said Lewis. 'Another cutlet?'

'Yes, please.' Walter had been rather flattered to be invited to Sir Lewis's house, and after Calvary's plain fare he was enjoying the food, which had been set out in covered dishes by a neat parlour maid who had then withdrawn leaving them to serve themselves. There was no sign of Lady Caradoc whom Walter had not met; when he arrived Sir Lewis had said briefly that she was away and had not referred to her again.

Sir Lewis served the cutlet, and said, 'Have you discovered anything about the other girl yet? The one they never found?' Walter looked up. 'Higneth's told me about the police request – it's unusual but not entirely unknown. Higneth knew I intended to talk to you about Fremlin, so if you want to discuss it with me it will be all right. You can trust me not to gossip afterwards, of course. But if you'd rather talk about something else I'll understand. I was curious, that's all.'

'I haven't found out anything,' said Walter. 'It's four days since Fremlin was brought to Calvary and I've seen him twice each day, but he hasn't talked about the murders at all. He'll discuss most things, apparently quite openly. Things he's done in his life that he's enjoyed: music, the theatre, books, studying for the pharmaceutical exams. But I'm wondering if he's playing a game. Taunting me – letting me think I'm getting near to a confidence, and then shutting up shop, so to speak.'

'Keep trying,' said Lewis. 'There have been gallows confessions.'

'Fremlin's perfectly polite when he closes that mental door,' said Walter, 'but once he's done it, he's unreachable.' He paused, his mind on the man in the condemned cell: the man who had said there would be style in going to the gallows reading Byron's poems. 'Sir Lewis, how usual is it for a man on the brink of being executed to play games of that kind?'

'Very unusual indeed in my experience,' said Lewis. 'It may simply be bravado and, if it is, Fremlin will probably crack near the end. But it's possible he's got a murderer's vanity and believes he'll find a way to slide out of this.' He glanced at Walter. 'I shouldn't think there's any danger of that, should you, Walter?'

'No,' said Walter at once. 'No danger at all.'

After Walter had left, chugging down the driveway in his little car, Lewis poured himself another glass of brandy, and sat by the fire with it. It was extraordinary how talking to Kane had sent his own mind scudding back across the years – it was the eagerness, of course that was so reminiscent of his son, and the idealism. Caspar had had exactly the same qualities – several times, talking to Walter, Lewis had thought it might almost be his son who sat there.

The idealism and eagerness had never been more apparent than on the late-spring day in 1915 when Caspar left for France with his regiment. Off to beat the Hun, he had said, with the light glowing in his eyes and the smile that people said was the very print of Lewis's own smile. Off to give the Kaiser a pasting. But he would be back before they knew it: the war would not last long – everyone said so – and they must keep the home fires burning for his return and have a hero's welcome ready.

Lewis had loved his son undemonstratively but very deeply, even though he had never cared much for the name Clara had insisted on. Surely they were not going to saddle the child with a name like Caspar Caradoc? he had said at the birth, half amused, half annoyed – but Clara had refused to give way. A romantic name, she had said. Names shaped people, she had always believed that, and this was a name that might lead their son to do great things. In those days it had been easier to give way to Clara and so he had agreed, thinking he would shorten it to Cas, which was a not unattractive diminutive, and which should not cause the boy too many problems during his school years. Clara had persistently called him Caspar, but to most people he had been Cas and Lewis had always thought of him as that, so much so that when the telegram arrived there had been a moment when he had not recognized it as referring to his son at all. Not my boy after all! he had thought. Thank God!

'Deeply regret to inform you . . . Lieutenant Caspar Caradoc killed in action, 23 March, 1916, at Verdun. A heroic death, fighting to save several of his comrades . . . Our deepest condolences . . .'

The fact that Cas's death had been heroic had not made losing him any easier. Lewis had been in agony at his son's death, and although he had done his best to comfort Clara she had shut him out. Months later, when Lewis was beginning to reach some degree of acceptance, she had seized on a mawkish custom of the long-gone Victorian era. She was already wearing black for Cas, of course, but now she had a lock of his soft baby hair made into one of the old-fashioned mourning brooches. She commissioned a large, elaborate marble stone for their local church and visited it every day, sitting in front of it, sometimes until it was dark, murmuring the engraved words over and over to herself. When this wretched war was over she would travel to France to find Caspar's burial place; no, she did not want Lewis to accompany her, thank you; she would prefer to be on her own to find her beloved boy. Lewis had been trying to hold on to the good things about Cas – his vivid enthusiasm and bright intelligence – but Clara's grief had become bound up with graves and cold stone memorials and worm-nibbled coffins in lonely foreign soil.

After a time he consulted Dr McNulty, Calvary's new doctor, who said that people dealt with grief in different ways, but that he would very gladly come to dinner to observe Lady Caradoc. Lewis did not much care for the man, but since 1914 so many doctors had joined the medical corps that Calvary had had to take what it could get, and what it had got was Denzil McNulty.

McNulty watched Clara intently throughout the meal: Lewis tried not to think there was a greediness in his eyes as he did so. After dinner, seated in Lewis's study, McNulty said the healing process progressed in stages, and he thought Lady Caradoc's present melancholy was one of those stages. The bereaved person repudiated the reality of death, he said, and sought to call back the spirit who had gone ahead. Whether it was conscious or unconscious, this was what Lady Caradoc was doing now; it was the reason for the visits to her son's memorial and her insistence on finding his grave after the war ended. It was not unusual to encounter such behaviour and there might be ways that he, McNulty, could help. Seeing Lewis's slight frown, he said smoothly that he had colleagues who might guide her thoughts onto more positive paths.

Lewis, thinking McNulty referred to psychiatrists, and disliking the rather flowery references to souls and spirits going ahead, said, non-committally, that he was most grateful for the advice and he would think it over.

It had not, of course, been possible to tell McNulty that one of the stages in Clara's mourning appeared to be an inflexible chastity. After an enforced celibacy of almost six months Lewis had made a tentative move to share his wife's bed again, only to be met with flat rejection. Her life was devoted now to the memory of her beloved boy, said Clara, and she was surprised and rather saddened to discover that Lewis could con-template anything of such an *earthy* nature. This was said with a delicate shudder and the implication that it was insensitive and even rather coarse of him to have made such an approach. Intimacy, said Clara, with her maddening air of closing a subject, was quite out of the question; Lewis must understand that.

What Lewis understood was that Clara – never overly impressed by the physicality of marriage was locking her bedroom door for good. It did not come as much of a surprise; the marriage had been lukewarm from the start, but it had been entered into in the days when such things were still as much a matter of business as anything else.

The young people of today would express incredulity and derision at such an outlook – Cas, if he had lived, would probably have done so, and so, Lewis thought, would Walter Kane – but in the closing years of the nineteenth century it was how people had behaved: your money, my title. Clara had been very pleased to become Lady Caradoc, and Lewis had been very pleased with the marriage settlement made by her wealthy merchant banker family.

He supposed he would have to accept Clara's embargo – he was damned if he was going to knock humbly on his own wife's bedroom door again, especially when there were other bedroom doors he might knock on and be reasonably sure of finding them unlocked. There were probably not many possibilities for that in Thornbeck, but despite his work at Calvary he was in London quite often; Clara's money made that possible, of course, just as it made the upkeep of the small elegant house in Cheyne Walk possible.

He had begun to consider which bedroom doors he would try, when the next stage of Clara's mourning presented itself. It was a stage that startled Lewis very much indeed.

CHAPTER SEVEN

November 1917

'Lewis,' Clara said, 'the most remarkable thing has happened.'

It must be very remarkable indeed because it had brought Clara into Lewis's study, a room whose existence she normally ignored, apart from regularly asking when he was going to discard the disreputable leather chairs and the battered desk because guests would think they could not afford good furniture. A nice chintz from Liberty's, and one of those fumed oak desks with a leatherette top, said Clara. It would be much easier to clean. She did not, of course, do any cleaning of the house herself but she was strict with the two housemaids and could not abide an undusted surface or a badly swept carpet. Lewis had given up saying he liked his study as it was; the chairs and the desk had belonged to his father and been part of the library. The desk still bore the inkstain where his father had knocked over the inkpot.

Cas, when he was very small, had said the mark was the shape of an elephant, and had made up a story about a miniature elephant that lived in the desk and had built itself a house from pens and inkpots and writing paper.

Two weeks earlier Dr McNulty had persuaded Clara to leave Thornbeck and the sad stone monument in the churchyard for the livelier environs of London and the Cheyne Walk house. Lewis was guiltily grateful for her absence which allowed him to concentrate on drafting a report for the Home Office on the rehabilitation of long-term prisoners before their release. This was a subject on which he felt quite strongly: he believed it was wrong to turn unprepared men and women into the world after several decades behind prison walls, and he thought he might one day want to focus on it more fully. He had been delighted to be asked to form part of an official inquiry into the subject.

Clara returned in the middle of the afternoon, and when she came into the study Lewis saw at once that something had wrought a massive change in her. Not only had she entered without her normal polite tap on the door ('I know that gentlemen, when engaged in business, do not like to be disturbed.'), she seated herself in one of the despised chairs. Her hands were clasped, her bosom was heaving with some suppressed emotion, and her rather large face was flushed. For a wild moment Lewis wondered if she had been drinking or taking drugs; this particular exalted well-being was something he had occasionally seen in prisoners who had managed to get their hands on a few grains of cocaine.

But he would have sworn that Clara knew nothing of drugs, and the only alcohol she ever took was a ladylike glass of sherry. He listened to the account of the last fortnight, which appeared to include such innocuous pastimes as a little dilettante shopping, visits to her family, and tea at Gunter's with her cousins. There was nothing in any of that to account for this astonishing change.

And then Clara said, 'But, Lewis, I have saved the real news until last. I have formed a new friendship.' She sat back, and Lewis stared at her and thought, A man? An affair? Is that what she's going to tell me? But Clara was surely the very last person to have an affair. And she was saying something about there being two friends. She had met them through the good offices of Denzil McNulty, who had been so kind. Lewis could not imagine how very kind Dr McNulty had been.

'I hadn't realized McNulty would be in London,' said Lewis. 'Who are the new friends?'

'A Mr Bartlam Partridge and his wife, Violette. They have a house in North London. Quite out of the fashionable part, of course, but one is not a snob, or at least, one hopes not.'

'Indeed no,' said Lewis, managing to keep the irony from his voice.

The meeting, said Clara, had been arranged before she left Thornbeck but she had deliberately not told Lewis about it. Yes, she knew he made no objection to her having her own friends and to coming and going as she wished – her dear mother often said how very modern that was. But she had thought Lewis might pour scorn on these new friends, so she had said nothing.

'When did I ever pour scorn on anyone?' murmured Lewis. 'After all, I spend most of my days with villains and murderers.'

Clara disliked it when Lewis talked about Calvary's residents and she ignored this. She said that she and Violette Partridge had taken to one another immediately and Violette believed they were intended to become the greatest friends. Bart – his wife always called him Bart – had said in a very jovial way that he could see he was going to have his nose put out of joint.

'It's always pleasant to make congenial friends,' said Lewis after a moment. 'I look forward to meeting them some time.'

'You must meet them as soon as possible,' said Clara earnestly. 'But you have not yet heard the really wonderful part about all this.'

A faint prickle of apprehension brushed across Lewis's skin. She's too happy. This is all wrong. 'Yes?'

'Violette Partridge is a – a medium. Able to call up the spirits of those who have passed over.'

'Dear God,' said Lewis.

'She and Bart hold seances at their house. Lewis, they are going to enable me to speak with the spirit of my dearest boy.'

Lewis had no especial prejudice against the practice of spiritualism. He considered the dead should be left alone, and in his heart he did not really believe it was possible to contact them. He thought most of the so-called conversations with spirits were the results of elaborate tricks, but, that aside, it seemed to him a harmless deception and something that apparently brought solace to a great many people. If it comforted Clara he would not object to her attending one or two spiritualist gatherings, although he did not much care for Denzil McNulty's involvement.

'Oh, you need have no qualms about Dr McNulty,' said Clara when Lewis mentioned this. 'He attends the seances as an observer only – he is extremely interested in all aspects of the Great Mysteries, you know.'

'I didn't know.'

'He is a member of several learned societies which study the subject,' said Clara. 'Groups of gentlemen who enquire into such matters in a scientific and scholarly manner.'

McNulty's kept all that quiet, thought Lewis. Still, a man's beliefs are his own, and providing it doesn't inter- fere with his work at Calvary – which I don't think it does – I can hardly object.

'Vita is very eager to meet you,' Clara was saying.

'Is she? I would prefer not, Clara. In any case, I'm far too busy.'

'Oh, your wretched murderers again. I should have thought the opportunity to talk to our boy would have been more important than a parcel of common felons.'

If Lewis said that for the next few days he would be absorbed in the death of a young man who made him think of Cas, Clara would succumb to one of her stately sulking fits and life would be unbearable. So he said, 'This Home Office sub-committee is taking up a lot of my time.' That ought to satisfy her; she liked to think of him having dealings with government ministers; she boasted about it.

'Then I must attend the meeting on my own.'

'I hope it brings you some comfort,' was all Lewis could think of to say.

*

Lewis had presided over perhaps a dozen executions during his time at Calvary. He had thought, at the beginning, that he would become accustomed to this business of taking a man's life, to the old biblical premise of an eye for an eye, but he had not.

'The trouble is, sir, that you see the killers when they're beaten and caged and meek,' one of the West Riding police inspectors said shortly after Nicholas O'Kane's arrest. 'Perhaps if you saw the victims, you'd feel differently.'

'O'Kane isn't precisely a killer.'

'O'Kane's a traitor,' said the inspector. 'I'll grant you he hasn't personally strangled with his own hands, or used a gun to shoot anyone through the head, but he's probably been responsible for a great many deaths. You know he was one of the rebels in the Easter Rising in Dublin last year?'

'Yes. He's half Irish.'

'The rebels paralysed the entire city to proclaim the birth of the Irish Republic,' said the inspector. 'O'Kane was at the centre of it all, Sir Lewis, although it wasn't until months later we finally tracked him down. Somehow – and I'll never know how he did it – he had inveigled himself into the Admiralty offices. Everything that went through his hands – anything that gave a clue about the whereabouts of our ships – went straight to the Kaiser's armies.'

'He was beside himself with bitterness and fury against the British,' said Lewis. 'They believed in a cause, those young men. Patrick Pearse and Eamonn de Valera and all the rest of them. O'Kane was distraught with grief and anger. He simply snatched the nearest weapon he could.'

'The nearest weapon,' said the inspector caustically, 'happened to be the selling of naval information to the enemy. Because of that information our ships were torpedoed. Lives were lost – the lives of young men fighting this country's enemies.'

Young men's lives . . . Lewis said, 'You're quite right, of course, Inspector. There's nothing romantic about a traitor.'

'Indeed there is not, sir. You've got extra guards on duty for the next three weeks, I hear.'

'Yes.'

The inspector glanced about him, at Calvary's bleak walls and locked doors. 'No one's ever escaped from here, have they?'

'No,' said Lewis. 'But we've never had an Irish rebel before.'

'You're thinking someone might try to get him out?'

'It's a possibility I have to consider. O'Kane will leave a wife and small son, and the Irish can be sentimental about such things.'

'I know about the wife and son,' said the inspector thoughtfully. 'But to my way of thinking O'Kane should have thought of that before he set about selling information to Germany. Murderers have no business having wives and children, and in my book O'Kane is as bad as any wife killer or mistress poisoner.'

'They're saying this one is as bad as any wife killer,' said Calvary's head warder, watching the porridge-faced warder finish the grim task of digging a grave for a man still living. 'And I don't know but what I wouldn't agree with that. To my mind it's a nasty affair, this selling out of your country. I shan't be sorry to see this one turned off.'

The porridge-faced warder, whose name was Saul Ketch and who had just come off guard duty on the condemned prisoner, would not be sorry, either. He disliked glossy-haired young men who behaved with unnatural politeness in the condemned cell, and who reminded the female warders of Rudolph Valentino, so that they sighed to think of the ugly death waiting for him. That was nothing but a lot of female nonsense to Ketch's way of thinking. If a man had committed murder, he should pay with his life.

He laid down his spade and straightened up, wiping his forehead with the back of his hand. Digging a grave made you sweat like a pig. He pulled the thick gardener's gloves from his pocket, because the next part of the task was to open the lime store. Ketch put on the gloves and made sure his trousers were tucked into the tops of his boots. You got two pairs of uniform trousers with the job, but Ketch and a few of the other warders ran a nice little business selling prison-issue clothes in a second-hand shop in Kendal. You did not really need both pairs; if you were careful, one pair could last you two or three years, and it was a nice little sideline. He had a few other sidelines as well, but the clothes one was the best, although it meant if he splashed lime on these trousers he had not a spare pair, so he had to be careful.

He had to be careful anyway, with Old Muttonchops watching him and very likely Lewis Caradoc glancing out of the window of his posh study as well. Ketch sent a sidelong glance to the steep wall of Calvary, but nothing seemed to be moving behind any of the windows –

unless, of course, it might be old Pierrepoint creeping through the deserted passages, trying to catch a glimpse of his man without being seen.

Ketch walked across to the corrugated iron door in a corner of the burial yard, and unfastened the padlock. He opened the door slowly, keeping well back because he was not going to get himself burned, not for Nicholas O'bloody Kane nor Lewis Caradoc, nor anybody. Even like this – before you poured on the water that slaked it – lime could be dangerous. Volatile or some such word they called it; Ketch did not bother overmuch about words. That tart Belinda Skelton brought in books to read when she was on duty which Ketch considered a form of showing-off. Belinda was trying to catch the eye of the governor, of course, Ketch knew all about that, and he was watching her very closely. Most people thought the governor was cold and strict – aloof they called it – but Ketch had seen a certain look in Lewis Caradoc's eyes at times, particularly when he looked at Skelton. It did not take fancy words or book-learning to know when a man was wanting to get between a tart's legs.

Ketch did not entirely blame Sir Lewis, what with being married to that cold-eyed Lady Caradoc. A man wanted a bit of warmth in his bed of a night, and if it came down to it, Ketch was not averse to giving any tart a good seeing-to himself, although Belinda had smacked his face when he once said that to her. Downright insulting, she had said. Women were not playthings or objects. Ketch had not understood what she meant, but he had gone away thinking Belinda would pay for smacking his face one of these fine nights. She gave herself such airs, the slut, but Ketch would even the score before much longer. Considering how to do that had warmed him on many a dull spell of night duty.

If the governor really did bang the slut, Ketch would go straight to the doctor with the information. The doctor had some odd ways – they said he went to those groups where people tried to contact the dead, which to Ketch's mind was downright daft – but he would be a bad person to cross. He liked knowing about people – he liked knowing their secrets – but if you gave him information you had to be able to prove it was true. The doctor would not pay for any made-up stories.

'You bring me information about people inside Calvary,' he said to Ketch. 'Things you see or hear or find out. If I can make use of it, you'll get your cut. But you have to bring me proof, mind that.'

Ketch was minding it. He was going to be watching Belinda Skelton and the governor to see if they got into bed together, and he going to enjoy the watching. He would enjoy getting money from Dr McNulty as well. The prospect of all this pleasurable watching and money-making enabled him to shovel out the dry lime with a good will. Even when Old Muttonchops told him off to move a bit faster because they did not want to be here all day, Ketch said, quite meekly, 'Sorry, Mr Millichip,' and got on with filling up the tin vat with lime in readiness for activating and then for chucking onto Nicholas O'Kane's body tomorrow.

Lewis had gone back to his office after seeing O'Kane's wife and son to Calvary's doors and making sure arrangements had been made for their journey home.

The interview had disturbed him. The woman had been distraught, her face had been marked by extreme pallor and her eyes were swollen with constant crying. Beneath had been traces of considerable beauty, although this was not surprising – O'Kane was not a man who would have married a plain woman. The boy had interested Lewis – he had reminded him a little of Cas at the same age. A bright child, he thought, and hoped O'Kane's wife would control her grief sufficiently well to handle the matter of the father's death with tact.

It was the custom at Calvary for the female warders to bring cups of afternoon tea to the staff; Lewis did not always bother to drink his, but he encouraged the small habit which seemed to him to maintain a fragile link with civilized behaviour in an uncivilized place.

Today it was the slant-eyed Belinda Skelton who was on tea duty. She set the cup down on his desk and Lewis noticed, as he had noticed before, that her nails were bitten but that the shape of her hands was beautiful. Was the skin of her palms as soft as it looked?

He went on writing some notes, and was aware she hesitated. When he looked up enquiringly, she said, 'Mrs O'Kane was dreadfully upset, wasn't she, sir?' and Lewis remembered he had assigned Belinda to the condemned wing that morning. He would not normally have put a female warder there, but Nicholas O'Kane had shown no signs of violence and even if he had, Saul Ketch had also been on duty. He had thought that the presence of a female might be reassuring for Mrs O'Kane and the child.

'Yes, she was very upset. It's difficult to find words of comfort at such a time, Belinda.'

'I'll bet *you* found them, though,' she said. '*Is* he guilty, sir? Mr O'Kane?'

'Yes, he is. He's a traitor.'

'Oh yes, sir.' She paused. 'They're saying – the warders – that you're worried someone might try to get him out before tomorrow.'

'Are they, indeed? Well, you can tell them I'm not worried in the least. No one will get into Calvary tonight.'

'Mightn't Mr O'Kane have had his reasons for doing what he did, sir?'

'I can't think of any good reasons for anything he did,' said Lewis a bit sharply.

'I s'pose not.' She looked at him steadily. Unusually for a fair-haired girl she had quite dark blue eyes with black lashes. Beautiful, thought Lewis, staring at her. Eyes you could drown in. With the thought came a throb of sexual desire, which he instantly tried to repress. He reached for a sheaf of papers at random, thinking he would appear to be immersed in work, and she would go away. He did not trust himself to look directly at her again. Had she sensed that sudden shiver of physical awareness? Yes, of course she had.

Belinda said, 'Sorry, sir, I'm forgetting who you are and who I am.' The words were correct, but the tone was not – Lewis recognized a note of parody. I know my place. Like one of those saucy music-hall performers around the turn of the century, burlesquing pert maids out to seduce the master. He looked up involuntarily, and she grinned at him like an urchin. The tension lightened at once.

'I'll leave you to your tea, sir.'

Despite his resolve, Lewis watched her go out, and had to repress a desire to follow her. He drank his tea, and saw that it was half past four and O'Kane had just over fifteen hours of life left.

'The weight's worked out to a whisker, Sir Lewis,' said Thomas Pierrepoint in his down-to-earth manner. Lewis had heard people say that Pierrepoint's manner was indicative of insensitivity, and that you could not be an executioner and have many of the finer feelings left to you. He did not agree with this; he believed Pierrepoint's matter-of-fact air was simply the countryman's calm acceptance of life and death.

'Everything's in place,' Pierrepoint was saying. 'I'll go along presently and try out the sandbags as usual. But I've not bungled one yet, as you know, sir.'

'Have you seen O'Kane? asked Lewis.

'Aye, I've seen him. I saw him when they exercised him in the yard earlier on. Reckless look he has. If it's agreeable to you, sir, we'll hood him before we take him in, just to be sure he doesn't try to jump at the last minute.'

Lewis was aware of revulsion at the thought of O'Kane led like a blinded animal to his death. It's because he's attractive and young, he thought, that's all. It's nothing to do with his fleeting resemblance to Cas – that way he has of tilting his head as if he's challenging every authority there is. Cas did that the last time I saw him, but the challenge then was for the Kaiser's armies. Nicholas O'Kane's challenge was with this country.

He said, 'By all means put on the hood early, Mr Pierrepoint.'

'These idealistic young men, sir, they sometimes like to make that last reckless gesture, you see,' said Pierrepoint, almost as if he was apologizing. 'As if they want to show they aren't afraid. So they try to leap down into the trap and meet death halfway, as they call it. Still, we've seen a lot of that these last three years. Young men going off to meet death, thinking it's a glorious thing.'

'Yes, we have,' said Lewis expressionlessly. 'Mr Pierrepoint, I'm staying here tonight, of course, and they'll bring me in some supper at about nine o'clock. You'll be very welcome to join me. And your assistant, of course.'

'Thanking you kindly, Sir Lewis, but I can never relish a meal in company on the night before a hanging. I'm not a fanciful man, well, I wouldn't be doing this work if I were. I'm not one to be having an attack of nerves, female-like, or saying I can't eat a bite, but it's true that food never lies easy on my stomach just before turning a man off. My assistant'll likely be off to the King's Head for a sup of ale later – boasting about who he is and what's he's doing here, I shouldn't wonder – but I'll take my bite of supper by myself. And I'll make an early night if that's agreeable.'

Lewis said, 'Then I'll see you tomorrow morning, Mr Pierrepoint.'

CHAPTER EIGHT

No one will get into Calvary tonight, Lewis had said to Belinda Skelton, but as he walked along the prison's dimly lit corridors he could not help thinking that something *had* got in. Cas would have said, with serious eyes, that death had entered the prison and was stalking the corridors, peering into the men's cells one by one, saying, Ah yes, that one is not for me, nor that one. But this one – oh yes, this is the one who is waiting for me . . . But then Cas would have smiled the narrow-eyed smile, and said, God, what fantastical nonsense and wouldn't you think I'd have grown out of all that stuff years since.

Lewis did not consider himself to be what Thomas Pierrepoint called fanciful, but he knew that on the night before a hanging something happened to Calvary. The change in atmosphere was largely due to the prisoners' unease and to the extreme fear and nervous tension within the condemned block itself, but he always thought it was as if the prison slid down into a half-haunted state.

The prisoners hated a hanging. The warders had instructions not to tell them about it, but they always knew. They heard the scrape of spade against earth in the burial yard and they saw the warders with the marks of quicklime on their boots, and they gathered in frightened little groups in the exercise yard, whispering together, half resentful, half fearful. It was extraordinary to see these men – many of whom were killers in their own right and had narrowly escaped the gallows themselves – so strongly and so visibly affected.

The gas lamps in the corridors were always turned down after the prisoners were locked into their cells for the night, but they were never turned off completely. Normally there was no one abroad in the evening, except the handful of night warders, but tonight was different. Tonight people came and went within the flickering bluish gaslight, occasionally pausing to exchange a word, frequently hunching their shoulders as if to ward off a cold breath of air, or glancing about them as if fearful of being watched.

Denzil McNulty was among them, subdued and deferential, but his normally sallow face showed a tinge of colour and he was unable to wholly conceal a self-important swagger. The chaplain, sombre and absorbed, walked the dimly lit halls as well, the prayer book clutched to his chest, a ribbon marking the page for the burial service. His lips moved as if in prayer and he looked at his pocket watch with nervous regularity.

Shortly after half past seven Lewis saw Mr Pierrepoint and his assistant shuffle their way through the gloom, the shameful bag of their curious trade in their hands.

Presently he heard the clang of gates being unlocked and then the scrape of the execution shed door opening and closing. The two men would carry out their sandbag tests as quietly as possible, but several times – perhaps as many as four or five – the prison would feel a dull thrumming as the gallows lever was released and the trap opened.

Before supper Lewis had talked to Denzil McNulty. Had the prisoner been given the usual bromide? Had he made any special requests?

'I haven't given the bromide yet, I'm just off to do so now,' said McNulty. 'There aren't any requests, as far as I know. He's very quiet. He'll go like a gentleman, this one.'

But Lewis knew Pierrepoint intended to put the hood on the prisoner outside the execution chamber, and could not stop thinking that O'Kane would go not so much like a gentleman but more like an animal made docile, unable to see the instrument of death that waited for him.

He knew, deep down, he was feeling this way because he liked O'Kane. There was no accounting for such things, and there was no law saying a killer or a traitor could not possess charm. It was nothing to do with his resemblance to Cas; there was no possible link between them. In fact, they were worlds apart because Cas would never have betrayed his country. But hadn't Cas fought for a cause he believed in just as Nicholas O'Kane had? Cas had known he faced death because of that cause, and O'Kane had known it as well. When it came down to it, both had been destined to die: Cas on a mud-drenched battlefield in France, O'Kane at the end of a rope. Lewis thought that Cas would certainly have been prepared to go into the Kaiser's realm to get information about German secrets to pass to his country. He would have seen it as brave and romantic and honourable – and he, too, might have ended in some dreary prison cell, watching the minutes slide by until morning.

He went back to his office. A small inner room opened off it, furnished with a narrow bed and a washstand. In accordance with custom soap and towels had been put out for him. Calvary's governor – any prison's governor – was expected to spend the night inside the gaol before an execution.

He ate his supper without tasting it. It was half past nine now – O'Kane must be watching the minutes tick by in much the same way. Or would McNulty's bromide have sent him into a dreamless sleep by this time? Lewis frowned and reached for his book. He would read until ten o'clock, and then go along to see if O'Kane slept. If he did not, Lewis would sit with him for an hour. After that he could talk with the chaplain.

He lay on the bed, trying to relax, wishing his muscles were not so tense. By tomorrow night every bone in his body would feel bruised, as if he had been struck repeatedly with a hammer. Blind bruising, he called it to himself, and wished, as he always wished on these nights, that there was a sympathetic female waiting for him at home, someone who would understand the nightmare that went with this part of the job, and who would apply whatever comforts might be available. Simple things like a hot bath, a stiff drink, a listening ear.

After presiding over his first few hangings he had tried to talk to Clara about this feeling but she had looked at him in blank astonishment, and said surely he had known what the post of governor would entail? It was to be hoped he was not developing some ridiculous senti-mental notion about clemency or forgiveness, said Clara. Murder was murder, and those committing it deserved their fate. She, personally, had no qualms whatsoever about the executing of a convicted criminal.

(But supposing the criminal in question is only a few years older than Cas, and supposing he has Cas's trick of tilting his head challengingly, as if he was prepared to take on the world?)

Lewis forced his mind to the pages of his book. He had chosen Somerset Maugham's *Of Human Bondage*, liking the gracefulness of the phrasing and the gentle unwinding of the hero's tribulations. But he could not concentrate. Every emotion and every feeling that dwelled inside Calvary tonight seemed to be settling on the condemned cell along the passageway, and the printed words danced meaninglessly before his eyes. If it was Cas in that condemned cell tonight, what would I do? With the thought came a sudden painful image of Cas, and the day he had left.

The countryside had looked so beautiful – the woods around Thornbeck had been smoky with the haze of bluebells, and the cuckoo was calling everywhere.

At the railway station there had been flags flying and military bands playing, and there had been crowds of family and friends to cheer the soldiers off. None of them had known what was ahead, although some of the old soldiers – the fathers and grandfathers of these heart-breakingly young men – might have guessed at some of it. But none of them could have guessed that those boys were going into a world of muddy battles, violent shelling, mustard gas and of men drowning in quagmires and dying squalidly from dysentery . . .

The ache of loss sliced through Lewis all over again and he lay back on the bed, pressing his face into the pillow, fighting for self-control. Through the muffled difficult sobs, he was aware that someone had knocked at the door. Oh God, no. No one must see me like this.

The tap came again, and then the door was pushed hesitantly open. Lewis managed to say, 'Yes?'

It was Belinda Skelton. She paused, looking round the main office, then turned to look through the partly open inner door. By now Lewis was sitting on the edge of the bed, more or less composed, although he thought the marks of his emotions were still visible.

'I didn't see you in there, sir. They've made coffee in the canteen – quite a treat for once. I thought you might like a cup after your supper.'

'Thank you, Belinda. Yes, I should.' Had his voice sounded all right? A bit false, maybe. She would not notice.

But she did. She set the cup down and came to the doorway of the inner room.

'Is something wrong, sir?'

'Not at all,' said Lewis. 'I'm only tired.' And now all I have to do is thank her for the coffee, pick up my book, and she'll go.

'You hate these hours, don't you?' she said, not moving. 'I mean – the last few hours before a hanging.'

'Yes, I do. How did you know?'

'I don't know. Is it just because of this particular one – Mr O'Kane? Or do you always hate it?'

'I always hate it,' said Lewis. 'But tonight is worse than usual.'

'Why? I don't mean to be prying, sir, but— Is it because he's young? Or because he's – I don't know the right word. Because he believes so strongly that what he did was right?'

'The word you're looking for is idealistic,' said Lewis, and saw her give a small nod as if she was tucking away the newly learned word. Her hair was lit from behind by the desk lamp. It was pinned under her cap, but little tendrils had escaped. Lewis suddenly wondered what she would look like with her hair loose and tumbling over her bare shoulders. He said, 'Nicholas O'Kane reminds me a little of my son, that's all.' *All?* said his mind angrily. *All,* when it's tearing me into pieces?

'Your son who was killed in France? I heard about that. It'll be a difficult thing for you, then, seeing Mr O'Kane hanged and all.'

'Yes.'

She was still standing in the doorway. Her skin was white, like alabaster or porcelain. She would be warm and welcoming, and she would drive away some of the ghosts. But I'd be mad, thought Lewis – it's insane even to think about it. But the ache for Cas was still with him and the black loneliness that always gripped him on these nights had bitten deeply this time. He looked at Belinda and thought, Would it be so disastrous? She's indicated more than once that she'd be willing. She hasn't actually said it aloud, but we both know. But supposing it's all a trick – or even a bet with the other warders? Or supposing she's deliberately set out to seduce me, intending to use it against me later?

But it was as if the normal values and rules of his world had turned upside-down. He stared at Belinda and thought, Just for company. Just for half an hour of human warmth and human sympathy. No, that's utterly selfish, I can't make use of her like that. I'll thank her for the coffee and she'll go away.

But instead of the cool words of thanks and dismissal he had intended, he said, 'Will you stay and drink the coffee with me, Belinda?' And then as she smiled, he heard himself say, 'And are we going to keep on playing this game, or are you going to come over here to the bed?'

It was as simple and as straightforward as that. No pretence about needing to be coaxed. No coy flutterings of, 'Oh, sir, I shouldn't . . .' or, 'What will you think of me afterwards?'

No genteel demurrals or protestations that she did not usually, but perhaps just this once . . .

Belinda closed the inner door and came to stand at the side of the bed. She pulled off the linen cap, tugging at her hair so that it cascaded around her shoulders. Her eyes narrowed in a sudden smile of intimacy, and she unfastened the buttons of the ugly prison uniform and slid out of it. Lewis saw with delight that there was no ungainly struggling with lacings or whalebonings: she simply unbuttoned the bodice and stepped out of the dark blue gown. Beneath it she wore a few wisps of white cotton and what looked like silk stockings. Lewis could not remember the last time he had seen a female's legs in such gossamer-thin silk stockings, and the sight was almost unbearably arousing. They were held up with little black garters. Had she worn the stockings and the garters deliberately tonight? If she had Lewis was beyond caring. He held out his hands to her and she took them eagerly and let him draw her down onto the bed.

She locked her hands behind his head, kissing him as if she had been thirsting for him for a very long time. Her mouth tasted young and clean and eager, and her thighs were firm and warm against his body. He finally managed to say in a gasp, 'Belinda, I'll stop in a minute.'

'No – oh, don't stop, Lewis,' she said, and the words and the use of his name seemed to lock them into such deep and exciting intimacy that Lewis gave a half groan, and pulled at his own buttons.

As he moved on top of her he had the feeling she was not quite as experienced as she had let him believe. She knows the opening moves, he thought, and she's not a virgin, but I think this means more to her than she's letting me see. This realization made him pause, and say, 'Are you sure?'

'I put on my only pair of silk stockings specially for this,' she said, her eyes narrowing in amusement.

'I love them,' said Lewis. 'I'll be careful, I'll stop before—'

'You're doing it again,' she said. 'Talking about stopping. Lewis, will you stop being such a fucking gentleman and make love to me.'

Saul Ketch thought if it had not been for the onion broth served at tonight's supper, he might never have known about that tart Belinda Skelton and her carryings-on with Lewis bloody Caradoc.

Ketch had gone along for his supper as usual. A

quarter past nine to the tick it was, although on night duty you only got fifteen minutes to eat and have a bit of a smoke, which Ketch considered mean. He might ask somebody to write a letter about it – there would be no need for him to add the painstaking scrawl that constituted his signature because you should always be able to swear off a thing if it went wrong. But a man could not be expected to eat his food in fifteen minutes. Ketch often took in a gulp of air with his meal on account of having to gobble it down too fast, and this sometimes led to awkwardness later on, particularly in the small warders' rest room. Old Muttonchops had once or twice pointed out that if Ketch did not eat such vast quantities in the first place he would not be continually letting off wind in such a disgusting way afterwards, and one of the female warders had very pointedly brought in some lavender bags to hang over Ketch's chair. Ketch thought the stink of lavender far worse that any internal rumblings or letting-offs that Calvary's onion broth brought about.

He had had two helpings of the onion broth tonight, defiantly slurping it up under the disapproving eye of Muttonchops who was on supper duty and who was always stricter than usual when they were about to turn a bloke off. But Ketch took his time because he did not see why he should not have as much supper as he wanted; it was not going to make any difference to Nicholas sodding O'Kane who ate what, and it was not going to help anybody if Ketch went hungry.

The broth sent him a bit hastily along to the necessary house, and on his way back he saw the tart Belinda padding along the corridors, a cup and saucer in her hand. And a button or two undone on her gown? Ketch stepped back from the flickering light of a nearby gas jet, and stood in the deep shadows, trying to see without being noticed. Yes, the slut had definitely unfastened her gown at the neck, Ketch could see a glimpse of white underneath the dark blue cloth. He could only think of one reason for the trollop to have done that; she was going to meet somebody, and it did not take a genius to guess who that somebody was. Ketch had seen the governor look at Belinda enough times, and he had seen Belinda look at the governor as well, and he felt a thump of pleasure when he thought of how gratified the doctor would be with this little nugget of information. But the doctor would want proof positive, that was always the arrangement, and so Ketch glanced up and down the passages to make sure no one else was around. Then he went after her.

He had been right! There she was, the saucy madam, going into the governor's office, as bold as you liked. Would she take her clothes off for him right away? Ketch remembered there was a bed in there for when the governor stayed in Calvary, and he had a sudden picture of Belinda getting undressed and getting into that bed. If he stayed here to listen, would he be missed? He would surely hear the sounds of the others coming out of the dining room. He tiptoed nearer to the door, hoping to hear what was happening.

And he did! He heard the low murmur of voices, and then Belinda laughed. Sir Lewis's deep voice said something in response, but Ketch could not make out the words. Greatly daring, he pressed closer to the door. If someone came along now and caught him he would be for the high jump, but he would risk it. As he listened, he could hear, beyond the closed door, the rhythmic creaking of a bed and cries and moans. A slow smile spread across Ketch's doughy features. No doubt about what those two were doing, and very thoroughly as well! Who would have thought the disdainful Sir Lewis could have tupped a tart as vigorously as that? It went to show you should not judge by appearances.

Ketch listened for a minute or two longer, still grinning to himself, because from the sound of it they were going at it like a pair of stoats, in fact they would be lucky if they did not bust the bed. He laughed silently at this possibility. But keep it up for a while yet, Sir Lewis – in fact keep everything up – because if I'm to get along to the doctor and bring him back to listen to you, I'll need at least ten minutes.

Lewis half raised himself in the bed and looked down at Belinda. Her hair was spilling across the pillow.

'I didn't hurt you, did I?' he said.

She reached up to trace the contours of his face with one finger. 'You didn't hurt me,' she said. 'It was sweet and loving and honest, wasn't it? But had I better go now?'

Lewis glanced at the time. 'Yes,' he said. 'I'd like you to stay. I'd like us to be together like this again. But tonight there are too many things I should be doing.'

'I understand.' She slid off the bed, and reached for her discarded clothes. She moved more gracefully than anyone Lewis had ever encountered. He was just thinking he would get dressed himself and make sure she got back to her spell of duty without anyone suspecting where she had been, when the outer door opened and footsteps crossed the room to the inner door. Before either of them could move, it opened and Denzil McNulty stood in the doorway.

The curious thing was that in that first crowded moment, the emotion that came to the surface was surprise at McNulty's expression. He's smiling, thought Lewis. That's extraordinary. I'd have expected him to be horrified or embarrassed, but he looks pleased.

Belinda had donned her clothes swiftly, and Lewis managed to find sufficient self-possession to say, 'Go along to your spell of duty, Belinda. We'll talk later.' He saw with gratitude that she did as he asked, and only when the door had closed did he turn his attention back to McNulty.

'Doctor, if you have something to say to me, wait in the office.' What will I do if he refuses? thought Lewis. Hell, this is appalling. I shouldn't have let any of it happen. But McNulty ought to have knocked before coming in, and he certainly oughtn't to have come into this room at all. Is the bastard up to something?

But McNulty left the room as requested. Lewis closed the door and got back into his own clothes as fast as possible. He paused to straighten his tie in the little mirror over the washstand and smooth down his hair, because he was damned if he was going to face that unpleasant little weasel looking dishevelled.

Opening the door into the main office took considerable resolve. McNulty was perched on the edge of the desk. He sometimes affected a monocle and he was wearing it tonight; it caught the flickering gaslight, making it appear that he had a single distorted eye. Lewis

110

said, coldly, 'Be seated if you wish, Doctor,' and took his own place behind the desk.

McNulty said, 'I do feel I should apologize for breaking in on such an intimate little scene, Sir Lewis.' His face was bland but it was impossible to miss the smirk in his voice.

Lewis said, 'Say whatever you have to say and then go.'

'An interesting situation,' said McNulty. 'I suppose it comes down to a matter of honour among gentlemen, and of discretion. The trouble is that discretion can sometimes be rather costly, can't it?' He let the monocle drop, and swung it on the end of the cord.

So it was blackmail. Lewis said, 'I've never found it so. Are you threatening me?'

'Dear me, no. Nothing so crude. Merely an idea I have. And curiously it's something I think your wife would find very interesting.'

Lewis had known it was inevitable that Clara's name would be brought up at some stage, and he waited to see what use McNulty would make of it.

'Lady Caradoc has become so interested in spiritual matters,' said McNulty. 'I've been very pleased to introduce her to one or two like-minded friends, and I do think it's been a comfort to her. That's why I feel – quite strongly – that she would give her support to the experiment I am about to suggest.'

'Experiment?' said Lewis.

The eye-glass stopped swinging on its cord, and McNulty leaned forward. Horrid eyes he has, thought Lewis, fish eyes.

'Yes,' said McNulty. 'And I should certainly like to talk

to Lady Caradoc about it, unless, of course, you felt it might be too – distressing a subject.'

'Suppose you talk to me about it first,' said Lewis guardedly.

'Very well. I daresay you won't have seen an article in this quarter's edition of the *Psychic Journal*, Sir Lewis? No, of course you wouldn't read such a thing, I don't suppose. But there's no need for you to make that involuntary gesture of distaste; it's a most scholarly publication. Many of its subscribers are very learned men – doctors, scientists, statesmen, writers.'

'The gullible and the credible,' Lewis could not help saying.

'That is your opinion, but they are men of enquiring natures, Sir Lewis. Men who allow their minds to remain open to all possibilities. I am proud to count myself as one of their number. The article I'm speaking of makes a remarkable claim.' He paused, clearly choosing his next words carefully. 'A group of medical men,' said McNulty, 'have recently become convinced that at the moment of death there is a change in the body's weight. They have not been able to measure this change with any precision, but they believe the human body under-goes a definite lessening of weight.'

'There must surely be any number of explanations for that.'

'Oh yes, and the writer of the article admits that. But,' said McNulty, 'he also suggests the answer may not be physical.'

'I'm sorry, I don't follow your meaning.'

'No conclusive experiment has yet been conducted,' said McNulty. 'But the writer strongly believes that this change in weight at the moment of death is due to the soul leaving the body.'

Lewis stared at him and could think of nothing to say.

'I'm deeply interested in this claim,' said McNulty. 'Indeed, I'm deeply interested in everything to do with the whole subject. You might say it has been at the core of my life for many years. I see you looking incredulous, Sir Lewis, but the ability to communicate with the spirits of the dead is a very old one. It's found in all cultures: the Ancient Egyptians; the Greeks and the Oracle at Delphi, Saul in the Old Testament asking the Witch of Endor to call up the spirit of Samuel . . .' His eyes gleamed with the fervour of the fanatic. 'As soon as I read the article I knew I must do all I could to further the research and take part in the search for the truth.' He leaned forward. 'Think of it, Sir Lewis, think of giving the world proof incontestable that the soul really exists. Of proving there is life after death.'

Lewis said slowly, 'It's a curious ambition. I can't imagine how you'd get proof.'

'Can't you? Oh, I can. Rigidly controlled conditions, of course. A very precise weighing of the subject in the minutes before death, and then again immediately after death has occurred. That is really all that's needed. But,' he said, jabbing the air with a bony finger, 'but, Sir Lewis, there are two major obstacles, and this is what has hampered the trials. The first is finding someone physically fit to be weighed just before death. That's very difficult, because most people approaching death are scarcely conscious let alone able to stand on a weighing machine.'

'I would have thought it was even harder to weigh

someone after death,' said Lewis. 'But what's the second obstacle?'

'Finding a subject who would die at a predictable time.' McNulty was still watching Lewis.

'Impossible,' said Lewis, after a moment.

'Is it?' said McNulty very softly. 'Oh, is it indeed impossible, Sir Lewis?' He paused, and then said, 'There is an ideal candidate for this experiment.' And then, as Lewis stared at him in sudden comprehension, he said, 'A man awaiting execution.'

CHAPTER NINE

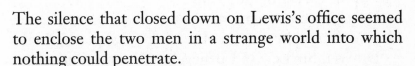

The silence that closed down on Lewis's office seemed to enclose the two men in a strange world into which nothing could penetrate.

Finally, Lewis said, 'It's an alluring area of enquiry, of course. The soul's existence – Yes, I can see you'd find it interesting. I can see many people would. But there must surely be other subjects you could use in hospitals, the workhouses, even.' He thought, McNulty's a fanatic. He's seeing himself as the man who proves the existence of life beyond death. Why the devil am I even having this conversation with him? But he knew why. This was McNulty's price for keeping quiet about Belinda.

'I have considered hospitals and workhouses, of course,' said McNulty. 'And although I could probably find a suitable subject, the authorities would not permit the weighing.'

I'm not surprised, thought Lewis, but he said, 'And you think I will permit it? On Nicholas O'Kane?'

'Well, d'you know, I do think it,' said McNulty. 'Particularly since your wife takes such an interest in these matters.'

Lewis said very flatly, 'Unless I agree to this, you'll tell my wife what you saw earlier in that room? Is that it? Yes, I thought it was. There's an ugly word for that kind of threat, McNulty. There's an ugly punishment for it, as well.'

'You mistake me. I intended no threat, merely the setting up of a scientific experiment.'

'Even if I agreed to it, you would need O'Kane's permission,' said Lewis.

'Would I? Wouldn't he just think being weighed was part of the execution procedure?'

'Deceive a man facing his death? That's an unpleasant idea, McNulty. In any case, I refuse to give permission.'

'Do you, Sir Lewis? I believe that if you think about it, you'll see it in a different light.' McNulty stood up. 'I'm going along to see the prisoner,' he said. 'To make certain the bromide's taken effect. You see, I do have some sensitivity about these things. Suppose I return in half an hour? I'm sure that when you've thought about this a little more you'll see it'll be much better if you agree.'

It was a pity Lewis had not agreed to come to London to meet Bartlam and dearest Vita. Clara Caradoc, enduring the rigours of the railway (even the first-class compartment was not as clean as she would have liked and a guard had been downright insolent at Kendal), supposed she should have known that his absurd prisoners at Calvary would take precedence.

Father said Lewis was a very dedicated man and Clara must understand he was trying to help the unfortunates who were under his care; there but for the grace of God go I, said father. But mamma said this was nonsense, a gentleman did not consort with thieves and murderers to the neglect of his family, and while a title was very gratifying in its way (yes, she *knew* how satisfying it was for Clara to use it in shops and restaurants), by itself it was not something that could escort you to dinner parties or help you entertain luncheon guests.

Mamma had not always disapproved of Lewis. All those years ago, with Clara still a hopeful girl in the big Dulwich house, she had thought the marriage a very good prospect. They would be extremely pleased at such a match, she had said. The Caradocs were a very good family indeed. Originally Welsh, so she believed – she had made enquiries. Clara would do well to accept this offer. So Clara, who had not actually received any other offers, and who had a dread of being left on the shelf like several of her drearier cousins, had accepted Lewis Caradoc's offer and married him in guipure lace and white satin.

During the wedding breakfast (lobster salad and champagne, because Clara's mamma was not having Lewis Caradoc's grand family look down their noses at City bankers), much speculation went on behind hands as to the precise amount of the marriage settlement. Estimates varied wildly and by the time the speeches began there had been a few lively differences of opinion, but on one thing everyone was agreed: Clara had made a very good marriage indeed.

Driving away from the church on Lewis's arm, Clara

had thought the same thing. She had thought so all through the reception, and she continued to think it on the night train to Paris for the honeymoon. She stopped thinking it when Lewis got into bed with her and performed the act that apparently constituted marriage. It had not mattered that he had been what he called *gradual* about the proceedings; to Clara's mind there had been nothing gradual about any of it. She had been shocked and revolted – at one stage she had even wondered if he might be a little mad and whether there was any insanity in the Caradoc family. Later, she could not help thinking that mamma or one of her cousins, or *somebody*, might have given her a hint about what she would be expected to endure on her wedding night and for a surprising number of nights afterwards.

But out of that messy undignified act had come her beautiful boy Caspar, whom everyone had loved and admired, and who brought that look of intense pride to Lewis's face. Clara felt almost loving towards Lewis when she saw him look at his son in that way. She had even allowed the marriage act a few times after the birth, because it could mean another child. Not a boy this time, she thought; you could not expect to get such a golden child twice, and a second son would inevitably be a pallid copy of Caspar. But perhaps a pretty, dainty daughter. It was disappointing when there were no signs of any child at all, and so after a suitable interval Clara considered she could justifiably close her bedroom door on Lewis. She was polite but firm about it. She dared say Lewis satisfied his masculine needs somewhere – by that time one knew men liked that kind of thing, but one also knew by then that there were women of a certain class who did not mind satisfying those needs. It was not necessary to know any details.

And then had come the overwhelming tragedy of Caspar's death in that senseless war, the war that to Clara's mind, the government should have been able to avoid. The German empire should not have been allowed to get so much above itself, and as for France – well, France had simply been petulant about losing some petty little province or other in the Franco-Prussian war – Clara did not know the name of the place and it had all happened years ago anyway. In Clara's view – also in the view of Clara's mamma – these things could easily have been nipped in the bud, or the countries involved left to sort out their own squabbles and deal with assassinations of grand dukes in unpronounceable provinces. (One thanked God that kind of thing did not happen in England!) When the news that Antwerp was occupied was announced, Clara's mamma even went so far as to say that if they had ladies running things there would not have been a war at all, which caused Clara's papa to laugh very heartily, and say, My word, ladies running the country, what an idea.

Clara had suffered what was known as a dark night of the soul after Caspar's death. It had been no use for people to say he had died a hero's death, fighting bravely for his country, and that Clara could be very proud of him. Clara was proud of him, but she would have preferred to have him alive and a coward. She did not say this, but she had been sure there could never be any happiness for her ever again in the world.

The train was chugging through the industrial Midlands. Clara looked out of the window to see where they were. Crewe, was it, where she would have to change trains? It was difficult to see because of the disgusting state of the windows. She might complain about that to the station master at Euston, although most likely she would only be met with rudeness again. People used the war as an excuse for slack service, but to Clara's mind the war was no excuse at all. She leaned back and opened the book she had brought to pass the journey, but she did not read it because her thoughts were still filled with memories of her dear boy.

Happiness had come back into her life when she met Bartlam and Violette Partridge – Dr McNulty's doing that had been. Clara would be eternally grateful to him for the introduction, although when he had first suggested it, she had been doubtful. She had listened to his explanations about how Violette had gifts as a medium and could contact the dead, and she had reminded him that the church frowned on such practices. Dr McNulty had said this was not quite so; the church was most interested in the latest discoveries, and his good friend Bartlam Partridge numbered two vicars among his little circle. If Lady Caradoc cared to come along one evening just to meet Bartlam and Violette, he, Dr McNulty, was sure her doubts would be allayed. Names were not, as a rule, exchanged between the members of the circle unless people particularly wished it, and Lady Caradoc could be assured that her identity would not be known, other than by her host and hostess. Nor would any information about herself or her family be given to them, she had his word on that.

And so Clara had gone along, combining the expedition with shopping and a visit to her family who were always pleased to see her. Her cousins took her to tea at Claridges and derived immense satisfaction from calling her Lady Caradoc loudly enough for the other patrons to hear. Clara enjoyed this, although it was a pity the cakes were not up to Claridges' pre-war standard and the waiter forgot the sugar tongs and had to be remonstrated with. Slack service, you see.

Afterwards Clara had set off in a cab for the address Dr McNulty had given her, shuddering to think what the cousins would have said about such a seedy area, not even daring to think what mamma would have thought of it. But Bartlam and Violette welcomed her so courteously, and seemed so delighted that she was visiting their house – 'A real honour,' Violette said – that Clara decided to overlook Violette's voice and her clothes and scent, which were both a little overpowering. She recognized the scent as Evening Violets – 'Expensive but rather common,' mamma would have said. 'I should not myself care to use it.' Clara would not care to use it either, but Violette Partridge appeared to have bathed in it.

None of this mattered though, because Violette knew at once about Caspar. She pressed Clara's hand with sympathy, and said she could see that poor dear Lady Caradoc had suffered a grievous loss. A child, perhaps? Yes, she had thought as much. She could always tell. A boy, wasn't it? Or no, not quite a boy, more a young man. And the initial of his name was – a pause ensued while Violette tapped her plump lips with a thoughtful finger. The initial was C, Violette was sure of it. Christopher? No, something more unusual. A name from one of the medieval legends, or from the biblical tales of wise men . . . Ah yes. Caspar, that was it!

There was a moment when Clara thought, Dr McNulty has told her! He must have done! But then she remembered Dr McNulty's promise that he had not passed any information to these two, and she stared at Violette, and said, 'Caspar was my son. He was killed in France a few months ago. It was a week before his twentieth birthday.' And then, without in the least realizing she had been going to say it, she said, 'Can you reach him for me?'

Violette Partridge thought for a while, and rolled her eyes a bit which Clara found embarrassing, and then said she believed she could indeed reach Caspar. Lady Caradoc would have to place herself completely in Violette's hands – and the hands of dearest Bart as well, of course, for he saw to the business side, Violette had no head for that kind of thing. From his chair by the fire, Bartlam smiled reassuringly, and said Lady Caradoc would be entirely safe with them.

'Then,' said Violette to Clara, speaking very seriously, 'if, and only if, you are prepared to trust us completely, I believe there is a very good chance of reaching your boy in the Great Beyond. Do you agree, Bart?'

'Indeed I do.'

'I already sense Caspar's nearness,' said Violette, clasping Clara's hands in hers. 'I think he will be eager to talk to his mamma.'

There had been two subsequent visits to the violet-scented house, during which Clara met several of Bart and Vita's other clients. Anonymity was carefully preserved, and no names were given in the introductions. Vita said things like, 'This is our friend from Clapham.' Or, 'This is a seeker after the truth.' When Clara was presented, Vita merely said, 'This is a new but very dear friend who wishes to reach a departed son.'

It was reassuring to find that Dr McNulty had been perfectly right about gentlemen of the church coming to the house. There was a Reverend Lincing who made no secret of his name or his calling, but who had a rather unclerical way of patting the hands and shoulders of some of the younger ladies, and who always smelled strongly of peppermint. Mamma said that gentlemen who sucked peppermint lozenges (unless as an aid to digestion after a meal, of course), should be suspected of intemperate drinking; she always, said mamma, considered peppermint an infallible sign. When Clara saw Reverend Lincing helping himself to Bartlam Partridge's sherry when he thought no one was looking, she considered it an infallible sign as well.

There were five other ladies. The two youngest seemed to know one another; they sat quietly in a corner, not saying very much to anyone. Clara thought they might be sisters. Of the other three, one always brought a piece of knitting which she said soothed her while she was waiting for the spirits to come through, but which Clara considered a very ill-mannered way to behave. One of the women brought a husband; a rather insignificant little man with thinning hair, a drooping moustache and a high, starched collar. He might be a shopkeeper or a bank clerk.

The other female brought neither knitting nor husband, but Clara did not speak to her at all because it was obvious that the creature painted her face. She mentioned this to Violette afterwards, but rather surprisingly Violette did not seem to think it important, saying they were all seekers after truth and searchers after consolation.

Bartlam, hearing the discussion, said, Come now, Lady Caradoc, a little powder and rouge was not frowned on nowadays, and the lady in question might well have endured several deep sorrows in her life. Clara was perfectly prepared to allow the creature any number of deep sorrows; all she asked was that she was not expected to sit by her.

There was a certain etiquette that had to be employed when dealing with the afterlife. Dr McNulty had drawn Clara aside on her first visit to tell her about this, and at first Clara had not been best pleased. She said frigidly that she did not need any lessons in behaviour, thank you very much, but Dr McNulty was quick to explain about such things as the holding of hands with one's neighbours at the table. Lady Caradoc would not be aware of that rule, he said, and it was very important to observe it. There was also the preserving of absolute silence unless directly addressed, which was equally important. The seances – they usually called them that for want of a better word, said Dr McNulty apologetically – were always held in the dark. The spirits did not care for bright lights.

It was not until the third meeting that Violette was able to tell Clara quite definitely that she had spent considerable time communing with her spirit guide – a most interesting woman who had actually been a Turkish slave girl: Violette would have to tell Clara all about her one of these days – and that as a result of it she had very good news to impart.

'In fact, Clara, I can say with complete confidence that

your dear boy is finally near enough for us to reach.'

'You are sure? Will I see him? Be able to talk to him?'

It was Bartlam who answered. 'You may not be able to actually talk to him,' he said. 'Or not very clearly.' And he smiled at her and said, 'But I think I can say with some assurance, my dear, that you will certainly see him.'

CHAPTER TEN

Clara did not know how she got through the days until the next meeting in the North London house, and she did not know whether to be relieved or disappointed when Dr McNulty had to return to Thornbeck to help deal with the execution of one of Lewis's murderers.

The seances always took place in the downstairs parlour of the house, which Vita had decorated with red flock wallpaper and carpeted with a thick Turkey carpet. Everywhere was be-bobbled and be-plushed, and most of the legs on the furniture were covered with trailing shawls and fringing. Clara had several times thought it a pity that Violette herself was not covered with shawls and fringing. For the promised seance – the seance at which they were to reach Caspar – Vita wore a tea-gown, mauve and puce as to colour, clinging and revealing as to style. Clara's mother had called that design of neckline a pneumonia blouse and wondered that any decent woman could be seen abroad in such a garment.

Before they began Bartlam turned down all the gas jets, and positioned a fire screen across the hearth, after which they were bidden to sit round the table, and to please keep absolute silence. Clara was not yet accustomed to sitting in a dark room holding hands with strangers – the knitting lady was on her left and the meek bank clerk on her right – but it was necessary to conform. It was curious how much difference the darkness made to the room, although after a few moments her eyes began to adjust to the dimness. She noticed that tonight Bartlam had not taken a seat at the table, but had remained quietly in an upright chair near the fire.

Clara was not given to silly fancies and imaginings like some hysterical young girl, but the longer the silence stretched out, the more uneasy she became. The ticking of the long-case clock in the corner which she had scarcely noticed before, was becoming unnaturally loud. Violette was calling on Fatima the Turkish slave girl – please to come into their hearts and guide them through the labyrinths of the afterlife, she said. Presumably it was necessary for Violette to roll her eyes and thrash about in her chair during this part of the proceedings, but Clara thought it regrettable that these antics caused Vita's exposed bosom to wobble so noticeably. It was even more regrettable that Reverend Lincing stared at this spectacle in a very ill-bred manner. Clara might have a quiet word with Vita afterwards, because it was most unseemly behaviour, and even when engaged in trying to contact the afterlife there was surely no need for such a display.

A series of erratic lights flickered across the room, and the bank clerk and his wife exchanged a pleased nod, as if recognizing them as a sign that Fatima was agreeable to tonight's expedition into the spirit world. There followed a series of questions to Fatima, most of which were incomprehensible to Clara, but which appeared to deal with the spirits and the souls of those who had passed over and whom Fatima had encountered. There were also several very regrettable references to Fatima's own life, which appeared to have been colourful, to say the least.

Then Violette sat up straighter, and with a sudden sharpness in her voice, said, 'There's someone else here. Someone has come among us.'

Clara's heart jumped and she listened intently.

'You are most welcome here,' said Violette after a moment. 'Please tell us who you are.'

For what felt like a very long time nothing happened. The clock was still ticking with its maddening rhythm in the corner; it was important to remind oneself that it was only a clock – a mechanical, man-made machine – and that it was not the rhythmic beating of a human heart, Caspar's heart, struggling to beat with life in its muddy grave somewhere in northern France ... No! That is the most ridiculous thought in the world, said Clara angrily to herself.

She was just becoming unpleasantly aware of the bank clerk's hand sweating slightly in hers, when a series of loud cracks split the silence. Several people jumped wildly, and Clara distinctly heard Reverend Lincing let out an oath quite unsuited to a man of the cloth.

Violette's voice rang out again, asking who was there, please to tell them, they intended only love and friendship.

Love and friendship and the inexorable ticking of a human heart that was steadily getting louder – Clara was sure of it.

And then the footsteps came.

They were slow, dragging footsteps, and they were not quite in rhythm with the ticking of the clock, which was somehow irritating of them. Like a night-train journey when the wheels were not quite in time with the rattling of the carriages. Tick-tick, step-step . . . Tick-step, step-tick . . . Nearer and nearer they came, and they seemed to *crunch* their way forwards. Is it Caspar? thought Clara, listening with every fibre of her being. It must be – Violette and Bartlam promised I should see him. If it really is Caspar, it's as if he's trudging across the battlefields to get here – across the splintered bones of hundreds upon hundreds of dead men – his comrades –, all those young men who died.

It was at that moment Clara became aware that Violette was frightened. She had released the hands of the people on each side of her and she was gripping the arms of her chair, and turning her head from side to side as if scanning the shadows. Whatever was happening was not something Violette had expected. Clara glanced across to Bartlam, and saw that he had half risen from his chair and was looking about him, as if he, too, had been faced with something unplanned.

The darting lights were still zig-zagging back and forth, occasionally showing up the faces of the watchers. Reverend Lincing was looking bewildered, and the younger of the two girls looked as if she might start screeching at any moment. For a moment it seemed as if something inside the lights struggled to take on a definite

form, and Bartlam put out a hand as if he might be trying
to ward something off.

The face of a very young man seemed to paste itself
onto the shadows, and Clara cried out, because it was
Caspar, it was her dearest boy, looking exactly as he had
looked before he went away from her – exactly as she
remembered him. He was there, in the room with them,
and Clara forgot the need to be dignified and correct,
and cried out his name. At once the shadowy outline
moved. Had he heard her? Was he searching for her?
The head turned again, a little more definitely this time,
but jerkily, as if this was a body no longer familiar to its
owner, or as if it did not obey the brain's commands as
easily as once it had done. One hand lifted itself in a half
salute, then the figure seemed to move upwards. He's
going, thought Clara, in agony. But he can't go, not yet,
they mustn't let him go.

As if the thought had been spoken aloud, the head
swivelled around and the half salute came again, touching the fingers to the lips. Did it make the gesture of
blowing a kiss?

As the outline vanished, the oppressive room with the
beating heart of the clock blurred, and Clara pitched
forward in a dead faint on Violette Partridge's polished
table.

One did not, of course, make a fuss over a trifling
indisposition, and Clara waved away the burnt feathers
(Violette and the knitting lady), the glass of brandy
(Bartlam, Reverend Lincing and the painted female) and
the offers of hot sweet tea (the two young girls).

She was quite all right, said Clara firmly. It had just

been the shock of seeing her dearest boy like that. Doubtless they would understand.

The little man with the depressed moustache said, diffidently, that his wife had smelling salts in her bag. A gentle application of ammonia – just a whiff under the nose – was wonderfully good for steadying the senses.

'She would do better to have some air,' said the knitting lady sharply.

'Beg pardon. Only wishing to help.'

'It's very kind of you,' said Clara.

Reverend Lincing was saying that perhaps after all a cup of tea would be a good idea if it was not too much trouble. A sovereign remedy for any shock, wasn't it? Well sugared, if Mrs Partridge would be so kind.

'I'm perfectly all right,' said Clara again. 'If a cab could be obtained for me, I shall return home.'

At this, the little man with the moustache, whose name turned out to be Henry Bingley, was prodded forward by his wife. A cab, it seemed, had been ordered for himself and his lady wife. Nine o'clock to the tick it would be; Mrs Bingley did not like to keep late hours. They would be honoured to take – ah – to take their fellow guest anywhere. Anywhere at all. No trouble whatsoever.

The Cheyne Walk address caused Henry Bingley to blink slightly, but Clara saw his wife give a pleased little nod. A social climber, you could always tell. Still, it was a kindly offer, and Clara said graciously, that if it was no trouble she would accept.

The tea was brought and the painted female came to sit by Clara while she drank it, and said in a brusque voice that it had been a remarkable experience. Presumably the young man they had seen had been a close relation?

'My son who was killed in the war,' said Clara, her mind still seething with that last image of Caspar who had made that heart-breaking attempt to send his dearest mamma a jaunty wave of his hand, and to blow her a kiss from beyond the grave.

'Then I'm not surprised you fainted,' said the woman and moved away before Clara could think how to reply.

Violette Partridge saw Clara to the door, helping her into her cloak, and pressing her hand emotionally.

'I am sorry you were indisposed – the emotions are unpredictable – but I am so pleased for you, my friend,' she said. 'To see your boy like that, even for that brief moment. Such a joy, my dear Clara. And especially tonight, when—'

'Yes?'

'It does not matter. I must not trouble you with it.'

Clara could not bear people to dither or prevaricate. 'Vita, if something is wrong, please tell me.'

'It is only that this may have been our last evening in this house.' There was a small, brave smile.

The last evening ... Then I may not see him ever again. Clara said, sharply, 'Why is that? You surely do not intend to end the meetings?'

'Not if it can be avoided. So much comfort we are able to bring to people who seek us out. We shall continue our work if at all possible, of course.'

'Then surely—'

'I do not understand business very well,' said Violette. 'But it concerns the lease of this house. It ends or has to be renewed or something of the kind, and Bart says it will mean paying considerably more money to the owners. That, he fears, is beyond our means.' She squeezed

Clara's hands. 'We shall try to rub through, though. Please do not worry. I shall write to you to let you know the outcome. And now here is the cab. Mr and Mrs Bingley will take very good care of you, I am sure.'

Clara was solicitously helped into the cab, and a blanket was tucked round her knees by Mrs Bingley. Such a nasty night, wasn't it? You had to be careful you did not take a chill, which was a thing as might easily happen after a fainting fit. An extraordinary evening, hadn't it been? The Bingleys were, themselves, hoping to contact Mrs Bingley's sister who had passed over in the spring. They had not precisely seen her yet, but they had twice smelled her perfume – lily of the valley which Elsie had always used and which was quite unmistakable. Violette Partridge possessed remarkable powers, and it was to be hoped she and Mr Partridge were not obliged to leave their house – Mrs Bingley did not quite know what she would do if that should happen. She was determined to reach Elsie. There had been a small rift between them before Elsie was killed by a tramcar – nasty dangerous things. She would not feel easy in her mind until she had spoken with her and put matters right between them as you might say. Mr Bingley made no objection to this, in fact he was enormously interested in the entire process, aren't you, Henry?

'I'm enormously interested,' said Henry Bingley solemnly. 'As the poet says, there are more things in heaven and earth. Is this the house? So pleased to have been of help.'

Once indoors, Clara thought back to the scrappy conversation with Violette. 'This may have been our last evening in this house,' Violette had said. 'The lease has to be renewed . . . it may be beyond our means . . .'

Remembering that jerky difficult salute that Caspar's image had made, Clara knew she would do anything she could to ensure that Violette and her husband remained in that house, and that the seances continued.

Extract from Talismans of the Mind, *by C. R. Ingram*

With the facts available it is not difficult to conjure up a seance in Violette and Bartlam Partridge's house. The room would have hummed with nervous anticipation – itself conducive to the seeing of spectres – and shadows would have clustered thickly in the corners, because the lights, either gas or electricity, would certainly have been turned right down. 'Spirits do not care for bright light,' visitors to the house would have been told.

Fraudsters do not care for bright light either, and this infamous pair could not risk any light shining on their various deceptions. They seem to have employed most of the tricks of their parasitic trade – the wax-filled gloves treated with luminous paint to represent ectoplasmic hands; the spring-loaded attachments clipped beneath the table to cause it to tip apparently of its own volition. It is tempting at this point to visualize the portly Bart's be-spatted ankles nudging the mechanism in the nether regions of the table, as he urbanely sipped his wine above it. Less tempting, perhaps, is the image of Violette's flowing tea-gowns judiciously draped over a pair of metal plates strapped to the insides of her dimpled knees: plates which could be rapped smartly together in response to the time-honoured question whether anyone was there (knock once for yes and twice for no).

There was a further refinement to these devices as well: a kind of fantastical pièce de résistance in the unseemly feast they spread before their victims. There is evidence that Bartlam created what seems to have been an ingenious adaptation of the magic-lantern principle, by which he projected jerkily moving images of his clientele's loved ones onto a wall, Violette having obtained photographs of them beforehand. ('Do please let me see a likeness of your dear son/husband/brother/ sister . . . Such a help if I can visualize the dear departed we are trying to reach . . . Oh, how perfectly charming/ handsome/distinguished . . .')

From all this it's a reasonable assumption that Bart had a working knowledge of the early kinotoscope machines, although rumours that after the Great Partridge Catastrophe he took to peddling sly peep-shows in the style of 'What the Butler Saw,' or 'The Widow Jones's Kiss' cannot be authenticated. We are, however, on firmer ground with the indecency charge in Brighton in 1924, since some of the court records are still extant.

The Partridges would have taken steps to guard against accusations of fakery, and Bartlam, certainly, was sharp enough to pretend fear at times. It seems he was also sufficiently twisty-minded to keep some of his tricks from Violette in order to ensure a genuine reaction from her. In a fragment of a letter sent in later life by Violette to a friend, she says of Bart, 'I never knew what he might have in store for the evening; more than once I was so startled by his inventions that I all but swooned.'

Trickery on trickery. Deceit on deceit. And yet, and yet.

Is it conceivable that these two occasionally tapped into

something they did not expect and could not explain? Something that owed nothing to the machinations of early cinema or photography, or to the clackety-rapping of metal against wood? The accounts that have survived indicate complete belief on the part of the people who went to the North London house, and also complete devotion. One lady who apparently sought a dead sister, wrote to a cousin that, 'Henry and I are resolved that if we can help Violette and Bartlam by selling our house, we shall do so. It should fetch a very good price, and I am sure we could find for ourselves a modest flat.'

The clients believed. The clients paid – or allowed themselves to be fleeced, depending on your point of view. Many of them were clearly intelligent, worldly-wise people, and it could be argued that they ought to have been able to spot the wolves in partridge's clothing. But they were almost all affected by deep grief, these trusting lambs. How objective were they?

CHAPTER ELEVEN

Vincent bustled up to the top floor of Caradoc House partway through the morning, taking a cup of freshly brewed coffee for Miss Grey. He had put on a new shirt in a deep raspberry, which was not a colour many people could carry off, and he was wearing it open-necked, which made him feel pleasantly modern. He had been careful to carry up a cup of coffee for himself so he could drink it with Miss Grey and hear how she was getting along, and what she had found so far.

She was sitting cross-legged on the floor, wearing a floppy shirt and jeans. Her hair was bundled up into a big tortoiseshell clip and strands had escaped to curl light brown tendrils around her neck. Of course it was sensible to wear old clothes when you were sorting through dusty papers and to tie long hair on top of your head. Mother had never done any kind of dusty work, but she had occasionally worn what she called a tea-apron if she had baked scones for one of her bridge afternoons or when she dusted the china figures in the cabinets.

Miss Grey seemed pleased at being brought the coffee and said she was finding the contents of the deed boxes quite interesting. There was a lot more to sift than she had expected – sheaves of papers had been stuffed into envelopes, and she was trying to sort them into appropriate headings. So far she had made three categories, starting with personal items – things like old theatre programmes or receipts.

'How interesting,' said Vincent.

'There are a few photos after all, but I don't think any of them are of Walter. I think they're just local places, or people he worked with at Calvary or who he met while he lived here. There are a few letters from other doctors – oh, and one or two requests for lectures. It sounds as if Walter became quite eminent after he left Thornbeck. I've put those in the second category – professional correspondence.'

Vincent asked what the third heading was.

'Strictly medical. Several editions of old medical journals. I wondered if there were any medical libraries who'd like to have them – for details about treatments that were in vogue in the thirties and forties. And there are a few records of patients – notes of treatments and medication prescribed. I should think they got in by mistake.'

'Patients from Calvary?'

'Not so far. There's a reference to a house in Switzerland – it looks as if Walter bought it. Oh, and I found an article about the Caradoc Society which I thought you might like. I put it over there on the table for you. It's from the local paper. It mentions Lady

Caradoc – I hadn't realized she was involved with the Society.'

'She was very much involved,' said Vincent, picking up the article and glancing at it. 'Her son was killed in the First World War and the story is that she never got over it. Apparently she spent the rest of her life trying to contact him through various mediums and spiritualists.'

'How sad.'

'The seances and spiritualists would have given her a good deal of comfort, of course.' Vincent said this with a touch of reproof, because it would not hurt to remind this modern young woman of the Caradoc Society's raison d'être. 'It's always been generally believed it was really Lady Caradoc's influence that caused the Caradoc Society to be created, but at the end of the First World War ladies didn't have much equality so it was Sir Lewis who actually set things up. Georgina, if there is anything else that relates to the Society, I'd very much like to see it. Even though things are being wound up. My articles, you know . . . One is always looking for new material.'

'Of course you can have anything I find,' said Georgina. 'I'll probably finish sorting it all out later today. D'you think I could stay on for another couple of days, though? I suppose strictly speaking I can just take everything back to London, but it's so nice up here, and I'd like to find out as much as I could about my great-grandfather. That local newspaper's still going, isn't it? I thought I'd see if I could look at their archives. Walter might have been involved in all kinds of things.'

'You'd be most welcome to stay,' said Vincent. 'This house isn't actually on the market yet, and even if it was we could arrange viewings so as not to disturb you. Is there much more to sort through?'

'There are still these envelopes,' said Georgina, indicating them. 'Jam-packed, as you can see. Most of the stuff in them seems to date from the late 1930s. That was when Walter was at Calvary, wasn't it? So they might yield all kinds of local information for your articles.'

'Indeed they might,' said Vincent feeling as if a steely hand had clutched at his stomach. Late 1930s. But he said, quite lightly, that he would leave her to her delvings. 'You'll probably have a more interesting after-noon than I will. I'm bound for a dull hour with the Society's accountants.'

'That does sound dull,' said Georgina, smiling.

Back in his own part of Caradoc House, the words, 'late 1930s' beat a horrid tattoo in Vincent's mind. The dangerous years. Walter Kane's Calvary years. The years that must at all costs be kept hidden.

Until today Vincent had been thinking he would be able to find a way of destroying the contents of the boxes. It was annoying. If only he had known of their existence earlier he could have staged some kind of break-in at Small's offices – even a fire – but he could not start a fire inside Caradoc House; some of the Society's valuable archives might be damaged or lost altogether. And this morning's conversation seemed to indicate that the problem might go deeper than merely destroying Walter's papers.

He thought back over the conversation and to how Georgina Grey had declined all offers of help in the sorting of Walter Kane's papers. Was there anything suspicious about that? She had made it politely clear she wanted to deal with them on her own, and twice at least she had seemed to pause before answering a direct question about her findings. Had she been thinking up a good lie? Working out how to put Vincent off the scent of something? If so, what? As he bustled about his office, Vincent began to see that it was not Walter Kane's papers that would have to be got rid of: it was Walter Kane's great-granddaughter.

As soon as the thought formed, he knew it had been lying under the surface all the time, like a basking shark. Get rid of her. Get rid of this modern confident girl who might drag the shameful past into the light, and who might as a result spoil Vincent's nice, ordered life and his standing in Thornbeck. *Get rid of her*. But how could he do that? *How?* And then – inevitably – what would Mother have done faced with Georgina Grey?

Mother had always said a plan could be worked out for any eventuality in life: the only thing to beware of, she said, was getting caught. Vincent could almost hear her saying this, and he could see how she used to look when she said it. He never remembered her as the pale sad creature she had been just before she died; he always remembered her as radiant and glowing and beautiful.

Exactly the way she used to look when she came back from murdering one of her lovers.

She had not called them lovers, of course; it was not a word she would have dreamed of using – it was certainly not a word that would have been used when she was a girl. They had been gentlemen friends, escorts, Mr Somebody who advises me on investments, Major

Something who accompanies me to concerts. There had been a major in Bournemouth where they had lived until Vincent was eight – a widower, rather friendless, very polite and respectful. He called Vincent's mother Mrs Meade, and he called Vincent, young sprog. In private, Mother said he was a bit of a bore but it was a kindness to befriend him.

The Bournemouth major had a big house in what was called the Avenue, and they went to afternoon tea there on Sundays. There were unfamiliar sandwiches and seed cake, and Mother and the major drank tea, and a little later on, Mother had a glass of sherry and the major had a whisky and soda. Vincent was given ginger beer which he did not much like, but the major was not very used to children and ginger beer was what he had had himself when he was a child.

Despite being boring and giving people seed cake and ginger beer, Vincent thought it sad when the Bournemouth major died. It happened one spring evening. Vincent had been going to his friend John's house straight from school; they would have tea there, and after homework they would spend the evening playing with John's Meccano set. Vincent had looked forward to it, because there were always extra-good cakes.

But when they got to the house the doctor had just called and it seemed that John's sister had whooping cough.

'It's a nasty thing to get,' his mother said. 'So we'd better not even risk you coming in, Vincent. Shall I telephone your mother to collect you?'

But Vincent said no, he would go home by himself, thank you. It was not very far, and if he went past the park he would not have to cross any roads. John's mother, who was distracted with whooping cough and a small baby who was yelling its head off, supposed this would be all right, but said he was to telephone them to let them know he had got home safely, was that clear?

'Oh, yes. Thank you very much,' said Vincent, and she went back into the house thinking what a nice-mannered boy and how sad for his mother to be a widow so young.

Vincent walked back to his own house, enjoying the small adventure of being out alone, which was not something that was normally allowed. It was not very far to walk and Mother would surely not mind.

It was slightly disconcerting to find the house locked up with no sign of his mother anywhere. Vincent tried all the doors and peered through the windows, and then sat down on the doorstep and tried to think what to do. It was getting a bit chilly to wait out here for any length of time and it would soon start to get dark. He did not want to go to any of the neighbours' houses, because Mother did not approve of being too friendly with neighbours. They could become familiar, she said, and it did not do to let everyone know your business. But the major was a different kind of friend and Vincent thought he could walk back to the Avenue and ask the major what he had better do. The major might know where Mother was or she might even be there with him. He set off.

It was already beginning to grow dark and there were lights on in some of the houses in the Avenue. There was a light on in the major's house as well, which was reassuring. But when Vincent knocked on the door the major did not appear, so after a moment he went round the side of the house to the scullery door and knocked a bit harder. Nothing. Perhaps the major was listening to the radio in his study and had not heard the knocking, or perhaps he had gone out somewhere and left the light on by mistake. Greatly daring, Vincent tried the door. It was not locked, it opened easily and he stepped inside.

He knew at once that the house was not empty, in the way you always did know. He called out a bit timidly, hoping the major would hear and call out one of his bluff greetings, but he did not. Vincent went cautiously through the scullery which smelled of Vim and into the breakfast room beyond which smelled of stored apples from the major's fruit trees. He stepped into the big hall with the black and white tiled floor and the dark-leaved plants in their brass pots. Everywhere was quite dim except for a light showing under the study door. As Vincent hesitated, there was a sound from the study. The floor creaked as if someone had walked across it and there was the chink of glasses.

He called out. 'Major? Are you there? It's me, Vincent.'

The study door opened at once and Vincent's mother said, 'What on earth are you doing here?' She stood in the doorway but the lamp on the major's desk was on and Vincent could see straight into the room.

At first he could not make any sense of what he saw because it looked as if the major was asleep in the chair. But he was asleep with his eyes open and his face was white and marbly. There was a mess of something all down his shirt front and a dreadful sour smell of sick. Vincent began to feel frightened. He looked at his mother and felt even more frightened because she was different. Her face was flushed and there was a shininess to her eyes as if a light had been switched on. But she said again, in an ordinary voice, 'What are you doing here? I thought you were at John's house for the evening.'

She glanced back at the major lying in the chair and then stepped out into the hall and shut the door firmly.

Vincent mumbled about whooping cough and having to come home and Mother said thoughtfully, 'Oh, I see.' In a sharper voice, she said, 'Did you tell anyone you were coming here? Or see anyone on your way?'

'No.'

'Ah.' Vincent had the feeling his mother was pleased with this.

She said, 'Well now, Vincent, I'm afraid Major Thodden was taken very poorly a little while ago.'

'Should we get a doctor?'

'Oh no,' said Mother at once. 'No, there'd be no point. I'm afraid – well, you're so grown-up these days I think I can tell you. He's dead, the poor man. A heart attack, that's what it was, I should think.'

They looked at one another and for a long time neither of them spoke. Vincent had never seen anyone dead, but he had seen pictures in comics. He was not supposed to read comics but they were sometimes passed round at school. He could not remember the dead people in comics looking anything like the major looked now. 'What do we have to do?'

Mother appeared to think for a moment, then she said, 'As you know, it's my rule not to become involved in unpleasantness. And people might be very unkind if they knew I had been here tonight. A widow alone with a gentleman – taking a drink with him . . .' She looked at the glasses she held in her hand. One was a small sherry glass; the other was the chunky tumbler the major used for his whisky.

'I thought,' Mother was saying, 'that it would be a kindness to just set the room to rights a little. Major Thodden would not like anyone thinking he lived untidily. And people would not believe I only drank sherry. Gin, that's what they would say. So I'm going to wash these glasses and put them away in the cabinet and there will be no trace of my visit. You can come into the scullery to help me. Don't go into the study, will you? And once we've dealt with the glasses, we will go home and remember nothing about any of this. That's the plan, Vincent. It's very important to have a plan and to keep to it. A wise man taught me that when I was very young.'

They washed the glasses and put them away in the dining-room cupboard. Then they went home and had scrambled eggs and Vincent did his homework. The next day he went to school as usual and he did not tell anyone what had happened. Mother had said he must not, she had been very firm about it.

'No one at all, Vincent, not even your very best friends. You are my brave boy and such a comfort to me. And I have brought you up to be a gentleman, and a gentleman never betrays a lady's secret, so I am trusting you. What happened last night must be our special secret.'

Vincent did not really see why the major dying had to be a secret, but he wanted to be worthy of Mother's trust and he wanted them to have the special secret together.

The major's body was discovered two days later by a cleaning lady, whose shrieks could apparently be heard halfway along the Avenue. 'How very vulgar,' Mother said disapprovingly when she was told. 'No self-control, that type of person.'

There was a report of the major's death in the local newspaper because he had fought in the war and been wounded at Gallipoli, and the newspaper thought that made him interesting to people. The article said he had had a heart condition. 'But,' said Mother, in what Vincent could not help thinking of as a *satisfied* voice, 'the post mortem concluded he died accidentally as a result of taking too much digitalis. That's heart medicine, Vincent. It helps the heart beat more strongly. Very important for people who have a weak heart. But they think the major swallowed his usual dose and then felt unwell and took a second one and possibly even a third. Perhaps as much as half a grain altogether.'

Half a grain did not sound very much to Vincent, but Mother seemed pleased. She read out how the amount might easily have been fatal to someone with low blood pressure and a kidney condition which was what the major had had. 'They make the point that the dosage of digitalis has to be controlled very strictly,' she said, and lowering the newspaper for a moment she looked directly at Vincent. 'But none of this is anything to do with us and we must stick to the plan.'

They had stuck to the plan and they had not told anybody anything. No one asked them where they had been on the night the Bournemouth major died; there was no reason why anyone would do so.

Not many people attended the major's funeral because not many people had known him very well. Shy, they said, reserved. Or simply downright aloof, depending on your point of view. Mother was asked by neighbours if she had gone to the service – she had known the major, hadn't she? – but she said she had hardly known him at all. 'Only to say good morning.'

When a man called from a solicitor's office to tell Mother Major Thodden had left her all his money, she shed some tears into a lace handkerchief. Then she pulled herself together and gave a sad smile. 'Poor man,' she said, 'he had no family and he was very lonely, you know. I'm glad if I gave him some companionship these last months, although I hadn't actually seen him for two or three weeks before his death. How extremely generous of him to do such a thing. I don't in fact need the money, of course, my husband was a prudent man and as you can see I am very well provided for.' One hand indicated the house and its comfortable furniture. 'I may decide to give most of Major Thodden's bequest to a charity. Not all of it – that would be like rejecting his kindness – but a large portion of it. Perhaps you would advise me on suitable charities. Distressed army officers, something of that kind – he would like that, wouldn't he? But I do wish I had been there with him when he died. A lonely death, it must have been.'

After a while they left Bournemouth and went to live in Chichester. A very cultured town, said Mother. There were theatre festivals there and a cathedral, and they would meet a very nice type of person. They had a bigger house in Chichester and a lady came in to clean three times a week and to prepare some of the meals. A man came twice a week to keep the garden in order because Mother found gardening exhausting. 'I'm afraid I haven't much stamina.' She liked to sit beneath the apple tree with a book and to talk about My Roses. Vincent went to a new school where the uniform was very smart indeed. The only other difference to their lives was that Mother coloured her hair a much darker shade. 'But we do not tell people that,' she said. 'It is still thought rather common to dye one's hair. When I was a young girl, it was taken to mean that one was rather fast.'

They made a few friends – not too many because it was best not to give people the opportunity to know all your business. But there were one or two boys at Vincent's school who might be invited to tea, and Mother joined a small gardening club and after a while found a new gentleman friend. 'A very nice person,' she said, pleased. 'A bachelor. Not a very young man, but that does not matter. You see, Vincent, how important it is to work out a proper plan and to keep to it?'

A plan. A proper plan that you had worked out and kept to. Those words had stayed with Vincent ever since. Mother's shining look when she came out of the dead major's study stayed with him as well. He thought of it as a beacon, lighting up his life.

After he left the Caradoc House flat he spent an hour in the office downstairs, but his mind was not on the Society: it was still busy with the question of Georgina Grey. When you were going to get rid of someone you needed a weapon, just as his mother had used the digitalis as a weapon against the Bournemouth major. Neither of them had ever said this, of course, and it had not been until many years later Vincent had understood what had happened.

Had Vincent a weapon he could use against Georgina? He frowned, thinking hard, and then quite suddenly saw the answer. Calvary. Calvary was the weapon he would use to get rid of this prying great-granddaughter of Dr Walter Kane.

The more he thought about this the more he liked the symmetry of it. But how should it be done? At mid-day he walked along to his own house and while he made himself some lunch, he reviewed what he knew about the place. At the moment it was owned by H M Prisons, which was to say the government, and Huxley Small's firm acted as agents, making sure it was not occupied by squatters or tramps, sending out a surveyor once a year to see it had not fallen down or been burned to a crisp. Managing the place, they called it. Keeping it secure. Vincent knew perfectly well that managing Calvary was a sinecure because there was nothing that really needed managing: even the surveyor only had to look out last year's report, tweak a few phrases to make it seem newly written, and send it along with an invoice for a fat fee. Very nice too.

So, to practicalities. First, he hunted out the sketch plan he had managed to acquire some years ago of the gaol's interior and spread it out on his dining table to study. It was a plan the indolent surveyor had drawn years earlier, and was very clear and exactly to scale. There were the cells and the communal rooms, the refectory, the governor's office, the medical block, the chapel and the old burial yard. The mortuary with its brick tunnel beneath the execution chamber. And the condemned block, which was a little apartment on its own containing the cell for the man awaiting execution.

The execution chamber itself with its grisly gallows trap . . . The lime store.

The lime store . . .

CHAPTER TWELVE

The more Vincent thought about his plan, the clearer it became and the better it looked. He put away the layout of Calvary's interior, and felt able to return to Caradoc House. Once inside he paused at the foot of the stairs, wondering whether to go back up to see Georgina, but decided it was better not to do so. He would get the details of his plan sorted out properly in his mind before he saw her again.

He was engaged in packing the Society's files away: labelling and dating things as much as possible, and tying folders into neat bundles. It was dusty and unproductive work, but it had to be done and Vincent would not have trusted anyone else to do it. So far nobody had told him what was going to happen to all these files, which was very discourteous; you would have thought he was owed that after so many years. But he was going to leave everything in apple-pie order for Huxley Small and the accountants, so that when they did move in, they would remark on what a very meticulous secretary the Society had had in Vincent Meade and wonder why they had not realized it before. They might even consider employing him in some other capacity, although if they made any kind of offer it would give Vincent great pleasure to decline; he was not going to be at anyone's beck and call, thank you very much!

In any case, he might have other fish to fry. A rather exciting project was starting to take shape in his mind: this was the creation of his own psychic society. It was quite an ambitious idea, but Vincent did not see why he could not make a success of it. He fancied he was rather well known in psychic circles, and people would recognize his name and be interested. 'Is that the Vincent N. Meade of the Caradoc Society?' they would say. 'What an enterprising chap to be starting his own society. And he'll know what he's talking about after all these years. We must certainly see about joining that.'

This was a very promising prospect, and Vincent was nearly sure he was going to do it.

While he worked, he considered how he might get Georgina out to Calvary, because clearly this was the next stage of the plan. Mother had always believed in keeping such plans as simple as possible and Vincent was going to follow her precepts. He thought he could offer to show Georgina the place where her great-grandfather had worked. He tried out a little dialogue to himself.

'I've been thinking,' he would say, 'that you ought to see where your great-grandfather worked. So I've arranged to borrow the Calvary keys from Huxley Small.

He took a bit of persuading, but he agreed in the end. I'll drive you out there if you like.'

Would she like? Vincent thought so; he had already seen how much Walter Kane intrigued her. If he implied that he had gone to some trouble to get the keys, she could not very well refuse. Yes, it ought to work very neatly.

At half past three he went home to change for the appointment with the accountant. He decided to be classy with a touch of flamboyance in a dark overcoat with an astrakhan collar. The coat was pleasingly similar to those favoured by the more ornate actors of the Edwardian era, and Vincent was considering buying a very wide-brimmed homburg to wear with it. He thought this would cut quite a dash, although he was having a little difficulty in finding such a hat because the local gentlemen's outfitters did not deal much in flamboyance or dash.

He got out his car to drive the short distance to the accountant's office. He did not actually drive very much and it was not really necessary for him to have a car at all – his house was just off Thornbeck's main street in a little cul-de-sac. It took him exactly five minutes to walk to Caradoc House, and he bought all his groceries and provisions in Thornbeck and rarely went any further afield. But he had a car because Mother had thought it important. In her day it had been a mark of success and wealth. 'I never learned to drive,' she used to say. 'Girls didn't when I was young. They expected to be driven. And I should not understand the mechanics. But a car will show people that we are comfortably placed, and now you are seventeen we will see about driving lessons

for you, Vincent, and ask about buying a little car –
although *not* a Mini car, I don't think. Undignified and
unladylike. They will turn out to be nothing more than a
fad, mark my words. But a car will be very useful. You
could take me for little drives on the days when I am
up to it.' She had, in fact, quite often been up to it, and
Vincent had become a very competent driver.

He was competent at the meeting with the accountant
as well, although the accountant was a glum sort of
person, who spread balance sheets all over the desk and
said they did not make very happy reading, did they?
Quite a bit of mismanagement had gone on, he fancied.
This was said rather severely and anyone else might
almost have thought the accountant was chastising
Vincent himself. Vincent knew he was not, however,
and so he settled himself cosily in the chair, put on
the spectacles he always fancied made him look rather
donnish, and frowned over the figures for several
minutes, finally agreeing that, Oh my word yes, they
were very depressing indeed, weren't they?

Georgina had deliberately not told Vincent Meade
she was going out to Calvary that afternoon in case he
offered to accompany her. It would be a perfectly natural
thing for him to do and it would be difficult to refuse,
but Georgina did not want anyone with her the first time
she saw the place where Walter had worked.

But Vincent had said he had a dull afternoon ahead of
him with accountants, so at half past twelve Georgina
made herself a sandwich and a cup of coffee, read a bit
more of Dr Ingram's *Talismans of the Mind* while she
ate, and by half past one was driving out of Thornbeck.

As she went past the King's Head she remembered with pleasure the lunch she had arranged for Friday with Drusilla and Phin. She would enjoy that, and it would be interesting to hear about the proposed TV programme on Calvary.

Calvary . . .

She turned into the lane she had seen on her way into Thornbeck. It was narrow and winding, and although vehicle-passing places had been cut into the bank at intervals if another car came hurtling around one of the blind bends there could still be a head-on collision. Georgina slowed to a snail's pace and hoped for the best. Walter must often have come along here, either going to Calvary or leaving it. Had the possibility of a prang worried him or had there not been very much traffic then? Or had he not driven a car anyway?

'After all we went through together I should be devastated to lose you,' Lewis Caradoc had written in 1940, and the words had burrowed into Georgina's mind. Had something really big – really life-changing – happened, or was it just that the two had shared the stresses of having worked at Calvary?

She had expected to see the prison from the lane because she had assumed it would be set on high ground – Calvary, the place of execution on the hill – but the lane's left-hand bank was high, and even at this time of year the hedges were so thick it was impossible to see over them. It was only when she rounded a curve that the bank fell away and without warning she could see it across the fields.

She slowed down and then stopped altogether, staring across the countryside. Calvary did indeed stand on a hill

– a small hill as hills went in this part of the world, but a hill for all that.

The building was four-square and constructed from what Georgina supposed was local stone – grey and bleak-looking. It was a bit smaller than she had expected but it was unpleasantly easy to visualize a jolting cart going up the steep track, pausing in front of the massive central doors while they were unlocked, and then going inside. Had the prisoners in those carts been handcuffed? Manacled?

After a moment she drove on. Was it possible to get up to the place from here? Yes, there was a narrow track, not much more than a footpath, but wide enough to take a car. She would not, of course, be able to get inside, even if she had wanted to, but she would like to take a closer look.

The car struggled up the hillside in second gear, its erratic suspension complaining loudly at the uneven terrain. Halfway up, the fold of the land caused the prison to vanish behind some trees and suddenly reappear, much nearer. Georgina was annoyed to feel a lurch of nervousness at this.

The track stopped abruptly in front of the impressive entrance and she switched off the engine and got out. It was very cold and very quiet. The doors reared up above her. How must it have felt to see them swing open, and then to hear them close as you were taken through in a windowless van or a cart? What would lie beyond? There was a small door inset on one side which must have been for gaolers and visitors, and there was the remnant of a thick old bell-pull near to it. Georgina had to resist a sudden desire to pull it to see what happened.

She walked cautiously around the side of the building. There was a paved path of sorts, but most of the slabs had cracked and weeds and rank grass made it necessary to walk close to the walls. Even so, Georgina almost missed the door halfway round. It was deeply set into the stonework, almost entirely hidden by moss and some kind of grubby creeper, and for a moment it looked so utterly unreal – so like something out of a child's storybook – that she was not immediately sure if it was just a pattern of cracks in the stones. But cracks did not form themselves into a hefty-looking latch, nor did they have hinges. She put out a tentative hand, causing the mat of leaves to rustle drily and rather eerily. Like the fingernails of murderers scratching against a prison-cell door, trying to get out . . .

If David were here he would laugh at that and say, Too much imagination, George, and suggest they walk briskly back to civilization. Georgina was glad David was not here because she did not want to walk briskly back to anywhere; she wanted to see if this door would open, and she wanted to find out as much as she could about this place that had been such a part of her enigmatic great-grandfather's life.

She glanced about her, but nothing stirred anywhere and her car was comfortingly within sprinting distance. If she saw anything she did not like she could be back at the car in a couple of minutes.

The door resisted slightly, but more of the ivy mat fell away and with a groan of disused hinges it yielded. Georgina hesitated, then went inside.

The door opened onto a courtyard which was enclosed on three sides by Calvary's bulk, and on the fourth by the outer wall through which Georgina had just come. It was dark and was not a place where sunlight ever penetrated. The stone flags were cracked and weeds pushed up everywhere, but at one time it must have been some kind of garden because there were patches of dried-out soil. Georgina stared about her, aware of a feeling of infinite loneliness.

Quite suddenly she understood where she was. She was in Calvary's burial yard. The patches of dried-out soil were not the remains of a garden: they were burial plots. The graves of murderers who had been hanged here. She took a tentative step nearer. Yes, there were tiny squares of stone marking each of the oblong plots, each printed with a name and date. The letters were faded, but they were still just about readable. She was standing by one that said, 'NICHOLAS O'KANE. NOVEMBER 1917'. What had Nicholas O'Kane done to be hanged in a year when most men were away fighting a war?

She moved along the row, reading the names as she went. None of them meant anything to her until she came to the one nearest the door. It was exactly the same as the others, and bore the legend, 'NEVILLE FREMLIN. OCTOBER 1938'.

Neville Fremlin. Calvary's isolation seemed to close down on Georgina and she glanced uneasily over her shoulder, because if ever a place was likely to be haunted . . . What would she do if Fremlin's ghost suddenly entered the walled courtyard, smiling the legendary charismatic smile and inviting her to step into the private rooms behind his chemist's shop. Waste of time, Neville; I haven't got nearly enough money to interest you, in fact I haven't got any money at all.

She went quickly out through the creaking door, closing it on the sad eerie courtyard, and half ran around the sides of Calvary Gaol to her car.

CHAPTER THIRTEEN

Extract from Talismans of the Mind *by C. R. Ingram.*

It can probably be argued that the downfall of Violette and Bartlam Partridge was inevitable. A cynic might have said that if Violette had even a small part of the psychic powers she claimed, she ought to have seen it coming and taken steps to avoid it.

The source for the facts is an unusual one: it's the archives of the Fidelity & Trust Insurance Company. (Motto: You can have perfect faith and complete trust in us.) Bartlam apparently possessed the Victorian/ Edwardian respect for Property – the conviction that a house, once acquired, must be suitably looked after. Having paid his premiums to the Fidelity & Trust people, he saw no reason why he should not claim his pound of flesh from them when disaster struck.

There are several clues as to what happened in the North London house on that last night. That useful source of information, the *Finchley Recorder*, provides several, but the main information comes from correspondence between Bartlam and the Fidelity & Trust Company. The Company's records date back to 1911, and, incredibly, copies of every letter ever sent out by them are preserved.

28th November 1917

Dear Sirs

Owing to the deficiencies of a gas supply to the drawing room, and an unfortunate incident involving Mrs Partridge's fondness for entertaining our supper guests by candlelight and her partiality for gowns with flowing chiffon sleeves, we find ourselves deprived of home and hearth.

I enclose for your early attention, a detailed list of extensive damage caused on 22nd instant, and am making claim in full against the policy I took out with you in 1915. I look forward to your early and complete settlement of same.

I believe you may be receiving similar claims from our neighbours, since, sad to relate, the incident caused shattered windows and the demolishing of a chimney pot (No. 22) and the complete annihilation of a wash-house and privy (No. 24), although it should be pointed out that said wash-house and privy had been in a disgracefully dilapidated condition for years and the smallest puff of wind would probably have rendered it a heap of rubble anyway.

All correspondence should be addressed to me in the care of Mr Henry Bingley, 13 Laburnum Avenue, Chiswick, a friend who most generously opened his doors to us in our travail and with whom I and Mrs Partridge are presently residing.

I am, dear sirs,
Yours very truly
Bartlam F. Partridge

1st December 1917

Dear Mr Partridge

We are in receipt of your letter of 28th November and beg to reply as follows.

Since the damage for which you are making claim is so very extensive, and your assessment of its cost so high, our assessors have visited the property. Their report, in summary, is as follows:

i) The gas jets have been completely torn from their moorings. However, this does not matter, since the fitments pre-date the 1847 Act of Parliament controlling the quality and allocation of gas which is directly contrary to the requirements of your policy. This means that this part of the claim is null and void.

ii) The outer wall, which had fronted onto the street has partly collapsed and since this was a load-bearing wall, the upper floors have since also collapsed. However, as the entire front of the house was severely affected by wet rot (*coniophora puteana*) and the roof joists by dry rot (*merulius lacrymans*) and as you had not taken the necessary steps to eradicate it as we asked (see our letter of 10th September 1915), this part of the claim is null and void.

iii) The roof has fallen in and buried most of the
     furniture, but since the furniture does not form part
     of the policy that is not our concern. The claim for a
     new roof can, you will be pleased to know, be met in
     full, although obviously we cannot provide you with
     a new roof until you have rebuilt the supporting
     walls.

Our assessors found among the rubble, two partly
dissolved cones of lime, in a format we believe is
used by theatrical gentlemen to create unusual and
startling effects for stage performances. We are at a
loss to account for this, and will be glad of your
explanation.

Assuring you of our best attention
at all times, we remain,
Yours very faithfully
For and on behalf of the Fidelity &
Trust Insurance Co.
('You can have perfect faith and trust in us')

2nd December 1917

Dear Sirs

Your letter is an insufferable example of bureau-
cracy run mad and a sad indication of what this
country is coming to.

I will have no truck with footling underlings or
trumpery two-a-penny assessors who poke and pry
in the desolate ruins of my home and have the
temerity to question my neighbours (and in any case
the inhabitants of No. 24 have always been known as

antagonistic to me and mine, so you should bear in mind that you will certainly not get an unbiased account of events from them).

I am requesting two very influential friends to take this matter up on my behalf. You may be interested to know that these are a doctor of considerable repute and a prelate of the Church of England. Both gentlemen were dining at my table on the night in question, and will provide unimpeachable authority and verisimilitude for my claim.

Despite my ire, I remain, sirs,
Yours very truly
Bartlam F. Partridge

Poor old Bartlam! He was left without so much as a roof over his head, although it seems that the roof could have been replaced for him, had he, on his part, been able to replace the walls to support it.

His claim form records six people as being present in the house on the night in question. 'A few friends for supper' is how he puts it. So let's not wonder too deeply as to the purpose of those friends, or question the authenticity of the 'doctor of repute' or the 'prelate of the Church of England'. Let's not wonder, either, if the sly old bird calculated that to admit there were more than six might cause the Fidelity & Trust officials to accuse him of packing too many people into too small a room and to dismiss the entire claim on those grounds. So let's assign a judicious eight persons to the evening.

It's not difficult to piece together the fragments of clues and to assemble a picture of what that night must have held. Whether six or sixteen people were present, and whether any of them really were doctors and church prelates, what with candlelight and lime cones it's very clear that Bartlam had set the scene for a major and important event in the Partridge calendar.

And it all went disastrously wrong . . .

November 1917

Clara Caradoc had found it quite difficult to get through a whole week before the next meeting at Violette and Bartlam's house, and when finally the evening did arrive she was annoyed to find her heart beating fast with excitement and anticipation.

She reached the house at the same time as Henry Bingley and his wife.

Violette was there to welcome them, taking their hands delightedly, full of hope for the evening ahead.

'My dears, I have the strongest feeling that tonight we shall see marvellous things. Muriel, I have the greatest confidence of reaching your dear sister – I feel she is very close to us – hovering on the outer edges as I like to put it. And Lady Caradoc – Clara – I know your boy is waiting eagerly tonight. Now that he has made the journey here.'

'Crossed the divide,' put in Bartlam.

'And knows himself to be welcomed and surrounded by loving friends, he will certainly come to us again.'

There were similar messages for the others: the Reverend Lincing would be reunited with the one he sought – there was a sidelong smile from Bartlam at this as if he might possess some information that Reverend Lincing would not like made generally known. And the dear ladies who were such earnest seekers would be rewarded as well, said Violette, beaming at the knitting lady whose name Clara still had not found out, and including the two young sisters and the painted female, who, as always, sat on her own.

They took their places around the table; Clara was between Henry Bingley and the Reverend Lincing, with the painted hussy directly opposite. She had half thought the room would be different after the last time – she had almost fancied that Caspar might have left some kind of mark on it – but it was exactly as she remembered: the dark red wallpaper and the brass Benares ware on the mantelshelf. The aspidistra in its heavy pot, the fringed curtains, shawls everywhere. Bartlam had left a gas jet near the door burning quite high which caught Clara's attention because he had previously been careful to turn them all right down, saying the spirits preferred the dimness. At the time Clara had wanted to say this would not tempt Caspar who, in life, had enjoyed light and noise and brightness, but she had not done so. But tonight, it appeared, they were to have a little more light.

Violette saw everyone was seated around the table and then left the room – 'To make my preparations,' she said, placing a finger to her lips to indicate silence. Bartlam smiled – he was always so agreeable Clara thought, despite not being *quite* a gentleman – and said Vita had been in a ferment of anticipation all day.

When Vita returned, she looked subtly different although Clara was hard put to it to say precisely why. Something about Vita's face, was it? She was decidedly on the plump side (all those violet creams she indulged herself in!), but tonight her face looked really fat – when she turned her head to one side, her cheeks were positively bulging. But most likely it was the light; the single gas jet was throwing odd shadows everywhere, and Bartlam had spent several minutes tinkering with it. It was to be hoped the jet was not faulty; Clara was always a little nervous of gas fittings.

Vita took her usual place at the table and they placed their linked hands on the surface, as always. Clara's heart began to beat faster, because if only Caspar would come again, and this time stay with them for long enough to speak.

Violette did not seem to be calling up her spirit guide tonight; she was staring straight ahead of her, not saying anything at all. Clara had no idea if this was a good sign or not; she risked glancing over her shoulder to where Bartlam was standing by the door. He still seemed concerned about the gas jet. Clara began to feel worried, which was annoying because she should have been concentrating on Caspar and not bothering about gas fittings.

Ah, now Violette was getting more into her stride. She was still not speaking, but she was turning her head this way and that and twice she brought her hand up to her mouth – she did this rather gracefully. The second time she did so it seemed to coincide with a popping sound from near the door. Clara had time to think it was the irritating gas fitment again, and then a flare of the most brilliant light seemed to shoot upwards in the room, and Bart gasped and cried, 'A spirit light! My dear friends, on no account move from your seats! An *ignis fatuus* at the very least!'

The light swooshed up and up, and as it did so Violette

gave a little cry and her hand flew to her mouth again. A stream of something cloudy and almost vapour-like began to pour from her mouth, and again Bartlam cried out.

'Ectoplasm! Spirit vapour! Do not attempt to touch it.'

The ectoplasm floated across the table. Against the glowing whiteness of the light it was like thin clouds of gossamer.

The painted female opposite said, rather sharply, 'What, precisely, is it? I've heard of ectoplasm but I've never known what it is.'

'Spirit energy,' said Bartlam repressively because the rule was silence at all times, and Violette said, 'The spirits are here with us – all our lost loved ones are here.' Her voice sounded slightly thick and flannelly; she must still be in a semi-trance.

The painted female said in a down to earth voice, 'It looks remarkably like bits of white chiffon to me,' and Clara turned to stare at her, because just for a moment the stuff did look exactly like that. Ribbons of feathery-thin cloth. Indian muslin, thought Clara.

'In fact,' went on the woman, 'if you aren't careful it's going to drift straight into that light you seem to be conjuring up in the corner, and if that happens it will—'

She did not finish the sentence. The cloth and the bright light finished it for her. The floating ectoplasm suddenly turned brown at the edges and shrivelled into threads. The glowing incandescence licked hungrily upwards and within minutes half the room was on fire.

Clara thought afterwards that you could never predict how people would behave in a crisis. If she had known that the half the house was to be set on fire that night, she would have said it would be Bartlam himself, possibly with the help of Reverend Lincing, who would take charge. She would have expected them to marshal the ladies to safety, while Violette wrung her hands and wept.

The reality was that Bartlam reeled backwards, and let out such a stream of curses that the two sisters squeaked with embarrassment, and Lincing let out a moan of distress. It was left to the painted female and – remarkably – to Violette Partridge to fling wide doors and windows (this last was rather a mistake, Clara noted, since it fed the fire considerably), and then to rap out sharp orders to everyone to leave the house immediately, and for someone – you, Mr Bingley – please to run as fast as possible to the police box along the street and summon help.

By this time Clara had recovered a little from the first shock, and made haste to help everyone out through the nearest door which gave onto the garden, and then to lead them along a narrow alleyway and so to the street. Muriel Bingley was dithering back and forth, telling everyone that Henry had gone straight along to the police box as requested, he was extremely good in an emergency, Henry, everyone said so.

Clara found herself standing next to the painted female, who seemed to have found time to snatch up a few personal belongings, and was in the process of restoring the knitting lady's beaded dorothy bag to her. Since it was a situation where etiquette must perforce be set aside, she said, 'What on earth happened? Is everyone safely out?'

'What? Oh, yes, everyone's out, unless there are any other occupants of the house we don't know about.'

'Servants, do you mean?' said Clara. 'I don't believe they have any live-in servants.'

The woman sent her a scathing look. 'I didn't mean servants,' she said.

'Then who?'

'Accomplices.'

Clara stared at her, forgetting for a moment about the fire which was by this time sending out clouds of evil-smelling smoke. 'I'm sorry, I don't understand.'

'You didn't swallow all that guff about spirit energy, did you? Good God,' said the woman in what Clara thought a very coarse way, 'you did, didn't you? I'd have thought you of all people would have more sense.'

'The lights—' began Clara.

'Probably produced by a cone of lime held over a flame. It's used for stage effects. And as for that image they contrived of your son at the last meeting, that would have been done by—'

'You're here,' said Clara, snapping the rest of the sentence off in case it might be hurtful.

'I'm here because I want to unmask them for the charlatans they are,' said the woman with suppressed anger in her voice. 'I'm a journalist.'

'A what?'

'A reporter,' she said with angry impatience. 'I write articles for newspapers. I'm working on a series of exposés about bloodsucking tricksters like these two. They're heartless and greedy and they batten on people's tragedies. I want to see them both held up to the ridicule they deserve!'

The suggestion that Bartlam and Violette were charlatans was ridiculous – you only had to see how concerned they were for their friends to know they were genuine. The implication that Clara herself was not able to recognize fraudulent behaviour was downright insulting; Clara was perfectly capable of knowing when people were being deceitful. And the remark about battening on people's tragedies was as melodramatic and vulgar a remark as she had heard in a long time, although presumably you had to expect such colourful language from a person who made money by writing things for newspapers. One had heard about the tricks these people adopted to make a good story and probably this female had some kind of grudge against Violette or Bartlam.

Clara was about to reply very sharply to put this woman right on the matter, when Henry Bingley came panting back to say, importantly, that he had spoken to the police station and help was on the way.

'They won't get here in time to save the house,' said the woman, studying it critically. 'It's burning like the deepest cavern of hell already. I'll bet a few bits of evidence have gone up with it, as well. Pity. I might have managed to get a photograph or two.' She looked across at Reverend Lincing. 'A shame you couldn't recite a few prayers to drive back the flames of Satan, Reverend, isn't it?' she said.

Extract from Talismans of the Mind *by C. R. Ingram*

There is evidence to suggest that in the aftermath, several of Bart and Violette's victims – most of whom refused to believe they had been duped – rallied round to help them. But the evidence of what actually happened to most of the victims is sparse and comes to us in tantalizing fragments.

'My sister and I sold our mother's jewellery in the hope of reaching her after she and our father died and left us orphans to be brought up by distant cousins,' one is reported as saying. Again the *Finchley Recorder* helps us with some information, giving an account of how an unnamed lady of very slender means paid her dues to the pair by knitting gentlemen's golfing sweaters, which she sold in a street market. The paper also provides a very vivid description of a careful arrangement of lime cones ignited over a gas jet, and of how Violette packed thin cheesecloth into her mouth with an end thread tied around a back tooth, and then sneezed or spat the cloth out daintily at the appropriate moment to suggest ectoplasm.

After the fire, the Partridges apparently stayed with friends in Chiswick, although the ungrateful pair do not seem to have found this to their taste.

'I am devoted to dearest Muriel,' Violette wrote to the unknown 'Clara' in December 1917. 'And I shall be for ever in her debt for allowing us to share her home when times were so difficult for us.

'But her house is furnished with Brummagem china-ware and our wine is served to us in thick sixpenny Woolworths glasses. The rooms smell of wet biscuits and of something that Henry rubs into his hair each night. Every Monday there is the additional smell of washing, for Muriel believes everything in the house must be thoroughly washed each week. Every Tuesday there is the smell of boiling cabbage which we have to eat with the cold remains of Sunday's roast. I do not believe Bartlam will be able to stand it for very long – he hankers for London or for some big city at the very least – and I should not be at all surprised to find one day that he has packed his bags and left.'

And so, of course, he did just that. By the spring of 1918, Bartlam seems to have broken the marital bonds and left Violette.

In the light of his later exploits (see references elsewhere to the Unpleasantness in Brighton in 1924, and also the misunderstanding in Greek Street in 1927), Violette was probably better off without him, although she doubtless did not take that view.

Whatever else emerges from the tag-ends of gossip, letters and newspapers, it is clear that during those years at any rate, she was firmly under Bartlam's thumb, and was never able to view his behaviour objectively.

CHAPTER FOURTEEN

'I want you to be as objective as possible,' said Chad Ingram to Jude in the small bedroom of the King's Head. 'Is that understood?'

'Certainly it's understood,' said Jude. 'I will be as an unwritten book, or as a virgin canvas facing a painter. I will clear my mind of all its irritating clutter and I will be as receptive as an insect's antenna or a cat's whiskers. In fact—' He broke off and half turned his head. 'Someone's coming along the corridor outside,' he said, and three seconds later there was a knock on the door.

'It's probably Drusilla.'

'It sounds a bit too polite for Drusilla,' said Jude, as Chad walked across to the door. 'It'll be Phin. He's very clever, isn't he, underneath all that breathless enthusiasm.'

'Yes, we're lucky to have him. He's only supposed to be here for a year, but I'm hoping to persuade him to stay longer. Phin – ah, it *is* you. Jude thought it was. Come in.'

Phin came in a bit warily. He was finding it quite difficult not to give away any clues as to where they were or about Calvary. The trouble was that they had been working on this project so intensely, they had got used to talking about the place without thinking.

'We're all ready downstairs. Drusilla's putting the dictaphone in the car, and we've asked reception to make up a flask of coffee. I thought it would kind of keep you company, Jude.'

'That's extremely thoughtful, Phin. I've got a bottle of a wine, and my MP3 player as well. I thought,' said Jude, with the air of one to whom this was a major concern, 'that I'd play Mozart as we enter the place, or possibly Mahler. He can be very dark, Mahler, and since I'm fairly sure this is one of Chad's upmarket ghost hunts I might as well heighten the atmosphere. While we're on the subject, Chad, how about breaking into the music industry afterwards and doing one of those compilation CDs as a tie-in? Music for Ghost Hunting.'

'Symphonies for Swinging Spooks,' said Phin with a grin, and then, without thinking, 'Are you frightened about all this?'

As soon as he said this he wondered if it was a bit too personal, but Jude did not seem to mind. He turned his head thoughtfully towards Phin. He was wearing dark glasses – Phin had not yet seen him without them – and there was an eerie impression of sight behind the lenses.

'No, I don't believe I am frightened,' said Jude, and for the first time the irony was absent. 'What I am is intrigued – as much by what I'm going to experience as by Chad's off the wall experiment. I'll even admit there are a few inexplicable things in this world. I'd have to say I've never yet met a ghost, however.'

'You don't believe in ghosts?' Phin could not help saying.

'Oh,' said Jude vaguely, 'I didn't say that. Are we ready to leave?'

Jude hoped he was striking the right note with Chad and Phin Farrell, and he thought neither of them had realized how deeply apprehensive he was. I must be mad to be doing this, he thought as they left the bedroom. I'm going to be on my own in an unfamiliar place and I'll be stuck there for much of the night.

As they set off, he reached for the Edwardian walking cane he had bought in a junk shop in the Portobello Road some years ago, liking it as much for its silver top as for its air of belonging to an era where gentlemen had used such things as an accessory. It had been useful on more than one occasion when he was travelling; suspicious customs officials in uneasy parts of the world had not regarded it as a weapon of menace, and once or twice it had extricated Jude and his team from a threatening situation. The village just outside Syria where a couple of mercenaries had thought it would be a great joke against these foreign journalists to disable the camera team's equipment. And the Afghanistan border where they had been attacked by soldiers whose nationality and loyalties had been ambiguous but whose enmity had been unmistakable. Since the bomb blast it had been useful for gauging the whereabouts of doors, walls and kerbs.

As they went down the stairs there was the buzz of

people talking, and the warm scents of food, wood smoke and beer. 'The stairs are narrow and they wind around to the left,' Chad said. 'Remember?'

'Since it's only three hours since I went up these same stairs, I remember perfectly well, thank you,' said Jude. 'This is quite an old place, isn't it? I can smell the timbers. I do hope it isn't chintz and self-conscious about being ye olde.'

'It isn't,' said Chad. 'In fact it's rather attractive, and— Oh, blast it.'

'What's the matter? Were you about to say something that would give the whole thing away or have you stubbed your toe?'

'Neither. I've just seen someone I want to avoid, that's all. No, it's all right, I don't think he saw me. We're at the door now. Straight through, and the car's over to your left.'

'Who were you trying to avoid?' demanded Jude when they were outside. It was sharply cold; he turned up his coat collar and imagined how everyone's breath would be vapourizing on the air.

'One of the locals who's been trying to muscle in on the programme. Harmless, but a bit of a know-all,' said Chad shortly. 'I don't think he saw us – he almost certainly didn't you see you, anyway. The car's here.'

'I hope,' said Jude, as Chad opened the car door, 'you've stowed the wine away safely.'

'It's in the boot.'

'Have you remembered the corkscrew and the glass? Because I'm damned if I'm going to drink wine out of the bottle or from a paper cup.'

'I've remembered the corkscrew and Drusilla's

wrapped the glass in tissues so it won't break. For pity's sake get into the car and let's get going,' said Chad sounding exasperated, and Jude smiled.

'Dear me, Professor, I might almost think you were agitated.'

'I am *not* agitated,' said Chad.

Oh yes, you are, thought Jude, getting into the car, moving slowly and deliberately so he did not miss his footing or bang his head on the car roof. It was something he had been taught to do early on. 'Unless you're absolutely sure of your surroundings do everything slowly,' the specialist nurse had said. 'Make a quick mental check of each move before you actually make it. Especially in an unknown place. If you don't, you'll fumble and probably get it wrong.'

Be blowed to mental checks, thought Jude, but he got into Chad's car slowly because he was damned if he was going to miss the seat, and then feel waves of silent sympathy from Chad and the other two as a result.

As Chad got into the back, Jude said, 'Aren't you driving us?'

'Phin's driving us.'

'Well, thank God for small mercies.'

'Don't you like the boss's driving?' said Drusilla, sounding amused.

'It's something no one should have to suffer more than once in a lifetime,' said Jude.

Jude was not like anyone Phin had ever met. For most of the time he was ironic and offhand – Phin had not yet decided how much this was a defence mechanism against unwanted sympathy – but he was also almost abnormally perceptive. There was no way of knowing if this was something the blindness had triggered or if it had been part of his personality anyway. Drusilla had said privately to Phin that Jude must have been a knockout with the women before he was blinded, and then had said, 'No, scrub the part about before he was blinded – he's still a knockout.'

Driving up the narrow track to Calvary, Phin was torn between excited anticipation and near panic. He leaned forward over the steering wheel to peer through the windscreen. He had not seen the gaol yet, only Dr Ingram had seen it, – he had, in fact, made a very careful exploration of the interior to make sure it was in an acceptable condition for Jude to spend the night. Phin had seen the photographs and the ground plan, but this was not the same.

As part of his research he had checked the origins of the name, partly because it might make a good snippet of information on the programme, but also because he was interested. Most of the books said the name usually indicated a place of execution and that the word derived from the Latin *calvaria*, meaning skull. According to one reference this lent some credence to the belief that the contours of the hill on which Christ was crucified resembled a skull. There was, it appeared, a further theory that the hill was the place where Adam's skull was buried. These were the kind of quirky details Dr Ingram liked so Phin had made notes, after which he had spent several enjoyable minutes visualizing Dr Ingram's politely ironic de-bunking of both theories in front of the camera. Polite irony was what the English were really good at when they put their minds to it.

Cumbria's Calvary also stood on a hill, but it was a gentle English hill and it bore no resemblance to skulls, biblical, mythological or otherwise. It did not need any legends to give it an air of the macabre; it did macabre very effectively on its own. On this late autumn night its squat bulk was menacing in the extreme, and as Phin parked in front of the main entrance he had to repress a strong compulsion to turn and run.

Jude did not appear especially concerned, however. Phin remembered he had spent most of his working life in war-torn parts of the world, dodging bombs and terrorists and the raggle-taggle mercenary armies of religious fanatics and power-mad dictators, and supposed spending a few hours in a deserted prison cell would be child's play by comparison.

Jude got out of the car – Phin had already noticed he moved slowly and rather deliberately – and put the MP3 player in a jacket pocket. Only then did he say, 'I'm ready when you are. If anyone's interested, I'm going to walk in to the first movement of Mozart's Piano Concerto Number Twenty-one. It's a prowling kind of music: it makes you think of walking alone through a dark forest with something malevolent creeping along after you. Classic fear theme, of course, and I daresay it's been plundered and plagiarized for the opening to a dozen horror films, but who cares? Mozart certainly wouldn't. He loved vulgarity.'

'Mozart notwithstanding,' said Chad, 'once we're inside, I think Phin had better walk alongside you. I know you've got that flamboyant walking cane, but I think it would be a good idea.'

'In case I fall? I've been known to fall into all kinds

of things, and sometimes in worse places than this,' remarked Jude, and Phin saw Dr Ingram smile.

'Yes, I know you have and I've been there when you fell, in fact I picked you up on a couple of occasions if you remember.'

'On a couple of occasions,' observed Jude drily, 'you fell with me. In your wilder youth, of course.'

'We'd like to hear about his wilder youth sometime,' said Drusilla.

'No, you wouldn't. Jude, the point I'm trying to make is that I don't want you to end up with a broken ankle in here.'

'I am silenced.'

'That'll be the day,' observed Chad caustically. He produced the keys – they were large keys on an old-fashioned ring and they clattered a bit.

'You've got all the sound effects, haven't you?' remarked Jude. 'Is this the moment when I switch on the MP3 and let Mozart screen everything out?'

'It is.'

Massive oak doors sealed Calvary off from the world, but there was a small door inset on one side and it was this which Chad proceeded to unlock. Beyond it was a small inner courtyard with guard rooms on each side, and straight ahead was another door. Phin felt another bump of apprehension. This is it, he thought.

Chad locked the outer door, and crossed the courtyard to the second one. He glanced at Jude, and then in a low voice said to Phin and Drusilla, 'There are three ways in. But when I checked the place the other two were both firmly locked or bolted from the inside. There's even a padlock on one of the doors.'

Phin was glad to know this, because it was a place where you wanted to be sure nothing was lurking in a dark corner watching you.

'As soon as we're in, I'll lock this door as well. Drusilla, you've got the torches, haven't you?'

'Yes, here you are. One each.'

'Then let's go inside.'

Even with the light from Chad and Drusilla's torches, Calvary was a dreadful place. Phin, keeping one hand on Jude's arm to guide him, instantly felt the swirling memories of Calvary's past pressing in on them. Or was it simply his own knowledge of the place's history influencing his reactions? He wondered what Jude was feeling, but he did not look as if he was feeling anything. He was using the silver-topped cane to test where he was going, but was apparently shutting out his surroundings with reasonable success. Phin had no idea if this was due to Mozart or to sheer force of concentration.

As they went further in Phin reminded himself that he did not believe in ghosts; ghosts were for kids. He liked a good ghost story as much as anyone, but you needed a few cans of beer and a gang of like-minded friends with you. Ghosts became quite cosy at that kind of party.

There would not be anything cosy about Calvary's ghosts if they turned up to join tonight's party. Did Neville Fremlin's ghost walk these unquiet halls? Fremlin was supposed to have killed five people – or had it been six? Phin could not remember, although the legend was that the police had never established the final number, and that Fremlin had never talked. Faced with the gallows had he begged for mercy in his final moments?

I'd bet the ranch that you didn't, said Phin to Neville Fremlin's ghost. You were the Silver-Tongued Murderer and I'll bet you kept up the image to the bitter end.

Chad was leading them along a wide corridor – it did not look to Phin as if anyone had been in here for about a hundred years and the atmosphere was getting worse all the time. It certainly seemed to be affecting the others: even Drusilla had stopped making languid remarks about the dust and saying things like, Oh God, this is ruining my boots. Phin thought if you came into a place like this wearing suede boots you should not expect much sympathy if they were spoiled. Drusilla had good legs for boots though, in fact she had good legs for anything, although Phin was not going to tell her so because she would only make some ball-shrivelling reply.

Their footsteps rang hollowly in the emptiness of the corridors and several times Phin caught a faint overspill of Mozart. Jude had been quite right about it being prowling through dark forests music.

They walked past what were unmistakably cells: rows of thick-looking doors with small grilles near the top. Some of the doors were sagging off the hinges, and twice they passed cells where there were no doors at all. Phin glanced inside and repressed a shiver, not because it was such a small soulless place but because it reeked of such loneliness and misery.

Veils of cobwebs hung everywhere and several times scuttling sounds came out of the darkness. Phin had known there might be rats but he had been trying not to think about it. He knew this was pretty cowardly of him but he could not help it. They would have to make sure there were no rats in the execution room before they shut Jude in and he hoped that particular task did not fall to him. Meantime he tried not to flinch every time the shadows scuttled.

Dr Ingram was saying something about the place being in quite good repair under the neglect and dirt – Phin suspected he said this more to break the brooding silence than for any other reason.

'It's in lousy repair,' said Jude. 'Dry rot everywhere.'

'I thought you were listening to Mozart.'

'It's the end of the first movement. And you can't really miss the smell of dry rot. Wherever this is, Chad, I hope you haven't bought it.'

'Of course I haven't bought it.'

'In that case I'll return to the London Philharmonic. Let me know when we get to wherever we're going.'

Chad stopped in front of a thick oak door. He did not say anything, but looked back at the others and Phin knew the condemned block – the separate little suite of rooms with the condemned cell and the execution chamber – was beyond this door. He felt his heart rate bump itself up a few notches. I wish I were a million miles away, he thought. No, I don't. I'd hate to have missed this, rats and all. It's nothing like I imagined, though.

But it was Jude who said, 'Is this it?'

'Yes,' said Chad. 'Yes, this is it.'

CHAPTER FIFTEEN

The minute they went through the oak door it felt as if a massive weight was pressing down on them. Phin saw Jude recoil and put up a hand as if to shield his face. He turned his head slightly as if he had heard a sound from the corridors behind them, and Phin's heart leapt. He thought – there's someone else in here with us. Jude's heard someone. But although he listened intently, he could not make out anything except the rustlings they had heard earlier on and the faint drip of water.

There could never have been much light in here. No windows looked onto the outside world and if Calvary had ever had electricity it had not been brought to this part. Rusted gas brackets hung from the walls at intervals and the stench was dreadful. Rats again, thought Phin. Or Jude's dry rot. Or is it the stench of despair and fear? No, I'm being absurd.

Drusilla suddenly pointed to a door on their left.

There was a hefty lock on the outside and the now familiar grille three quarters of the way up. She looked at Dr Ingram enquiringly. 'Yes,' he said softly. 'That's it.'

Condemned cell, thought Phin, remembering the layout plan. He wondered if it would be locked.

It was not locked, but when Chad tried to open the door it groaned and seemed to be stuck. Phin went to help and under their combined pressure it yielded slightly.

'Harder,' said Chad, and they tried again. This time a shriek of hinges tore through the dimness like a hundred souls in torment. There was a splintering noise and the door fell inwards, crashing onto the floor of the cell, sending clouds of dust and debris billowing upwards. Drusilla and the other two jumped back.

'Angels and ministers of grace defend us,' said Jude, removing his earpieces. 'What in the name of heaven was that?'

'A door collapsed,' said Chad shortly. 'Phin, are you all right?'

Phin had been at the forefront and had consequently received the entire dust cloud in the face. His eyes were streaming and he would probably never stop coughing from the ancient dust that had gone down his lungs, but he said, a bit gaspingly, that he was fine.

'Have some coffee from the flask,' said Jude, and Phin gulped it down gratefully and managed to stop coughing.

'Are you sure it was only a door that fell in?' demanded Jude. 'It sounded as if the roof had collapsed at the very least. I suppose this isn't a wild elaborate joke? You haven't brought me to a film set where they're remaking Dracula, have you? Because between rotting doors and groaning locks this is starting to be almost too good to be true.'

'You've been listening to Mozart's Twenty-first too much,' said Chad. 'But no, it isn't a film set and it isn't an elaborate joke.'

Drusilla suddenly said, 'What's that?' and Phin's heart leapt all over again.

'What? Where?'

'That sound. It's like something vibrating somewhere.'

Phin started to say he could not hear anything and then stopped, because Drusilla was right – there was a faint thrumming sound coming from somewhere quite close to them.

'It's not exactly machinery, I don't think,' said Jude. 'But something's been disturbed by the door crashing in. Like when you pluck the strings of something and it goes on resonating all by itself.'

The thought of something resonating all by itself somewhere in the darkness of Calvary was almost more than Phin could bear. He saw Dr Ingram's expression and realized with horror that the sound was coming from the execution chamber. It's something to do with the gallows, he thought.

'It's stopping,' said Chad after a moment, and shone the torch inside the condemned cell.

It was larger than the other cells, perhaps twelve by fifteen feet, and incredibly some furniture remained in place. There was a square table in one corner, with a couple of chairs drawn up to it. That's where the prisoner would have sat, thought Phin. He'd have turned his head to this door if anyone came in. There'd have been two warders with him and they would have played cards or chess or chequers. Would they pretend to care who won?

'Is this where I'm spending the night?' demanded Jude. 'In the room where the door fell off? Because if so . . .'

'No, this isn't it,' said Chad. 'But wait here with Drusilla, will you? Phin, come with me. Bring the other torch and your notebook, will you? Oh, and the camcorder.'

In American prisons there was, Phin thought, a macabre procession across courtyards and along corridors, but in Calvary the execution shed was just along the corridor from the condemned cell. Phin, the camcorder slung around his neck, counted the paces as they went. A dozen. Twelve steps between cell and scaffold. He tried not to wonder if the rats might have got into the execution chamber.

'This will be it,' said Chad, and opened the door.

The thrumming of the machinery had not completely died away and with the opening of the door it seemed to shiver under their feet. Phin stopped dead on the threshold, because if the condemned cell had been bad this was like stepping into a huge suffocating blackness. Waves of anger and fear came at him like invisible smoke. We're not wanted here, he thought. Whatever ghosts – whatever memories – are trapped in here, they're boiling with hatred and resentment and they're trying to beat us back. But he set his teeth and forced himself to go inside and examine the room objectively so he could make suitable notes. Size of room, objects in it, condition, construction. The camcorder would pick up a lot of it, but it was as well to have notes in addition.

The room was approximately the same size as the condemned cell. Chad shone the torch around, showing up the bleak decay. There was a small window high up in one corner, the glass thick with the grime of years. The brickwork directly beneath it was leprous with damp.

The gallows trap was near the centre: it was about four feet square.

'Double trapdoors,' said Chad, shining the torch directly on it. 'D'you see? They're sunk into the floor. Not absolutely flush with it, but nearly so. And that's the mechanism for the trap alongside it.' The torchlight fell on a heavy iron lever jutting out of a small square aperture in the floor.

'It's nearer to the trap than I thought it would be,' said Phin after a moment. 'You'd think they'd have tried to hide it a bit. Had a screen tucked in a corner, or something. But the – um – the condemned man would have seen it.'

'They nearly always blindfolded them at the end, I think,' said Chad, walking around the edges of the trap.

'The mechanism's still humming a bit, isn't it?'

'Yes. The crash must have disturbed the metal rods under the floor – they've probably worked a bit loose over the years. It's quite a simple mechanism from the look of it – can you see, Phin? The lever works horizontally. When the executioner slid it across, it pulled the metal rods back, and that removed the plugs holding the doors in place.'

'And the doors would have dropped,' said Phin.

'Yes. The plan shows a vault directly beneath the trap. There's a stairway from this level, leading down to it.' He shone the torch onto a second, much smaller trapdoor in a corner of the room. 'It won't move,' he said 'I tried it when I checked everywhere. There's a ring handle, but I can't budge it.'

Phin knelt down to try, but he could not open the flap either. 'I don't think it's locked or bolted,' he said. 'It's just warped.'

'That's what I thought. But it doesn't materially affect tonight's shooting, although I'd still like to know what's down there. We'll see if we can force it tomorrow.'

Phin looked up at the thick crossbeam directly over the trap. There was a massive metal bracket clamped to it and a thick iron chain hung down, clearly for the rope itself. The end of the chain was just over his head; if he reached up he could grasp the last few links. They felt harsh and cold and he let go at once. It was difficult to decide if the crossbeam and chain were more grisly than the trapdoor mechanism.

'Should I try for some stills?' he said. 'The light won't be good though, and flash isn't ideal for this kind of thing, is it?'

'We'll get the stills tomorrow,' said Chad. 'But we'll take some footage now, just to get the flavour and scale of the place, and then some of Jude actually entering. It'll be shadowy but it'd certainly indicate the atmosphere. Will you do that, Phin? Get as much as you can. Both sets of trapdoors and the levers, of course. Once Jude's in here we'll leave the camcorder running.'

'Shooting the ghosts,' Phin could not help saying.

'Yes.' Chad waited until Phin had recorded the room from all possible angles, and then went across to the edge of the gallows trap and knelt down to examine it more closely. 'Switch the camera off for a moment,' he said. 'I want to double-check these doors are safe. Because if they aren't, and if Jude walks onto them without realizing it— Close the door first. I don't want him to hear what we're doing and pick up any clues.'

Phin closed the door and at once felt the room's atmosphere jump up at him again. Don't shut us in this place, said the memories and the ghosts.

They tested the trap, cautiously stepping on it one at a time, and then both together. The wood creaked loudly and sagged a bit, but both trapdoors appeared to be sound and firm, even when Phin jumped up and down a few times as an extra test.

'They may be lined with something on the underside,' said Chad, studying them critically, 'but we'd need to operate the lever to see, and we'd better not do that. I think they're all right though, don't you?'

'Yes.'

Nothing about any of this was really all right, of course. The room was seething with terrible memories; the shadows moved and slithered with the play of the torchlight so it was dreadfully easy to imagine bowed-over shapes swinging to and fro on the end of a rope.

'What about the lever?' said Phin, speaking a bit too loudly in order to thrust the images away. 'How moveable is it? Because if Jude were to explore he might activate it without realizing what it is. And if the mechanism's still working, the trap would open and he might – uh – fall into it. Or should we tell him to stay put in one place?'

'We can try telling him but he probably won't take any notice. Let's see how pliable the lever is.'

Phin had thought he was coping with the room quite well, so he was annoyed to find that when they tried to move the lever his hands were shaking.

'Is the room getting to you?' said Dr Ingram, glancing at him.

'Um, yes, a bit.'

'I thought it might be. It's getting to me, as well,' he said, and grinned, and Phin instantly felt better. Dr Ingram's work had taken him to about a zillion places like Calvary and if he was unnerved by the atmosphere it must be really bad.

'I think it's still moveable,' said Chad, after a moment. He frowned, and Phin said, 'Could we stuff something around it? To kind of wedge it a bit more firmly? It might stop Jude catching his foot if he explores.'

'Good idea. That particular danger hadn't occurred to me. What have we got?'

In the end they used Phin's long woollen scarf and Chad's gloves, wadding them up and pushing them into the square aperture around the lever. 'I think that's padded it quite well,' said Chad, inspecting it critically. 'It's as immovable as we can make it. Good. We'd better get back to the others.'

Phin said, 'Jude will be all right on his own in here, won't he? Has he got a cellphone? Should we leave one with him if he hasn't?'

'Yes, he's got one,' said Chad. 'But I don't think there'll be a signal in here.'

'Let me try,' said Phin, producing his own phone.

'Any good?'

'No. Damn. He really will be cut off, won't he?'

They rejoined the other two and Chad said they were

all set. 'It's just along here, Jude. Phin's going to film you going in.'

'All right,' said Jude. He put the earpieces of the player in his pocket. 'It's bloody cold, isn't it?' he said, as they walked along the passage.

Phin walked backwards, carefully keeping Jude in the camcorder's view-finder, trying not to bump into the walls as he went. He was dismayed when Drusilla said, 'I suppose you have remembered to put a tape in, have you, Phin? Boss, d'you remember that time when we were shooting *Talismans of the Mind*, and that girl – what was her name? – forgot to wind a new tape back to "Start" and there was only about five minutes on it. It ran out without anyone realizing, and we filmed for two whole hours before we discovered it. We had to re-shoot the entire thing. I've never seen you so angry with anyone.'

Phin would not put it past Drusilla to have said this with the deliberate intention of panicking him. It did panic him. Tonight was not something you could go back and re-shoot and he would never get over it if he screwed up. He sneaked a peek at the counter meter and the battery levels while Drusilla was not looking, and saw that everything was whirring along just as it should. There were times when he absolutely hated Drusilla.

'Personally, I couldn't give a tuppenny damn if Phin's filming this or not,' said Jude. 'Because I'm going to write up my own account of it anyway and sell it to – well, to whoever will pay the most. You weren't bargaining for that, Chad, were you? Listen though, if you ever ask me to take part in one of your wild experiments in future, could you make it somewhere with central heating. It's as cold as a nun's embrace in here. Phin, if you're taking sound as well, you'd better edit that last remark out.'

'It doesn't matter about the sound,' said Chad, 'because we're going to do a separate voice-over, so you can curse and blaspheme to your heart's content.'

They had reached the doorway of the execution chamber by this time and Phin went in first, still walking backwards so as to get the actual entrance squarely in shot. He was trying not to notice the atmosphere, but Jude stopped dead on the threshold and Dr Ingram and Drusilla exchanged a quick glance as if worried he might change his mind about the entire thing and demand to be taken back to the King's Head. I wouldn't blame him if he did just that, thought Phin.

But Jude did not change his mind. He stood very still for a moment, gripping the silver-topped stick, his head slightly to one side. He's listening to the room, thought Phin. God knows what it's telling him. Then in a voice that was very nearly his normal offhand tone, Jude said, 'Well, wherever this is, it certainly isn't the Plaza Suite or the Ivy, is it? What a good thing I brought my own food and drink. Where do you want me, Chad?'

'Over here, I think. Halfway along this left-hand wall. I'll guide you.'

'No thanks, I'd rather make a mental map of the room.'

Using the stick, he went along the wall on the door's left, reached the corner and turned down the long wall facing the gallows trap. 'About here?'

'Yes, good. You're about halfway along. Drusilla's brought a couple of cushions and a blanket, so we'll put those out on the floor for you.'

'Thanks.'

'And the camcorder in that corner I think, please Phin,' said Chad. 'Jude, it'll be on the left of the door.'

'On my right?'

'Yes. From there it'll take in most of the room and you should be in shot all the time.'

'I'd better make sure not to knock over the wine, then. I'll submit to a good deal in the cause of research, but I'm damned if I'll be caught on film sloshing Merlot all over the floor.' Jude moved to the cushions and sat down, laying the cane beside him. The MP3 was still in his pocket, and the wine and the flask of coffee were next to him. He checked these with his hands, and then said, 'There should be a box with food in it as well somewhere.'

'I've got it,' said Drusilla. 'Caviar and water biscuits, I see.'

'And pâté. If I'm going to do this at all, I'm going to do it in style. There should be the dictaphone in there, as well – yes, thank you, that feels like it. Chad, I'll record what I feel as it occurs to me. All right?'

'Yes. You're a pro, so I don't need to tell you how to phrase anything or what to put in or leave out. You know the kind of stuff I want,' said Chad. He shone his torch onto his wristwatch. 'It's just coming up to eleven o'clock. I'd like to give you three hours here. Can you bear that?'

'I thought you'd want the witching hour including,' said Jude. 'Yes, I can bear it. You're going to lock me in, aren't you?'

'Don't you want me to?'

'I think you'd better.'

'I'd like to ask you to stay put,' said Chad. 'But I know that's a useless thing to say. So I'll just say that if you do decide to take a stroll around, be careful.'

'Why? Is there a yawning pit in the centre of the room, or a spiral staircase?'

'No. It's almost empty,' said Chad, and Phin recognized that he was choosing his words carefully. 'But it's an old place and I'd hate you to trip over any odd bits of uneven floor or bump into anything. You've got the stick though, haven't you?'

'I have. And I'll prod the air with it before every step I take. All right?'

'I suppose that's as good as I can hope for. We're going back to the King's Head,' said Chad. 'I want to work on an intro while this is all still fresh in my mind. We'll probably plan out tomorrow's schedule as well. Phin and I will drive back at half past one, and we'll be here at two o'clock.'

'I'll tell the ghosts to admit you,' said Jude gravely. 'But there's no guarantee that they will. You can't get staff these days.'

There was a rather awkward pause, then Chad said, 'Jude, will you be all right?'

'Not if I can't find the corkscrew, I won't. Oh wait though, it's here, isn't it?' The dark head turned to where Chad was standing. 'I'll be perfectly all right.'

'Sure?'

'Sure. Never better.'

CHAPTER SIXTEEN

Jude listened to their footsteps receding. It was remarkable how distinctive footsteps could be: he was able to identify Chad's brisk tread, the light tapping of Drusilla's heels and Phin Farrell's eager steps scurrying along. This last made him smile. He liked Phin who reminded Jude of himself at that age – all that enthusiasm.

The acoustics of this place must be either very powerful or very unusual because the footsteps seemed to go on for a long time. Jude listened, thinking that surely Chad and the other two must have reached the outer doors by now. Or perhaps the corridors doubled back in some way before actually reaching the outer door and the way out was alongside this room. It had felt a bit maze-like in here. He waited for the footsteps to die away, thinking that once he knew he was really on his own he would start dictating his initial impressions.

There was the sound of a door clanging. Then that's it, thought Jude, they've gone and I'm about to spend a night in the classic haunted house – at least, I'm assuming it's haunted in some way. Probably nothing at all will happen. I'm certainly not expecting a clutch of spectres to erupt out of the walls on the stroke of midnight. There's never been conclusive proof that ghosts actually exist anyway. Oh, yeah? Are you sure about that?

Could anyone really be sure about it? Supposing there were ghosts in the world but the people who encountered them did not live to tell the tale? Or lived but were driven mad by the sight? Would Chad return in a few hours to find a gibbering wreck on the floor of this grisly place, and cart Jude off to the nearest psychiatric ward? He spent a few minutes considering this possibility. It might even be a benign, rather quirky, madness in the end. 'Poor Mr Stratton,' the nurses would say, 'he often talks about spectral highwaymen and martyred monarchs – we hear him gossiping with the ghost of Ann Boleyn or Charles the First. Some night's it's as good as the Open University or BBC Two, and we've all got quite knowledgeable about history since he came.'

The black humour of this pleased Jude so much that he reached for the dictaphone to record a few sentences along those lines before he could forget them. Always kick off on a note of comedy if you can: it grabs the listeners' attention from the start. Not that there had been much comedy about the last few years, nor was there likely to be much tonight, either. His voice, as he talked into the machine sounded eerie, but he was used to dictating reports in all kinds of odd places and he disregarded this and ended on a more sombre note.

'Headless monarchs and spectral midnight coaches aside – to say nothing of Falling Houses of Usher – this is undoubtedly a place where there's been very great sadness and fear, and you would have to have the mental skin of a rhinoceros not to feel that.' He switched the tape off and it was only when the silence closed around him once again that he realized Chad's team were still around – he could hear their footsteps. Probably they were getting some extra shots, although Chad had left the camcorder in here – it was whirring away quietly – Phin must be taking stills as well.

Jude opened the wine and poured it into the glass, doing so slowly and deliberately because of being filmed, pleased at managing these small manoeuvres smoothly. He set the bottle down far enough away not to knock it over by mistake and marked the position of it in his mind. Right-hand side, a bit more than an arm's reach away. The specialist nurse had taught him to create a mental plan of a room and then file it for future reference. Then, when he went into that room or house again, he had only to refer to the plan, she said. Jude had resisted this, as he had resisted most suggestions for making his life easier, but in the end he had tried the small ploy and found it worked surprisingly well. He knew the layout of his recently acquired flat, even though he had never seen it.

But maps, mental or otherwise, would not help him tonight because tonight he was on his own in the dark. Nothing new there; he had been locked in his own particular darkness for the last two years. Don't whine, Jude, just be glad you survived the bloody bomb and remember what the medics told you. They had said, Yes, of course it was tragic that he had not been rescued from the chaotic hell on the Syrian border much sooner and taken straight to a hospital: there was a chance that earlier treatment might have saved his sight. But they had also told him he had been extremely lucky there were no other injuries. Brain damage, amnesia or pronounced personality change, visible trauma to skull or cheekbones. There were worse things than bilateral detachment, they said, and in time he would learn to accept the blindness. Stuff that, Jude had thought, I'll never accept it!

He set the wine glass down and leaned his head back against the wall, which would probably give him lice or something equally disagreeable, and deliberately opened his mind to his surroundings.

Chad and the other two had been very guarded, but there had been several half clues. Clearly this was a very run-down, very large old building, and its approach was along what was little more than a cart track. But wherever and whatever it was, it was thick with misery, anger and chock-full of the most dreadful despair Jude had ever encountered. It had not seemed to have the layout of a house. An institution of some kind? That seemed a strong possibility. One of the old Victorian asylums? A disused fever hospital or a workhouse? He switched on the dictaphone again.

'One thing's unpleasantly clear: this room doesn't like me being here – it's absolutely seething. There's fear and bitterness in here – it's almost as if they've soaked into the walls and as if they're bouncing back at me now. I don't believe in ghosts, but I certainly believe that strong feelings can leave an imprint.'

He found the Pause button, pressed it, thought for a few moments, and then went on.

'There's also an impression of some kind of very precise, almost formal event that used to take place here – something so carefully arranged, its pattern followed so strictly, that it might almost have been a ritual.'

He played this back, frowning over the final word. Ritual. The Black Mass? Devil worship? That seemed a bit hackneyed for Chad.

But the impression of solemnity was very vivid. A deconsecrated church? There was the feeling of prayers of some kind and the sense of figures moving in a procession. The feelings sharpened in his mind, like a fuzzy piece of film coming into focus. Men walking through a smeary early morning ... And with them someone who could not walk on his own and was having to be helped ... This last impression was so vivid that for a moment Jude thought he could hear the hesitant footsteps. He listened, but there was nothing. It was probably water dripping somewhere.

A ritual. A procession. But what had been at the culmination of that ritual? Jude frowned, trying to project his mind into the darkness to pick up something more. Nothing. He checked the Braille watch on his wrist. Half past eleven. Two and a half hours still to go. How about exploring the room a bit more to see if it felt different anywhere else?

Moving cautiously, he began to work his way around the walls. They felt like stone, and the floor felt like stone, as well, but everywhere seemed to be intact. He counted his steps as he went. It did not seem to be a very big room – perhaps it was twelve or fourteen feet square – but Jude still had no clue as to its purpose. He found his place with the cushions, dictated a couple of sentences to this effect, then set off again, this time walking outwards from the wall.

He had taken five paces when without warning the floor level changed. It was only a small change – nothing so deep as a step, but the stones vanished and in their place was timber, and the surface suddenly dropped by about an inch. If Jude had been able to see, he probably would hardly have noticed it, but without his sight the sudden change threw his senses out of kilter. He stumbled, lost his balance and fell. Something hard and angular struck his shoulder and he grabbed it as he went down.

Whatever it was he grabbed, moved, and beneath his feet something shivered. There was the sensation of old mechanism struggling to engage, and then a loud crack rent the air. This time the floor did not just shudder, it shook like the first tremor of an earthquake, and something stale and foetid seemed to gust straight into his face. There was a banging clatter, like a door slamming against a wall.

Jude gasped and instinctively curled into a ball, throwing his hands protectively over his head. For a dreadful moment the abruptness and intensity of the sound rocketed him straight back to the Iraqi village, with the world exploding in agonizing starbursts of colour before blackness seeped inexorably over his vision. But almost at once his senses steadied, and after a moment he was able to stand up. He was a bit shaky, his shoulder felt as if something had kicked it and the evil-smelling dust was still making him cough, but other than that he was all right. The Braille watch indicated five minutes to midnight.

He groped for the walking stick, at first only encountering the stone floor but eventually finding it. The clattering was dying away but the echoes of the original crash were still going on. In a moment Jude would try to find his way back to the familiar wall with the cushions, but first he would record what had just happened. He rescued the dictaphone from his pocket, and thankful to find it still working, managed to give a brief, businesslike account of what had happened.

'The camera should have picked up all this,' he said. 'I have absolutely no idea what's happened, but whatever it was, it's certainly stirred the atmosphere up – it's like sitting inside a vat of boiling hatred and terror.'

He played this back. If there was the smallest hint of fear in his voice he would wipe the whole thing off and begin again, because he was damned if he was letting anyone know how frightened he had been. His voice sounded a bit tinny, which was because the dictaphone was small and not very powerful, but it did not sound frightened. He switched the machine off and tapped around with the stick, trying to get his bearings. Behind him was the bare cold stone. To his left and right was the wooden floor, its surface that disastrous couple of inches lower than the rest. And ahead of him—

Jude froze and panic scudded through him. Straight ahead – no more than three steps forward – the floor ended abruptly. An open cellar? Had he opened it by falling against that lump of iron? Had it been a handle? If so, it was a peculiar arrangement to open a cellar. But whatever it was, if he had taken those three steps without knowing he would have fallen over the edge and God knew how deep the cellar might be. He fought for calm, but his heart was racing and images of himself standing on the edge of a steep cliff swept through him. Despair overwhelmed him. This was how it would always be – this fear, this compulsion to stand absolutely still because he believed he was on the edge of a precipice. This choking fear of the impenetrable blackness.

But the floor behind him was stone and perfectly sound, so surely to God he could work his way around the yawning hole. He tested the floor immediately behind him and heard the cane's tip ring reassuringly against solid stone. Good. If he moved carefully and checked the floor before each step he would get back to his place with perfect safety and he would stay put until Chad appeared. This would be the sensible option.

But Fenella had once said, in the days when Jude still had his sight, that he was as curious as a cat – she had made it sound rather an attractive quality. It was only after the bomb that she had begun complaining he asked too many questions; a person did not always want to give chapter and verse, she had said irritably, which was when Jude had known she was bored with his limitations and spoiling to be with someone else.

But although Fenella had gone, the cat-like curiosity had remained and it was strongly with him now. He wanted to know what had happened. It seemed as if some kind of cellar or under-floor space had been opened, but what sort of cellar needed that grating mechanism to open it?

Jude knelt down and felt around with his hand. Yes, here was the opening. He explored further and began to form a mental picture of a rectangle set into the floor, made from timber, roughly four feet square. In two parts, was it? Yes. Two doors – trapdoors? And the mechanism must have caused them to open. But either it had been faulty or it had simply been old, because only one door seemed to have opened – Jude thought he was kneeling on the other one. He tested it cautiously and felt the creak and the sag of old timbers. He crawled back to the safety of the stones, and then worked his way around the edge of the timber sections. This felt like the lever he had fallen against; he explored it gingerly with one hand, disliking the cold feel of its surface. And here was the open section of the cellar again. Were the doors hinged? Thinking he would reach around the entire frame to find out about hinges, he leaned cautiously over the open half.

As if something had reared up from the cellar and bitten his face, an image hurtled straight into his mind – a nightmare thing, dreadful. The staring face of a man, the cheeks suffused with crimson, the eyes bulging and glaring malevolently. Jude gasped and recoiled, scrambling back from the open edge as if he had been scalded, throwing up a hand in an automatic gesture of defence. The appalling thing vanished from his mind almost as quickly as it had come, but its ghost stayed with him, like the after-dazzle from staring at the sun for too long in high summer. He realized he was gripping his cane as if prepared to ward off a blow and that he was turning his head from side to side as if he could pierce the darkness. Stupid! he thought angrily. This is a darkness you'll never pierce, remember?

He forced himself to take several deep breaths and, crawling on all fours, feeling his way as he went, finally managed to get back to his cushions. His mind was churning. Presently he located the wine bottle and poured himself a glass. He drank it gratefully and tried to arrange his thoughts into some kind of logical order.

When the doctors had eventually made the grim pronouncement that the damage to his eyes was irreversible, they had said the mind was a strange thing and the nervous system could play cruel tricks. Just as people continued to have sensation in an amputated arm or leg, so the brain might think it received the signals for seeing. It was known as phantom limb syndrome, and it was possible that Jude might experience a form of it – that he might get the occasional flashes of vision. Sadly though, they said, it would not mean his sight was returning. Jude had understood this, but in the two years since the bomb he had not experienced any such flashes of vision at all. That did not mean he had not experienced one tonight, although it did not make the experience particularly pleasant. Could the violent crash of the trapdoors have jarred the nerve-endings into this false vision? Jude supposed this was just about possible although it seemed a bit far-fetched.

He considered the possibility that there had been someone hiding in the cellar, and that whoever it was had stared balefully up at him when he leaned over the edge. It was just conceivable that his brain could have picked that up and conveyed it to him, but again he did not think this a very likely solution.

What about the more spiritual answer? What about the possibility that he had picked up a fragment of the room's memories – an echo that had briefly taken on substance? Jude thought he could just about concede that one. Just about. It was no more far-fetched than the idea of a sudden phantom vision caused by the crash.

He forced himself to recall the image and examine it in more detail. He had seen enough bodies in Afghanistan and on the Iraqi borders to recognize death, and he was fairly sure that the fixed glaring eyes he had just seen had been a death-stare. There had been some kind of collar around the neck. But why would a dead man be wearing a collar?

His thoughts spun this way and that, like a child's kaleidoscope shaken into whirling meaningless patterns, but nothing made any sense, and if there was a pattern he was not identifying it. *Think*, damn it! Put the facts together. The face, the cellar at the room's centre, the mechanism . . .

The fragments of thoughts stopped tumbling and suddenly and startlingly Jude understood. What he had taken for a collar had been the flesh of the man's neck, purple and swollen. It had been the neck – and the face – of a man who had been hanged.

He knew now where he was. He was in the execution chamber of a deserted gaol. The wooden doors were the trapdoors over the gallows pit, and the face he had seen was the face of a man who had been hanged.

'After that there was nothing,' said Jude to Chad, Drusilla and Phin. 'But I'll freely admit it was a very long two hours.'

It was just on three a.m. Chad and Phin had collected Jude an hour earlier; Phin had expected Jude to be exhausted: he thought if he had spent half a night inside Calvary he would have wanted nothing more than to crash out until lunchtime the next day. But when they got back to the King's Head, Jude merely went up to his room to wash away Calvary's dust, and then joined the others wearing jeans and a clean sweater. The dark glasses were in place, and so far from being exhausted or wanting to crash out he crackled with energy like a cat's fur in a thunderstorm.

The manager had left the coffee room open for them, and had also left out a percolator. Drusilla made coffee which Phin handed round. While they drank it, Jude played the recording he had made, occasionally stopping the machine to explain or elaborate. He spoke fluently and easily, conjuring up the brooding atmosphere of the old gaol and the curious echoes that it harboured. The recording ended with a description of the odd vivid image that had printed itself onto his mind.

'I'm convinced he had been hanged,' said Jude, when the tape finished. 'I saw a couple of bodies in Syria – men who had died that way. Some kind of local punishment it had been – we got there after it was all over, but once you've seen—' He broke off and then said, 'It wasn't until I saw that – face, that I guessed where I was. It was the execution room of a disused gaol, wasn't I?'

'Yes,' said Chad after a moment.

'I thought so. My God, it's no wonder it held all that hatred and despair and terror. You all felt that, didn't you?'

'Oh yes,' said Chad.

'I'm still sceptical about ghosts in general,' said Jude, 'but I've been in enough odd places in the world to know that strong emotions can linger in quite peculiar ways. I think that's what happened tonight. You've got your theory proved, Professor, because I picked something up

– something from the past. It's the only explanation I can come up with.' He frowned. 'Was it really a gallows trap I opened when I tripped over my own feet?'

'We'll have a look at the footage tomorrow – today, I mean,' said Chad. 'But there's nothing else it could be.'

'It was like taking the lid of a bubbling cauldron,' said Jude, half to himself.

'At least you didn't fall in,' said Chad. 'I did tell you to be careful if you went on a voyage of discovery.'

'We tried to disable the lever,' said Phin, 'but it was only a very makeshift arrangement. Actually we thought it was old enough not to work properly any longer, or cause any problems.'

'It wouldn't have caused a problem if Jude had stayed put,' said Chad. He looked back at Jude. 'The gaol's called Calvary,' he said. 'It was known as the murderers' prison, and it was used almost exclusively for executions in this part of England, although they had some life-sentence prisoners as well. But life sentences were quite rare until comparatively recently – killers were usually hanged or transported.'

'The murderers' prison,' said Jude thoughtfully. 'No, I haven't heard of it.'

'Neville Fremlin was hanged there.'

'The Silver-Tongued Murderer from the thirties? I've heard of him, of course. Calvary,' said Jude thought-fully. 'The name's very evocative, isn't it? The place of execution. Then where exactly are we, Chad? Fremlin was from York or Harrogate or somewhere like that, wasn't he?'

'Knaresborough,' said Chad. 'We're in Cumbria – the west edge of the Lake District.'

Jude half nodded, as if absorbing this information, and then said, 'Very early on I thought I heard footsteps, but I think now it was either my imagination or maybe you were still around.'

'Unless it was the ghost of some old warder who prowls around every night, clanking a bunch of keys,' said Drusilla.

'Of course. Tommy the Turnkey, that's who it'll have been,' said Jude at once.

'Well, nothing but a ghost could have got in,' said Chad. 'We checked everywhere before we left, if you remember. There are only three ways in – and one's through the door we used. Then there's a door opening onto the mortuary, and a little scullery door right at the back, but they were both locked. And we locked the main doors after we left, as you know.' He leaned forward. 'Jude, can we talk some more about that image you saw?'

'We can talk until the start of the next millennium,' said Jude. 'Or until breakfast time at the very least. I can't offer any opinion on it, though. And before anyone starts talking about hallucinations, I should point out that I was in my right mind and I had only had half a glass of wine. It's true that I fell against the gallows lever and the crashing in of the trap was a hell of a shock. But I wasn't knocked out by the fall or even knocked into dizziness. You'll probably see that when you run the film.' He paused and then said, curtly, 'Also, I'd better say that I'm physically unable to experience visual hallucinations in the accepted sense, and at that stage of the night I had no idea where I was – you were all very careful about not giving out any clues, and I honestly didn't know. So there was no subconscious knowledge at work.'

Phin leaned forward, and said very hesitantly, 'Jude, I – um – I'm not sure how to put this, but there's a thing I'd like to ask.'

'Ask away.'

'You said you "saw" the image. The man's face. Well, you haven't put it quite like that, but – and I hope it's OK to ask this, but—'

'How exactly did I "see" it?'

'Well, uh, yes.' Phin pushed back the flop of hair that had tumbled forward, and thought he had probably committed the worst discourtesy in the world. He supposed Dr Ingram and Drusilla were staring at him in horror, but he did not dare look at either of them.

But Jude appeared to give the question serious consideration. He said, 'Phin, I can only explain it by saying that I've still got the memory of sight. I still know what a tree looks like, or a car or a whisky bottle.'

'Especially a whisky bottle,' murmured Chad. He sounded amused and Phin was deeply relieved he had not offended anyone by his question.

'But,' said Jude, 'those images I have are mind images. Like closing your eyes and conjuring up a memory. Seeing with your mind. Does that explain it sufficiently?'

'Yes,' said Phin. 'I'm glad it was OK to ask.'

'Whatever it was, we're going to use it in the programme, aren't we?' asked Drusilla. 'Maybe with some kind of mock-up?'

'Yes, of course we're going to use it – it's exactly what we hoped to get,' said Chad. 'But I'm not very keen on mock-ups. I'd rather present the facts and let people make up their own minds.'

'You need something to fire people's imaginations, though,' said Jude thoughtfully. 'Something about the history of the prison, maybe.'

'Dru and Phin are working up some stuff about Neville Fremlin,' said Chad. 'And Phin's trying to find out about any other reasonably dramatic murderers who were executed there.'

'I love the phrase "dramatic murderers",' murmured Jude.

'How about if we use the relevant bit of footage from tonight – showing Jude's reactions and so on, and then segue into a mock-up of a hanging?' put in Drusilla. 'We could dub some sounds onto it – the footsteps of the condemned man's last walk to the gallows, stuff like that.'

'And superimposed photos of Fremlin?' said Jude. 'No, that'll detract from the programme's aim, won't it?'

'Wouldn't a mock-up detract from it as well?' said Phin. 'Because isn't the point here that Jude got that hanged-man image? I don't think we ought to fuzz that with simulations and dubs and whatnot.'

'Phin's right,' said Chad. 'We set out to see if buildings could have imprints of their past – we made an experiment using someone who didn't know where he was – and we got that extraordinary, perfectly genuine result. You had no idea where you were, Jude, but the image you picked up was of a man who had been hanged. Absolutely classic.'

'Does it weight the evidence in favour of the spooks?'

'I don't know about spooks, but it goes a long way to

proving that buildings can store up their histories,' said Chad. 'That's the angle we need to use, I think.'

'He'll be sub-titling the programme QED in a minute,' said Drusilla.

'Well, I think that'd be pretty neat,' said Phin firmly.

They watched the footage the following day and Phin had several anxious minutes while they waited for the film to begin. The viewing screen they had brought was a small one and at first there was only a fuzzy snow storm. He chewed his knuckles, wondering what he would do if it turned out he had put the batteries in back to front, or accidentally left the Pause button on. Dr Ingram would certainly kick him out if that happened. Phin was just visualizing the disappointment of his tutors at Harvard ('We never thought he'd make such an asshole of himself') when the screen suddenly spat into life, and there, oh blessed sight, was the dim room with the trap-doors and the crossbeam with its dangling iron chain. There was Jude in one corner, pouring a glass of wine. The images were shadowy because the light had been so poor, but they had not wanted to use any kind of night imaging because of using this footage in the programme.

'We can use quite a lot of this,' said Chad, watching intently. 'It portrays the atmosphere beautifully – it's a brilliant shot of the gallows trap, Phin. Jude, you've put the wine glass down now, and you're moving around the room.'

'I was pacing it out. Trying to get a mental map of it.'

'Dru, will you fast forward a bit – thanks. You're walking out to the centre of the room now,' said Chad to Jude.

'And falling over the trapdoor.'

'Oh God, yes, so you are. You've smashed straight into the lever.'

'And there goes the trap,' said Phin, wincing.

'You were right that only one half of it opened,' said Chad.

'Jeeze, look at the dust – it's like a socking great sandstorm.'

'You're leaning over the edge – recoiling—'

'So would you have recoiled,' said Jude. 'I do wish there was some way of finding out who it was I saw,' he said. 'I know that's impossible, of course.'

'It is,' said Chad. 'There must have been dozens of men executed there. Women as well, I should think. It's a very old gaol.'

'I know. And I know we'd never track him down, even if I could identify him, which I can't. It's just that I keep wondering . . .'

'What he was hanged for?'

'No, not that,' said Jude. 'I'm assuming he'd been found guilty of murder. But I can't stop wondering if he really was guilty.'

CHAPTER SEVENTEEN

October 1938

'I do know Neville Fremlin is guilty,' said Walter, facing Edgar Higneth in his office on Calvary's upper floor. 'I've read the reports of the trial, and it's all as damning as it could be.' He hesitated, and then said, 'I don't suppose there's such a thing as typical behaviour for a condemned man, sir, but I'm finding Fremlin's attitude surprising. He's not behaving as I thought he would.'

This, thought Higneth, was one of the problems a prison governor occasionally hit: the idealism of the inexperienced. That was the trouble with employing these younger men at Calvary; you got the enthusiasm and the learning which were all very fine, but you also got the idealism which could be tricky to deal with.

But he liked Dr Kane and was pleased with his work – also, they still needed to know if Fremlin was intending to take any secrets to the gallows with him next week – so he said temperately, 'In what way is his attitude surprising you, Dr Kane? Is it something he's said?'

'It's more what he hasn't said. I haven't any real train-ing in psychiatry,' said Walter, 'but I'm working on the assumption that Fremlin has his fair share of murderers' vanity.'

Higneth recognized this as one of Lewis Caradoc's tenets, but did not say so.

He said, 'More than his fair share I should think.'

'Then in that case,' said Walter, 'I'd have expected him to behave in one of two ways. Either to be over-whelmingly contrite – almost to the point of religious fervour – or to taunt us with the crimes, even to gloat a bit. But there's no sign of contrition as you know, and he certainly hasn't taunted us with his crimes. In fact, he hasn't talked about them at all.' He frowned. 'And that brings me back to whether there's a typical behaviour with condemned men.'

Higneth did not think there was. 'When they're as close to the execution as this, there's usually one of three attitudes,' he said. 'Either they're deeply contrite, as you've said, or they're defiant: "I'm guilty so hang me and be damned." We can deal reasonably well with either of those two: it's the third attitude that's the difficult one. The ones who plead their innocence all the way. "Don't hang me, I didn't do it." That's the one that'll cause you nightmares.'

'Fremlin doesn't fall into any of those categories,' said Walter. 'He's an enigma, and I think he'll stay an enigma to the end. Which means the family of that miss-ing girl – Elizabeth Molland – will never know the truth.' He hesitated, and then said, 'With your permission, sir, I'd like to talk to her parents.'

'The police talked to them, of course,' said Higneth. 'And the usual enquiries were made. But it wasn't until much later, that they began to wonder if she might have been one of Fremlin's early victims. They found five bodies, but there's no knowing if that was the final tally.'

'He might have had another burial ground,' said Walter.

'Exactly. One they never found. There are acres of lonely mountainside and woodlands in that area – the Yorkshire Dales and the Moors. Impossible to search everywhere. And it's a sad fact that solitary women can vanish without anyone noticing they've gone.'

'I won't talk to the parents if you dislike the idea,' said Walter, 'but I think it might be worth it. I might just pick up something that would help me reach Fremlin.'

Higneth thought about it and could see no objection. The Molland girl's parents had themselves been anxious to know if Fremlin had killed their daughter – the police would like to know as well, although as the inspector had remarked, if it was proved that Fremlin had murdered a hundred times they could still only hang him the once, more was the pity. They had talked to the parents, he had said, but nothing useful had emerged. Edgar Higneth thought Dr Kane might just disinter an odd fact or two that would be of use. Also, he was polite and considerate and could be trusted not to do or say anything that would bring himself or Calvary into disrepute. It was probably a bit absurd to care about Calvary's reputation – in fact when you considered the cut-throats and villains that Calvary housed, it was doubtful if it actually had a reputation at all. But Higneth took his work seriously and he had taken over the guardianship of the gaol from

Lewis Caradoc, thus imbibing some of Sir Lewis's standards along the way.

'I have no objection, although I'm doubtful anything will come of it. I'm glad you've been open about your intention, by the way. See now, Knaresborough's just the other side of Harrogate from here, isn't it? It's a good couple of hours' drive I should think, but if you set off early you could get there and back in one day.'

Walter said he had looked at the map and thought it was a fairly easy journey.

'You normally take Thursdays as a free day, don't you? Then since tomorrow is Thursday, I suggest you try to see Mr and Mrs Molland then.'

'That's what I thought of doing. Molland is semi-retired, so there's a good chance he'll be at home. If not, I'll try to arrange a visit when he is at home.'

'There isn't much time left to us.'

'Five days,' said Walter.

As he drove away from Thornbeck, down the winding lane that was now so familiar, past the field beyond which he could see Sir Lewis's house, Walter was already wondering if he was doing the right thing. He was uneasily aware that he liked Neville Fremlin far more than was professional – or even safe – and he was not sure how much this feeling was influencing his judgement. He wondered if he might be making this visit in order to satisfy himself of Fremlin's guilt.

But how much proof do you need? he asked himself. The entire West Yorkshire and Cumbria police force had irrefutable evidence of Fremlin's guilt. Large sums of money had been paid into his bank account on dates that fitted with the disappearances of two of the victims. He had been identified as being the man who had sold, to second-hand jewellers in Carlisle and Lancaster, jewellery that had belonged to three of the victims – quite a lot of jewellery, and much of it valuable. One of the women had drawn a bank draft two days before her death, and that draft had been paid into Fremlin's account by Fremlin himself. Finally, most damning of all, the police had followed Fremlin and had seen him actually burying the body of the last victim in Becks Wood. Near the other four bodies.

It was incontestable. Was that why Fremlin had never bothered to contest any of it? Why he had politely declined to give evidence at his trial? Why he had sat silent and graceful as a cat in the dock, listening to the parade of facts being unrolled, inclining his head slightly when the jury convicted him and when the judge pronounced the death sentence. The judge, Walter remembered, had agreed so wholeheartedly with the jury's verdict that he had given a little homily on how Fremlin must surely be soulless and the personification of evil to have battened on these lonely defenceless women. The press had seized on that with relish, of course.

And yet, thought Walter . . . And yet . . .

Yes?

I can't square that business about evil and soullessness with the man inside Calvary, he thought. I can't see the man I've talked to coldly seeking out rich women for their money, then stabbing and strangling them.

He pushed the macabre images away and concentrated on the journey. It was pleasant countryside – the Yorkshire Dales and the Pennine Hills were ahead of him. He reached Knaresborough halfway through the morning and drove through it, liking the bright little market town with the ruins of the castle looking down from its hill and the glimpses of the river.

It was necessary to ask for directions to Ivy House which was a few miles outside the town, but Walter found it without too much difficulty. Edgar Higneth had described the Mollands as prosperous middle-class people, and the house was quite large and affluent-looking. A neat maid opened the door and after a brief wait Walter was taken to a long drawing room, furnished in the rather heavy style of forty years earlier. Mr and Mrs Molland were older than Walter had been expecting – she was certainly well over fifty and her husband looked as if he was approaching sixty. They were rather like their house: solid and well upholstered. Years of large meals and security, thought Walter. I dare say they haven't lived especially exciting lives, but they're a decent couple. A spurt of anger went through him that these nice, ordinary people had had to suffer such anguish.

He explained his errand, careful to emphasize that he was here unofficially, but that he had talked to Neville Fremlin in his professional capacity. At the mention of the name Mrs Molland gave a shiver and Walter saw Molland put out a hand to comfort her. Yes. Nice people, once living normal happy lives. And that monster in Calvary had ruined their lives for ever. (That's better, said the inward voice. Think of him as a monster.)

'I'm not exactly spying on Neville Fremlin,' he said carefully. 'But the police have asked me to be alert for any clue that might lead them to the truth about your daughter. Mrs Molland, I'm so sorry – I know this must be deeply distressing for you.'

'Tell us what you need to know, Dr Kane,' said Molland. He was a large, rather portly man, and Walter thought he had probably been indulgent in his treatment of his wife and daughter. There was a slight northern accent and an aura of no-nonsense business dealings and aldermen's public duties.

'It's not knowing what happened to our girl,' said his wife. 'We haven't even a grave to tend.'

The voice in Walter's mind said, Remember these people's grief when you go into the condemned cell tonight. Keep remembering it. Aloud, he said, 'Could you tell me a bit about Elizabeth? She used to go into Fremlin's shop sometimes, didn't she?'

'Indeed she did, Dr Kane. Lotions and scented soaps and suchlike she'd buy. Girl's fripperies, but we made no objection. She had her allowance to spend as she liked. She'd go into Knaresborough with a friend or with her mother, and they'd do some shopping and have a cup of tea in one of the little teashops.'

'She was a bit frivolous at times,' put in his wife eagerly, 'but she was only nineteen. And she was a good girl, Dr Kane Not one to have her head turned by – by that man.'

'Not by any man,' said Molland firmly, and Walter thought: well, if she didn't have her head turned once or twice, she was probably the first girl of nineteen who didn't.

'She'd wrap her dad round her little finger,' said Mrs Molland indulgently. 'She had such pretty ways, Dr Kane.'

'It's a sad man who can't let his daughter coax him,' said Molland.

This is dreadful, thought Walter, but he set himself to go on, and choosing his words with care, he said, 'Had she a young man?'

'Oh no,' they both said at once.

'One or two young men had admired her, of course.' This was Mrs Molland, displaying an eager pride that cut through Walter like a knife. 'What with her being so pretty and dainty. I have a photograph here if you'd like to see . . .'

The photograph, predictably, was in a silver frame and had pride of place on the mantelpiece. Walter studied it with interest. Elizabeth Molland had been a very pretty girl indeed. Masses of fair hair and dark, slightly upward-slanting eyes. Yes, she would have coaxed her doting father into doing anything she wanted. He would have known he was being coaxed, but not minded.

'Thank you,' he said, carefully replacing the photo-graph. 'She's very lovely indeed. Beautiful eyes.' He was glad he could say this with complete truth; he did not want to lie to these people and he thought they would have known if he had done so.

'I make no doubt there was a bit of giggling with her friends about the young men they met at various little parties and social gatherings,' said Molland, studying the photo fondly. 'That's natural at nineteen, Dr Kane. But we always knew where she was. She never spent an hour out of our sight but what we knew where she was and who she was with.'

'You hear such dreadful things, these days,' put in his wife. 'Girls getting themselves into trouble— But we'd brought her up right, you see. We made sure she had friends of her own age – daughters of our own friends they'd be in the main. Or Mr Molland's business acquaintances and the like.' Again there was the note of pride.

'Church every Sunday, of course,' said Molland. 'And I made no objection to Elizabeth joining one or two of the groups attached to St Luke's.'

A picture was forming in Walter's mind of an ordinary lively nineteen-year-old girl, perhaps a bit rebellious at her elderly, old-fashioned parents, possibly occasionally telling a harmless fib or two to escape their protection. Laughing with other girls, and exchanging secrets about young men – possibly meeting one young man in particular and permitting a few guilty embraces. All entirely normal and harmless. A girl who, in a year or two's time, would have married some nice, suitable young man, and had children of her own.

He said, 'That last evening . . .'

'Dr Kane, I shall never forgive myself,' said Mrs Molland. 'A musical evening it was – such as we often used to attend, being so fond of music. And Elizabeth enjoyed coming with us. A grown-up night, that's what she used to say. And she'd dress up in one of her best frocks, and wear her jewellery and we'd be so proud of her.'

'The police believed it was the jewellery that attracted him,' said Molland. 'That man, I mean.'

They can't bring themselves to say Fremlin's name, thought Walter, torn with pity all over again. He asked if the jewellery had been valuable.

'Not especially. Trinkets we'd given her over the years

– birthdays and Christmases, you know. Seed pearls and turquoise. But they made her look – prosperous. Cared for.'

'He liked the rich ones,' said Mrs Molland simply. 'He liked to go where there was money.

'Yes.' Walter remembered how Fremlin had talked about attending first nights at the theatre and concerts, enjoying drinks at the interval and supper afterwards.

'The police notified jewellers in the area, thinking the pieces might be offered for sale, but they got no information,' Molland was saying. 'Not surprising though, when you think of the number of jewellers even in this county.'

'Not surprising at all,' said Walter. 'Mr Molland – you've both been very frank with me and I'm grateful. If I can find out anything at all that would bring you a little comfort, I promise I'll let you know. I talk to Fremlin each day.'

'If we could just know what happened to her,' said Mrs Molland, twisting her handkerchief between her hands. 'If we knew for sure she was dead. We'd cope with that after so long. We'd have a little memorial tablet in St Luke's, wouldn't we, Joe?'

'It'd be a comfort,' said Molland briefly.

'Yes, I understand that.' Walter's mind slipped back over the years to his mother saying, 'I can't even have a memorial stone for your father, Walter. I wish I could; it would be such a comfort.' But there could be no memorial stone to a man hanged for betraying his country.

He got up to go. 'There's nothing you can think of that would help me to – to find a way into Fremlin's mind? Anything about her friends, her life? Her child-hood, even?'

He felt, rather than saw, a response to this last question. Like the flicker of an electrical current before it springs into life in a dark room. Like the faint quiver of a pulse in an unconscious man's body. Unmistakable. The silence stretched out, and Walter tried to think of something to say that might encourage them, but he could not and the moment passed.

Molland saw him politely to the door, shaking hands. 'We're grateful for your concern, Dr Kane.'

'The execution is in four days' time,' said Walter. 'I expect you know that, though.'

'We do.'

Of course they would know. They would be counting the days away until the man they thought had killed their daughter himself died.

'I'm only sorry we couldn't tell you anything to help,' said Molland.

Walter drove back into the town centre, and parked his car. There was one more thing he wanted to do while he was here, and there was plenty of time. Had he got the directions right? Yes, here was the street, quite near to the centre. It was a lively little part of the town – there were a number of smartly painted shops selling a variety of goods: a ladies' dress shop with costumes and svelte evening dresses, labelled 'Paris Fashion, Latest Mode'. Next to it was a milliner's. Then a leather goods shop with handbags and dressing-cases. After that a draper's, with a discreet display of silk stockings and wisp-like underwear. Several doors along was a rather fussy-looking teashop with potted palms and wicker basket chairs, advertising 'Morning Coffee and Cream Teas'. It was exactly the kind of little street that ladies would enjoy visiting: there would be an inspection of the frocks, hats and bags, and then a cup of coffee or tea to discuss purchases made or being considered.

The bow-windowed shop beyond the draper's was like a dark blemish on the street. The windows were boarded up and a tattered fly poster hung from one pane. It was unkempt and uncared for, and the paint was already peeling from the once-scarlet shop door. Someone had tried to paint out the legend over the door itself, but the letters were still readable and they proclaimed the little shop as the place that had been splashed across the national newspapers.

N. FREMLIN PHARMACIST AND DISPENSER

This is where he worked, thought Walter staring up at the words. This is where he mixed his potions and prepared his draughts. This is the place the police examined over and over again for clues – for tattered fragments of humanity, for bloodstains or gold rings or fingernails or shoe buckles. In the end they had found nothing to add to the evidence already gathered, but it had not mattered because the evidence they had was more than enough to send a man to the gallows in five days' time.

Walter had expected to find the place firmly secured, and probably it had been until recently. But time or neglect, or both, had rusted the door lock from its hinges and when Walter put out a cautious hand, it swung inwards with an unpleasant scrape against the wooden floor. He glanced up and down the street, but the afternoon was already sliding into evening and most shoppers had long since gone home. Into the murderer's den, then . . .

It was larger than he had thought: reading the newspaper reports he had visualized a mean poky little place. But of course, the man who had enjoyed London first nights and who had requested poetry to read in the condemned cell, would not have associated himself with anything second rate or down at heel. The interior of the shop was spacious and even with the accumulated dust everywhere, it was plain that this had been a very classy establishment. There was a counter for the business of selling and buying, but there was also a section devoted to cosmetics and lotions – the 'fripperies' that Elizabeth Molland's father had referred to. The remains of display cabinets stood against one wall, and there was a small area furnished with several comfortable chairs and a low table, where, Walter supposed, customers might have been invited to wait for their prescriptions to be dispensed.

He crossed the dusty floor, his footsteps echoing. Any furniture that might have been here had been removed, but a built-in cupboard remained and a long marble-topped slab was affixed to one wall. At the back was another door, partly open, with two deep steps leading down. After a moment he went down the steps. His heart was beating fast and he felt as if he was prising open a dark and bloodied fragment of the past.

This is it, said his mind. This is where he brought them after he killed them. There's the long table where he must have laid them out and removed everything that might identify them. Clothes, engraved wedding rings or lockets that he didn't dare try to sell. That's the range where he burned their clothes. Did he work by night? Putting up the shutters and lighting oil lamps? Walter glanced back up to the front of the shop. Yes, the windows did have shutters.

He was suddenly aware of self-disgust. I'm behaving like a voyeur, he thought, or like one of those characters in Dickens who went jauntily along to Newgate to watch a public hanging. Or the crones that Fremlin himself talked about, the ghoulish women who had sat knitting at the foot of the guillotine.

The feeling was so strong that he went quickly from the shop, closing the door as well as he could, and drove back to Calvary.

CHAPTER EIGHTEEN

Walter sat at the table in the condemned cell. It was late; the gaslights were flaring and popping in the corridor outside, and there was a faint sound of rain beating against a windowpane somewhere. Walter liked night rain; as a child he had always liked to lie in bed and hear the rain outside and know himself safe, warm and secure. But how would it feel to lie in this room and listen to night rain?

He said, 'I was in Knaresborough earlier today.'

'Were you?' Neville Fremlin had been reading the poems of Wilfred Owen which Walter had managed to get for him, but had politely put the book aside when Walter came in.

'As a matter of fact I went past your old shop.'

'Oh, did you? I was meaning to have it freshly painted. I daresay it's looking a bit sorry for itself by now.'

'It wasn't looking so bad,' said Walter who had not expected this response.

'Nevertheless, the lease specified . . .' Fremlin paused as if considering whether he had given too much away, and then seemed to shrug as if to say, What does it matter? He said, 'The lease specified it should be re-painted every three years. I always kept to that.'

'Because you like to have things orderly?' said Walter.

'Bright and clean, anyway.'

Having got Fremlin onto the subject of Knares-borough, Walter said, 'I also saw Mr and Mrs Molland while I was in the town. Elizabeth's parents.'

Fremlin did not move a muscle, but something seemed to shift behind his eyes and a stillness crept over him.

Watching him, Walter said, 'They showed me a photograph of her – she was an outstandingly pretty girl, I thought.'

'All girls of nineteen are pretty, Dr Kane, or are you not yet old enough to appreciate that?'

'How did you know her age?' said Walter at once.

'I read the newspapers.' The tone had returned to its former carelessness. But I've shaken him, thought Walter. He wasn't expecting me to mention her and there was definitely a reaction at her name. 'And,' said Fremlin, 'she came into the shop once or twice. I remem-ber her fairly well.' He studied Walter thoughtfully. 'That was a curious visit for you to make, Dr Kane.'

'I was interested,' said Walter.

'Ah.' It was so non-committal a sound that Walter wondered if he had been mistaken about the reaction to Elizabeth's name a moment ago. He let the silence lengthen but Fremlin appeared to have withdrawn again. Quite suddenly, he said, 'You'd like to get me out of this, wouldn't you, Dr Kane?'

Walter felt as if a hand had squeezed itself around his heart. This is it, he thought. This is the moment he's going to propose some wild escape scheme. At a purely superficial level he was aware of being thankful that neither of the warders was in the cell, although he supposed Fremlin would not have said it if anyone else had been there. 'You'd like to get me out of this ...' Walter's mind whirled chaotically for a moment but finally a vestige of professionalism returned to him and he was able to say, 'I have mixed feelings about the death penalty. I do admit that.'

'That's not what I asked you.'

This time it was not Walter's professionalism that came to his aid, it was the thought of how Lewis Caradoc would handle this situation. He'd play it by the rules, thought Walter gratefully, and he said, 'Fremlin, you know I can't possibly comment on your case. You're here to answer for crimes. I'm here to help you through the last few days of your life.'

Fremlin regarded him for what seemed to be a very long time. Then he said, softly, 'Is that all it is, Walter? Just part of the job to you? Am I just a – just a statistic? A name on Calvary's death register?'

Walter struggled for a moment, and then said, 'Of course it's more than just a job. You must know that. I have compassion for you and I hope I'm helping you. But I haven't sufficient knowledge of the facts to make any kind of judgement.'

'And yet,' said Fremlin in the same soft voice, 'you drove out to see Elizabeth Molland's parents today.' He leaned forward, his eyes glowing. 'You would like to get me out of this, wouldn't you, Walter? Because—' He stopped and seemed to be searching Walter's eyes. Then he said, 'Forgive me,' he said. 'Perhaps I misread you.' He leaned back, and in a completely different voice, said, 'Did I thank you for getting Wilfred Owen's poems for me? I've been enjoying rereading them. I always admired the idealism of those young men who fought in the Great War.' Then, without missing a beat, he said, 'If you go into Kendal before Monday, d'you think you could bring me a bottle of wine? A good claret for preference.'

'I don't think the governor would allow it,' said Walter, managing to match Fremlin's lightness of tone.

'No? Ah well, it was worth a try,' said the man who was going to die on Monday morning. As Walter got up to leave, he said, very casually, 'You're ready for Monday, are you, Dr Kane?'

'Yes,' said Walter. 'Yes, I'm ready.'

He was not ready, of course, and he would not be ready if he had ten years to prepare.

The day after his visit he sent a careful note to Mr and Mrs Molland, thanking them for their courtesy, and saying he feared there would not be any information from Fremlin about Elizabeth. If, however, there was anything that either of them remembered – anything that might help him – he hoped they would get in touch. He did not really expect very much, and when he received a rather flowery little note from Mrs Molland, expressing their appreciation of his thoughtfulness but saying nothing more, he was not surprised.

Time seemed to have become uneven and unreliable. At first, after the visit to Knaresborough, it went with such dragging slowness that Walter wished there was a way to shunt it along and get to Monday morning so that the appalling thing waiting there could be faced. But then it seemed to double and triple its pace, flying like a weaver's shuttle, like a runner racing to reach a finishing post, wastefully spilling the last hours of a man's life.

During those days a great deal of Walter's time was taken up with prisoners whose health had to be regularly checked – two had heart conditions and three had the miners' lung disease from working in the Yorkshire collieries. The oldest of these was becoming quite seriously ill, and although Walter was making the man as comfortable as he could, he knew and the man knew, that the condition would inexorably worsen.

The day before the execution was one of the lowering days in which this part of England seemed to specialize. Clouds scudded across Mount Torven and flurries of rain spattered down.

Walter attended morning service in the small chapel. The prisoners were brought in as usual; Sunday attendance was compulsory for them, but Walter thought they would have been there anyway because it made a change in the strict routine of their lives. They liked Sunday services even if it was for the wrong reasons; they liked to sing loudly to the hymns and some of them would furtively ogle the female warders. But today they were quiet and watchful; several of them looked as if it would not take much to make them erupt into rebellion. Walter had known there would be things he had not expected, and this odd unease among the other prisoners was one of them.

He had lunch with Edgar Higneth and the chaplain. It had been an invitation he could not refuse although he would have preferred to drive to the King's Head in Thornbeck where the landlady roasted an enormous side of beef each Sunday and served it pink and tender with home-grown vegetables. Several of the local people who did not have families usually came in to eat in the small dining room and Walter had made one or two cautious friendships among them. Men who did have families often looked in for a half-guilty glass of beer before their own dinner, reluctantly returning to obligatory domesticity for the afternoon.

Walter had come to enjoy this pleasant Sunday ritual, but today he had to eat the peppery soup and over-cooked meat which was Calvary's idea of a Sunday roast, and to forgo any kind of drink since the regulations did not permit alcohol inside the gaol. Edgar Higneth would not have been above smuggling in a couple of bottles of wine for his guests, but the chaplain had strict views on temperance and probably would have reported the smallest glass of sherry to Higneth's masters at Whitehall, so they drank barley water.

After lunch Walter spent some time in the small infirmary where a couple of patients were recovering from operations that had been performed in Kendal Hospital – neither were serious but both were suffering some pain and Walter was administering morphia. As the afternoon wore on, one of them said, 'No more of that stuff, Doc.'

'But a hernia operation is very painful.'

'I know, but they're topping Fremlin in the morning. I need to stay awake.'

'For the – topping?'

'They think we don't know,' said the man. 'They have

235

all these tricks for keeping it a secret. But of course it never is a secret and we always do know. It's as if something creeps into the place.'

Walter sat with Fremlin for an hour during the early evening, but Fremlin seemed to be withdrawing into some private world of his own and for the first time scarcely seemed to care who was in the cell with him. Is this the start of the disintegration? thought Walter, and in the deepest part of his mind knew that he did not want Fremlin to disintegrate; he wanted him to go to his death with the same ironic courtesy he had displayed all along. That's because it's the first hanging I've dealt with, thought Walter, that's why I'm so deeply affected.

As darkness fell the gas jets were turned up and soft-footed steps stole along the dim corridors. A spiteful little wind crept into the gaol and whispered up and down the halls, as if it wanted to join in the low-voiced discussions that went on in corners. 'Is the hangman here?' 'Will the prisoner die quietly – or will he die hard?' 'Have they put the rope in place?' 'Have they dug the grave?' As the hours went by Walter could no longer tell which were the furtive conversations of the warders and which was the sighing of the wind. The impression that something invisible and implacable was stirring Calvary's bones grew on him. Something creeps into the place, the prisoner had said in the infirmary. Something creeps in . . .

Shortly after nine o'clock he was called to Edgar Higneth's office to meet the executioner and his assistant who had arrived that afternoon. The executioner obviously sensed Walter's apprehension, because he said it would all be done very swiftly and cleanly. He had a

Yorkshire burr which was oddly reassuring, and although he did not quite pat Walter's shoulder or call him 'lad', he nearly did. There was a discussion as to the weight and height of the prisoner, which had a direct bearing on the length of the drop. Tables were produced with columns of weights and heights. By this time Walter felt oddly distant from it all, as if he was encased in glass. He felt as if he was seeing and hearing everything from a distance, but he thought he managed to take a reasonably intelligent part in the conversation.

He looked in on Fremlin, who appeared to be asleep from the sedative Walter had given him after supper, and then went back to the room near the infirmary, which was used as a temporary bedroom for Calvary's doctor. He lay down on the bed although he did not expect to sleep. Calvary seemed alive all around him – three times he heard footsteps go past his door but when he looked outside the corridors were empty and he went back to the bed. But Fremlin's words danced endlessly through his mind. 'You'd like to get me out this, wouldn't you, Dr Kane, wouldn't you, *wouldn't you* . . .'

'No!' cried Walter and came abruptly awake, his heart racing, the sounds of his own cry still echoing in his mind. He saw he had slept after all and for longer than he would have thought possible, because a cold dawn light was trickling into the room through the small, high window. The little bedside clock said six a.m. The day of execution. And whatever had crept into Calvary last night was still here.

The room felt cold and unfriendly and Walter shivered as he washed in the basin of cold water. But he felt better now that the hour was almost here and as he stepped out of the small room he was grateful to think he would be in the company of Higneth. (And Fremlin? Who would Fremlin have for company on this final morning? Which of the warders were on death watch?)

A cup of tea was brought to him. He could not drink it, but he curled his hands around the cup to derive some warmth from the hot liquid. There were not many windows on Calvary's ground floor, but there was a small one in this room. Walter stood looking down the hillside, seeing everywhere still shrouded in early--morning mist and the moisture dripping from the trees.

Fremlin would be given breakfast at seven o'clock. Would he eat it? Was there any point in him doing so? Walter remembered, and wished he had not, the stories of men vomiting or losing control of their bowels and bladders on the scaffold, and wondered if he ought to have put an anti-emetic in last night's sedative. Was it too late to do it now? What about one of the ergot compounds? His mind automatically went to the side-effects but then he saw the absurdity of this. Still, he would make sure that Fremlin had a second, stronger, sedative in the next fifteen minutes.

Everywhere was unnaturally quiet as he went along to his small surgery, to mix a hefty dose of bromide in the little dispensary cubicle, and when he went into the condemned block he saw that strips of thick coconut matting had been laid along the passage between the condemned cell and the execution chamber. Walter had not known about this procedure, which was obviously meant to muffle the footsteps on that final walk to the execution chamber and prevent the other prisoners from hearing anything. It probably would not make any difference to them if they heard or not: they knew what was happening anyway.

Fremlin was wearing the regulation prison shirt and trousers – Walter noticed the shoelaces had been removed from his shoes and that there was no belt on the trousers. He proffered the bromide and Fremlin nodded slightly as if he had expected this and was grateful for it. But it's all right, thought Walter, studying him. He's perfectly composed. There aren't going to be any embarrassing scenes. He'll go like a gentleman – he might even take Byron's poems, as he said on our first meeting.

He supposed he ought to have known Fremlin would disconcert him in some way. He drank the bromide in one go, and setting down the empty glass said, 'I'm glad you'll stay with me, Walter. One day—'

'Yes?'

'One day,' said Fremlin, 'you might understand me a little better.' And then, before Walter could think how to respond to this, he turned away.

'I'll be back very soon,' Walter said, and remembering what the executioner had said yesterday, hesitated, then said, 'They tell me it will be very quick and very clean.'

Again Fremlin gave a small nod of acknowledgement.

At twenty minutes to eight Walter, still feeling as if he was separated from everything by a sheet of thick glass, went along to Edgar Higneth's room.

The under-sheriff of the county had arrived, and Higneth introduced Walter to him. From behind his glass wall, Walter made polite conversation, agreeing that it was a distressing business and saying the prisoner seemed fairly calm. No, he did not anticipate any problems. The under-sheriff had brought the notice of death to post on the gates; he made a great play of showing it to Higneth – Walter thought this was to hide his own nervousness.

He had thought this would be a difficult part of the proceedings: standing around trying to find something to say, watching the clock tick away the last minutes, but time, having been erratic, suddenly speeded up, and almost before he knew it they were walking along to the condemned block and Higneth was unlocking the outer door. In the sunless morning the thick slabs of matting looked like pieces of dead animal hide; Walter thought he would never be able to look at pale brown mats or carpets again without remembering today.

Fremlin's words went through and through his mind. 'I'm glad you'll be there, Walter.' 'One day you might understand me a little better.' Had that been an admission of something? But of what? Innocence? Guilt? Did Fremlin expect Walter to do something about it?

He had expected disturbance from the other prisoners – he knew the legends about them rioting or banging trays on their cell doors when there was a hanging – but there was nothing.

When they entered the condemned cell Neville Fremlin stood up. He looked at Higneth for a moment, then his eyes went to Walter, and although he did not move, it was as if he put out a grateful hand. ('One day you might understand me a little better, Walter.')

'Mr Fremlin,' said Higneth, and Walter was absurdly glad that Higneth had given the man this last small courtesy.

'Mr Higneth,' said Fremlin, his tone faintly ironic. It's

all right, thought Walter suddenly. He didn't mean anything – he didn't mean me to do anything.

'You are ready?' said Higneth, and Fremlin at once said, 'Never readier.' His eyes went past Higneth to the chaplain. 'Are you going to read from the Book of Lamentations, Padre? "He hath led me and brought me into dark places but not into light." That would seem appropriate, wouldn't it? How does it go on? Something about, "He hath filled me with bitterness, he hath made me drunken with wormwood, and removed my soul from peace." There's nothing to match the rodomontade of the Old Testament, is there? But I suppose it has to be the burial service, doesn't it?'

Walter saw Higneth's brows go up and the chaplain's lips draw together as if uncertain how to handle this. Neville Fremlin saw it as well, because a faint smile curved his lips.

'These things are set out to give us comfort,' said the chaplain after a moment.

'They're not giving *me* any comfort,' said Fremlin. 'Given the choice I'd have preferred a paean of praise to one of the livelier pagan gods. Bacchus would do nicely. No? I thought not. Then the good old Church of England let it be.'

He won't keep it up, thought Walter as the solemn grisly walk began. He'll break down before the end. Oh God, it's three minutes to eight. 'I am the resurrection and the life . . . he that believeth in me, though he were dead, yet shall he live . . .' Don't let him break down.

Would the other prisoners be watching the time ticking away the final minutes? As far as Walter could remember only a few of them had clocks or watches, but he thought that in some way he could not understand, they were here with Neville Fremlin now. So strong was this impression that for a second Walter almost thought he could see them, indistinct forms in the winter greyness, prison garbed and prison pale, but walking alongside the man who was healthy and whole, but who, in three minutes' time would be dead. Or were they present-day prisoners he was seeing? Mightn't they be those other prisoners who had been here eighteen years ago? 'Say goodbye, Walter . . .' How much of an imprint did people leave on buildings? How much of an imprint had Walter's father left? How much would Neville Fremlin leave?

'Man that is born of woman hath but a short time to live and is full of misery . . .' It had been misery for Elizabeth Molland's parents, and it must have been misery for the families of all the other victims.

Here was the door of the execution shed – Higneth pushed it wide and as they went in, the executioner, who had been waiting quietly in the corner stepped forward. His hands were gloved and in them he held the leather straps and pinions, and the white canvas hood. Fremlin glanced at these with distaste.

'I believe a blindfold is part of the ritual,' he said. 'But I should prefer to look death in the eye, if you don't mind. I suppose the straps are obligatory, though.'

He stood on the trapdoor, on the chalked mark as neatly as if he had rehearsed it. He's almost there, thought Walter. It's almost over. The assistant bent to loop the ankle straps in place, and it was only then that Walter saw that the executioner's hand was already on the lever. It'll happen before he realizes it, he thought, his eyes never leaving Fremlin's still figure.

'I'm glad you'll stay with me, Walter.'

There was the faintest shiver of the wooden floorboards, and the trapdoors fell abruptly downwards. Neville Fremlin jerked violently, and then sagged.

The shadowy prisoners who had walked alongside the grim little procession, had vanished. From the cells came the ordinary sounds of the morning: men being taken to the shower blocks in groups of four and five; others being herded along to the exercise yards. It's an ordinary day at the gaol after all, thought Walter. Except that no day will be ordinary to me for a very long time.

When he went past the condemned cell, the door was open and he glanced inside. The table and chairs were still where they had always been. The bed was in its corner; the sheets were pushed back, and a pair of pyjamas was still lying by the pillow. On the wooden locker at the side of the bed was a mug. All those ordinary things, thought Walter. Wearing pyjamas in bed, getting up, getting dressed, drinking a cup of tea.

And then walking twelve paces along a corridor to die.

Walter dined at Lewis Caradoc's house that evening. He was grateful for the invitation, and when Sir Lewis asked him about the execution – not prying, thought Walter, but interested and concerned – he found that for the first time he was able to speak of the curious little conversations he had had with Fremlin.

'What did you make of them?' asked Lewis.

'I still can't decide,' said Walter. ' "You'd like to get me out of this, wouldn't you?" that was what he said last night. I don't know if it was a subtle approach to help him escape or whether I should just have taken it at face value. And then this morning. "One day you might understand me a little better." I haven't been able to get either of those things out of my mind.'

'They could have meant several things.'

'I know.' Walter frowned, and said, with difficulty, 'He used my first name. He called me Walter – two or three times. I can't get that out of my mind, either.'

They had finished dinner and were having coffee in the low-ceilinged drawing room. A fire burned in the hearth and there was a faint scent of wood smoke and good furniture polish. The curtains were drawn against the night but in the summer there was a view towards Calvary's lane. Walter loved this room and he loved the house.

Lewis was drinking his coffee, clearly thinking over what Walter had just told him. He said, 'Fremlin could have been trying to find out if you'd be prepared to help him escape.'

'From the condemned cell?' said Walter, staring at Lewis. 'That's impossible.'

'It's been known. He had nothing to lose by trying.'

'I think he was simply turning on the charm,' said Walter. 'It didn't matter to him that he was about to die; charming people was just something he did automatically.'

'Would you have helped him escape, d'you think? No, I'm not testing you, I'm just curious.'

'I'm sure I wouldn't,' said Walter after a moment. 'But I can't help wondering what would have happened if

I had said, "Yes, I would like to get you out." I wonder if he had a plan ready to put to me.'

And if he had? thought Lewis. But he did not say it, instead he said, 'Walter, what you're going through is something I went through every time a man was hanged. When I was Calvary's governor, I questioned the guilt of every single man who was executed. Even today I sometimes look back and question it all over again for some of them. You don't come out of it unscathed. But you can only accept the court's decision and do the job you're there to do.'

'I know.'

'It's a pity you didn't find anything out about that girl,' said Lewis thoughtfully. 'I do feel for her parents, you know.' He glanced at Walter, wondering if the boy was going to talk about the execution any more, guessing how it would have dredged up the memories of his father.

But the only other reference Walter made was to the executioner, Albert Pierrepoint. He had been surprised, he said, to find him such a quiet-mannered man.

'I believe he is,' said Lewis.

He did not say that it had been a Pierrepoint who had come to Calvary to hang Nick O'Kane all those years ago – Thomas Pierrepoint, uncle of the man Walter had met earlier today. He did not let Walter see that their discussion had brought the memories painfully to the surface all over again.

CHAPTER NINETEEN

November 1917

After McNulty went out, Lewis had no idea what to do. It was as clear as a curse that McNulty was in the grip of an obsession about this macabre soul-weighing theory, and that he would do anything to further it. Including telling Clara about seeing Lewis in bed with Belinda Skelton? Lewis thought McNulty would not hesitate.

What would Clara do in that situation? Lewis was fairly sure she would leave him – probably she would go back to live with her parents. It would not be a particular sadness; there had never been a great deal of fire between them although he thought they had rubbed along tolerably well. Would she sue for divorce? Yes, almost certainly. She had most likely known about his other occasional affairs and had turned an indifferent eye to them, but she would regard this business with Belinda as sordid and disgusting. A girl of that class, she would say, not understanding that the war was sweeping away such differences, that class was starting to matter less to people, and that Belinda had a bright intelligent mind and humour and sensitivity.

Divorce was not the disgrace it had once been but there was still considerable stigma attached to it. And there was a tacit understanding that people in certain positions in life should lead unblemished private lives. People such as churchmen and ministers of the Crown. And governors of His Majesty's Prisons. Clara might want to keep things quiet and discreet, but McNulty would not. McNulty was set on achieving a bizarre fame, and cheated of it he would be bitter and angry. Lewis would not put it past McNulty to give the story to the newspapers, and the newspapers would seize glee-fully on such a juicy titbit. 'Sir Lewis's adulterous liaison with twenty-four-year-old prison wardress . . .' 'Love nest in governor's office . . .' 'Eminent governor of Calvary Gaol sued for divorce . . .'

Lewis did not consider himself eminent but the newspapers would like the word. They would drag in his involvement in the Home Office inquiry for rehabilita-tion of long-term prisoners, and he would be forced to step down.

Would the papers unearth Clara's attendance at seances? If they did, they would wring every shred of pathos from it. They would talk about a bereaved mother, desperate for a last glimpse of her dead hero son – Cas would have laughed at that and said, What nonsense, he had not been a hero, he had only been helping a few friends out of a tight spot. A stab of pain sliced through Lewis, and he thought he would give everything he possessed to hear Cas laughing at the idea of himself as a hero.

But there was the other side of the coin. What if he gave in to McNulty and the truth about that got out? Mightn't the headlines be even worse? 'Calvary's governor presides over bizarre experiment in execution shed . . .' 'Baronet in quest for the soul's origins . . .'

It was a bastard choice. On the one hand he would be made out to be a faithless husband who indulged in bed games with a bouncing trollop, and on the other he would be a fanatic who abused his position and inflicted unnecessary mental torment on a condemned man. Either way he would lose the work that meant so much to him.

A tiny treacherous voice in his mind said, But you wouldn't really be inflicting mental torment on O'Kane, would you? It would be simply a question of O'Kane stepping onto a weighing machine, that's all. Two minutes at most, McNulty said. You wouldn't even need to give O'Kane a reason: he's been weighed by Pierrepoint once already; he would think this second weighing was simply a confirmation of the first. And you'd be in the clear with Denzil McNulty. But would I? thought Lewis. Don't blackmailers always come back for more? And the thought of lying to Nicholas O'Kane was deeply distasteful. O'Kane's idealism might be misplaced but he had believed in his cause with the same passion that had ultimately sent Cas to his death.

O'Kane deserved to die – he had been indirectly responsible for the deaths of a great many English sailors whose ships the German navy had torpedoed, but he did not deserve to be deceived on the threshold of death.

Lewis frowned, reached for the whisky he kept in a locked cupboard, poured a hefty measure and went on thinking very deeply.

Saul Ketch had also been thinking very deeply. He had been thinking ever since he had found out about the Skelton tart and the governor, and he was now feeling mightily disgruntled.

You might have considered that a man taking a juicy bit of information along to the doctor – all according to their arrangement – would have been welcomed and given money there and then. You might also have thought you could trust a doctor not to rook you.

Ketch had trusted the doctor and what had it got him? Bugger all, that was what it had got him. 'Sorry, Ketch,' he had said, swinging that stupid eyeglass that made him look like a lopsided toad. 'This information is not worth anything. It's unusable.'

Ketch, stung, had demanded to know why. The doctor had proof of it, hadn't he? Well, Ketch knew he had proof, because the doctor had gone capering along to Sir Lewis's office to see for himself there and then. That made this a prime morsel of information, worth at least half a sovereign of anybody's money, and Ketch would bet the doctor would get a lot more than half a sovereign out of Lewis Bloody Caradoc for keeping quiet.

'It's worth nothing,' the doctor said when Ketch put forward this point of view, turned on his heel and went away to his own room, leaving Ketch staring after him.

Well! Well, if Doctor Toadface McNulty was not going to use this prize snippet, then Ketch was going to do so on his own account. That would just serve

Toadface right, the spidery old miser that he was, not even giving a man his proper name, calling him 'Ketch' as if he had been no more than the sweepings of the gutter.

The more he thought about using the information himself, the better he liked the idea. He would go along now, this very night, and he would say what he had seen and heard to Sir Lewis Cocksure Caradoc. The small bawdiness of this pleased him. Cocksure. Sir Lewis would soon be very cock *un*sure if Ketch handled this right.

He thought very carefully about what he should say, and then went along to Old Muttonchops and said he had a bellyache, and please could he be excused duty in the condemned cell for a while.

Muttonchops was not best pleased, what with it being death watch. They were always busy on death-watch nights, what with so much to be done, and what with having to make sure the prisoner did not top himself beforehand and cheat the hangman.

But however much Muttonchops disliked it, he could not very well refuse permission. He said, Oh, very well, Ketch had better go off and deal with whatever his problem was, and there was no need to tell the details either, thank you very much. But he was to be back on duty at midnight or they would ask Dr McNulty to take a look at him. He reminded Ketch that his spell of duty took him through to nine o'clock tomorrow morning, and added a remark about Ketch's unwise consumption of onion broth, which annoyed Ketch because it was nothing to do with anybody what he ate and drank. But he said, quite meekly, Thank you, Mr Millichip, and promised to be back on duty at midnight and to be there to take the prisoner to the execution shed. Ketch had, in fact, bullied another warder into switching duties with him, because there would be O'Kane's clothes to be got hold of. These were presently folded in a locker in the condemned cell, and very nice clothes they were too: Ketch had looked through them when O'Kane was being exercised. He had marked out some shirts to sell in the King's Head four-ale bar, and there were trousers and underthings as well. Three pairs of shoes – good leather ones. Muttonchops would have marked those for himself, the sneaky old greed-bug, but Ketch was going to get in ahead of him. You could get at least five shillings for a pair of good leather shoes. There were no flies on Saul Ketch, not if there was money to be made.

There might very well be money to be made in the governor's office tonight, and Ketch smiled to himself as he went along the corridors. He liked the feel of Calvary on an execution night and he liked the feeling of what he was about to do.

Sir Lewis was in his office. He looked pale and his eyes were darker than usual. Ketch had a little inward snigger at that, because he knew why Sir Lewis was looking pale and dark-eyed, didn't he just!

He said politely, 'Begging pardon, sir, but there's a matter I need to discuss with you.'

'Yes?' Caradoc did not quite say, make it quick, but he nearly did.

'It's a bit difficult, really,' said Ketch. 'It's about Dr McNulty, sir. It's a bit – like – delicate.' Aha! That had made Sir Lewis look up and take notice!

'In what way delicate? Is McNulty ill?'

'Oh no, not ill, sir. But I thought – well, several of us thought – as how you ought to know what's been going on.'

'What do you mean?'

Ketch had decided that at this stage, worried innocence was best. He said, 'Well, sir, he's been – I hardly like to say it – but he's been trying to get a few of us to spy.'

'Spy?'

The word came out so sharply, so much like a gun-shot, that Ketch flinched, and then he realized Caradoc thought he meant spy in the way O'Kane had spied. He said firmly, 'Spying on the people here, sir. In Calvary.'

'On the prisoners?'

'Not the prisoners, sir. The people working here.'

'The warders? D'you mean Dr McNulty has asked you to spy on the warders?'

'Well, yes, sir. And,' said Ketch, looking Caradoc straight in the eye, 'others as well.'

The governor frowned. 'You're making this up, Ketch. Have you been drinking?'

Ketch was stung by the injustice of this. A liar and a drunk, that was what he was being called, which was rich coming from a man who not an hour since had been ramming away between Skelton's thighs!

He said indignantly, 'I haven't touched a drop. And it's all the truth. The doctor tells us to watch and listen and find out things. We have to let him know what we've found, and he gives us money.' Too late he saw he had made it sound as if he had gone along with the arrangement. But he could not take the words back

252

and so he plunged on. 'Tonight I told the doctor what I heard in this room an hour ago.' He stopped and waited.

The governor's expression did not alter, but when he spoke again his voice held a new note. 'And what did you think you heard, Ketch?' he said, and although the words were soft, for the first time Ketch wondered if he had been altogether wise to come here.

But he was not backing down now. He thrust out his jaw and said, 'We both know what I heard, don't we, sir? You and Belinda Skelton.' Artfully he let his eyes stray to the closed door that led to the little bedroom leading off the room.

'Scurrilous lies,' said Sir Lewis at once. 'Did you think McNulty would pay you for your mad lies?'

Ketch did not know what that word – scurry-something – meant, but he knew that was twice the governor had called him a liar. He said, 'The doctor pays for knowing things like that. I told you – he's got a whole string of people he gets to listen at keyholes and the like.'

'Why would he pay you for that?'

'He makes money out of knowing things that go on,' said Ketch.

'Blackmail,' said Sir Lewis slowly. 'Yes, I see. And tonight you thought you'd try your hand at a little blackmail on your own account, did you?'

'I supposed you'd like to know what the doctor was up to,' said Ketch righteously. 'That's why I come here, for to tell you.' He edged nearer to the desk. 'Also, sir, I thought you wouldn't want people knowing what you'd been up to.'

'What you thought,' said Sir Lewis, his words like chips of ice, 'was that I'd give you money to shut you up.' He eyed Ketch with dislike. 'You're a disgusting little weasel, Ketch, and you're dismissed from your post here and now. I'm not having liars and blackmailers working in Calvary. Collect your things and go straight away. If you're still in the gaol in half an hour's time I'll have you thrown out.'

'You can't dismiss me!' blustered Ketch.

'I most certainly can. I've just done it. Think yourself lucky I'm not turning you over to the police.'

Ketch was not worried about the police. What he was worried about was the prospect of penury, which was suddenly opening up before him. And he was even more worried that if he had no job they might send him into the army – conscription or some such word they used nowadays. Ketch was not going off to fight the Hun, not for Lewis Caradoc, nor King George nor nobody. That was why, once he was seventeen, he had come up to Calvary. Reserved occupation they called it.

He gripped the edges of the desk and said angrily that Sir Lewis could not throw him out. There was his week's money. He was owed a week's money, he said pugnaciously.

'You're owed nothing. Now get out before I break your neck.'

There was nothing for it but to go. But as Ketch walked along the corridors to the warder's room and his locker, he was already planning how he would be revenged on that cool-as-a-cat Lewis Caradoc and that whore Belinda.

*

So, thought Lewis, as the door closed, I'm between the devil and the deep blue sea. No, I'm not, I'm between the devil, Denzil McNulty, and that unwholesome slug, Saul Ketch. And an unholier trinity I never wish to meet.

He considered how far he should believe Saul Ketch. Denzil McNulty operating a sly little spy network inside Calvary? Gathering information and making use of it? Making people pay for his silence? Was that likely? Oh yes, thought Lewis, pouring a second drink and making it a stiffer one this time. Oh yes, it's more than likely.

He did not think Ketch had the wits to make up such a tale, and it was plain that Ketch had been McNulty's scavenger, carrying unwholesome pieces of information to his master. But tonight, it seemed as if there had been a falling-out between the two, and Ketch had taken the initiative. He could not have known that McNulty had been here before him, or that McNulty's price was not money but something infinitely more macabre.

Lewis was not particularly concerned about Saul Ketch. He did not have the intelligence to do any real harm, nor would he be able to tell his tale in quarters where it would do harm. If he talked in Thornbeck, people would think it the pique of a man dismissed for some squalid little misdemeanour. Lewis thought he must make sure the senior warders knew he had dismissed Ketch for— What? Stealing? No, better not be specific; better just say he had caught the man in a flagrant flouting of the rules, and leave it at that.

But McNulty? Oh, Dr McNulty, thought Lewis, what a deeply unpleasant creature you are. Of all the crimes blackmail's one of the most vicious.

He would have to do something about Clara's

association with McNulty, but for the moment he could not think how he would grapple with that. If he forbade her to have anything to do with him, she would want to know why. And Lewis could not tell her why; he could not tell her about any of this. My God, he thought bitterly, this twisted little slug has really got me tied up. I can't see any way out of this situation. Or can I? The speck of an idea had dropped into his mind, and he sat very still, the minutes ticking away.

When McNulty returned, and said, without preamble, 'Well, Sir Lewis, have you come to a decision?' Lewis smiled and said, with perfect politeness, 'I believe so. But first of all, doctor, I should like you to tell me about the blackmail network you've been operating in Thornbeck.'

The extraordinary thing was that McNulty did not deny any of it. He said, quite frankly, that he had made use of two or three warders to gather snippets of information in Thornbeck and a few of the surrounding villages. Yes, Calvary was part of the hunting ground as well, he said. Why not? When Lewis used the word scavengers he nodded and said, Yes, that described it well enough. He displayed no contrition and appeared to feel no guilt.

'The remuneration for a prison doctor is pitiful, Sir Lewis.'

'So you extorted money from people.'

'You don't understand,' said McNulty impatiently. 'It's for my work. My research on the soul – the existence of life after death. That can't be done without money, Sir Lewis. The truth must be uncovered, no matter the cost. And if I can be the one to uncover it – to make the discovery—' He broke off, breathing as if he had been running hard, and Lewis said, in his coolest voice, 'The discovery of the existence of the soul?'

'Yes.' A shrug. 'As for the extortion charge – well, we all take the pickings from our work. What were your pickings, Sir Lewis? The likes of Belinda Skelton?'

Lewis did not dare let this jibe touch him or he would have been across the desk throttling McNulty there and then. He said, 'You blackmailed people.'

'I merely suggested payments to safeguard people's secrets. Things they would prefer to keep private. Adulterous liaisons, illegitimate children, a liking for bed partners of the same sex. People pay for keeping those things quiet.'

'You haven't asked me for a payment.'

'Not in money. But you can provide the one thing no one else can.'

'The soul experiment,' said Lewis softly.

'Yes.' The hunger was in McNulty's voice again.

'You do realize I can't ignore this,' said Lewis. 'Quite apart from the criminal nature of blackmail, there's your medical standing. As well as the police, I must report you to the General Medical Council.'

'Must you?' said McNulty softly. 'I don't think you'd better, Sir Lewis. I've already got you in a cleft stick with Skelton. If you really do tell your masters what I've been doing, it would be easy for me to say you had been part of it. That you had controlled it, even. I could say that faced with exposure you were trying to shift the blame onto me.'

'I don't think that would be believed,' said Lewis after a moment. 'I'm not immensely rich but I have sufficient money for my needs.'

'Do you? Does any man ever have sufficient? And if Lady Caradoc should decide to sever the marital tie because of your fondness for other women mightn't that sever a large part of your income as well?'

'You'd never do it,' said Lewis.

'Believe me, I would. If I go down, you'll go down with me,' said McNulty, and there was an edge to his voice Lewis had not heard before. 'It would be my word against yours, and even if you were cleared, people would look at you sideways for a very long time. Mud sticks. And I will do anything to further my work, *anything*—' He broke off, and then in his normal tone said, 'Is my request so very bad? We weigh a condemned prisoner each day anyway. Let me make one extra weighing tomorrow morning. Let me record Nick O'Kane's weight immediately before the execution and again after it, and then report my findings to my colleagues. Your name need never come into it, not now and not ever. And then, next week or next month, I'll leave Calvary and you need never hear from me again.'

'Have you really no ties to keep you here?'

'Oh no. As you know I'm unmarried and I have no close family. I'm free to roam where I wish,' said McNulty.

Lewis said slowly, 'If I could be sure you mean that about leaving . . .'

The smile that Clara Caradoc had found reassuring, but Lewis thought sly, showed briefly. 'You can't be absolutely sure, of course, can you?' said McNulty.

'No.'

'But between gentlemen . . .'

Lewis thought, You're no bloody gentleman, in fact

I almost think I prefer Saul Ketch. At least he's honest about his villainy.

McNulty eyed him for a moment, then said, 'Well, Sir Lewis? Have we an arrangement? Are we making the soul experiment on Nicholas O'Kane?'

Lewis said slowly, 'It looks as if we are, Doctor.

CHAPTER TWENTY

Lewis finally went to bed at one a.m.

McNulty had remained in the governor's room for over an hour, discussing the exact details of the experiment, considering how they should deal with the actual weighing of O'Kane's body. There was an unhealthy excitement in his voice as he talked about body weight and about allowing for the evacuation of the body's fluids at the moment of death. Lewis had thought himself hardened to the sometimes messy spasms of a hanged body, but he found it repellent to be discussing this when it was Nicholas O'Kane.

Around midnight he conducted a brief interview with the senior warder, Arthur Millichip, saying he had found cause to dismiss Saul Ketch, and that Ketch had left Calvary and was not to be allowed back under any circumstances.

Millichip did not ask about the cause for dismissal and he did not seem particularly surprised. He said Ketch had always been a bit unsatisfactory, although there had not been anything you could actually get hold of, if Sir Lewis took his meaning? A bit of a slippery customer, was Millichip's opinion of Ketch, and it would not surprise him if the man came back to Calvary one day as an inmate. In any event, it was good riddance to bad rubbish as far as he, Millichip, was concerned.

'Did you want me for anything else, Sir Lewis, because with Ketch gone I'll need to re-arrange my rotas?'

'Yes, of course,' said Lewis. 'But there's nothing else. Thank you, Millichip.' He watched the man go out. He was reasonably sure Millichip was not one of McNulty's scavengers but he was not sufficiently sure of it to ask for his help in tracing the others. It flickered in his mind that he might ask Belinda to help on that score, but then he wondered how far he could trust Belinda and how far he could trust anyone at all. He wondered where Belinda was tonight. Was she asleep somewhere – in her own bed or someone else's? He did not know if she was on duty tonight, and he realized he did not know where or how she lived. Did she have a house of her own, or did she live with family?

When at last he went to bed, he dreamed about Cas. He dreamed Cas was laughing at the idea of being dubbed a hero and saying that far from being any such thing, he had betrayed his country and sold naval secrets to the Kaiser's armies. There was nothing wrong with doing that, said Cas, not if you believed in your cause. He had believed passionately in what he did, but because of it, in a few hours he would die for a dream. That was what all traitors did, said the shadow who had Cas's voice but Nicholas O'Kane's eyes. Traitors died not for flag, nor king, nor emperor, but for a dream born in a herdsman's shed . . .

Lewis came fully and abruptly awake, the lines of the Irish poem still ringing in his ears. He stared up at the ceiling, the dream still strongly with him. To die for a dream, a dream born in a herdsman's shed. O'Kane had read the poem to him shortly after coming to Calvary; he had a good voice for reading, soft and just very slightly touched with an Irish accent, and Lewis, listening, had instantly had a picture of the poverty-stricken Irish crofters, gathering round their peat fires, planning how to overturn English domination and rule their own land. The Irish were the dreamers and the rebels of the world, of course. Irresponsible and erratic, but filled with such charm.

O'Kane had said that if possible he would like the poem to be incorporated into his funeral service. Could that be done? Lewis had seen no reason why not.

In accordance with custom, the kitchen staff set out a light breakfast in the governor's rooms for McNulty, the chaplain and Mr Pierrepoint and his assistant. McNulty arrived punctually, and Lewis, who could never eat on such mornings, saw with faint nausea that the man piled his plate with eggs and toast. Their eyes met briefly and there was the sly glint of the conspirator in the doctor's expression; Lewis was glad that the chaplain and Pierrepoint came in almost at once. He managed to drink a cup of coffee and felt slightly better for its warmth.

Then he said, 'Gentlemen, because of the nature of this prisoner's conviction, I have decided that Dr

McNulty and I will prepare him for execution in the condemned cell.' He glanced at the chaplain. 'Mr Pilbeam
I should like you to be outside while we do so.'

'Very well, Sir Lewis. I shall commence reading the
order of service when you bring the prisoner out. Is that
agreeable to you?'

'Perfectly. You've got the verse of the Irish poem,
haven't you?'

'I have.'

'Good. Dr McNulty, are you all right?'

'Yes, why?'

'I thought you sounded as if you had a cold. Perhaps
not, though. Mr Pierrepoint, may I have a word before
you go?'

Pierrepoint had been at the door with the others, but
he turned and came back. 'Yes, Sir Lewis?'

Lewis said, 'Can you trust McNulty and me to pinion
O'Kane's hands and ankles before he's brought out?'

It was many years since a condemned man had had
to make the slow, shambling walk to the scaffold with
his wrists already pinioned, the leather strap binding his
elbows against his body, and his ankles loosely fettered,
so Pierrepoint looked a bit surprised. Before he could
speak, Lewis said, 'I realize it's not the custom any
longer, but this is an awkward case and there have been
whispers of trouble.'

Would Pierrepoint assume this meant Lewis had
received information that O'Kane's Irish companions or
his German masters might be planning a rescue attempt
and that there had to be extra security as a result? Yes,
he seemed to have done. He still looked dubious but he
was nodding his agreement.

'Although we'll need to check the straps and the pinions at the last moment, Sir Lewis.'

'Yes, of course. That needn't take more than a few seconds, though. In strict confidence, we have definite word of trouble brewing over this execution. We may need to seal off the prison at least until after the funeral. You're booked into the King's Head, I think? Ah, good. Then I'm going to arrange for you and your assistant to be taken straight back there after the execution. I don't want you caught up in any violence – you could be a target. Dr McNulty or I can bring the death certificate down to you later today.'

'It's not according to regulations, Sir Lewis.'

'The Home Office were quite clear on the point,' said Lewis smoothly.

'Good enough.'

At twenty past seven the under-sheriff of the county was admitted, and five minutes later, McNulty and the chaplain returned. Lewis felt his heart start to beat faster. This is it, he thought, and picking up the leather straps the assistant had brought, he said, 'Gentlemen, if you're ready, shall we go?' He was immeasurably relieved to hear that his voice held its usual cool note of polite authority, but when the under-sheriff glanced questioningly at the straps he ignored him.

As they walked towards the condemned block Lewis heard the other prisoners banging their tin mugs against the doors or the barred windows of their cells. It was strong and rhythmic as if a giant iron heart was beating at Calvary's centre. They would keep it up until the clock had finished striking eight, and then, as if a command had been given, they would stop abruptly. Just as the condemned man's heart would stop.

Lewis glanced at McNulty. The doctor was silent and apparently composed, but his eyes darted this way and that like a watchful snake's, as if they were the only part he could not keep suppressed. The few mouthfuls of coffee Lewis had managed to drink stirred uneasily and he had to take several deep breaths to steady himself.

Millichip, solemn and hushed-faced, met them at the entrance to the condemned block, and touched his cap respectfully before turning to unlock the door. He would have been with O'Kane all night; he was not precisely the man with whom Lewis would have wanted to share his own final night on earth but at least he was better than Saul Ketch. Keeping the leather straps out of sight behind his back, Lewis stepped inside, leaving the chaplain and under-sheriff in the passageway.

O'Kane's chair was facing the door and Lewis saw that there was still a trace of light in his eyes. But as he looked at Lewis and McNulty, he gave a small nod and the thread of light was quenched. It almost always happened like that and it was one of the things Lewis hated so much; it was as if the condemned man had been valiantly clinging to the last shreds of hope but, with the unlocking of the cell door, had finally accepted that hope must be relinquished.

McNulty must have arranged for the weighing machine to be brought here earlier on, which angered Lewis because it had not been part of the arrangement. But it was pointless to protest now, and he stood aside as Millichip, obedient to Lewis's brief order, went out.

McNulty gestured to O'Kane to step onto the machine. A faint puzzlement flickered in O'Kane's eyes, as if he might be thinking, but we've already done all this, then he gave a half shrug and did as he was bidden. A tiny nerve was jumping in McNulty's cheek, but he worked swiftly, moving the tiny metal weights along the rack, and scribbling his findings in a notebook. He repeated the process, but when he seemed set to make a third check, Lewis said, 'Enough. Mr O'Kane, I'm sorry but we must fasten on the straps in here.'

'Here? I had hoped to walk unfettered to my death, Sir Lewis.'

'I'm truly sorry, but it's necessary.' He handed the ankle straps to McNulty.

'Doctor, would you—'

But McNulty had already taken the looped leather straps with the thick buckles and was half kneeling, fastening them about O'Kane's ankles. His head was bent, and Lewis glanced behind him to the quarter-open cell door and the waiting men just out of sight in the corridor. He took a deep breath and pulled from his pocket the heavy glass paperweight he had taken from his desk earlier on. He brought it down hard on McNulty's head, and there was a dreadful dull crunch and then a grunt as McNulty toppled forward. He lay prone on the floor, and a faint rim of white showed under his eyelids. Nicholas O'Kane backed away, and turned wide uncomprehending eyes on Calvary's governor.

Keeping his voice low, Lewis said, 'Quickly, man. Change clothes with him, and help me to put the straps on him.'

'But what—'

'Don't ask questions, just do it. Then you'll be free and so will I.' He shot a quick look towards the door again, and gestured to O'Kane to move so that he was out of its line of sight. 'We have just over ten minutes if we're lucky.'

'I guessed you were a risk taker,' said O'Kane, pulling off McNulty's distinctive frock coat and then his own things. 'But I didn't know you were an outright gambler.'

'I'm many things.' Lewis was dragging off McNulty's shoes and his trousers. 'Don't bother about the underclothes. Just get your prison things onto him – you're much the same height. Pull on his coat. The shoes might not fit, but do the best you can.'

'Believe me, I'd walk over burning coals to get out of this place,' said O'Kane.

They pulled the blue serge shirt and trousers onto McNulty's unconscious form. Just over six minutes left, thought Lewis, glancing at his watch. We're cutting it dangerously fine. He looked back at O'Kane who had donned the coat and the dark trousers. 'Yes, that's all right. Hunch your shoulders a bit. You'll have to keep your wits about you now, because for the next few minutes you're Denzil McNulty, and this man is Nicholas O'Kane.'

'Caradoc, this will never work! I'll be recognized—'

'Not if you keep a handkerchief to your face,' said Lewis, handing him his own. 'The only two who really know McNulty are the chaplain and Millichip, and I've already planted the idea of a head cold in their minds. It's a dark morning, but keep well back from the others. No one will be looking at you, though – everyone will be concentrating on the man they think is the prisoner.'

He took a second handkerchief from his pocket and pushed it into McNulty's slack mouth. 'I'd like to gag him properly in case he comes round and cries out, but this is the best I can manage.'

'But they'll know McNulty isn't me,' said O'Kane in a strained voice.

Lewis produced the hood – the canvas bag with its drawstring neck and eyelets for breathing, largely intended to hide the worst of the gallows' stark ugliness from the condemned man. He pulled it down over McNulty's head and adjusted the strings. 'They won't know,' he said.

'God Almighty,' said Nicholas O'Kane, half under his breath, staring down. 'That's a faceless creature you've made of him.'

O'Kane was right. With the pulling on of the hood, the thing they were supporting between them no longer seemed to be Denzil McNulty: it had turned into a macabre puppet, the head formless inside its pale sack. Take away a man's face, and what is left of him?

'You'll have to pronounce death immediately after-wards,' said Lewis. 'Can you do that?'

'God, how do I know?'

'You've been fighting in a war, O'Kane, even if it was on the wrong side. You must know what death looks like. And it won't be much more than a formality – Pierrepoint's never bungled an execution yet and every-one knows it. He'll leave a timber plank in place across part of the trap and there's a stethoscope in your pocket – I've checked that. All you do is step onto the plank, then kneel, and reach down. His chest will be about level with the floor – you'll be able to apply the stethoscope.

Listen to the heart for a few minutes. It'll get weaker and then stop. All right?'

'No, it's not all right,' said O'Kane. 'But I'll do it. What about afterwards?'

'Afterwards,' said Lewis, 'you and I will have to go down to the brick vault and cut the body down. Pierrepoint would normally supervise that, but I've got rid of him. Just take your lead from me. And when it's over, we let a blackmailing villain be buried in a grave intended for you.'

'And I walk free?'

'And you walk free.

Two minutes to eight. There was a sound from beyond the cell door. We're behind the usual timing, thought Lewis, and they're wondering what's happening. But before he could give way to real panic he heard his voice calling out, quite coolly, that the prisoner had swooned.

'We've tried to rouse him, but he's out cold. We're going to carry him out in a minute.'

Millichip murmured an assent and Lewis heard with thankfulness that there was no suspicion in his voice. It was not, indeed, a suspicious situation, because it was not unknown for a man to faint from sheer terror in the final moments.

'Sir Lewis – wait. Are you actually letting him go to the gallows in my place?'

'Yes.'

'In God's name, why?'

'I don't know if it's in God's name at all,' said Lewis. 'But I'm letting him go to the gallows because he's a blood-sucking blackmailer, and he deserves to die.' He met Nicholas O'Kane's eyes very straightly. 'Although unlike you, he hasn't a dream he's prepared to die for,' he said. 'O'Kane, I'm trusting you more than I've ever trusted any man in my whole life.'

'Why?' said O'Kane again.

'Too many reasons to list. Now take his feet, and keep in the shadows.'

For an incredible moment he thought O'Kane was going to protest, but he did not. He made a half gesture with one hand as if saying, on your head be it, and bent to pick up McNulty's ankles. As they carried McNulty out into the corridor the prison bell began the sonorous tolling. That means we should already be inside the execution shed, thought Lewis, hearing it.

'Sir Lewis, shall I take him?'

It was Millichip, respectfully anxious to take on the task of carrying the unconscious man. Lewis said, 'Thank you but I have him securely and Dr McNulty is helping me. It'll be easier if we stay with him. You go ahead of us, please. Mr Pilbeam, begin if you will.'

'Man that is born of woman hath but a short time to live . . .'

The dozen steps from the condemned cell to the execution shed seemed to stretch out like something in a nightmare. We'll never do it, thought Lewis. At any minute they'll realize this isn't O'Kane we're carrying. McNulty's harsh breathing filled the narrow passage, mingling horridly with the chaplain's sombre tones. We're going to be late, thought Lewis, panic rising once again. No, it's all right, we're at the door of the execution chamber. But at any second McNulty might recover from the blow to the head, and if he did, would he have time to realize what was happening? Lewis could not begin to think what he would do if McNulty managed to spit out the makeshift gag and shout out the truth.

At least Millichip knew the procedure from here. Open the door, stand respectfully back and let them get on with it. Lewis's arms were starting to ache with the strain of carrying the dead weight that was Denzil McNulty and a sudden pain tightened around his chest. Heart attack? For pity's sake, I can't die of a heart attack in here! He nodded to O'Kane to let go of McNulty's ankles, and leave it to him from here on, and O'Kane did so. Thank God, at least, for a man who could pick up a meaning from a look. Millichip started forward intending to help, and there was a movement from the under-sheriff as well, but Lewis shook his head.

'I'm just placing him on the trap and then leaving it to Mr Pierrepoint,' he said, doing so before anyone could intervene, seeing that the plank was in place for the doctor's pronouncement of death. So far so good.

He stepped back. 'Will you need the chair?' he said to Pierrepoint.

'I'd prefer not, Sir Lewis. It upsets the balance of the weights.' He surveyed the unconscious man. 'Difficult for us when this happens,' he said. 'But happen it's best for him. If he's lucky he'll go out not knowing.'

Pilbeam was reaching the end of the service as the five-minute tolling bell stopped and the first chime of eight sounded. Pierrepoint had drawn down the waiting rope from the crossbeam and adjusted it around McNulty's neck. The second chime of eight sounded. It was then that the hooded head moved.

'He's coming round,' said the under sheriff, sounding panic-stricken.

Lewis said sharply, 'Stay where you are. Mr Pierre-point knows how to handle this.'

'He's not really conscious, anyway,' said Pierrepoint.

But McNulty was conscious. He turned his head from side to side, and then, clearly finding himself unable to see, feeling the presence of the handkerchief in his mouth, he began to draw in panic-stricken breaths so that the hood was frenziedly sucked in and out. The clock's still chiming, thought Lewis in agony. He's supposed to be dead by the time the last stroke sounds, but he won't be, he won't—

At least the clock was drowning whatever grunting cries McNulty might be making, and the canvas hood and handkerchief muffled his cries. That's the last stroke of eight, thought Lewis. Pierrepoint, for God's sake do it, move the lever, draw the bolt, break his neck . . .

The lever was drawn across and there was the faint shuddering of the floor. The gallows trap fell inwards and down and McNulty's body dropped like a stone into the brick-lined vault and hung there, swaying slightly.

I've done it, thought Lewis, staring at the dreadful figure. I've killed a fellow human being. And the utterly terrible thing is that I feel no compunction whatsoever. I don't feel anything at all. He caught O'Kane's eye, and O'Kane moved onto the plank at once, taking the stethoscope from his pocket as he did so. Lewis was glad to see he had the sense to keep his back to most of the room so that no one saw his face.

Still keeping his face turned away from the watchers, O'Kane knelt and reached down, placing the stethoscope on McNulty's chest which was level with the floor as Lewis had told him. He bent his head, listening through the earpiece. There was absolute silence in the room, and Lewis, trying not to clench his fists, waited. Two minutes. Three. Surely the heart had stopped now? Five minutes. Six. Oh God, let him say it, let him say the man's dead.

Then Nicholas O'Kane removed the stethoscope and stepped back, and before anyone could speak, Lewis said, 'He's gone, doctor?'

'Yes.' No one could have told that the single syllable was not McNulty's voice.

'Thank you, gentlemen,' said Lewis, and made a gesture to usher them out. As they moved to the door, he drew a deep sigh of relief. O'Kane was still at his side; it was a strange feeling to know that the young man who had betrayed his country and consorted with rebels and dissidents – who must have known people high up in the German intelligence services – was unsure and nervous.

They both waited until the other men had gone out, and then Lewis moved to the door.

Behind him, O'Kane said in a low urgent voice, 'Caradoc – wait.'

'What is it? What's wrong?'

'I don't think he's dead.'

Lewis spun round at once.

'The heart didn't stop beating,' said Nicholas, 'but I didn't dare risk leaving it any longer.'

'It happens like that sometimes. The heart muscle keeps going for a little while. It doesn't mean anything.' But Lewis was staring at McNulty's body. The trap had sent him half inside the vault.

'He's moving,' said O'Kane suddenly, and cold horror flooded Lewis's body.

'Muscle spasm. Quite common.'

'Are you sure?'

'No. Oh God, no, I'm not sure.'

'Nor am I. Can we bring the trapdoors back up?'

'Yes, but it's a slow process and it's noisy. Can't you reach him from there?'

'Of course I can't bloody reach him from here!'

Lewis was just grasping the lever when McNulty began to struggle.

CHAPTER TWENTY-ONE

His hands were pinioned behind his back and his ankles were fettered, and he squirmed like a fish on the end of a hook. He really is alive, thought Lewis, his mind spinning. He's alive and he's slowly strangling. I meant him to die swiftly from a snapped neck, I didn't mean this to happen . . . Oh God, oh God, we've got to free him.

The execution chamber was filling with Denzil McNulty's grunting cries, and O'Kane was kneeling on the edge of the yawning gallows trap, trying to grasp his body and lift it to take some of the weight off the rope. There was a bad moment when the writhing shape seemed to turn its faceless head accusingly towards him and swing straight at him. Nicholas flinched, but he had managed to get McNulty's upper body in a grotesque half-embrace and to lift him slightly which had reduced some of the rope's tension.

Lewis was at the lever by this time. He drew it back, and the trapdoors shivered, hesitated, then slowly – far more slowly than they had opened – came back up into place. As they levelled out, the taut rope slackened, and Denzil McNulty was pushed back up into the room. He fell forward on the trapdoors, knocking the plank to one side, his body jerking in spasms, retching drily. Lewis bent over him, tearing at the rope and the canvas hood, hardly even remembering that this was the man who had been prepared to ruin him.

'Is he all right?' said O'Kane, kneeling down to help.

'I think so. He's breathing freely.' Lewis managed to drag the rope off, and after it the hood and the saliva-soaked handkerchief. He laid McNulty flat, and then glanced over his shoulder, praying no one had heard the trap being closed. 'We'll have to get him down into the gallows vault and along to the mortuary. There's a tunnel leading out of the vault straight to it. Can you help me, O'Kane? We can take him down the steps.' He indicated the second, smaller trapdoor in the corner and saw with gratitude that O'Kane was already opening it and peering down.

'It's all clear, Caradoc.'

'Good. Wait a minute, I'll lock this door. No one should come in, but we'd better make sure.'

Nicholas was inspecting McNulty again. 'He's just about conscious,' he said. 'He'll have the devil of a sore throat for a few days but he's breathing all right. I'd say he'll live to tell the tale, wouldn't you?'

'Yes,' said Lewis, coming back from the door and pocketing the keys. 'He'll live to tell the tale.'

'And there's the rub, isn't it?' said O'Kane, softly. 'Because he will tell the tale, won't he?'

They looked at one another. I don't know if I

altogether trust O'Kane, thought Lewis, pocketing the keys. But I can't see I've got any choice, although I still don't know what I'm going to do with him. He said slowly, 'You're right, McNulty will tell the tale. Unless . . .'

'Unless we bribe him? Strike a bargain with him? Is that what you're thinking?'

'Yes. But we'd need to offer him something he wants very much.'

'Can we do that?'

'Yes,' said Lewis meeting Nicholas O'Kane's eyes. 'I think we can.'

'I have,' said Nicholas, 'conducted discussions in some very odd places. I've helped to hatch plots against the English in places you two gentlemen wouldn't even know existed – places that oughtn't to exist on God's earth in this enlightened century. But I don't think I've ever conducted a discussion of any kind in the mortuary of a gaol.' He glanced about him. 'Is anyone likely to come in here, do you suppose? Because if so I may need to get under a sheet and pretend to be my own corpse.'

He was seated on the ground, leaning back against a wall. His hair was untidy and there were marks of extreme strain around his eyes. But for all that and for all the bizarre nature of the situation and the surroundings, the remark about pretending to be his own corpse was said with a carelessness bordering on the flippant. Lewis was half sitting on the edge of one of the stone tables and McNulty, his face still blotched with ugly red patches and his neck mottled with bruises, had the only chair. His feet were still tied – Lewis had not dared free him completely – but they had removed the wrist straps.

'No one will come in here yet,' said Lewis. 'The body's always left on the rope for an hour.'

'Why?'

'Partly to let the muscle spasms die away. Partly as a mark of respect. I know it might not sound respectful at all, but it's what's always done. Doctor, isn't that right?'

'It's perfectly right,' said McNulty. He spoke with difficulty and his voice sounded as if the whole inside of his throat had been scraped raw.

'We're down here,' said Lewis, 'because we need to talk without fear of interruption.'

'And because none of us wanted to stay in that loathsome death chamber any longer than necessary,' put in Nicholas, glancing over his shoulder at the door to the brick tunnel leading to the gallows vault. 'I never thought that, given a choice, I'd find a mortuary preferable to anywhere, though.' He looked about him. 'It's a dark old place, isn't it?'

It was dark because the mortuary was partly underground, but O'Kane had found and lit an oil lamp. Lewis had filled a tin cup with water from the sink and after sipping this for a few moments, McNulty was able to direct them to one of the medicine cupboards for a small phial containing some kind of restorative crystal. He inhaled this a few times and as the room filled up with the smell of ammonia, his face regained some of its normal colour. He's recovering, thought Lewis, and thank God for it. I'm not a murderer after all. I've been saved that. Was I mad to do what I did? The problem's still there, of course. How am I going to get out of all this?

'I find it a remarkable eventuality,' said McNulty in

the raw, difficult voice, 'that I should be sitting down here with the two villains who intended to kill me. Lewis Caradoc you're a cold-blooded murderer.'

'And you,' said Lewis at once, 'are a greedy blood-sucking blackmailer.'

'If either of you are thinking that puts you on an even footing,' said O'Kane, 'I'd have to tell you it does not.' He studied McNulty. 'So you're a blackmailer, are you, Doctor? Well, in my book, blackmail's a far worse crime than murder.'

'Where, in your book, does treachery come, O'Kane?' said McNulty coldly.

Lewis saw Nicholas's hands curl into involuntary fists, but he said, 'I wouldn't expect you to understand the – the anger and the bitterness your countrymen generated in Ireland, McNulty. When we held Dublin, the British opened fire, but they were so bloody inept they shot civilians. And d'you know, when they executed the ringleaders James Connelly was already dying. But they propped him up in a hospital bed for the court martial, and afterwards carried him out to the firing squad and tied him to a chair to shoot him. Someone like you couldn't imagine the – the disgust and outrage Connelly's execution caused. It's the stuff that brews hatred and lets it ferment in men's minds, McNulty. It makes men throw in their lots with enemies of your bloody country. I hated the British for what they did to Connelly. We all hated the British for that.'

'So you spied against us.'

'For God's sake, man, you have spies on your side! Spying's a part of war. And if you really are a black-mailer, then I wish I'd left you to choke your guts out at the end of Pierrepoint's rope. Caradoc's too much of a gentleman for his own good.'

'Your opinions don't matter,' said McNulty. 'By tonight you'll be back in the condemned cell, and this time tomorrow you'll be a corpse on that table and there'll be no pretence about any of it. As for you, Caradoc, you'll be in one of your own cells on a charge of attempted murder.' He stared at Nicholas with dislike. 'Did you really think you'd go free after this? That I wouldn't turn you – both of you – over to the police? Or were you thinking you'd finish me off here and now, and throw me into the grave that Saul Ketch dug yesterday?'

'We'll have to throw someone into that grave,' said Nicholas at once. 'So don't tempt me, McNulty, because you haven't recovered from being hanged yet and it could still be you in there.'

'We'll make a dummy for the burial,' said Lewis who had already worked this out. 'Blankets and old pillows tied inside a sheet. Not difficult to fool people if it's done properly.'

'And the coroner's verdict? The "death by judicial execution" certificate? How will you manage that?' said McNulty.

Lewis said, 'You can write out the death certificate yourself. I've already sent Pierrepoint back to the King's Head. He thinks we've had warning of reprisals for O'Kane's execution. The coroner can be told the same story.'

'Reprisal for the death of a hero?' said McNulty a bit sneeringly.

'Don't sneer, McNulty; I'm using what's to hand to get us out of this,' said Lewis.

'Neither of you are getting out of anything,' said McNulty. 'I'm making sure of that. After all, I'm the innocent one in all this.'

'Are you sure about that?'

'I'm not the one who tried to commit murder,' said McNulty. 'And it's only because of the difference in weight that you really didn't murder me. Pierrepoint had worked out the length of the rope allowing for O'Kane's weight and height,' he said. 'We're much of a height, but I'm thinner than he is, so the hanging went wrong.'

'For want of a few pounds of fat, the battle went the other way,' remarked Nicholas.

'And,' went on McNulty, 'unlike you, Nicholas O'Kane, I haven't sold my country to the enemy. How many people d'you suppose died because of what you did?'

'I have more contrition for that than you could ever understand,' said Nicholas. 'But I'm damned if I'll account to you for any of my sins. But I'll be straight with you both and say I haven't the mind to go back into that hell hole and wait to have my neck ceremoniously broken. So, Caradoc, if you have a plan let's hear it.'

Lewis frowned, arranging his thoughts. 'It's said that every man has his price,' he said. 'And I'm fairly sure I know yours, McNulty. When we began this, it was because you blackmailed me into your macabre experiment to weigh a soul.'

'Jesus God,' said O'Kane from his corner. 'He wanted to weigh a soul? Was that what all that fiddling about with measures and balances was this morning? And this is the man who accused you of being cold-blooded!'

'I think,' said Lewis, still addressing the doctor, 'that

if I offered to set up your own research society – to fund it for you but allow you all the kudos of heading it and being its founder – then you'd agree to keep quiet about what happened here this morning. I think you'd write out that death certificate and back up my story about a threatened attack from O'Kane's countrymen.'

'And help us tie up a bolster and drop it in the grave for the chaplain,' put in Nicholas.

Lewis was still watching Denzil McNulty. An immense stillness had fallen over the doctor, and Lewis knew he had read the man right. McNulty was not only a fanatic, he was immensely vain. He could not resist being hailed as a new star in the psychic firmament and he could not resist having his name attached to research and experiment into that subject. Lewis could almost hear the thoughts scudding through his mind. To head a new and prestigious research facility, with the eminent Lewis Caradoc as its sponsor. Perhaps to be known as the man who gave the world conclusive proof of the soul's existence.

McNulty said slowly, 'I could certainly be known for the work, but the General Medical Council might frown if such a society actually bore my name. They might see it as a form of advertising and, as you know, that's strictly forbidden.'

Lewis, who had partly foreseen this, said, 'That needn't be a difficulty. You could use my name, but we could ensure people knew you were the true founder of such an organization. The guiding light.'

McNulty had already taken the bait, of course, but he pretended a little longer. 'It would all have to be done properly,' he said, frowning consideringly. 'An official headquarters, a properly registered association. It might be quite costly.'

'Short of the outright ridiculous, the money can be made available.'

'This morning's experiment failed,' said McNulty suddenly, and Lewis thought, he's going to say he'll try again somewhere else. What will I do if he tries again at Calvary?

But he only said, 'I should, of course, require your absolute assurance that nothing that has happened here this morning will ever be spoken of beyond the three of us. That goes for you as well, O'Kane.'

'I'm not likely to speak, am I?' said Nicholas with some force. 'If I speak out I put myself straight back in the condemned cell.'

'You're letting him go?' said McNulty to Lewis.

'We're letting one another go,' said Lewis. 'Think about it. Each of us has committed a crime on his own account. You are a blackmailer; O'Kane is a convicted traitor. I am guilty of attempted murder – and I would have been an actual murderer but for the difference in your two weights. As well as that, we're all guilty of covering up the substitution of McNulty for O'Kane – oh yes, we are, Doctor. Calvary's clock has just struck ten o'clock; that means it's two hours since the hanging. But you've done nothing to bring either myself or O'Kane to justice. The law would consider that to be condoning the crime.' Lewis knew he was on thin ice with this last statement, so he went quickly on before McNulty could question it.

'We each have a weapon we could use to bring down the other two. But if one of us speaks out, he damns himself as well. If you were to bring a charge of attempted murder against me, I should bring a counter-charge of blackmail against you. It would probably be a charge that would stick, as well. But if we all remain silent, no one need ever know what happened inside Calvary today.'

'An unholy trinity,' said Nicholas. 'A gallows pact. Well, I'm with you, Caradoc. You might not count my word as meaning much, but you have it anyway. I haven't so very much money – I left what I had for my wife and the boy. She said it was tainted money, but for all that she'll have used it.' A sudden sadness showed in his eyes, and Lewis knew he was remembering the small boy with intelligent eyes who had been brought to Calvary to bid him farewell. 'And even if she hasn't,' said Nicholas, 'I can't see any way of regaining it. I'll have to work for my living.' He considered for a moment, and then said, 'But I can't stay in England, that's for sure – not for a few years at any rate. The world believes me to be dead and the world will have to go on believing that.' He broke off, and in a voice Lewis had not heard him use, said softly, 'The hardest part will be never seeing my son.'

Lewis said, 'I can't make any promises but if ever it's in my power to give him any help, then I'll do so.'

'Thank you,' said Nicholas after a moment. 'I trust you on that.'

'McNulty?'

'I don't pretend to any kind of honour,' said McNulty, 'and I shan't forget that you intended to murder me this morning, Sir Lewis. But providing you keep your promise about founding a society for psychic research with me as its head, I'll agree never to speak of any of this.'

Extract from Talismans of the Mind, *by C. R. Ingram*

In the latter years of the First World War and in the years immediately following it, psychic societies mushroomed and flourished everywhere as lushly as the Old Testament bay tree flourished in the wilderness.

They travelled different roads and they went by different names, those societies, but stripped of frills and verbiage, they all had the same aim: to prove or disprove the existence of life beyond death – the soul, pre-existence, post-existence, the human essence, the quiddity, the survival of the human spark. The quick, the dead, the heart and the soul, the flesh and the devil. It was all grist to the mills of these people, some of whom may have believed themselves genuine, but too many of whom battened on the weak and the gullible and saw the pursuance of the soul's origins as a means of amassing a fat bank balance.

The enquirers numbered among them the ascetic – Carmelite nuns, Trappist monks, and followers of Buddha, with fasting commonplace and shoulders to be kept to the wheel no matter if it was tantric, tarot, or merely chariot. They touched on the downright sybaritic – the infamous, self-styled black magician of the 1920s, Aleister Crowley, pursuing Pan down a number of priapic paths – and gentlemen (often also ladies) whose tastes ran ghoulishly to human sacrifice and virgins.

And then, of course, there's our old friend Bartlam Partridge, he of the two-tier sherry and the velvet smoking jackets and that unfortunate predilection he developed in later life for the company of very young ladies. The 1924 indecency case was not very widely reported, but it seems the unrepentant Bartlam importuned teenage flappers on Brighton Promenade, and invited them back to his rooms which were at a boarding house called Seaview. The only views the flappers were given, however, were of Bartlam wallowing amid bedsheets wearing nothing but a silk dressing gown and suggesting that in order to achieve a higher plane of consciousness, the flappers should disrobe, join him in the bed, and perform what he liked to call the rite of creation. (It has been called a great many other things in its time, that particular rite, but Bartlam always liked to dress these things up a little.)

When one of the young ladies squeaked in alarm (because Bartlam, unclothed cannot have been the best of sights), the Seaview landlady came running up the stairs and Bartlam was hauled to justice. Perhaps if Violette had still been sharing the nuptial couch, Bart might have behaved with a little more decorum, but Violette, who had grumbled at having to share the cabbage-and-laundry scented rooms with the nameless friends, seems to have vanished without trace.

However, it must be said that not all the psychic societies of the era were quite so venal or so artificial. Indeed, a number of them were perfectly reputable, and some could even be described as scholarly. One such is the Caradoc Society, founded early in 1918, its name taken from Sir Lewis Caradoc who sponsored its creation. Not a great deal is known about Lewis Caradoc, other than his work for various prison reform inquiries during the First World War and the early 1920s which caused him to be regarded with considerable respect. He did not take much part in the Society that bore his name;

the first actual chairman was a doctor: a man who seems to have worked with Sir Lewis on prison reform and rehabilitation.

His name was Denzil McNulty.

CHAPTER TWENTY-TWO

Georgina had wondered whether she ought to include Vincent Meade in the modest lunch party. It was, after all, the Caradoc Society's house, and it seemed a bit discourteous to invite people there without at least telling him. In the end, she wrote a careful note which she put through the door of the office; not precisely saying she hoped there was no objection to her having a couple of guests, but explaining she had met two of the television team in the King's Head, and they would be calling around lunchtime to take a look at some of the material she had found. She read it through twice, to make sure it did not sound as if she was inviting him to come along as well.

Drusilla telephoned shortly after half past nine, to ask if Georgina would mind another guest for lunch.

'We're bringing some culinary offerings with us, of course. It's Jude Stratton who's the extra one – he's been helping Chad with the research.'

Georgina asked who Jude Stratton was, and Drusilla explained.

'Yes, of course bring him. Only . . .'

'Yes'

'You'll be looking at photographs and letters and we'll all be talking about them. Will it be all right to do that with someone there who can't see?'

'Oh, perfectly,' said Drusilla. 'Jude will simply ask you to read things aloud for him. As far as I can tell it makes him furious if people seem to make concessions.'

'Thanks for the tip.' Georgina had made the connection now; she remembered seeing Jude on one or two newsclips after he was blinded by the Iraqi bomb. A cameraman or a sound engineer had been killed as well and the news programmes had made quite a feature of it at the time. She asked if he was anything like the TV news reports.

'He's exactly like that, only more so, if you know what I mean,' said Drusilla. 'Impatient, aggressive, frequently bloody rude. But,' she had added thoughtfully, 'he's devastatingly attractive as well.'

Georgina rang off wondering if Drusilla was intending to lay siege to the attractive, aggressive, rude Jude Stratton and if she was warning Georgina off as a result. If so, Georgina would have to find a way of telling Drusilla that she did not need warning off anybody, because she was going to give all men a wide berth for about the next ten years, especially aggressive attractive ones.

Vincent read Georgina's note with astonishment. The bitch had actually had the effrontery to invite the television people to Caradoc House! The very people Vincent had intended to befriend! The people for whom he had written those really excellent notes about Thornbeck and Calvary.

If you were sufficiently charitable, you could say Georgina had been quite polite about letting Vincent know she had asked people to Caradoc House. Mother would certainly have approved of the note. 'The correct thing to do,' she would have said, although she would have added, 'I see she does not include you in her luncheon party, Vincent, which would have been a mannerly thing for her to do, I would have thought.'

Vincent would have thought so as well. He would have enjoyed having lunch in such company, discussing the television programme, talking about the introduction he had written. He would have been at his best among such people – gently witty and erudite.

But this was not the issue. The issue was that Georgina Grey and Dr Ingram's team would be pooling their resources. They would be exchanging information, and anything might come to light in that kind of situation, *anything*. Vincent felt quite ill with panic when he thought about it. If he had had any doubts as to whether Georgina must be dealt with, he had them no longer. She would have to be attended to as swiftly as possible.

Vincent kept a watch for the arrival of Dr Ingram and the others, doing so discreetly, of course, since he was not going to be noticed peering through windows as if he was a common snoop. But he saw them arrive: Dr Ingram, the Drusilla female, and the American boy. With them was a man Vincent had not seen before – a dark-haired man in his middle thirties. He studied this man with interest. Some women might regard him as rather striking, although it was Vincent's opinion that most ladies preferred manly men with a good healthy colour to their cheeks and neatly trimmed hair, rather than thin-faced creatures who looked like untidy eighteenth-century poets. He watched for a moment because any information about Dr Ingram's team might come in useful, and it was only when the American took the man's arm to guide him through the main door of the house that Vincent realized he was blind. Or was he? Yes, the boy was keeping hold of his arm, guiding him through into the main hall. Vincent thought vaguely that it was unexpected that Dr Ingram should have a blind man involved in his work.

He waited until they had all gone upstairs to the little flat, and until he heard the door close, then he locked up the office, and went along to his own house and got out his car.

He always liked the drive to Calvary even though the lane was overgrown and rutted. You would have thought the council would have done something about it years ago but they had not. He parked three quarters of the way up the narrow track, tucking his car into the semi-concealment of some trees and walked the rest of the way, keeping a sharp eye out. It was a lonely spot but you sometimes got people exercising their dogs out here or pretending to take vigorous exercise, or engaging in back-seat bonking which Vincent always found sordid, especially when the collapsed-balloon consequences were left to litter the ground. It was a pity the council did not do something about that, as well.

For years no one had ever gone to Calvary, not even a tramp looking for a night's shelter. Then one Halloween a group of teenagers had broken in and held a drunken seance in the condemned cell, and there had been a great outcry when it was discovered. After that the prison authorities had employed Huxley Small and the local surveyor to check the place regularly.

But Calvary was not as secure as old Small and the surveyor thought. There were three ways in and out and Vincent knew them all. There was the main entrance – the huge iron-studded gates you stepped through into a little inner courtyard with guard rooms on each side, and from there through the door into the prison itself. Then there was the door inside the burial yard which led down to the mortuary. The mortuary door did not have a lock, but was secured by two heavy-duty bolts on the inside, which were always firmly in place. Finally, there was a third door at the very back of the building, which opened onto the big stone-floored kitchens. Few people knew about this door but Vincent knew about it and it had been absurdly easy to make it his private door into the prison. He had simply waited for a holiday week and then driven out to Keswick which was always busily full of tourists at that time of year, and at a big anonymous DIY store he had bought a small but sturdy lock and key. Then he had waited for a rainy weekday when people were unlikely to be around, and had driven to Calvary, taking with him an old shooting-stick that had been at the back of his wardrobe – he thought it had belonged to one of mother's gentleman, probably the Southend Bachelor who had liked going to race meetings as a young man.

He had done a very good job on the door. It had taken a bit longer than he had thought to break off the existing lock, but the shooting stick was a good solid one and in the end it did the trick and Vincent was able to attach the new lock. He made a neat job of it – he was quite good with small carpentry tasks – and when he finished he was confident no one would realize what he had done. The surveyor, on his six-monthly inspection, would use the main door at the front. He presumably checked the fabric of the place, made sure all doors were secure, and left. If he noticed a newly fitted lock he would assume it to be part of the solicitor's caretaking work and was unlikely to realize that the bunch of keys labelled 'Calvary Gaol' no longer included a key that fitted the scullery door. Which meant, providing Vincent chose his times carefully, he could come and go inside Calvary as much as he liked.

He did like. Calvary drew him like a magnet – it had done so ever since he had first heard its name as a child. It was a castle, his dark enchanted realm and the people of the past walked there. The first time Vincent, greatly daring, walked there, he knew that as long as the past stayed here it was secret and safe, shut away from the prying eyes of the present. He saw himself as a guardian of that past, keeping it safely sealed away behind the massive walls.

When he first went into the execution suite, he saw at once that the heavy oak door – the door that separated the condemned cell and the execution chamber from the rest of the prison – had its own lock. How useful might it be to have a key to this door? To the door of the execution chamber itself? Think ahead, Vincent, said Mother's voice in his mind.

And again, it was absurdly easy to take the big old keys that no one had ever thought it worth removing from the thick oak door and from the door of the execution chamber, and drive over to Lancaster (Vincent was not going to risk the same DIY store twice!), to get duplicates cut. An elderly aunt's house, Vincent said, handing them over. She was always losing keys and they – the family – were making sure they all had extra sets. He conveyed the impression of a slightly scatty old lady, living in a big house with old-fashioned locks, and of himself as an affectionate, slightly exasperated nephew, collaborating with other family members. Both images were light years away from Calvary Gaol.

But this afternoon he had only brought the scullery key, although he did not think he would even need that. He went around the outer walls and opened the door into the burial yard. The latch crackled as he pushed it, like dead finger-bones in a coffin, the flesh eaten away by burning lime . . .

Lime. *Lime.*

The burial yard was dank and sunless, and Calvary's darkness seemed to lie heavily over it so that for a moment it was difficult to breathe. Was this how it had felt for all those men and the few women who had died here? This choking constriction? It would have been a very bad thing to die here.

Yes, it was, it was . . . To die here was a very bad thing, Vincent.

On his right were the burial plots of all the murderers

executed here: the men who had strangled or shot their wives; the wives who had poisoned or stabbed their husbands; greedy nephews or nieces who had wanted rich aunts or godfathers out of the way so that they could inherit . . . The traitor Nicholas O'Kane was here. Vincent glanced across at O'Kane's grave. There was a story that he had gone to his death reciting poetry, which Vincent thought affected, but people had remembered him for quite a long time. 'Nick O'Kane,' they said in the bitter hating way they were later to say, 'Adolf Hitler', or 'Saddam Hussain'. Often, they added, with contempt, 'O'Kane was the man who sold England's secrets to the Kaiser and who quoted Tom Kettle's poetry on the gallows.'

But O'Kane had been almost forgotten by now and the poem he had clung to in the last moments of his life had also been forgotten, which just went to show that affectation and poetry availed you absolutely nothing in the end.

In one corner of the burial yard was a second court-yard, almost hidden from view by a jutting piece of wall, but opening into another small courtyard. Set against the main prison wall was a jumble of what, in a house, would be regarded as outbuildings: little more than lean-to structures with rather flimsy doors. Two were open and clearly empty, but two were padlocked. One of the padlocked doors had a sheet of corrugated iron across it and Vincent regarded this with a thump of anticipation. The lime store.

This was a door that would have been kept firmly locked all down Calvary's history, and it looked as if it was still locked today.

It was important not to get too carried away because there were two very negative possibilities here. The first was that there would not be any limestone left. The second was that even if there were, after so many years it would have lost its effective properties. Vincent was not very well up on chemical matters but he knew that in Calvary's hanging days, lime had been burnt in a massive kiln a few miles outside Thornbeck village, after which the rocks had been brought to the burial yard and stored. When there was a hanging, the warders shovelled the lime into metal buckets and then added water after which they simply tipped the steaming, smoking, corrosive lime straight into the grave. Vincent had an idea that in later years they had not always bothered with the slaking but had just poured the dry lime in. But people did not have much use for lime these days, although Vincent thought farmers still used slaked lime putty as a wash for out-buildings.

The door had a bolt across it, held in place by a small padlock, and Vincent inspected this carefully. It was very rusty: it looked as if it could be snapped off easily.

As far as possible, he had come prepared to tackle the lime store – he had certainly come prepared to make a small experiment on it – but he was not going to take any risks. He wound a thick scarf around his neck, and put on a rainhat of the oilskin sou'wester kind used by fishermen, and dark glasses. He was wearing gloves which came well over his wrists, and he had again brought the Southend Bachelor's very useful shooting stick. Keeping to one side of the lime store, he reached this across to the padlock. A sharp blow knocked it to the ground, the door gave a little sighing groan, and an inch of blackness showed around the rim where it had sprung slightly open. As easy as that.

Still standing at arm's length, he levered the end of the shooting-stick into the gap and coaxed the door open, taking his time so that there would not be any sudden gusting out of anything noxious. The hinges creaked, but eventually Vincent had pushed the door all the way back to the wall.

A thin wisp of something like pale smoke curled up from inside the open stores and he instinctively stepped back. A little gust of wind blew in and there was a faint pallid flurry from within. Keeping his face well covered, Vincent looked inside. It was quite a small place: not much bigger than the coalhouses that used to be attached to quite ordinary houses. The lime blocks were irregularly shaped lumps of rock of various sizes, but here and there were mounds of chalky powder where some of it had crumbled.

The lime was still here, it was *still here*. But how harmful might it be? After so many years the chances were that it had completely dried out. It might sting the skin a bit if someone were shut in here for any length of time, but it would not actually kill. And in any case, it was not necessary for Georgina to die. Or was it? Mightn't that be the safest thing?

Could the lime still be slaked? Made to fizz up into a hissing corrosive mass? Vincent was prepared to make a small and careful experiment, but if it succeeded, how would he then manage things out here? How could he carry enough water all the way out here, and how would he activate the lime without getting burned? *How?* It was unlikely that the water supply was still connected to

Calvary, although he could try the taps in the stone sink in the mortuary.

He would not need to try any taps! There, just a few feet away, was an old rain-water butt, three quarters full! Vincent stared at it, his mind working. Water. Water all ready to hand. There was a tap near the bottom – it looked very corroded, but it might still turn. He studied the courtyard afresh, seeing with a tiny thump of excitement that the surface of the courtyard was not entirely level: it dipped slightly near the row of outbuildings. Was there a gap at the bottom of the lime store's door? Yes. After heavy rain, surely the water butt would overflow and flood beneath the door? Ah, no, there was a small drain about a foot away; that would take the overflow. But what if that drain were to be blocked or covered? An ordinary plastic bag, a supermarket carrier held down by a stone, would do it.

Stepping cautiously inside the store, avoiding the powdery heaps which might cloud upwards into his face, he took from his pocket the small metal box he had brought. It had belonged to the Bournemouth Major who had used it to store the cigars he was not supposed to smoke. The box was barely six inches square, but it was big enough to hold a small piece of rock on which to experiment in the privacy of Vincent's garden shed. In his other pocket were tongs from his kitchen, and, using these, he picked up two chippings and dropped them in the box. Then he closed the lid tightly and wrapped the whole thing in several folds of a garden refuse bag.

As he walked back down the slope, not troubling to be furtive, simply being a local man out for an innocent walk, the thump of excitement was still with him because all the details of his plan were coming together beautifully. A corroded tap that had finally broken away from its moorings and caused an old courtyard to flood . . . a drain that had not dealt with the flood because a plastic carrier bag had blown into the courtyard and stuck across the grid . . . and as a result, water trickling across the old stones and seeping under the door of the lime store . . . all he needed to do now was make sure the lime could still be activated.

CHAPTER TWENTY-THREE

Georgina had recklessly bought Camembert and Brie and some sinfully rich pâté, together with ruinously expensive avocados and olives for the salad. She had set it all out on the little gateleg table by the window with the breathtaking sweep of Torven beyond. There would not be room at the table for everyone, but they could have their lunch buffet-style, which would be easier anyway.

She had expected to feel slightly disconcerted by the presence of Chad Ingram and the other three in the tiny Caradoc House flat, because although she was perfectly used to talking to people about how they could furnish their houses or offices or showrooms, she was not at all used to talking about disinterred fragments of her family's past. She was certainly not used to television presenters or journalists who had been spectacularly blinded in the Middle East. David would have said, 'Oh dear, George, this isn't your kind of thing at *all*, is it?' and Georgina would instantly have thought that David was quite right, concluded she was going to make a fool of herself, and abandoned the whole project.

But so far nobody had said anything disagreeable or confidence-shrivelling: on the contrary, they were all completely friendly and seemed genuinely interested.

She saw what Drusilla meant about Jude not making any concessions. He treated the blindness as an inconvenience, only occasionally displaying a flash of anger if he had to be helped to do anything. Georgina had gone downstairs to unlock the street door to let them in, relieved Vincent did not seem to be around to muscle in on the party, and the eager young Phin Farrell had guided Jude up the narrow staircase in a very understated way. When they sat down to eat, Georgina simply put Jude's hand on one of the chairs by the table and left him to sit down. It ought to have been a completely detached manoeuvre but, incredibly, she felt a brief prickle of electricity spark between them. This was disconcerting and startling, and she had no idea if he had felt it as well.

She said, 'The food's on the table and the papers are on the floor in the middle of the room. It's mostly articles about the Caradoc Society – psychic research journals from when the Caradoc Society came into being as far as I can see. Walter took over as Calvary's doctor from a Dr McNulty—'

'McNulty was the Caradoc Society's first chairman, I think,' said Chad. He was eyeing the papers with a light in his eyes.

'Yes, he was,' said Georgina.

'Your great-grandfather probably inherited a lot of material from him. It's how things often happen. Really useful bits of history get stuffed into cupboards for decades. Are any of the articles illustrated at all?' He sat on the floor and immediately began to sort through the nearest pile. Phin sat opposite to him, cross-legged, a notebook open on his knee, the quiff of hair tumbling forward.

'There are one or two photos of McNulty,' said Georgina. 'I've only just identified him, actually. I'd have to say he looks very earnest and humourless, although that might just be the photographic techniques of the day. Dr Ingram—'

'Chad.'

'Chad, I told Drusilla to copy anything that might be useful.'

'We'll probably want to copy quite a lot of it,' said Chad, in an absorbed voice.

'And then make use of it,' said Jude.

'The thing I thought you'd want to see above the rest,' said Georgina, scooping up portions of salad and pâté, and handing the plates round, 'is something my great-grandfather seems to have called an Execution Book. It's a record of everyone who was executed while he was there. Dates, names, times, and so on. Height and weight. Amazingly, there are photographs for most of them.'

'Mug shots,' said Drusilla.

'I read up on that,' said Phin. 'You had an Act of Parliament passed – uh, I think it was about 1870 – that ordered the gaols to keep registers of all the inmates. Some of the prison governors saw that as meaning photographs as well, although I guess that varied a good deal. By Walter's time it would have been standard procedure.'

'The book's a bit battered,' said Georgina, producing

it. She glanced uncertainly at Jude, and then said, 'And the binding's come loose all down the spine. It's got a sort of suede leather cover, and the photographs are just pasted onto thickish paper inside, with names and dates handwritten underneath, but it's perfectly legible.'

'I don't know about legible, it looks impossibly grisly.'

'Other people have ancestors who leave jewellery or photographs or medals,' said Georgina. 'My great-grandfather left me a record of all the hanged murderers he attended. But the thing is that there's a name in the Execution Book that jumped straight up off the page – partly because of *Talismans of the Mind*,' said Georgina, and looked at Chad. 'I'm hugely enjoying reading it, by the way. You wrote quite a lot about a couple who held fake seances during the First World War.'

'Bartlam and Violette Partridge,' said Chad, smiling.

'Yes. But did you know that one of them ended up in Calvary Gaol?'

'Good God, no, I didn't. Which one?'

'Bartlam,' said Drusilla at once. 'I knew he'd come to a bad end, the old goat.'

'No,' said Georgina, 'it wasn't Bartlam. It was his wife, Violette. She was hanged in Calvary on the first day of 1940.'

'As entries go, it isn't very informative,' said Georgina, half apologetically as they pounced on the book and pored over it. She saw that Drusilla and Chad both did exactly what she had been doing herself: they touched the surface of the paper lightly as if to draw out the story inside the faded writing and the brittle paper.

'It's primary source stuff,' said Chad. 'What a find!'

'Violette was executed under her real name, which was apparently Violet Parsons,' said Georgina. 'But you can see where Walter wrote in "also known as Violette Partridge", and that's what I recognized when I was flipping through.'

Chad studied the photograph intently. 'It's an extra-ordinary feeling to see her,' he said. 'She's not quite as I visualized. But she probably looked a lot different when she was younger and cavorting around at all those seances.' For Jude's benefit, he said, 'She's plump-faced, with piebald greying hair, and probably in her early fifties. My God, I wish I'd known about this when I was writing *Talismans*. What did she do that finally brought her to the condemned cell, I wonder? I'll have to find out.'

'He's already drafting out another book on the strength of this, Georgina, so make sure you get due acknowledgement, never mind a hefty share of the royalties.'

'You don't need to pay any attention to Jude, Georgina,' said Chad, looking up. 'He makes a career out of being rude to people.'

'Yes, but I'm not going to be rude to Georgina,' said Jude promptly. 'Because she's given us a delicious lunch and she has a beautiful voice.' And then, before Georgina could think how to respond to this, or even whether she ought to respond to it, he said, 'Did somebody say I had some wine somewhere? Oh, thanks Phin.' He located his wine glass which Georgina had put on a side table by his chair.

'Is Neville Fremlin in here?' said Drusilla suddenly.

'He is.' Georgina reached over to turn the pages back.

'Oh yes. Neville Fremlin,' said Drusilla. 'Nine a.m. on 17 October 1938.'

'He's a bit older than I imagined,' said Phin, reading over Drusilla's shoulder. 'Born in 1889, it says. Hanged in 1938. So he was forty-nine when that was taken.'

'In his prime,' murmured Chad.

'Whatever he was in, I don't mind admitting that if he'd said to me, "Come into my chemist's laboratory, my dear," I'd have gone like a shot,' said Drusilla, still staring at the photograph. 'He's very attractive.'

'You get weirder by the hour.'

'It's the company I keep.'

Phin bent over the book again, looking absurdly young. 'It shouldn't be difficult to find out what Violette's crime was,' he said. 'There'll be court records and stuff, won't there?'

'I'll bet she bumped off Bartlam,' said Drusilla. 'And serve him right, nasty old lecher. He'd be the kind who stands too close to you on the Tube.'

'A real ass-pincher. Excuse me, Georgina.'

'There's an added grisliness about the date of Violette's execution, isn't there?' said Georgina. 'Having to die on the first day of a new year and a new decade.'

'I lost her altogether after 1920 or so,' said Chad. 'There simply weren't any threads to pick up – no death certificate or marriage certificate, although that probably means Partridge wasn't their real name. It's remarkable, isn't it, how the different name changes the entire image? You can imagine a Violet Parsons being a very ordinary, rather colourless lady.'

'Good works, and never married,' said Jude at once. 'Whereas Violette Partridge fits beautifully with seances and table-turning. Plump as to build and gushing as to manner.'

'And don't forget the tea-gowns and the scent,' said Chad. 'If you knew the trouble I went to to track down shop records for that part of London – Oh, yes, please, Georgina, I'd love coffee. No, I couldn't eat another crumb.'

'If,' said Jude getting out of his chair, 'you would like to take me by the hand and lead me to the sink, Georgina, I'll help with the washing-up and the coffee while they delve into the past.'

'Yes, all right,' said Georgina, slightly startled.

'I don't promise not to break anything, though,' he said.

He did not, in the event, break anything at all. He simply washed the cutlery and crockery Georgina put in the sink, located the draining board, and stacked everything on it. He did this offhandedly, telling her a bit more about the night inside Calvary as he did so. Georgina, listening and enjoying the story, laughing at the concept of Tommy the Turnkey, could not help wondering how hard won this unfussed smoothness had been.

It was when they were seated around the little coffee table, with papers strewn over the floor and Phin enthusiastically making reams of notes and explaining how he would go about tracking down Violette and her trial, that Jude suddenly said, 'Professor, I've got a suggestion.'

'Yes?' Chad was still studying the Execution Book.

'It occurred to me while I was talking to Georgina over the washing-up,' said Jude. 'I'd like to spend a second night in Calvary. Only this time I'd like to be actually down in the gallows pit.'

There was an abrupt silence, then Drusilla said, 'That's the maddest idea I've ever heard.'

'Is it?' said Chad. He had put the book down and was staring at Jude. 'I'm not so sure. What's your reason, Jude?'

'Last night,' said Jude, 'I was observing without knowing anything. If I went in there again I'd be observing with knowledge. It'd be very interesting to see if the reactions are at all similar.'

'Difficult to find fault with that, boss,' murmured Drusilla.

'Can we keep the keys for any longer, though?' asked Phin anxiously.

'I'd have to check with the solicitor, but I don't see why not. Although I'd better make sure that wretched trapdoor wasn't damaged,' said Chad. 'Jude, you do realize that if it is, you've probably used up the whole of our professional indemnity?'

'You're so mercenary,' complained Jude. 'Now me, I have a soul above money and property. But if I must descend to the mundane, I'd have to say it didn't feel as if the trapdoor was damaged.'

'It didn't look damaged when we collected you,' said Phin hopefully.

'No, but we didn't make a very close examination,' said Chad, 'and we must.'

'If,' said Jude, 'I do make a second foray, I'd like to have someone with me this time. But it needs to be someone completely objective.'

'Why?'

'To observe the observer. So if I think I'm hearing Tommy the Turnkey yomping up and down the corridors, there'd be someone there who could either confirm it, or say I've flipped and am hearing things.' He paused, clearly listening for reactions, and when no one spoke, said, 'Chad, you obviously can't do it because you're supposed to be masterminding everything. So how about the rest of you? Any takers?'

To Georgina's utter horror, she heard herself saying, 'If you feel like drafting me in as a temporary part of the team I'd do it.'

For what felt like several minutes nobody said anything, but Jude's head turned towards her and Georgina had the impression she had disconcerted him. 'Would you really? Do you mean it?'

'Yes,' said Georgina, although she had no idea if this was true.

'Well,' said Jude lightly, 'at least I'm still able to persuade a lady to spend the night with me.' And before Georgina could think how to answer this, he went on, 'What about it, Professor?'

Chad said slowly, 'I can't see anything against it in principle. We'd better talk about it a bit more, but Georgina, if we do go for it, you'd be perfectly safe. At worst you'd have an uncomfortable few hours – the worst part of that would be Jude's undiluted company. There's also the possibility you might stop him from smashing up any more of the place.'

'We could do it tonight,' said Jude, ignoring this. 'We can leave about ten as we did last night – Georgina, would that be all right?'

'Fine.' I'm clearly mad, thought Georgina. I've just offered to spend the night in that spooky old prison with a man I've only just met, who's blind. But Calvary was

Walter's place. And something happened to him while he was there – something that caused him to leave his money to the Caradoc Society, and I want to find out as much as I can about why he did that.

'Have an early dinner with me at the King's Head beforehand,' Jude was saying to her. 'Seven o'clock? We can plan the campaign and apportion the ghosts. Because that's what this is, really: a massive ghost hunt. You're looking for Walter, Chad is probably looking for Violette, Drusilla's looking for Neville Fremlin. And so on.'

'Yes, all right,' said Georgina, and caught herself being glad that when she was packing in London, at the last minute she had put one reasonably decent outfit into her case – a jade-green silk skirt and a black silky sweater. She had brought the jade necklace that went with it as well. Then she remembered that Jude would not see any of this which was annoying because the outfit was one that always made her feel good. Then she thought she would wear it anyway. She could take jeans, a sweater, jacket and trainers to the King's Head with her; Drusilla would not mind if she changed in her bedroom before they set off for Calvary.

After they had all left, it occurred to her that the small working lunch she had originally intended seemed to have progressed from being a casual snack, to a slightly more distinguished party which, in its turn, had ended in creating an offbeat ghost hunt in Calvary Gaol.

As Georgina tidied Walter's papers back into the box, she thought that at times life took some rather unexpected turns.

July 1939

'The Fremlin case has taken a rather unexpected turn,' said Edgar Higneth coming into Walter's surgery just after lunch. 'I've just been told that the police have found Elizabeth Molland.'

Walter had been rather abstractedly writing up his notes on that morning's patients and wondering what he was going to do about offering his services for the war that was undoubtedly coming. People were not saying, as they had said in the last war, that it would all be over by Christmas; no one thought Hitler could be defeated in a few weeks. This was going to be a long haul once it got going, said everyone, although please God it would not be a four-year haul this time.

Walter had been thinking about this, and about when and how he would join the medical corps, and Higneth's entry into his room had startled him, his words had startled him even more.

'Elizabeth Molland? You mean they've found her body?'

'I don't mean that at all,' said Higneth drily. 'The lady is still very much alive. She was living not far out of Knaresborough – a few miles west of Keighley in fact – and she was seen wearing a piece of jewellery that had belonged to one of Neville Fremlin's victims – a local girl. That was what tripped her up. Odd how they do that, murderers, isn't it? They take the most painstaking care to conceal their crimes, and then overlook some small detail that betrays them.'

'Someone recognized the jewellery?' asked Walter.

'Yes. A friend of the dead girl was in a teashop and

Molland was there as well. Taking afternoon tea. The friend recognized the locket Molland was wearing – apparently it had been a family heirloom and quite distinctive. She told the parents of the dead girl, and they kept watch on the teashop for the next few days, hoping Molland would go back there. She did go back, and, very sensibly, the parents didn't approach her, but followed her at a distance to find out where she lived. Then they alerted the police.'

'And?' said Walter.

'At that stage they had no idea of Molland's identity,' said Higneth. 'They just knew that this was a girl who was wearing their dead daughter's jewellery, and they thought it was suspicious.'

'She might have bought it quite innocently from a jeweller's shop,' said Walter. 'Fremlin presumably sold his victims' things.'

'Oh yes, and that was why they treated it so cautiously for a while. But then the police realized who it was they were watching, and that Elizabeth Molland, far from being dead at Neville Fremlin's hands, was living in furnished rooms – quite smart and expensive furnished rooms from the sound of it. Normally they would probably have just gone along and tried to persuade her to return to her family, but—'

'But the locket made them suspicious,' said Walter.

'Exactly. It was all too much of a coincidence. But at that point there was nothing definite they could fasten on, so they kept watch for a few more days, to see what she did. And sure enough, on the afternoon of the fourth day she took an omnibus out to Becks Forest – but this time the east side, rather than the north side where

311

Fremlin had buried the victims. She led them straight to the cache of jewellery from the victims.'

'The other burial ground,' said Walter, half to himself. 'So there really was one.'

'Yes. There's a bit of a lake there and there was an old boathouse. Very ramshackle – no one had bothered about it for years. The jewellery was under the floorboards.'

'She must have known about the murders,' said Walter, remembering the wide-eyed stare of the girl in the silver-framed photograph.

'She more than knew about them,' said Higneth. 'They've just charged her with being an accomplice to them and with a murder on her own account in Lancaster in May. They're still preparing the evidence, but it's likely the trial will come on early in September.'

'But she's only a child,' said Walter. 'Nineteen or twenty.'

'Walter, some of history's most lethal killers have been under twenty-one. If Molland's found guilty we'll probably see her here.'

'She'll hang?'

'Don't sound so appalled. Yes, she'll hang unless she can bat her eyelashes at the jury and the judge to let her off,' said Higneth caustically and Walter thought, It's all very well for you to sound critical; you didn't see her photograph. 'I'm not making any predictions about that, however,' said Higneth. 'I shan't like it one bit if she does get the death sentence. I've never had to oversee the hanging of a woman.'

CHAPTER TWENTY-FOUR

September 1939

If it had not been for the outbreak of war, the trial of Elizabeth Molland would probably have attracted much more attention than it actually did. Walter, half guiltily driving to the courthouse at Lancaster, thought the newspapers would normally have had a field day with such a young and good-looking girl who was on trial for murder. It was an odd quirk of fate that because Hitler had marched into Poland and Britain was not going to let him get away with it, Elizabeth Molland looked like missing out on the circus normally surrounding a cause célèbre.

He had no idea why he had come to watch the winding up of the trial, unless it was simply that he was curious to see the girl whom everyone had thought of as another of Neville Fremlin's victims, but who had apparently been more of a fellow murderer. Walter recognized Mr and Mrs Molland in the public gallery; when they saw him Mr Molland made a brief nod of acknowledgement. Returning the nod, Walter saw anguish in the man's eyes. Was it worse to discover your beloved daughter was a killer instead of the poor butchered corpse you had thought? Mrs Molland was wearing a coat with a high collar which she had turned up to hide most of her face. They both looked modestly affluent but unremarkable and Walter hoped they would not be recognized and subjected to any kind of attack. It occurred to him that the families of the real victims might be here. He looked round the gallery, but although there were a number of people who had the right air of understated wealth, none of the faces held the same pain as that of the Mollands. Walter was sickened by the eagerness in most of the faces, then he thought, But I'm here as well. Am I any different?

When Elizabeth Molland was brought up from the cells and put into the dock Walter forgot about victims and killers, because he could not believe – he simply could *not* believe – that this fair-haired, velvet-eyed waif was a murderess.

It seemed as if he really had chosen the final day of the trial; the defence had finished putting forward the case for the prisoner's acquittal, and the judge was pulling all the separate threads of evidence and statements together, making of them a neat, understandable bundle to hand to the jury. Walter listened carefully to this summary of the facts: how the friend of one of Fremlin's victims had seen Molland in the teashop and how the police, alerted and moderately suspicious, had followed her, as Edgar Higneth had already said. They had kept watch and seen her take the jewellery from the hiding place in the old boathouse on the east side of Becks Forest – Neville Fremlin's hiding place which had never been found and he had never disclosed.

'It is not in question,' said the judge, speaking directly to the jury, his severe old eyes sharp and bright, 'that Neville Fremlin, who was justly executed almost a year ago, killed five females. Two were quite young girls, but two were older, rather lonely women. They were from all walks of life, but they had one thing in common and that was their wealth.'

Walter thought, But none of this is evidence of Elizabeth's guilt. She knew where the cache of jewellery was, but that doesn't make her a killer. There must be more than this.

And, of course, there was; a great deal more.

The police, it seemed, had not immediately arrested Miss Molland, but had continued to observe her from a discreet distance. For the first time Walter heard that Elizabeth had not been alone in the teashop on that afternoon; she had been with another, much older, lady.

'An unmarried lady in her sixties,' said the judge. It was noticeable that although he had his notes before him, he hardly referred to them. Only twice did Walter see the thin well-shaped hand turn a page, and then it seemed to be to check a date or a place.

'She was a lady recently returned to this country because of the worsening situation in Austria where she had been living,' said the judge. 'And she was a lady who must have thought herself fortunate to have got back to the safety of her home country after the turbulence of Europe. It was her tragedy that she fell into the malevolent clutches of the prisoner.'

Walter saw a little stir of unease go through the jury at these last words. There were eight men and four women. The women don't like her, he thought. But the men aren't sure. The judge is sure, though. He's trying to guide them to a verdict of guilty. He glanced along the benches and saw Mrs Molland pressing a handkerchief to her lips. Pity for her twisted through him, and he remembered how she had wanted to be able to mourn properly; to put a memorial tablet in the local church for their lovely, lost girl.

'Over the next week,' said the judge, 'it became apparent that the prisoner had befriended this lady. She visited her home on a number of occasions; she accompanied her to concerts and resorts – the jury will recall that this was during the month of May. The weather was hot and most people were relaxed after Mr Chamberlain's return from Munich the previous autumn. There was no need to feel nervous of travelling – in this country at least – and the prisoner and her prey did travel. We can reasonably assume that the lady was rather flattered at the attentions of such a pretty, well-mannered girl.

'And then came the final day, when the police followed them here to Lancaster,' said the judge. 'A day's outing for shopping was how it seemed: an entirely ordinary thing for two ladies. Molland was attentive, carrying parcels, helping her companion across busy streets. The streets were very busy indeed,' he said, 'there were omnibuses and trams and a great many cars. But despite the heavy traffic, the police officers had a very clear view of what happened. They saw Elizabeth Molland deliberately and calculatedly push her unsuspecting companion under a tram.'

The court and the jury already knew this, but it was like a blow across the eyes to Walter. He stared at Elizabeth, totally unable to imagine the soft white little hands giving that spiteful push, or to visualize the doe-like eyes hard and shrewd.

'Having listened to the evidence of the police officers in question,' said the judge, 'and also to the separate accounts given by three bystanders, I think, members of the jury, that you will already have accepted the evidence that Molland did indeed send this unfortunate lady to her death. As to the benefits Molland might have expected to get from that death – well, they are a little less clear. We cannot know what her intentions might have been; she has pleaded not guilty to the charges and defence counsel has not called her to give evidence. But we have the testimony that the victim possessed some very valuable jewellery: jewellery which it would have been fairly easy to sell.' He paused as if choosing his next words carefully, and then said, 'You should perhaps bear in mind that Neville Fremlin's victims were all apparently killed for their money. In three cases large sums had actually passed into Fremlin's bank account, and in another case some share certificates had been transferred. As well as that, jewellery is known to have been sold. So you will see the similarity. Elizabeth Molland does not have a bank account of her own, but jewellery – gold and precious stones – are universal currency.'

He's saying she learned from Fremlin, thought Walter. He's saying she learned about killing for money and turning jewellery into cash. But how well did she know Fremlin? He remembered her parents telling him Elizabeth used to go into the shop in Knaresborough, but surely it had only been as an occasional customer? He looked across at them again, remembering that curious flicker of unease he had picked up when he had asked them about her childhood. There's something there, thought Walter. Something they want kept secret. Could it be something to do with her knowing Fremlin?

The judge was saying, 'You will also want to keep in mind, members of the jury, the testimony we have heard from certain hotel staff where the couple stayed once or twice, or lunched. From those testimonies, it's clear that Molland and Fremlin knew one another very well indeed. It saddens me greatly to say this, and it must cause the parents deep grief to hear it, but there seems little doubt that these two had an intimate and immoral relationship.'

An intimate and immoral relationship. Walter stared at the smooth features of the girl in the dock. She looked as if the only thing she had ever taken to bed with her was a doll or a teddy bear. Could she really have had what the judge called an immoral relationship with the urbane man whom Walter had seen die a year ago? What was the age difference between them? Twenty-five years? Thirty?

'Molland's counsel,' said the judge, 'has very eloquently painted for us the picture of an impressionable young girl in thrall to an attractive older man – so completely under his spell that she came to believe killing people for money was acceptable. That is certainly one way of viewing this relationship and of viewing Elizabeth Molland's behaviour, and you must take it into account. But I will remind you that this is a girl from a loving and happy home. She has been properly brought up by

respectable parents who taught her the difference between right and wrong. She knew – as we all know, I
hope, members of the jury – that to live with a man in
a marital relationship without the blessing of the church,
is very wrong indeed.'

Walter thought one or two of the jury looked a bit
sheepish at this. A thin-faced acidulated spinster seated
at the end of the jury bench compressed her lips, and
made a note on a small pad.

'And she knew,' said the judge, 'that murder is the
greatest and most evil sin that can be committed. And
now the court will rise, and the jury will retire and
consider its verdict.'

Walter knew he should speak to the Mollands. At the
very least he should exchange a word of friendship with
them.

He could not do it. He could only see the fragile
beautiful face of the girl in the dock, and the sudden
blinding smile of Neville Fremlin, who had possessed
such charisma and subtle magnetism. He heard again
Fremlin's words in the condemned cell; Fremlin had
talked about good wine and first nights in London
theatres, and whether he might walk to the gallows
with a book of Byron's poetry. He had not mentioned
any relationships with females, other than a single
oblique reference to the fact that supper after the theatre
had always been more enjoyable in the company of
a friend.

An intimate and immoral relationship. Which way
round had it been? A dazzled young girl, bewitched,
mesmerized or bullied, Eliza Doolittle-style or Svengali-

style? Or an ageing man, boosting his ego and recapturing his youth by taking a mistress thirty years his junior? Never that, thought Walter angrily, whatever else Neville Fremlin was, he was no ageing roué with a pathetic gratitude for a young girl's flattery. But let's not forget that these two killed – not out of defence of a cause or a loved one, or out of pity – they killed out of simple greed.

He thought he would not return to the court for the jury's verdict, but found himself remaining in the precincts of the court until late that afternoon. It was ridiculous; the jury would not return their verdict today.

But they did return it that afternoon, and Walter went back to hear it. He saw the jury return, saw Elizabeth Molland stare at them with pleading in her eyes and thought they could not possibly pronounce her guilty. And even if they did – even if the evidence had been overwhelmingly against her during this past two weeks – then the judge would give her the lightest of light sentences.

The jury did pronounce her guilty. It was, said the foreman solemnly, the verdict of them all. A unanimous verdict.

The judge did not give her a light sentence. He reached out his thin old scholar's hand and placed the square of black silk on his head, and spoke the dreadful words.

'Elizabeth Molland, you have been found guilty by this court of wilful murder, and that is a verdict with which I entirely agree. I would earnestly urge you to seek for your soul the only refuge left for you, in the mercy of God through the atonement of our Lord, Jesus Christ. It only remains for me to pass upon you the sentence of the law, which is that you be taken from here to the place from whence you came and from there to a place of execution, there to be hanged by the neck until you are dead, and your body to be afterwards buried within the precincts of the gaol. And may the Lord have mercy upon your soul.'

Behind him, Walter was aware of Mrs Molland crying out, 'Oh, no. Oh, no,' then fainting and being carried out.

'She may well get a reprieve,' said Edgar Higneth, listening to Walter's account of the trial and the sentence the following morning. 'Or they may commute the death penalty.'

'To a life sentence? I should think that would kill her,' said Walter.

'Better than being hanged, though.'

'I wonder if she'd think so.'

Higneth looked at him sharply. 'Walter, I hope you aren't in any danger of losing your detachment over this.'

'No, I'm not,' said Walter, 'but I think she'll be a difficult prisoner.'

'Hysterics and pleas for freedom, you think? Ah well, that's probably to be expected.'

'I didn't mean that, exactly' said Walter. 'I think she'll be more subtle.' Doe-eyed sorrow, that appealing fragility. What had Mrs Molland said? 'She'd wrap her dad round her little finger.' And Molland, proud and indulgent, had said it was a sad man who could not let his daughter coax him. But Elizabeth had not been able to coax the judge or jury.

'But you think she'll cause us problems?' Higneth was saying, and Walter dragged his mind back to his surroundings.

'Yes, I do.' Only they won't be quite the problems you'll be expecting, he thought and wondered if Elizabeth would wrap Edgar Higneth, this good, rather stolid man, around her little finger. Then he remembered she would only have three weeks to do so.

'If you really do think that,' said Higneth, sounding harried, 'I'd better draft in extra warders for the death watch. We're in a thin situation at the moment, with half the men going off to war. You know we've lost four more of the warders to the army?'

'Yes.' Walter did not say that Calvary might shortly lose its doctor as well.

'Still, I'll see if there are any females in Thornbeck who might come up for the evening watches. Sir Lewis quite often employed female warders here, but I've always been hesitant, as you know. I have taken on one man, though; someone from Thornbeck village. He's just too old to be called up – about forty I think – but he was a warder here some years ago, so he'll know the ropes. I think he's a bit of a fly one though, and I don't know that I entirely trust him, but needs must. I'd be glad if you'd keep a discreet eye on him, Walter.'

'Yes, of course. What's his name?'

'Saul Ketch,' said Higneth.

CHAPTER TWENTY-FIVE

Walter had been wrong when he said Elizabeth Molland would be a difficult prisoner. She was not difficult at all. She was quiet and well behaved, and submitted to the indignities of her captivity with a docility that he found heart-breaking.

On the first morning he explained to her there must be a particular examination to establish that she was not expecting a child. He thought this a very unlikely circumstance, but there had been occasional cases of condemned women postponing the hangman by getting impregnated by a warder or another prisoner, or even by a prison chaplain, and the rules were clear. Elizabeth had been in prison for the last two months but Walter intended to follow the rules to the letter.

He had asked the new, temporary female warder to attend the examination, in order to satisfy medical etiquette. He had met the woman briefly. She was in her mid-forties, and had seemed agreeable, willing to please and grateful for the work. She wore a wedding ring; Walter thought she might be a widow.

Elizabeth Molland had not, at first, seemed to understand about the pregnancy examination. She stared at him and said that of course she was not expecting a child, how could he think such a thing? She was unmarried. An unmarried girl.

'Nevertheless,' said Walter, indicating the examination couch and screens and leaving her to undress.

While she was doing so the wardress tapped at the door and came quietly in. Walter nodded to her to wait by the door, and called to Elizabeth to let him know when she was ready. He was feeling awkward and slightly nervous; he had not, in fact, had to make a pelvic examination since his stint at the big teaching hospital where he had spent six months after qualifying before coming to Calvary. When Elizabeth timidly called out that she was ready, he had to beat down a wish to be a hundred miles away, but he stepped behind the screens, and reached for the jar of lubricant he had put ready. She was lying on the bed, clutching the thin robe around her, her eyes huge and frightened. Walter said, with what he hoped was a gentle firmness, 'This won't take a moment.'

But she still seemed not to understand, or to know what was expected of her for the examination, and Walter had to part her thighs himself. As he did so there was a disturbing feeling that an intimacy was being created between them, and he had to school himself to detachment. Even so, he found himself thinking that it was remarkable how you forgot the soft feel of the female body when you had only ministered to men for two years. There had been one or two girlfriends during his student years, but since he came to Calvary most of his energies had been directed into his work and he had scarcely given a thought to female companionship.

He was glad that his training held good when it came to it; he was able to be professional and impersonal about checking cervix and uterus, first with his hand and forefinger, then with the speculum. The uterus showed no sign whatsoever of being soft or in any way distended by pregnancy.

Nor would it. Elizabeth Molland was a virgin. There was absolutely no doubt about it. Walter had felt her wince of pain when he slid his forefinger inside her, and when he inserted the speculum she shrank in unmistakable discomfort and her hands came instinctively down to push him away. Extraordinary. He heard himself say, 'I've made you bleed a bit. I'm sorry about that. There's warm water in the bowl there and a clean towel.'

He washed his hands and stepped outside the screen. The warder was still standing by the door, and he thanked her for attending. 'When the prisoner's dressed you can take her back to her room, if you would.'

'Yes, sir. Is she all right?'

'Oh yes. It's just a routine examination.' He moved back to his desk, and had just reached for his pen to enter up his notes, when Elizabeth, once again dressed in the drab prison grey, came out from behind the screen. The wardress looked at her and let out a cry of such shock and deep pain that Walter looked up, startled. The woman was staring at Elizabeth Molland with distended eyes and a sheet-white face. One hand was clapped over her mouth in the classic gesture of horror or fear and she looked to be on the verge of fainting.

Walter said, 'What on earth's the matter? Are you ill?' He half reached for the alarm bell by his desk, because the possibility of an escape had always to be remembered. But there seemed to be nothing but puzzlement in Elizabeth's expression, and when she spoke she sounded concerned. 'Will she be all right?'

'Yes. But you'll have to go back to your cell at once,' said Walter, pressing the button that would summon a warder, and then taking the wardress's wrist to check her pulse, which was erratic. 'Put your head down for a moment,' he said to her. 'Right down – yes, that's good.' He filled a tumbler with water for her and when she straightened up, handed it to her. 'Sip it slowly.'

'It was only a moment of dizziness. I'll just sit for a minute if I could.'

'Of course.' Walter was grateful when a male warder appeared to take Elizabeth out. She went with him at once, but when she got to the door she turned back and looked at Walter for a moment. She's trying to create a link, thought Walter uncomfortably, she's trying to make something of the intimacy of the examination. No, I'm wrong; she's simply looking at the wardress and wondering what's wrong with her.

When the door closed, he turned back to the woman who was still sitting in the chair. Her hair had escaped slightly from the prison cap; Walter saw it was fair and soft. She must have been very attractive when she was young. Unusual, rather striking.

He said, 'Now, will you tell me what's wrong? Clearly you're unwell and clearly it was something to do with seeing Elizabeth Molland, wasn't it? But you knew she was here – you must have known about the case.'

'I did know about it, of course. I read an account of it in the newspapers and there was something on the wireless. But I hadn't seen her – there weren't any photographs in the papers. It's almost all war stuff nowadays, isn't it?'

'It is.' Walter waited.

After a moment, she said, 'So it was a shock.'

'Why?'

She paused, and then said, 'Anything I tell you – it's confidential, isn't it?'

'Of course.'

'Like – like when the Catholics confess to a priest?'

'Very much like that.' What on earth was coming?

'That girl – the one they call Elizabeth Molland—'

'Yes?'

'It's not who she really is.'

'Not? You mean—' Walter broke off, grappling with wild ideas of switched identities, of false names. But Elizabeth's parents had been in court, and he had seen the photograph in their house. 'It is Elizabeth,' he said, gently, 'that's beyond question.'

'I mean she isn't . . .' She sat up a little straighter, setting down the glass of water. 'Dr Kane, Elizabeth Molland is my daughter.'

And then, before Walter could say anything, she said, 'Her father is Lewis Caradoc.'

'I gave her up for adoption straight after the birth,' said Belinda – Walter had by this time established her name. He had asked one of the attendants to bring a tray of tea; when it arrived he drank his own cup as gratefully as his companion.

'It was 1917,' said Belinda, sipping the tea. 'The war was still going on, of course. I remember, we had the Irish traitor here. Nicholas O'Kane was his name.'

Something clicked into place in Walter's mind, and he stared at her, and thought: Yes, of *course*! You were the J. M. Barrie creature in the condemned cell. A slanting face and tip-tilted eyes – I recognize the eyes. You were the person I thought about all the way home from seeing my father just before he died; you're the one who took the edge off the pain for me.

It was impossible to say any of this, and in any case she would not have room in her mind at the moment for Walter's twenty-year-old memories. He said, 'You and Sir Lewis were lovers?'

For the first time the glint of a smile showed. 'Yes. Quite briefly. He was governor then.'

'These things happen,' said Walter. 'Did he know you were pregnant?'

'No. He would have helped me. If you know him, you'll know that.'

'Yes. Oh yes.'

'I just – went away, not telling him,' said Belinda. 'I went to live with distant relations just outside Thornbeck. Near enough to feel I was still with people and places I knew, but far enough away for no one to recognize me. I posed as a young widow. There was a lot of shame in an unmarried girl being pregnant in those days.'

'There still is,' said Walter drily.

'I suppose so. I don't know if he ever tried to find me: there was no reason why he would. He was married, his wife was a fine London lady.'

And a cold and humourless one as well, thought Walter.

'There was a vicar there who helped me,' said Belinda. 'He was very kind. He arranged an adoption – I never knew the details; he said it was better that I shouldn't. But he promised me they were good and kindly people. A couple who couldn't have children of their own, he said, but who dearly wanted them.'

So that was what they were hiding, thought Walter. Nothing sinister, nothing dark and grim in Elizabeth's childhood; just the fact that she was not their own child.

'They were quite comfortably placed, so the vicar told me,' said Belinda, 'but I didn't care too much about that, Dr Kane, only that the baby should have enough for her wants and be loved and cared for.'

'She was,' said Walter, remembering the distraught couple in the Kendal house. 'He told you the truth about that.'

'After a time the woman sent photographs of the child,' said Belinda. 'Not direct, of course. She sent them to the vicar and he passed them to me. She thought I'd want to know my little girl was safe and well and growing up. It helped seeing those photographs. It made me feel better about what I had done.'

'And that was how you recognized her today.' Walter could easily imagine Belinda secreting the photographs away, poring over them in privacy, touching the black and white images with love and with the pain of loss.

'They were good photographs,' she said. 'Very clear. One when she was a toddler, and then two later ones: when she was ten, and another on her sixteenth birthday.

They'd given her a party, and the photograph was in their garden with other girls and a nice tea all set out on a big lawn. She looked so lovely, and I could see she was happy. So I didn't mind quite so much. But now . . .' One hand came out to grip Walter's wrist. 'A killer,' she said. 'A murderess. My little girl is a killer. And they say she was with that man for all those months – that evil, dreadful man. In his bed – loving him— Dr Kane, I don't think I can be here when they hang her.'

'I don't think you can, either,' said Walter at once. 'I'll report you as being ill, Belinda. You'd better have an attack of gastric flu or something like that.'

'Does he have to know about this? Lewis? Does he have to know about – about Elizabeth?' She said the name as if she was trying it out in her mind.

'Yes,' said Walter, who had been grappling with this for several minutes. 'Yes, Belinda, I think he does have to know. Do you want to see him to tell him? I could be there as well, if you like.'

'I don't want to see him,' she said at once.

'Because you still love him?'

'I suppose I did love him,' said Belinda. 'I suppose I still do, in a corner of my mind. But you mustn't think he took advantage of me, Dr Kane.'

'I don't.'

'I made the approach,' she said. 'Shameless, wasn't it?' She smiled at him, and in that moment the years fell away from her and suddenly and disconcertingly it was a sexy, mischievous pixie who sat there. Walter saw why Sir Lewis had fallen for her twenty years ago.

'No, it's not shameless, Belinda. I'm sorry you had to lose Elizabeth, though.'

'Would she have turned out any different if I'd kept her?'

'I honestly don't know. She had two good and loving parents. No, I don't think it would have made any difference.' He had no idea if he believed this or not, but it would give Belinda some comfort.

'Did they call her Elizabeth, do you know? That couple? Or did they shorten it, just in the family? To Betty or Beth. Beth's pretty.'

'I think they called her Elizabeth. Sir Lewis really must know about this. Would you like me to tell him?'

'Would you?' She looked at him with eager gratitude.

'Yes. I'll go to see him this evening, and I'll call on you afterwards to tell you what he's said. Would that be all right? Where are you living?'

'I have a little house just outside Thornbeck. I live on my own, so you could come at any time at all. I'll write the address down and directions to find it.'

She did so in a neat, careful hand, and then said, 'How am I going to live with this? Knowing my own daughter killed people? That she helped that man to murder them for their money and their jewellery? And that poor woman she pushed under the tram . . .'

'I'll do whatever I can to help you,' said Walter, and thought: and I understand your agony more than you could ever realize. Your daughter. My father.

She said, 'Thank you, Dr Kane.' She got up to go, and then hesitated. 'I'd like to hear you saying that everything will be all right,' she said. 'But it won't, will it?'

'I don't think it can be,' said Walter. 'But I think it will get easier for you.'

*

There was a feeling of reassurance about the familiar low-ceilinged room with the views across the fields. The curtains were drawn against the night, and a fire crackled in the hearth.

For once Lady Caradoc was there, although Walter saw she was wearing street clothes, clearly about to go out. She stayed long enough to make a little stately conversation. The war news was quite encouraging, did Dr Kane not agree, but oh dear, what a very shocking thing about that young girl who had just been sentenced to be executed.

'There are many evil people in the world, Dr Kane. Of all ages.'

Walter said that was so.

'You are here to see my husband,' stated Clara. 'And I have an engagement in Thornbeck – my work with the Caradoc Society, you know.'

'Yes, of course. It must be very interesting,' said Walter politely.

'It is deeply important,' said Clara Caradoc solemnly. 'Deeply. My husband is inclined to scoff, but we are finding out so much. So many spiritual things are to be discovered and offered as help and support to people. I would not, of course, expect you as a young man and a doctor of the body, to be entirely in sympathy with our aims, however.'

This bland assumption annoyed Walter, but he said he tried always to have an open mind, and that perhaps one day he might be allowed to attend a meeting.

'All seekers of the truth and all searchers for the Light are welcome,' said Clara, adding, more prosaically, that the Society met every Tuesday at eight o'clock and it was as well to arrive early to be sure of getting a seat and a voucher for the cup of tea served at nine.

'Sorry about that,' said Lewis Caradoc after Lady Caradoc had gone. He poured Walter a whisky and soda and waved him to a chair on the other side of the hearth. 'She's very earnest about all this psychic stuff; she's been involved in it for years. I can't see that it does any harm, and at least she's out of the clutches of some very dubious people she met in London some years ago. A pair of very ripe ones they were, and I have a feeling Clara gave them quite a lot of money although I've never actually asked her. Is your drink all right? You don't need to tell me why you're here. Elizabeth Molland, yes? It'll be hard for you to attend the execution of a young female. I never had to. I'd have found it an ordeal.'

Oh God, thought Walter, and drank some of the whisky, and then said, 'It *is* about Elizabeth, but not quite in the way you think. Sir Lewis, twenty years ago you were – you knew a young wardress called Belinda.'

At the name a stillness came over Lewis Caradoc. He said, 'I did know her. But she left quite suddenly. I should have liked to keep in touch with her, just to be sure she was all right.' He made an impatient gesture. 'Dammit, Walter, I don't have to pussyfoot around with you, do I? Belinda and I were lovers, quite briefly. It wasn't the wisest of liaisons, but it was a difficult time for me just then – But no excuses. You know – you must have realized – that Clara and I have a very barren marriage.'

Walter said bluntly, 'Belinda had a child as a result. A daughter.'

For a moment Lewis stared at him blankly, as if not

understanding, and then one hand went up to shield his eyes as if a blinding light had suddenly been turned on to his face. He did not say anything, but after a moment he went back to the drinks cabinet and reached for the decanter; for the first time Walter saw that for all the sharpness and the quicksilver intelligence and humour, this was a man approaching old age. Lewis's hands were shaking so badly he was unable to pour the whisky, and after a moment Walter got up and poured the drink himself.

'Thank you. Bit of a shock.' He seemed to make a tremendous effort to regain control. 'A daughter,' he said, half to himself. 'Of all things.' Walter saw, with something like despair, that some of the light was already returning to his eyes. 'Can you tell me any more? How do you know about this?'

'Belinda has come back to Calvary for a while. A temporary wardress.'

'I didn't even know she was still in the area. Is she all right?'

'She didn't want you to know where she was.' Walter leaned forward. 'She's been living just outside Thornbeck it seems, and as far as I can make out she's perfectly all right. But there's something else.'

'Yes?'

'The daughter.'

'Yes?' There was a note of hope in Lewis's voice now. 'Tell me about her.'

'Belinda put her out for adoption. It was the only thing she could do in those days.' Oh God, thought Walter, he's beginning to look so delighted at the prospect of a daughter he didn't know existed. Is he remembering his son who died and thinking that this is a sort of second chance for him? Help me find the words for this, he thought. Help me to help him.

He said, 'Sir Lewis – the child was adopted by some people called Molland. She's Elizabeth Molland. The prisoner awaiting execution in Calvary.'

The light that had begun to shine in Lewis Caradoc's eyes went out and a dark and terrible pain took its place.

Clara Caradoc was glad that Lewis kept a car these days, and that there was usually one of the household to drive her to and from wherever she wanted to go. You might say a number of things about Lewis but you could not say he was mean, although Clara made due allowance for the fact that it was her family's money with which Lewis was not mean.

It had perhaps been a little casual of Dr Kane to call at the house tonight without notification or invitation, but that was modern young men for you. The visit would be something to do with that dreadful prison because Lewis had never quite relinquished the running of it to Mr Higneth. Her father said men like Lewis never really gave up their commitments, even if they lived to be a hundred. *Noblesse oblige*, that was what it was, he said, and Clara ought to remember it. Clara thought whatever name you gave it, it still meant Lewis went gallivanting off to committees and served on various boards and trusts. It was all very well to talk about *noblesse oblige* but ordering meals and household provisions was extremely difficult if you did not know whether your husband would be at home or in London, and if it was the latter how long he might be away. This war would make life a great deal worse, with the stupid government already warning about bringing in rationing for perfectly ordinary things. Clara had no opinion of governments and even less opinion of wars, although it would not do to allow that vulgar little man with the absurd ranting voice and the awful moustache to go rampaging wholesale over Europe.

Tonight's Caradoc Society meeting did not promise to be particularly interesting, but it was Clara's clear duty to attend. She nearly always did attend; Lewis had tried to dissuade her from doing so over the years – he had actually said he would prefer her not to associate with Dr McNulty. Of course Clara had taken no notice. Dr McNulty was a most conscientious and dedicated man; he gave unstintingly of his time, and it was a great shame Lewis could not understand how serious and important the Society's work was. It was even more of a shame that he had this unreasoning dislike of Dr McNulty himself. Clara had never been able to discover the reason for that, and nor had she been able to discover why, having allowed the Caradoc Society to come into being and to bear his name, Lewis refused to have any involvement with it. They had not had an argument about it, because Clara did not allow such uncivilized and undisciplined things in her house, and Lewis always walked fastidiously away from arguments anyway. But Clara was occasionally and uneasily aware that they had come close to it several times.

This evening they would discuss the recent theories about a person's aura being captured on photographs. Electrographic photography it was called, and Dr

McNulty was very enthusiastic about it; he had been in correspondence with people in Russia who were making experiments in the field. Clara would sit politely through the lecture but the real interest would come afterwards when they would gather round the table in the big meeting room, and Violette would make yet another attempt to reach Caspar. She had never been successful in this, not since that terrible night in the North London house, but she continued to try. 'One day I shall succeed,' she always said. 'After all you have done for me, dear Clara – after your generosity when the fire destroyed all our possessions – well, it is the least I can do.'

Clara thought it *was* the least Violette could do, but naturally this could not be said. She usually replied that she had been very pleased to help after the shocking business of the fire – to say nothing of the even more shocking business of Bartlam taking himself off in that cavalier fashion, leaving poorest Vita absolutely bereft. Clara had been glad to suggest that Vita came to live just outside Thornbeck – really a very nice little house Clara had found for her, and it had been her pleasure to buy the lease for her friend. (There had only been five years left on the lease, so the cost had actually been extremely modest.)

It had all been rather timely, what with the Caradoc Society so newly created and just finding its feet. Vita had been a great help in those early days, and Clara had been overjoyed to have her so near. She had foreseen many private sessions in which they would together try to bring Caspar back.

Vita knew, of course, that Clara had never given up the hope of reaching Caspar, and she had agreed that this war would bring him closer to his mamma. He might feel a comradeship with other young men going out to fight, said Vita. You never knew with the Departed Ones. They would speak with him yet, vowed Vita.

The trouble was that Vita's powers seemed to have diminished with the years. Clara supposed this was the shock of the fire, and perhaps the distress of Bartlam's leaving but as the years wheeled by, she wondered once or twice if it might have been Bartlam who had possessed the mediumistic qualities rather than Vita. If this was true, looked at purely selfishly it was a very great pity he had gone, but viewed in a spirit of friendship it was better for Vita to be rid of the dreadful man. Clara had been very much shocked to hear of Bartlam's squalid activities in Brighton and that dreadful business in Greek Street. It had been a blessed release for Vita when news of his death reached her a few years later.

'Heart failure, and in unpleasant circumstances,' was all Vita would say, and Clara had not wished to enquire any further. She had, however, been quite surprised when Vita re-married a year after Bartlam's death. One would have thought that at her age she would not have cared for marriage in any form, although it had to be said that Vita was a little younger than Clara herself. Perhaps she was just over fifty. Her new husband was a rather common sort of person – a local business-man – but he did not object to his wife's involvement with the Caradoc Society which was the really important thing.

Getting into the smart little Ford that Lewis kept at Thornbeck, Clara hoped tonight might be the night

Caspar would come, although it was a pity she had got to sit through an hour and a half of photographing auras first.

CHAPTER TWENTY-SIX

'I suppose,' said Lewis Caradoc, 'there isn't any doubt about this girl's identity?'

He can't quite bring himself to use her name yet, thought Walter. But he said, 'I don't think so. Belinda was sent photographs of her by the Molland couple. We'd need to check, but she seemed very positive.'

'She was an intelligent girl,' said Lewis, staring into the fire. 'I was going to help her to something – well, to something a little better in life. I do wish she had confided in me all those years ago.' The pain was still in his eyes, but Walter could almost feel him forcing his mind back to a semblance of control.

'When is the execution?' he said, at last.

'The twelfth.'

'Have they lodged an appeal?'

'I don't think so.' Walter realized that Lewis was focusing determinedly on the practicalities of the situation – practicalities with which he was so familiar – and was not allowing any other emotions to come to the surface.

'I read quite a lot of the reports of the trial. It all sounded fairly straightforward.' His voice was so down-to-earth they might have been discussing some anonymous prisoner, convicted and about to be brought to Calvary.

'The evidence seemed quite clear,' said Walter. 'But there's something a bit out of kilter. Something I've since discovered which doesn't fit with everything else.'

'What?'

'This is difficult, because there's the confidentiality of a patient's condition to take into account – Oh hell,' said Walter, 'I can't think it matters in this situation, and if I can't trust you, I can't trust anybody. Sir Lewis, the evidence at the trial said Elizabeth and Neville Fremlin had been lovers. There had apparently been testimony from people who knew them – I don't mean friends, I don't think they could have had any, not in the normal sense, but customers and hotel people. I didn't hear the prosecution case, but I heard the judge's summing up and it was fairly clear that they were making quite a lot of that.'

Lewis said, 'Fremlin exerted his charm over her and she thought it was acceptable to kill?'

'Yes.'

'It's a fair assumption,' said Lewis thoughtfully. 'Maybe he persuaded her it was – what's the word the Americans use? Glamorous. Maybe she saw it as that.' The shock had gone and the sharp intelligence was driving him again. Only a strained look around his lips betrayed him.

'But,' said Walter, 'the thing that's out of kilter is that

they weren't lovers at all. At least, not in the physical sense. I've examined her – the standard pregnancy examination – and she's *virgo intacta*. I'm trying to decide if it makes a difference.'

'It could throw the rest of the evidence into question,' said Lewis, frowning. 'Or could it? The relationship might have been non-sexual. An older man looking on a pretty young girl in a fatherly way.'

Walter said drily, 'Did you ever meet Neville Fremlin?'

'You know I didn't. I was retired by the time he came to Calvary. I saw his photograph in the newspaper reports of the trial, though.'

'I don't think Neville Fremlin would have thought of any pretty young girl in a fatherly way,' said Walter. 'In any case, he was only in his late forties when he met her.'

'All right. But she could still have been in thrall to him – sorry, that sounds rather melodramatic, doesn't it?'

'Not given the two people involved,' said Walter. 'She's very quiet, but she's somehow a very dramatic person.'

'Is she?' It came out a bit too eagerly and as if realizing he had lowered his guard but as if it would take too much energy to put it back in place, Lewis said, 'Walter, what are we going to do about this?'

'I don't know.'

'You do realize,' said Lewis slowly, 'that I can't let her hang.'

Walter had known they would reach this point; he had known it since Belinda's astonishing revelation. What he had not known was how he would react: he had not expected Lewis's words to churn up the long-dead memories: the ugliness and despair of that dreary day in Calvary's condemned cell. The fragment of the Irish poem that Nicholas O'Kane had wanted to pass to the small Walter: the poem about dying not for flag, nor king, nor emperor, but for a dream . . . Nicholas O'Kane had died for a dream that day, and in the stuffy little church that smelt of wintergreen, Walter's mother had tried to pray for him but could not because she was crying when the church bell chimed eight o'clock. The sound of his mother's crying had stayed with him ever since, and the look in his father's eyes had stayed as well. And surely, no matter what you had done, no matter what your beliefs or creeds were, you should not have to be tied up with leather straps and have your neck broken while stern-faced men stood in a coldly lit room and watched?

The memories blurred and spun, and from deep within them, Walter heard his own voice saying, 'I don't think there's anything we can do to prevent it.'

Saul Ketch had been very pleased to be asked to go back to his old duties at the prison; he had found life a bit hard these past years. You picked up what you could, and you took what you could find and sold it – clothes, jewellery, information. Especially information. But gathering information was not as easy as it had been in Ketch's youth – in the old Calvary days when he had gone along the corridors, listening and watching. For one thing, people were more suspicious now, particularly since this war business. They wanted to know where things had come from, or how Ketch had come by them.

They saw Germans behind every bush or hiding in every cellar or barn. For another thing, Ketch himself had got a bit podgy over the years and could not nip around as fast as he used to.

So taking it all in all, Ketch had been very glad of the work at Calvary, although he had not let on about that, not he! He had said, a bit grudgingly, that he supposed he might help them for a while. He would not come for tuppence farthing, mind. If they wanted him, they must pay him a decent wage. The decent wage had been agreed – it was not too bad a wage, either, although Ketch had not said this.

He had told the doctor about it almost immediately, going along to the house the doctor had taken on the Kendal road. It was a nice house, although a bit of a lonely spot for Ketch who liked to be at the centre of things with people around him.

The doctor had not worked at Calvary since that business with Nicholas O'Kane – Ketch had never got to the bottom of that, but he might do so one day. (It might be worth something to get to the bottom of it!) But they still had their little arrangement, Ketch and the doctor, even though he was so taken up with that dopey society Lewis Caradoc – *Sir* Lewis Caradoc if you wanted to be particular – had set up. But when Ketch was given the push by Lewis bloody Caradoc on account of that tart, Belinda Skelton, the doctor had said no need to worry: he always looked after people who had helped him. And give the devil his due, he had done so. There had been many a little job the doctor had passed to Ketch – finding out things about people it mostly was. Keeping an eye on people and passing on the information. The doctor liked to know as much as he could so he could put the squeeze on people and make them pay to stop their secrets being told. Ketch was all for getting money where you could, and did not in the least mind squeezing people. He did think old McNulty must be a bit mad to spend all the money he got on his daft experiments – seeing if the soul flew out of the body and suchlike.

Still, the doctor had managed to squeeze quite a few people over the years – with Ketch's help, of course. You wouldn't believe some of the things going on in Thornbeck and the villages around it. People pretending to be respectable citizens, when in fact they were no such thing – Ketch had certainly learned a thing or two about what went on behind closed curtains and locked doors, but he never told anybody anything unless he was paid.

The doctor thought it was a very good opportunity for Ketch to work at Calvary again. All kinds of things might be happening there, he said. Things that could be made use of. Ketch must be sure to bring him all the titbits of information – he knew what was wanted, said Dr McNulty. As for Ketch not being as nippy as he once had been, oh pish, said the doctor, all he needed was to stop gorging on pies and puddings and glasses of beer, that would bring the podge off!

It was all very well for the doctor, who had got a bit dried-up and wizened over the years; Ketch often thought a few good platefuls of steak and kidney pudding, or dumplings and beef, would do the doctor a lot of good!

But anyway, Ketch went back to Calvary, and at times you might almost have thought there had been no twenty-year gap, because not much had changed. The governor had changed, of course. Edgar Higneth, that was the new man's name. Ketch did not care for him, but at least he did not know the story of Ketch's disgrace all those years ago. And now Lewis Caradoc was away in London so often, being on stupid committees all the time, there was no one likely to spill those particular beans!

Ketch was glad to find he had not lost his old cunning when it came to Calvary and its inmates. He knew almost at once that there was something odd going on, and thought it was to do with the posh tart in the condemned cell. There was an uneasiness, almost as if somebody knew something about her. It might just be that they did not like the idea of hanging a young female, but it might be something more than that. Ketch was going to listen and watch very carefully.

He had made sure to take a look at the tart for himself, doing so when they took her into the little yard under the condemned cell window for exercise and fresh air, although why anyone would want to bother with exercise and fresh air with old Pierrepoint gobbling in the background and measuring the hemp, Ketch could not think. Liz Molland, that was her name. He supposed some men would find her nice-looking, although she was a bit skinny for his taste. She'd be one of those Die-away Doras, as well: no energy and lying around on sofas, and oh dear, poor little me, I can't cope with life. Expecting everyone to wait on her hand and foot. Neville Fremlin had waited on her, in fact if you could believe the reports, Neville Fremlin had done a lot more than wait on her, the dirty old sod. Ketch sniggered to think of Fremlin and this whey-faced tart together, but while he was sniggering he kept his ears alert for any nice little snippets of scandal the doctor might like.

Walter always slept at Calvary when a prisoner was awaiting execution; it was only a matter of three weeks and he thought it important to be on call in case of any difficulties.

He was doing so now for Elizabeth. The small room near the infirmary was familiar to him by this time; he had moved one or two of his own things in – some books, a couple of paintings he liked, an amber silk bed cover he had bought on a brief holiday in Italy which reminded him of a Tuscan sunset. No photographs, though. Photographs might cause one of the older warders to spot a familiar face, and say, 'Isn't that Nicholas O'Kane?'

Sir Lewis had to be in London a good deal at the moment – he was involved in the setting up of internment camps for prisoners of war, and he had recently been appointed to one of the committees of the International Red Cross. 'I thought when I left Calvary for the Home Office rehabilitation work, it would be a stepping-stone to retirement,' he said to Walter once. 'I thought I would eventually take up growing roses or keeping bees like Sherlock Holmes was supposed to have done. But it's not quite working out like that.'

'You'll never retire,' Walter had said. 'You'll never want to.'

He had seen Sir Lewis only once since that appalling night he had told him about Elizabeth, but he had been able to visit Belinda twice, using the pretext of checking on her health. Neither of them asked to see Elizabeth – Walter thought Belinda would not do so. But he saw the longing in Lewis's eyes and thought that very soon Lewis would want to see his daughter so much he would make some discreet arrangement to visit her.

He had given both Lewis and Belinda carefully edited reports, knowing quite well they were both aware of the scenes that sometimes took place in the condemned cell. But they appeared to believe him when he said Elizabeth was perfectly calm, and that she apparently accepted her fate. He did not mention how her behaviour had gradually changed – he did not tell them about the storms of weeping, or the pleas for a reprieve, or the night she had clung to him for more than hour, sobbing and hysterical, begging him to save her, because it was all a terrible mistake, and she could not bear to die.

He said Elizabeth had not talked about Neville Fremlin or the murders, and he had not pressed her on the subject. He would stay with her on the night before the execution; he would be with her to the end. There would be sedatives given, of course; he would increase them gradually as they neared the last morning. But just as he did not tell them about Elizabeth's hysteria, nor did he tell them about the resentment and unease that seemed to be filling Calvary because a young and good-looking female was awaiting the death penalty.

He worried a lot about what he would do if Lewis proposed an escape plan to him, but he could see no way in which Lewis could save Elizabeth from being hanged.

CHAPTER TWENTY-SEVEN

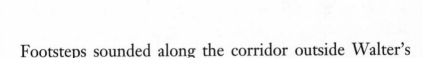

Footsteps sounded along the corridor outside Walter's room shortly after one a.m., and the knocking on his door was loud and urgent.

Walter had been in an uneasy half sleep in the narrow bed; he had developed a throbbing headache earlier so he had not bothered with supper, thinking he would try to sleep it off. But the sleep was a very shallow one, and he came fully awake at once and called out, 'Yes? What is it?'

'Dr Kane, can you come? It's Molland.'

Molland.

'Hold on a minute, I'll put some clothes on,' said Walter, and reached for the sweater, shoes and trousers he always kept ready.

The warder outside his door was one of the new, temporary men Edgar Higneth had recently recruited. Walter did not know his name, but thought he was normally put on duty with the unprepossessing Saul Ketch.

'What's the matter with Molland?' said Walter as they hurried along the dimly lit corridors to the condemned block.

'She's sicking up her guts and rolling around moaning in pain,' said the warder. 'It's my opinion she's trying it on – wants the attention, or she's managed to swallow something to cheat the rope – but Mr Ketch said I was to fetch you anyway, Doctor.'

'Quite right,' said Walter tersely.

The door of the condemned cell was open and the shifty-eyed Saul Ketch was waiting. He darted a sideways look at Walter, which Walter found disconcerting. 'Ketch, isn't it? I'll go in on my own; you'll wait outside, please.'

'Orders are to stay with the prisoner at all times, Doctor.'

'Be damned to orders,' said Walter. 'This is a young girl who might be genuinely ill, and I'm her doctor. So you'll stay outside the room until I call you.'

Ketch looked sullen, but he did as he was told and Walter closed the door. Elizabeth was lying on her side, hunched over. Her face was twisted in pain and it had a feverish flush. Tendrils of sweat-soaked hair were sticking to her forehead. There was sour smell in the room, and Walter saw they had given her a basin and a towel and that she had been sick.

He sat on the edge of the bed, and said, quietly, 'I'm here to help, Elizabeth. You know that. Just say where the pain is.'

'Stomach. Low down – this side.' She indicated the right-hand side, and Walter nodded.

'I'll give you something for the pain in a minute, but

I need to examine you first and take your temperature.'

He put the thermometer into her mouth, and made a careful examination of her abdomen. She watched him from half-closed eyes, wincing several times. Halfway through she struggled up in the bed, and reached blindly for the bowl to be sick again. Walter held the bowl for her and wiped her mouth afterwards, giving her a sip of water from the jug. Her temperature was 101.

'I'll give you a shot of morphine, Elizabeth,' he said. 'You'll feel better presently.'

'Thank you, Dr Kane,' she said on a gasp, and one hand came out to take his briefly.

Walter opened the door and stepped outside; the two warders looked at him.

'She's gammoning us, isn't she?' said the man who had knocked so hard on the door. Ketch said nothing, but his eyes were on the figure on the bed.

'No, she isn't,' said Walter sharply. 'She is very ill indeed. Ketch, stay with her – keep the bowl handy in case she's sick again.'

'I ain't no nursemaid to a murderer—'

'You'll have to be for the next ten minutes,' said Walter.

'I think it might be appendicitis,' said Walter.

Higneth stared at him in horror. 'Are you sure?'

'No. Appendicitis can mimic other conditions – diverticulitis, an abscess on the right-hand kidney, pelvic inflammation – although I've examined her for that and I think it can be ruled out.' He frowned. 'But taking it overall, the symptoms fit for appendicitis – the pain's in the right place and there appears to be rebound tenderness, particularly around McBurney's point. There's sickness and some fever. And she's the right age.'

'Appendicitis,' said Higneth, trying out the word. 'Oh God. What do you advise?'

'With most patients the best thing is to wait a few hours and see if it develops any more strongly – or if it calms down. But this isn't an ordinary patient,' said Walter, 'so I don't think we can take any risks. We need to get her to a hospital so more precise tests can be made. Blood and urine and so on.'

'If it is appendicitis?'

'Left untreated it may well burst, and peritonitis will set in. That's treatable, but it can be fatal.'

Higneth stared at Walter, as the appalling complexity of the situation washed over him.

'I don't know if there are any rules that govern you in this situation,' said Walter. 'But there are certainly medical rules that govern me and I'm afraid I'll have to follow them.'

'I don't think this situation has ever arisen before,' said Higneth. 'Walter, if we wait – and if it does worsen and you think it's appendicitis, can't you – isn't it possible for you to do the operation here?'

'Good God, no. It needs a properly qualified surgeon.'

'Could we get a surgeon here?'

'No,' said Walter. 'It needs full operating facilities: anaesthetic equipment; properly trained nurses. It would take far too long to set up.'

'You mentioned blood tests – Could they be done here? If we got Kendal hospital to send out anything you'd need and a laboratory technician and so on?'

'The trouble is,' said Walter slowly, 'that if she does need an appendectomy . . .'

'She needs to have it as soon as possible so that she can recover in time for – Yes, of course. This is the most macabre situation,' said Higneth.

'I know. But let's take it a step at a time. I could be wrong. I'll telephone the hospital and see if they'll send out an ambulance for her. They'll do the tests and if I'm wrong, she could be back here by lunchtime tomorrow. But if I've made the right diagnosis, they'll be able to operate at once. I'll go with her, of course.'

'You should have at least one warder with you,' said Higneth. 'A female – only I don't think any of the women are on duty – we're so wretchedly short-staffed at the moment.'

'If I travel in the ambulance with her, wouldn't that do? I've given her a shot of morphia and she's barely conscious – she isn't any danger to anyone. If necessary, we can send one of the women out to the hospital tomorrow. If they need to operate, I mean.'

Higneth said, 'An operation to save her life so that she can be executed. Walter, would she be—'

He stopped and Walter finished the sentence for him. 'Would she be sufficiently recovered in time to be hanged?' he said, and Higneth winced. 'Yes, I should think so. Just about. But we really shouldn't jump to conclusions yet. I'll make the call from the surgery now.' He went to the door and then turned back. 'We're letting her family know, are we?'

'I haven't done yet, but I must, of course. Apart from anything else, she's under twenty-one. Technically still a minor.'

'Would you like me to telephone the Mollands?' said Walter. 'There's someone with her now, and she'll be all right until the ambulance gets here. You must have a great many other things to do.'

'Would you mind?' said Higneth gratefully.

'Not at all. I've met them which will make it a bit easier.'

'I feel so sorry for that couple,' said Higneth. 'Whatever she did, they're still Elizabeth's parents.'

Elizabeth's parents . . .

'Mr Molland? It's Walter Kane from Calvary Gaol. I'm so sorry to be telephoning you at this time of the night, but we wanted to let you know about a rather unexpected development.'

'Has there been a reprieve?'

The sudden hope in Molland's voice sliced through Walter like a knife. He said quickly, 'No, I'm sorry, nothing like that. But Elizabeth's been taken ill – severe abdominal pains and some sickness. We're worried in case it's appendicitis, so I've arranged for her to go into the infirmary at Kendal: there's a big new one on the outskirts.'

'Oh, I see,' said Molland. 'It's very kind of you to telephone us yourself, Dr Kane. Is she very ill?'

'She's certainly unwell,' said Walter. 'I can't be sure that it's appendicitis. If it is there'll have to be an immediate operation but it could turn out to be a wasted journey for everyone.'

'I'm very grateful to you for telephoning. I'll let my wife know what's happened – I don't think she heard the telephone.'

But he did not seem as if he wanted to ring off and after a moment, Walter said, 'How is your wife?'

'It's an odd thing,' said Molland. 'But since the trial – since all that evidence came out – she's been better. It was the not knowing that was so bad, you see.'

'Yes, of course.'

'After the trial, she seemed to pick up. She said it was as if it wasn't our girl any longer. As if we'd lost her over a year ago. That's how Edith sees it, Dr Kane – that we'd lost our bright lovely girl, and that a – a cruel vicious monster had taken her place.'

'Do you feel the same?' said Walter.

There was another pause, then Molland said, 'Have you children yourself, Dr Kane?'

'No.'

'Ah. Well, a man looks on a daughter as a bit special like. But I go along with my wife, of course.'

'Of course.'

'Will the – the execution still be on the same day? I mean, if there's an operation, will that delay it?'

'I don't know yet,' said Walter. 'I don't think it's a situation that has ever happened before. At the moment the plan is for it to be on the original day, but I think we have to be prepared for that to alter. An ambulance is collecting Elizabeth shortly. It'll be here in about three quarters of an hour.'

'I understand,' said Molland. 'Thank you for telling me all this. I'm very grateful to you, Dr Kane.'

Elizabeth's parents . . .

'Sir Lewis? I'm sorry to phone you in the middle of the night.'

'Walter? What's wrong? Is it the prisoner?'

'Yes. Taken ill. I suspect appendicitis.'

'Good God.' He started to speak, and then hesitated. Walter waited, and Lewis said, 'I saw her earlier today.'

'I thought you'd visit her at some point.'

'Higneth knew, of course,' said Lewis. 'But hardly anyone else saw me. Most of the staff were in the warders' recreation room. She wasn't in the least what I expected, Walter.'

'She wasn't in the least what I expected, either,' said Walter.

'I didn't tell her anything,' he said. 'I just said I still took an interest in things at Calvary – in the people who came there. I only stayed for about half an hour. She seemed all right then. Are you taking her to the infirmary yourself?'

'I've asked them to send out an ambulance,' said Walter. 'It'll be easier all round. And the hospital will have the facilities to make a more definite diagnosis. It's not very far from here to Kendal anyway.'

'Nor it is,' said Lewis, 'in fact if they use the high road it'll only take half an hour.'

'It may turn out to be a false alarm, of course.'

'Does everyone know about it – everyone who ought to know, I mean?'

'I've phoned you and I've phoned the Mollands,' said Walter. 'I thought you should know. And if you know of anyone else who ought to be told . . .'

'I understand,' said Lewis, exactly as Molland had said. He added, 'Thank you, Walter,' and he, too, rang off.

He'll tell Belinda, thought Walter. We understood one another over that.

'It's all arranged,' said Walter to Higneth, who was standing rather helplessly at the open door of the condemned cell. He glanced inside. Elizabeth was lying as he had left her, but it looked as if the morphia had taken effect. He thought for a moment, and then said, 'Will you tell the officer on the gate to let the ambulance through when it arrives? I'll get Ketch to help me carry her down on one of the stretchers. She can be put in the guard room until the ambulance comes. She's not fully conscious, and it'll save a bit of time.'

'A good idea,' said Higneth, and went along to his office to give the order to the gatehouse.

Ketch was annoyed to be sent for the stretcher, because he did not want to miss whatever might be happening in the condemned cell. There were some very interesting things inside Calvary at the moment, and Ketch's nose was telling him that something was happening tonight. It was all about the Molland bit, Ketch knew it in his bones. But McNulty did not deal in bones – he would not pay money for feelings in bones – so Ketch would have to get proper facts. He dared say McNulty would be very pleased if something could be found against Walter Kane. Something dark and sly that Kane would not want knowing. That would be worth a lot of money to McNulty, which meant it would be worth a lot of money to Ketch as well. So he was keeping his eyes open and his ears on stalks.

He got the stretcher from the stores, took it back, and

helped Dr Kane lift the Molland tart onto it. She was wailing fit to wake the dead, thought Ketch, pleased with the humour of his thought, although what with the wailing and what with her chucking her guts up again, it was a dismal task. Ketch would have to have a word with somebody about the mess all over his uniform shirt. He would have to request a brand new one, in fact now he came to think about it, he might insist on new trousers and boots as well.

They might need to operate on Molland at the hospital, or so it seemed. Ketch listened to Dr Kane talking about this with Old Hedgehog and thought what a waste of time to operate on somebody who was going to die in a couple of weeks anyway. But Molland had all the men feeling sorry for her; Ketch had seen that for himself. Fluttering her eyes at Old Hedgehog and saying, Oh, Mr Higneth, you're being so kind to me. Putting on that, I am a meek little lamb and the wolf got me air with everybody. She was tough as old boots, Elizabeth Molland, and none of them could see she was working on them to get out of Calvary and out of reach of old Pierrepoint's rope! Ketch could see it, though. Ketch knew a thing or two about women, and he knew a thing or two more about frail waifs who were about as frail as a drunkard's hobnailed liver, and who pretended to be poor little victims when they were really vicious little vixens. A survivor, that was what this one was.

Operations were tricky things. Ketch had had a cousin who had 'pendicitis or something that sounded very like it. The cousin had been fifteen at the time and healthy as you liked, but he had died from being cut open. Everyone had said it was a scandal and a disgrace but there was nothing anyone had been able to do about it. You would not get Ketch on an operating table, not for any sum you cared to name. It was too much of a risk.

'It's too much of a risk,' said the ambulance driver truculently.

'There's no risk,' said Walter angrily, but the driver did not agree. He said he was not having a convicted murderess in the back of his vehicle without some proper safeguards. Guards and suchlike.

'This is the one who went with that Neville Fremlin, isn't it? Five females they did in between them, and then she did another one by herself. And now you're asking me to drive forty bloody miles through the dark with her in the back? S'posing she tries to escape? S'posing she clumps me on the head and makes off into the night? Where'd I be then? Up shit creek without a paddle, that's where I'd be, never mind a dose of concussion.'

'I'll be with you in the ambulance,' said Walter in exasperation. 'In any case, she's so drowsy from the morphia she's barely conscious, never mind making off into the night.'

'I'd rather face Hitler's bloody bombs than this one on the loose, morphine or no morphine,' said the driver obstinately. 'There's the weather as well, that's to be taken into consideration, isn't it? Coming down bloody stair-rods out there, it is. I might skid – half the lanes are under inches of mud, in fact I reckon I was lucky to get up the hill to this place. S'posing I were to skid and land us in a ditch? I wouldn't put it past her to take advantage of that, the sly little madam.'

He would not be budged and he would not be

convinced that Elizabeth was in no state to take advantage of anyone. He said he had his rights and he was not risking being clumped on the head by no silver-tongued murderer, not for Dr Kane, nor the governor of Calvary Gaol, nor King George himself. Handcuffs, that was what he wanted to see here.

'That's inhuman,' said Walter angrily, 'and totally unnecessary.'

All right, said the driver, if there were not to be handcuffs, he wanted another guard in the van – preferably somebody as could provide a bit of muscle if so needed. His disparaging glance at Walter when he said this suggested he did not reckon much to Walter if it came to a fight.

'Ketch,' said Edgar Higneth resignedly, 'sign yourself out for outside duties for the next two hours. And get yourself a heavy coat – whatever else the driver's said, he's right about the rain. I'll see you when you get back, Walter.'

It was raining even harder by the time they carried the stretcher out to the ambulance. Walter shivered and turned his coat collar up against it, but it seeped coldly into his bones and clung to his hair. Behind them, Calvary was dark and lowering with only the guardhouse lights showing, and below them the countryside was black and impenetrable.

Walter was starting to feel light-headed. He reminded himself that he had hardly slept for the past week and had missed supper tonight and that neither of these things were conducive to clear thinking or well-being. But seated in the jolting ambulance with Saul Ketch, Elizabeth on the shelf-bed covered by blankets, he began to feel as if he had entered a strange dark world where nothing was entirely real. The whole world seemed to have shrunk to this creaking metal box jolting its way along the rutted lanes, with the sound of the rain pattering down on the roof and the drugged breathing of the semi-conscious girl under the blanket. His headache had returned, and he wished he had taken a couple of aspirin before setting out.

'You all right, Doctor?' said Ketch's voice, and Walter looked up.

'Just a bit tired.'

'Hellish journey to have to make, ain't it?' said Ketch.

'Yes.'

'Old bone-shaker of an ambulance, as well. Reminds me of the old line they used to tell us about going to hell in a handcart.' He jabbed a finger at the figure on the stretcher-bed. 'You reckon that's where she's going? Hell?'

'I don't know.' Walter leaned his aching head against the ambulance's sides and as they jolted through the night Ketch's words repeated themselves in his mind, over and over again, forming a maddening little rhythm. Going to hell in a handcart. That's where she's going. Hell in a handcart. That's where we're all going, sooner or later.

'Will she be all right?' said Ketch, breaking into this.

'What? Oh yes, I should think so. It should be straightforward.'

All straightforward, but when you're going to hell in a handcart you can never be sure, can you? said a little voice inside his mind. You can never be sure what might happen on the road to hell. It's a very smooth road, but there are often some surprises along the way, remember that, Walter and watch out for the surprises on the way . . .

The ambulance had tiny slitlike windows in the rear but when Walter wiped the condensation away with his coat cuff there was nothing to be seen but dense blackness. He tried to see over the driver's shoulder. Surely they were nearing the junction with the main Kendal road? Their headlights were cutting a swathe of light through fields and hedges; once a little scurrying animal dashed across their path and they swerved to avoid it and went on as before, but for a second Walter's stomach had tightened with nervousness. Surprises on the way to hell, Walter, remember?

He thought they were just coming up to the main thoroughfare that wound across to Kendal proper, which was about the halfway mark of the journey. No sooner had he reached this conclusion when headlights coming from the other direction suddenly appeared. The driver swore and Walter's heart skipped several beats.

'Christ Almighty, the idiot's driving straight at us!' shouted the driver. 'He's on the wrong side of the road – is he mad or drunk?'

He swung the ambulance sharply over to the right to avoid the oncoming vehicle, and it bounced and skidded. The headlights of the other car flooded the interior: Walter saw Ketch throw up a hand to shield his eyes from the glare, but he had no time to spare for Ketch; he was concerned that Elizabeth, semi-comatose from the morphia, was not thrown from the bed. He dived forwards, trying to wrap his arms round her as the ambulance bounced off the road.

The ambulance tipped violently to one side as the wheels sagged into a pothole or a ditch and this time Ketch was flung hard against the sides, his head banging against the metal with a dull crunch.

The headlights skewed crazily upwards, and there was a crackle of brilliance on Walter's vision that might have been lights or might be something exploding behind his eyes.

He had no idea how much time had passed before he returned to a full awareness of the scene inside the ambulance.

It was very quiet. Ketch was lying where he had fallen, but he was groaning slightly and sounded all right. Walter managed to call out to the driver, asking if he was hurt, deeply relieved when he said no he wasn't bloody hurt, but he had known from the start that something would go wrong with this journey, and hadn't he been right!

'What happened?'

'Some silly bugger drove straight at us, that's what happened,' said the driver explosively. 'Drunk most like. He swerved at the last minute or we'd have done a lot worse than land in a ditch. Bumped my head on the windscreen.'

'Were you knocked out?'

'Bit stunned for a few minutes, but I ain't seeing double or anything if that's what you mean.'

'Thank goodness for that.' Walter was checking Ketch's vital signs, but the man's pulse rate was steady, and he seemed to be coming round. 'Is there any means of having a light here?'

'There is if it hasn't smashed in the jolt. Wait a bit . . .'

A rather subdued light came on, and Walter said, 'Oh God.'

'What's wrong?' said the driver, turning round to look.

In a voice from which all expression had drained, Walter said, 'The prisoner's gone.'

CHAPTER TWENTY-EIGHT

'It wasn't your fault, Dr Kane,' said the police inspector, seated in Edgar Higneth's office. 'Clearly the journey had to be made and you arranged it in the only way possible.'

'If any blame's to be apportioned,' said Higneth, tired and old-looking in the grey dawn, 'it should be apportioned to me.'

'Well, sir, I can't see how else you were to get Molland to the infirmary other than in an ambulance,' said the inspector. 'You had two people guarding her, which I'd have thought more than enough. I'd have to say, though, that it doesn't seem very likely she got herself out of the ambulance, not in that condition. You'd definitely given her the morphia, had you, Dr Kane?'

'Yes. You can see the record of it and the dosage. There are a few people who have a high tolerance to morphia, of course,' said Walter. 'But she seemed to be drowsy enough. It's difficult to fake the effects of morphia, Inspector. Pinpoint pupils, for instance.'

'To my mind, there are only two possibilities here,' said the inspector. 'The first is that she wasn't as ill as she seemed.'

He glanced at Walter as he said this, and Walter said at once, 'That's got to be considered. I'm not infallible and my diagnosis was never definite.'

'You might not be infallible, but you're very good,' said Higneth.

Walter shot him a grateful look, and then said, 'But she seems to have managed to escape from the ambulance while the warder and the driver were knocked out – and while I was dazed.'

'So you think she might have been faking after all?'

'People in here do fake illness,' said Walter. 'But by now I'm aware of most of the tricks they pull and I can usually spot them. I thought she was genuine, but . . .'

'But it's not that difficult to induce vomiting and a fever,' said the inspector thoughtfully. 'Had she any opportunity to take anything from the dispensary?'

'No,' said Walter. 'And the drugs book balances with the drugs in stock – I've checked – it was one of the first things I did when I got back.'

'Well, it only needs something as homely as mustard stirred in hot water or a good swig of ipecacuanha, and most households have both those things. What about visitors? Did anyone visit her in the last twenty-four hours? Anyone from outside?'

'No one,' said Edgar Higneth at once, and Walter glanced at him. He's not going to tell the police about Sir Lewis's visit, he thought. Is that because he knows the truth? Or because he thinks Lewis is involved in this? For a moment he wondered whether to mention his own phone call, but that might throw suspicion on Lewis. It might also mean Elizabeth's paternity coming out, and Walter could not see it would do anyone any good to make that public – not yet, at any rate. Hopefully it would never need to come out at all. So for the moment he would follow Higneth's lead.

'If Molland genuinely did have appendicitis,' the inspector was saying, 'it's unlikely she could have got out of that ambulance and walked anywhere, that's right, isn't it, Dr Kane?'

'Yes, certainly. Especially allowing for the morphia.'

'And even if she had managed to crawl a few hundred yards, my men would have found her by now. Which brings us to the other possibility.'

'The driver of the car who forced the ambulance off the road,' said Walter.

'Bit of a coincidence, wasn't it, that car?' said the inspector. 'Coming along that stretch of road just at that time. You're sure you couldn't make a stab at identifying it, Dr Kane?'

'No, I told you. It was pouring with rain and dark. I think it was a black car, but it could have been any make.'

'Pity,' said the inspector. 'Still, we'll work on it being black. There wouldn't be too many cars on the road at that time of night, in those conditions. And it does sound as if the driver could have got her out while you were all unconscious.'

'I wasn't out for long,' said Walter. 'I don't think the ambulance driver was, either. I think we were more dazed than anything.'

'Yes, but look here, Inspector, if the car driver did get her out, that argues pre-knowledge,' put in Higneth.

'And hardly anyone knew Dr Kane was making the journey. In any case, who would take such a massive risk? Friends? It's a lonely business being a murderer and from all the accounts Elizabeth – and Fremlin – lived very much withdrawn from the world for all those months they were together.'

'Everyone inside Calvary knew she was being taken to Kendal though,' said the inspector. 'Her parents knew it.'

Her parents. Walter said, 'Yes, but would her parents have had time to set things up? I only phoned Molland an hour earlier, if that. And if Elizabeth was taken, she had to be taken somewhere safe. That couldn't have been arranged so quickly, could it?'

'Whoever took her could just have driven her as far away as possible and booked into an hotel or a guest house,' said the inspector. 'There're hundreds of them for miles around. We'll check as many as we can, but that's a long-winded process.'

'They'd say they were father and daughter, I suppose,' said Walter.

'Or mother and daughter.'

'You think a woman could have been driving that car?'

'It's not out of the question. Whoever it was could say the daughter was unwell – recovering from flu or something of the kind, but they had a family commitment to attend. A funeral or a wedding. But I don't think it was the parents. We've talked to them, and we're watching the house, of course, in case she goes there, but I don't think that's likely.'

'You think the car driver really was part of it?'

'If not, it means Molland got away under her own

steam with no means of transport, presumably no money, and wearing just night things. Drowsy from the morphia, as well. All a bit unlikely, I'd say. We'll keep searching, but if she was taken in a car it's a pointless exercise; by lunchtime she could be in another country.'

'With this war?' asked Higneth.

'Not impossible, sir. There's a lot of confusion over travel at the moment; she could have been taken to Scotland and from there to Norway. Or she could have gone across to Ireland on the ferry and be on the west coast by tonight.'

'But that brings us back to the idea of it being pre-planned,' objected Walter.

'There have been madder escapes than this, and some of those people who escaped were never caught,' said the inspector. He stood up. 'We've alerted all the ports – also the hospitals, because if your diagnosis of appendicitis was right, Dr Kane, she'll need treatment in the next few hours.' He frowned. 'In that situation, how long would you give her?'

'It's difficult to be precise because her youth and general good health would be fighting the infection for her. But if the intestine were to rupture peritonitis could set in. Without medical attention that could be fatal.'

If Ketch had not seen it with his own eyes, he would not have believed it. But it had been plain as plain. Dr Walter Kane, that correct, saint-like doctor everyone said was wonderful, so dedicated and kind, had deceived everyone. And if he, Ketch, had not been as cunning as a fox, he would never have known it.

To start with, he had not wanted to form part of the stupid guard on the Molland female when they took her off to Kendal infirmary. It was a filthy night, and Ketch had taken a very sour view of the entire expedition, in fact if he had had any say in the matter, the murderous bitch would have been left to die and saved old Pierrepoint a job! But it had not been possible to get out of it, so Ketch had gloomily put on a heavy topcoat, and gone sulkily out to help load the stretcher. The Molland tart was rolling her eyes like a demented thing on account of something Dr Kane had given her but they had got her onto the ambulance, and he and Dr Kane had got in after her and off they had driven.

Ketch had not liked the journey. He had not liked the way Dr Kane seemed to be in a dream: staring out of the window every five minutes and hardly hearing when Ketch spoke to him. He wondered if the girl had got to him, although he would not have expected Dr Kane to be taken in by this doe-eyed tart. To Ketch's mind Molland was nothing but a cheap little whore who had let Neville Fremlin tup her for all he was worth, and had then gone on killing after he was dead.

And then that other car had come swooping down on them, and the ambulance had swerved violently and they had rolled into the ditch. Ketch had rapped his head smartly against the metal sides – a bad bang it had been and he had a lump on his head like an egg, not that anybody cared, or even asked if he was all right. All anyone had been worried about was that tart and her stupid belly-ache.

And then – just as Ketch had suspected – the whole belly-ache business was a sham! A put-up job! Ketch knew this because when he banged his head he had not really been knocked out, but he had pretended to be. This was so the others would have to deal with getting the ambulance out of the ditch: Ketch was buggered if he was going to do himself a damage pushing the great heavy thing back on the road, never mind being out in the pouring rain which could cause a man to catch his death. So he lay still and quiet, but after the first couple of minutes he opened his eyes to narrow slits to see what was going on.

He saw a lot more than he had bargained for. The other car came alongside and a figure got out. He – Ketch thought it was a 'he' although he was not absolutely sure – came up to the back of the ambulance, opened the doors, climbed inside, and began to help Molland off the narrow shelf-bed. Ketch went on being deeply unconscious, but he managed to dart a quick look at Dr Kane.

And Kane was watching them! He was lying half-against the side of the ambulance, much as Ketch himself was doing, but Ketch saw him open his eyes and look straight at Molland and the stranger. Dr Kane knew exactly what was going on, but he shut his eyes again and let them get on with it!

Molland had got off the shelf-bed by this time, although she was clinging to her rescuer's arm – Ketch still could not tell who it was because of the deep-collared coat and the hat with the brim pulled well down. But when they got down onto the road they left the ambulance doors open, and he saw, very clearly indeed, that Molland was not so knocked out by Dr Kane's medicines that she could not walk almost unaided to the waiting car and get herself into the front seat. Well! If that was a girl with 'pendicitis then Ketch was Winston Churchill!

He watched and waited and presently the other car drove away into the night, and Dr Kane sat up as if he had recovered from the effects of the crash, and came over to Ketch, so that Ketch decided to recover consciousness. Then Dr Kane called out to the driver to put on some lights in the back, and when the lights were switched on he pretended to be shocked and horrified to find the prisoner had gone.

That was when Ketch knew he had something really valuable to carry to Dr McNulty. He did not think Dr Kane had had anything to do with the escape plan; what he thought was that Dr Kane had guessed it might happen and that he had deliberately pretended to be unconscious and let them get on with it. But who had it been in that car? *Who?*

When they got back, Calvary was in an uproar, policemen crawling all over the building, everyone talking about what had happened. Old Hedgehog was scuttling to and fro with a face the colour of porridge, saying they had never before had an escape from Calvary and it was terrible, catastrophic, and the head governor of prisons would have his balls on a plate. Ketch thought Old Hedgehog must be in a real stew to use such an expression because normally he never swore at all. Ketch was going to enjoy watching Hedgehog being brought to book for all this. He liked other people's misfortunes.

When he thought about it all a bit more, he thought Dr McNulty would probably want evidence, so he set himself to look for it. He knew what he needed to find;

you did not grow up in Ketch's family without learning a few ways to dodge unpleasant things or to get out of a punishment; his father had had a quick hand for the leather belt. Ketch did not grudge that; if he had ever had a son of his own, he would have given him a belting when it was necessary. He had not had a son, as it happened, in fact he had not had a wife. He did not mind that. Women pried and fussed; Ketch could not be doing with either.

But having that kind of childhood meant he knew the tricks. He knew about the stuff you could take to make yourself sick, or give you what some people called the Other. There were ways to make your temperature high, as well. All you had to do was put the thermometer into a cup of hot tea or against a hot water bottle when no one was looking, and then perhaps tousle your hair or dampen it with water – better still with something oily – so it looked sweat-soaked. If you were being what they called artistic, you could rouge your cheeks as well to make them flushed and hot-looking; Ketch had never done that himself but he thought you could trust Molland to have a few bits of paint and powder in her cell!

Ketch knew about all of this, and Dr Kane, with all his doctor's training would know it as well. So he had a good look round Dr Kane's room when no one was about, opening cupboards and drawers, thinking that when he had more time he might try to fathom the records Dr Kane kept for the various drugs. A man might do very nicely out of selling drugs; Ketch would try to find out what people wanted.

But there was nothing! This was so annoying Ketch

felt the bile rise in his throat. He knew – he knew absolutely and surely that this had all been a put-up job! That bitch sitting in the condemned cell had—

The condemned cell. Would there be anything in there? Something there had not been time to get rid of – something that might incriminate Dr Kane – or anyone else for that matter. Ketch did not much care who was guilty and who was not, providing he had something definite to carry along to the doctor.

He made his way to the condemned cell, not being furtive or sly, simply walking quite normally, as if he had a task to do. Look furtive and people suspected you of all kinds of things. Look open and normal, and nobody thought twice about it.

Looking open and normal, Ketch went through to the condemned cell. He did not completely close the door which might have attracted attention – people were still running round like demented ants – but left it half open. He could hear if anyone came along the corridor, but if there was anything to be found, then Ketch would find it. As he pushed the door, he glanced at the board affixed to it, listing the people who had been in and out of the cell today. Mostly it was just the names of the warders going on or off duty – eight-hour shifts it was. Old Hedgehog was strict about keeping these kinds of records, although they were a lot of rubbishy time-wasting to Ketch's mind.

They were not time-wasting tonight. The list of names made very interesting reading. As he began to search the cell, he was smiling to himself.

A lot of people were saying Molland was innocent, that she had been under Neville Fremlin's influence, and that

the police, and then the judge and jury, had not understood her. This was all rubbish. Ketch knew that one for
what she was and he understood her very well indeed.

CHAPTER TWENTY-NINE

People had never really understood mother; Vincent knew that. Mother had said so herself, on a number of occasions.

'I was always misunderstood,' she said. 'People did not know how to treat me. If I have kept my looks after all I've been through, it is one of God's mercies.'

Mother had kept her looks, of course; Vincent was always able to reassure her on that score. She always looked so pretty and so ladylike. Despite what they had tried to do to her in Calvary, despite the disappointments she had suffered, she still had soft fair hair like spun silk, and a complexion like one of the porcelain figurines she was so fond of. She collected figurines, and insisted on cleaning them herself; she would not allow any of the cleaning ladies they had to so much as dust them.

'They are very precious to me,' she said. 'A gentleman I knew – oh, many years ago – told me I was exactly like one of those china ladies. Exquisite and fragile, those were his words.' When Mother said this, Vincent had waited hopefully, wanting to hear more about the gentleman who had said this. Had it been someone like the Bournemouth Major?

'Oh no, no one like that,' said Mother.

Greatly daring, Vincent said, 'Was it my father who said it to you?'

Mother sighed. 'No, my dear, it was not. John Meade was a very quiet, very ordinary man. He could never have talked so . . . so persuasively or so charmingly. That was a marriage of convenience, really. After my ordeal in that place, my life was very lonely – I felt I needed someone to take care of me.'

'That place' was Calvary; Vincent knew that. Calvary, the grim dark prison-house where Mother had been locked away.

'I was very grateful to John Meade, and very sad at his death,' she said. 'No, the man who likened me to a porcelain figure was someone I met when I was a very young, very impressionable girl, not even twenty years old. But he betrayed me, Vincent.'

Vincent could hardly bear to think of it, and he could hardly bear to think of her taking the burden of the man's crimes, which was what she always said had happened. 'He took advantage of your innocence,' he said, which was a phrase from one of the books Mother liked to read.

'I paid for his wickedness,' she said. 'I was a mere child, but that did not stop them from accusing me of dreadful crimes. They threw me into a dreadful place, little better than a dungeon, and vulgar people laughed at me. I was made to wear ugly prison clothes and eat coarse food.'

It was like one of her books: the poor misunderstood heroine who had to endure hardships and privations, but she had finally been set free.

'I do not care to talk about it nowadays,' she said. 'Justice triumphed in the end, although for a long time life was very cruel to me. That is why I have to redress the balance here and there.'

The Bournemouth Major had been one redressing of the balance, and the widower in Reigate who had tripped over the wire stretched across the top of his stairs had been another. Vincent had never been able to pronounce the Reigate Widower's name because he had been Polish but Mother said he had very courtly manners.

'The Poles are extremely civilized people,' she said.

What a sad accident, people had said about him. What a tragedy. He had been on his own in the house that afternoon, but there you were, life was often tragic. After Reigate they had gone to live in Chichester and then in Southend, where Mother had met the lonely, not so young bachelor.

Mother did not discuss her men friends very much. If Vincent questioned her, she would firm her lips and make a dismissive gesture with one hand. They would not talk of it, she would say. Instead, Vincent should take her for a little drive. Would he do that? And when Vincent said that of course he would, mother would look out one of her chiffon scarves to drape over her hair. She did not want to be seen driving around looking a fright, she said; people noticed such things. She was not going to lower her standards after so many years. And perhaps while they were out they might have afternoon tea somewhere. When she was a girl afternoon tea had always been a great treat. Such a civilized thing, afternoon tea at half past four.

Afternoon tea was no longer the institution it had been in Mother's youth, in fact people did not really bother with it any longer, but Vincent thought it was still a polite time to call on someone.

As the church clock was chiming the half hour, he went along to Caradoc House and up to the little flat. Probably Georgina would offer him a cup of tea, and while he drank it he could find out about her movements over the next twenty-four hours which should give him a way in to his invitation to take her to Calvary.

But she did not offer him tea. She did not even invite him in! Vincent could not believe it. She was quite polite: she said she was busy, there was still a lot of sorting out of Walter's papers to do, and she kept him standing at the door, the bitch! The really infuriating thing was that he could see, even from the door, she had laid out some kind of black and green outfit on the back of the little settee. Well, that was not the kind of outfit you would expect someone to wear for sorting out musty, fifty-year-old papers! It was, in fact, what Mother would have called a dinner dress, not that Mother would ever have dreamed of wearing such a clingy-looking skirt, even if she had had Georgina's figure and legs. A bit cheap, she would have said. Not ladylike.

Vincent went back down the stairs and out into the street with his thoughts in disarray. Georgina Grey was going out to dinner tonight, that seemed clear. And since she had told Vincent she did not know anyone in Thornbeck, logically it must be with Dr Ingram and his people. This was increasingly worrying. It was as well he had such a good plan worked out.

But if Georgina really was dining out, he had better get on with his experiment on the lime right away. He had not got very much time.

Once inside his own house he put on gardening gloves, the scarf and the dark glasses, then went along to the potting shed. His garden was enclosed by a high brick wall, and it was impossible for anyone to see over it. This garden was one of the reasons Vincent had chosen this house; you never knew when you might need real privacy, although he had not taken experiments with lime into account when he made this decision.

The potting shed smelt of earth and damp; it was small and dark and it felt secretive. Vincent tipped the lime fragments into an old metal bucket, and then put a large plastic bag of commercial compost within reach. After this he connected the garden hosepipe to the outside water tap, and, careful to stand well clear, trained a thin trickle of water onto the bucket's interior. He was only half-expecting a reaction because of the lime being so old.

But the lime reacted at once. It fizzed up in an angry boiling cloud, and Vincent was so astonished he almost forgot to turn the tap off and douse the hissing lime with the compost. But he pulled himself together and did so, relieved when the bubbling lime seemed to be completely quenched. He carried the metal bucket to the end of the garden, and tipped the whole thing onto a small unused patch, sprinkling another thick layer of compost over it all.

As he locked up the shed and went back to the house he was smiling because the plan for getting rid of Georgina Grey was moulding into a very good shape indeed.

The little hall clock was just chiming the half hour. Six thirty. Just time to put on his normal clothes and go back to Caradoc House. He did not much like the image of himself as some Peeping Tom, lurking sleazily in the shadows to watch, and perhaps even follow, Georgina, but it had to be done.

In the event, he did not have to lurk for very long; shortly after seven o'clock Georgina came out of the house, slamming the door behind her. Vincent was glad to see that at least she was sufficiently responsible to try the door to make sure the catch had dropped.

She walked quickly along the street, and as she passed under a street lamp Vincent saw that she was wearing the black and green outfit he had seen earlier with a black woollen cape over it. The one unexpected note was her bag; it was not an ordinary handbag such as ladies usually carried in the evening, but a large haversack-sized affair. This was puzzling, but Vincent would be the first to admit he was not absolutely abreast of modern fashions. For all he knew haversacks on dinner dates might be the latest look in London.

She went into the King's Head as he had expected and he hesitated, then followed her in, pausing in the little reception area. She went through to the small dining area, and Vincent saw the dark-haired man he had noticed the previous day – the one who was blind and whom he had thought an odd addition to Dr Ingram's team. Were these two having dinner together? It looked like it. Would they be discussing Walter Kane and

Calvary? That was highly likely. It did not look as if the plan could be left in abeyance any longer; with a jolt of pleasurable anticipation, Vincent saw that he had got to put it into action at once, now, tonight. Clearly he could not get Georgina out to Calvary tonight, but he could arrange to do so first thing tomorrow morning. How about appearing to bump into her later this evening and making the suggestion then? He considered this and thought it would work very well indeed.

'Why, hello,' he would say, feigning surprise. 'I didn't know you were in here tonight.' And it would be the most natural thing in the world for him to accompany her to Caradoc House – in fact it would be the gentlemanly thing to do, particularly since the blind man probably would not be able to do so. As they walked along the street, the offer to drive Georgina out to Calvary in the morning could be dropped quite casually.

Vincent looked across at the dining area again, to make sure Georgina and the man really were having dinner. Yes, they were seated at a table, and they had been brought a menu. Georgina was reading it out to her companion, and something he had said had made her laugh. She would not be laughing by this time tomorrow.

It would be better to return here later – Vincent could hardly sit here for the next two hours or so, watching those two. He walked towards the bar and then stopped abruptly and patted his inner pocket in the way of a man checking his wallet. Then he gave an exasperated *tsk* of annoyance, and turned to re-trace his steps. Anyone watching would have seen a man bound for a pleasant evening's drink suddenly realizing he had left his wallet at home.

Vincent filled in an hour at his own house by eating a hastily put together meal, and at ten to nine he returned to the King's Head. Were they still here? Yes, it looked as if they had just been served coffee. Very good, he would be able to have a drink at the bar and wait for Georgina to leave. Really, it was all working out very neatly.

But no sooner had he requested his glass of sherry than Georgina and the man left their table and walked out to reception. His hand was lightly on her arm, but Vincent had the impression that this was not so he could walk without bumping into anything, it was more because he liked the feel of her arm under his hand. Slightly flustered by dealing with sherry and change all at the same time, and by being elbowed out of the way by some rude person loudly demanding lager, Vincent prepared to go after them. Surely the man would not be seeing her back to Caradoc House after all? How would he find his way back here?

They were not going back to Caradoc House, they were going up the stairs to the bedrooms! Had they known one another previously, or was Georgina the kind of cheap little tart who went to bed with someone a couple of hours after the first meeting? Or was it something to do with the TV programme after all? Vincent did not know whether to be shocked at the possible promiscuity or panic-stricken by the potential Calvary collaboration.

He drank his sherry unhurriedly in case anyone was watching, and exchanged a few words with one or two of the locals because it was important to seem entirely normal. He was trying to decide what his next move should be, when Dr Ingram, the American and Drusilla came down the stairs, followed, more slowly, by Georgina and the blind man.

The bar was quite crowded, but Vincent was able to get nearer to reception. He was just in time to hear Drusilla say that Calvary at two a.m. ought to be quite a memorable experience.

He saw Georgina had changed into jeans and a thick jacket. Vincent followed them out and stood in the deep porch of the King's Head, pretending to turn up his coat collar against the rain that had started earlier and to pat his pockets as if trying to find his keys. All five of them got into the big estate car and drove away. Vincent frowned. It looked as if they were going to Calvary for night filming of some kind – moonlight shots of the place, perhaps? But Drusilla had made that remark about two a.m. and it was still only a quarter to ten. As the estate car's tail lights disappeared into the darkness, Vincent walked quickly to his own house. His mind was teeming with ideas and possibilities, and the pieces of the plan he had made were starting to come together in absolute symmetry.

A plan originally evolved for one person could as easily be used for two. Perhaps for more than two. Afterwards, everyone would say it was all very sad but the old lime store always had been dangerous and it should have been properly demolished years ago. But there you were, people could be careless, especially people who had their minds on other things. On the making of television programmes for instance, or on the sifting of a great-grandfather's possessions. And the result would be that Calvary's ghosts would be safe.

Vincent smiled, thinking of the lime store with its

unreliable door that might so easily close and shut some-one inside.

In the next couple of hours he would have to do what people called think on his feet. He would have to be alert and aware and he would have to adapt to whatever presented itself. But he could do it. He could be as quick-thinking and as nimble-minded as the circumstances required.

There were a few quite simple preparations to be made. Vincent went about making them, pleased at the way everything was working out. Last of all he collected his own keys to Calvary – the old scullery key and the key to the execution suite and the execution chamber itself – and went out of the house. On his way through the hall, he caught sight of his reflection in the mirror. He looked almost exactly the way Mother used to look when she had disposed of one of her gentlemen. Flushed, exalted, confident. He smiled at his reflection, and went out to his car to drive to Calvary.

It was raining quite hard by the time Vincent reached the track, and everywhere was very muddy. He switched off his headlights, and parked unobtrusively beneath some trees, reversing in and going as far back as possible. He pulled on the hat he kept in the car against bad weather – a deer-stalker it was, which he sometimes liked to wear with a glengarry cape – then he walked up the hill, keeping a sharp look out for Dr Ingram's people. Were they here? Yes, there was the estate car parked at the front entrance. He went a bit nearer and saw that the little inset door in Calvary's main entrance was closed, but that there were footprints in the wet mud, leading up to the doors. Then they were inside and Georgina was in there with them. Vincent glanced about him. Nothing moved on the quiet hillside, and there was only the sound of the rain pattering lightly on the few sparse trees out here. He went back down the track to his car, and edged it a couple of feet forward so he could see Calvary's main doors reasonably well. He settled down to wait, switching on the engine a couple of times for the heat to de-mist the windows.

It was almost half past ten when they came out and got back into the car. But now there were only three of them. Vincent peered through the darkness. Was he right? Yes, there was Dr Ingram, the American getting into the driver's seat, and Drusilla getting in next to him. The car revved up and drove down the hillside. Vincent saw it pause at the far end of the lane and then turn left towards Thornbeck.

As Vincent sat there, the rain blurring the landscape through the car windows, his lips curved in a smile at the thought of a sightless man and a single female completely alone inside the dark, deserted prison-house.

CHAPTER THIRTY

It had not been until they actually reached the execution chamber that Georgina felt Calvary's atmosphere close down on her. Thick waves of fear and despair seemed to fasten around her throat, and there was a moment when she thought she was not going to be able to do this.

Then Jude's voice said coolly, 'I suppose you've given us the same penthouse suite, have you, Professor? Yes, I thought I recognized the ambience. Well, Georgina? As a trysting place I don't suppose it's the best, but the company might be entertaining.'

It's all right, thought Georgina gratefully. I'm not going to make a scene. I'm going to carry this thing through with perfect panache – well, not perfect, per-haps, but pretty damn close to that.

She said, 'By entertaining company, d'you mean you or the spooks?'

'Oh, the spooks, every time,' said Jude at once. 'Now

listen, what I want to do is go down into the gallows pit while Georgina stays in the room up here.'

'The more I think about that, the less I like it,' said Chad, frowning. 'I certainly don't like the idea of you leaving Georgina here on her own. But I suppose if I ask you not to do it that way, you'll do it anyway as soon as I'm out of earshot.'

'The very second you've gone,' agreed Jude. 'The whole point is for me to see what the atmosphere's like down there. We've got a mobile phone each, haven't we? I know we can't get a signal in here, but if Georgina stays up in the room she can go outside to call you if we need to.'

'That's true. Georgina, you'd better have a key to the main entrance. There was a second one on the keyring.'

'Thanks.' Georgina took the key and slid it into the pocket of her jeans. 'What about the door to these rooms? Wasn't there a lock on that?'

'Yes, and the key was in it,' said Chad. 'But obviously we won't lock that door, so if you do need to summon us you can get straight outside.'

'I shall probably regret asking this,' said Georgina, 'but why might I need to summon you?'

'Half a dozen reasons,' said Jude promptly. 'I might break my ankle exploring. Or I might have a heart attack or succumb to a bout of drunken ravings—'

'Or become possessed by the ghost of Tommy the Turnkey?'

'Or a combination of all those things. What's the present situation on the trapdoor? Did I actually break it or just disable the mechanism?'

Chad was examining the lever. 'There are the two doors,' he said. 'They would both have dropped inwards, of course – but only one opened when you grabbed the lever.'

'It looks as if the hinges of the other one have rusted into place,' said Phin, shining his torch.

'Yes, and I don't think we'd better try closing the half that Jude opened,' said Chad. 'In case it causes any damage or in case it sticks. Jude, if you really do intend to spend the night down there you'd better make sure to stay directly under the door that's already dropped.'

'OK.'

'What's the other trapdoor over there?' asked Georgina, indicating the far corner.

'We think it's stairs leading down to the vault,' said Chad. 'But we haven't been able to open it. It's either stuck or locked, so you'd better disregard it altogether, I think. Dru, is the camcorder set?'

'It is and we've put it in the same place,' said Drusilla, pointing. 'And I've shown Georgina how it works.'

'I'm going to check it every twenty minutes to make sure it's running,' said Georgina.

'Jude's got the dictaphone again and Phin's taken a new set of stills,' said Drusilla. 'You've each got a flask of coffee, haven't you? Oh, and Georgina's got a notebook to make her own record.'

'Sounds all right.' Chad walked across to the partly open gallows trap. 'Jude, can you spring down into the vault if we guide you?'

'I can spring as nimbly as a mountain goat if I have to,' said Jude. 'Show me the way.' He paused and in a completely different voice, said, 'Georgina, are you sure about this? No one's going to think any the worse of you if you back out.'

'I don't want to back out,' said Georgina, who did want to back out but was not going to admit it.

'On a practical note, how deep is this bloody drop?'

'About eight feet from the look of it,' said Chad. 'If you sit on the edge, you should be able to sort of lower yourself down.'

'It's here,' said Phin, taking Jude's arm and leading him forward. 'About six steps forward. 'OK, we're there.'

'Thanks, Phin, I've got it.' Jude sat down, his feet over the trap. 'I'm on the edge, aren't I? No rude comments, please. Oh listen, you'll throw the walking stick down after me, won't you?'

'Yes. Get on with it,' said Chad, and Jude grinned.

'Here I go. Down, down, to hell, and say I sent thee thither. I bet I'm the only person ever to have quoted Shakespeare on the edge of the gallows.'

'I bet you're not,' said Chad.

'If you prefer it, I can do Sydney Carton. "It is a far, far better thing I do, than I have ever done;—"'

'If Sydney Carton's the anti-hero in Tale of Two Cities, he died on the guillotine not at the end of a rope.'

'Messier but more heroic,' said Jude, and half jumped, half slithered down. He seemed to land reasonably easily, although he let out a curse as he hit the ground below.

'All right?' said Chad anxiously.

'Never better.' His voice came up a bit muffled. 'It was a bit more of a drop than I expected, that's all. My God, this is an appalling place.'

'Your idea,' said Chad a bit shortly.

'Yes, but I hadn't realized it would feel quite so ...
No, it's fine. Had we better check that I can get back up
under my own steam before you all leave?'

'Go ahead.'

They were all crouching on the edge of the gallows
vault; Georgina saw that it was a brick-lined cellar-like
place, roughly five feet square.

'I can't do it,' said Jude, having made several attempts
to reach the edge. 'Hell and damnation. I certainly won't
be able to pull myself back up.'

'There's a length of rope in the car,' said Drusilla.
'Would that be any good?'

'I don't know, but we'll try. Phin, would you and
Dru get it?'

They set off, Phin galloping eagerly along, and were
back very quickly.

'You've got it?' said Chad.

'Yes, and Tommy the Turnkey says hello.'

'I'll bet. Try the rope, would you?'

But the rope was of no help at all in enabling Jude to
climb out.

'There's nothing to secure it to,' said Chad. 'Only the
lever, and we daren't use that. And Georgina wouldn't
be able to pull you out just using her own strength.'

'I'd try if necessary though,' said Georgina.

'It shouldn't be necessary. Jude, you'll have to stay put
until we get back, then Phin and I can pull you out.'

'That'll be something to look forward to,' said Jude
expressionlessly.

'We'll see you at two,' said Chad, and glanced at
Georgina. 'You've got my phone number on your
mobile, haven't you?'

'I have. We'll be fine, truly. But I'll summon you for help if anything unexpected happens.'

'We can be here within fifteen minutes,' said Chad. His voice was reassuring, but Georgina had to repress a shiver as they closed the door. She listened to their footsteps going away along the deserted corridors, then checked the camcorder which was whirring quietly to itself in the corner.

Jude's voice said, 'I'm going to kick off by having some of Drusilla's coffee. You have some too, Georgina. It's going to be a long night.'

Vincent waited until he was absolutely sure Dr Ingram and the other two had driven away back to Thornbeck, then he locked his car, and made his way up the slope. It was a wild night – the rain was still falling and gusts of wind drove it into his face. He did not mind any of this; there was an odd satisfaction in enduring the savagery of the weather, almost as if he were saying, You see what I'm prepared to suffer for your sake, mother?

He kept a weather eye open for anyone who might be lurking around, but there was no one – he had not expected there would be, but he was not taking any chances. He went around the side of Calvary's main walls, and let himself in through the old scullery door, closing and locking it behind him, careful to pocket the key. Calvary's darkness closed around him like a cloak, and he felt very close to Mother as he went through the dim corridors, past the workshops and the cells and on to the execution suite. I'm keeping the secrets, he said to her memory. Just as this place has kept them. No one shall ever know all those things you did, because no one would understand in the way that I understand. You did all those things in order to survive. I know that.

Ahead of him was the condemned wing. Had they locked the interconnecting door? No, they had not; the key was still there, on the outside. He had not needed to bring his own key after all, although it was better not to make assumptions. Vincent removed the key from the door and pocketed it, doing so gently and slowly so as not to make any noise, then pushed the door open carefully and stepped into the short passageway beyond, his heart racing with excitement and nervous tension.

He was fairly sure Georgina and the blind man would be in the execution chamber – it was the heart of Calvary – but he tiptoed along to listen. Yes, that was Georgina's voice. Vincent waited for the man's reply, but when it came, he was puzzled, because his voice was muffled, distant, almost as if it was not coming from within the room at all but from somewhere outside it.

Understanding flooded his mind. The man's voice was coming from beneath it! He was in the gallows vault! That must be the experiment they were conducting for the television programme – that must have been what Drusilla meant when she said Calvary at two a.m. ought to be memorable. He was actually spending the night in the vault. Vincent could not think why Georgina would be here with him rather than Dr Ingram, but her presence fitted so well into his plan that he did not care. He reviewed his plan quickly, and saw it was going to work – they were playing straight into his hands.

The first thing to do was separate them. In a moment he would make them aware of his presence, and with luck

Georgina would come out to investigate. First he went stealthily back to the oak door and turned the key in the lock. The lock was old and it protested a bit, but Vincent did not think the sound could be heard at the other end of the corridor through the closed door of the execution chamber. He pocketed the key, making a mental note to return it later so that nothing appeared to have been tampered with.

After this, he came back along the passage as far as the rather grim shower room next to the condemned cell. Could he hide in there? Yes, he could stand behind the door and anyone looking in, even shining a torch around, would be unlikely to see him.

It gave him a deep and satisfying pleasure to think that these two were locked in here with him.

'Why did you agree to tonight?' asked Jude. His voice, coming from the gallows pit, still sounded peculiar but Georgina was getting used to it. 'Is it about your great-grandfather? Are you laying his ghost? Sorry, I sound as if I'm prying, don't I? But after so many years in journalism it's an incurable habit to ask questions. Dreadfully antisocial, of course.'

'It's not prying and it's not really antisocial,' said Georgina. 'And yes, it is all mixed up with Walter, although I'm not entirely sure why. He intrigues me.'

'He intrigues me, as well. Did he really leave a lot of money to the Caradoc Society?'

'Yes, he did, and I don't know why. I don't know why he ignored the existence of his wife and daughter, and I can't square that with someone who worked with convicted killers and who fought in the war. It's a bit unnerving to keep uncovering fragments of information about him but not get to the end of anything.'

'Yes, one wants the full picture,' said Jude. He was silent for a moment, then he said, 'Had you seen Calvary before this?'

'I drove up here earlier in the week and had a look round the outside. It's a bleak old place, Jude. It's smaller than I was expecting, but I suppose that's because it was originally designed as a place of execution rather than a House of Correction. But I don't think anything could have prepared me for the atmosphere in here. How about down there?'

'Dreadful,' said Jude's voice. 'If you weren't up there to talk to, I'd begin to wonder if I'd fallen into one of the Old Testament equivalents of hell, although it's a lot colder than I'd have expected hell to be. Isn't there a line from something about hell being a soundless pit with no beam of comfort peeping in? Whoever wrote it must have been in a place like this.'

'I do wonder—' began Georgina, then stopped.

'What's the matter?'

'I thought I heard something. Out in the passageway.'

'Tommy the Turnkey?'

'Oh God, I hope not. It was a kind of scuffling.'

'Mice?'

'It might be. As long as it's not rats.'

'Can you still hear it?' asked Jude after a moment.

'I think it's gone. You didn't hear it?'

'No, but half a dozen people could be doing a clog dance and I wouldn't hear a thing down here. Has it stopped?'

'Yes.'

And for a moment Georgina did think that whatever she had heard had gone – whether it was rats or mice or ghosts, or even just the rain outside. Then she thought the sound of rainfall would not penetrate into this room. But probably it had only been Calvary's old timbers contracting against the night cold.

She was about to call down to Jude that it must have been her imagination, when she heard the sounds again and this time there was no doubt about them. They were not being made by mice or rats or by anything four-legged or spiritual or architectural. They were footsteps, clear and recognizable.

Someone was walking along the corridor outside.

Georgina was not aware of having moved, but she discovered she was kneeling on the edge of the gallows trap and calling softly down to Jude.

'It's most likely just Chad or one of the others,' she said. 'But . . .'

'But they'd call out – let us know that they were back.'

This was undeniable.

'A tramp?' said Georgina, a bit doubtfully.

'It might be. But how would he get in? Chad locked all the doors, didn't he?'

'Yes, except for the inner door to these rooms.' Georgina glanced uneasily over her shoulder towards the closed door. 'Whoever it is, it's pretty damn spooky of him to be stomping around at this hour of the night. Had I better phone Chad to check that he or Phin haven't come back – No, damn, there isn't a signal in here, is there? But you're probably right about it being a tramp. There must be a way in Chad doesn't know about.'

'Yes, but you're up there on your own, and tramps

aren't always harmless,' said Jude. And then, explosively, 'Oh God, if I could just bloody *see* for five minutes—' He broke off. 'Georgina? Are you still there?'

'Yes, but I'm going to find out who it is,' said Georgina, crossing the floor to the door before she could change her mind.

'For pity's sake, *don't!*' he said at once.

'I'm only going to call out to ask who's there. I've got the torch.'

'No, wait a minute. I'll find the stairs to that other little trapdoor and see if I can dislodge it from down here.'

'I'm really only going to take a quick look,' said Georgina.

Even with the torch, stepping into the corridor beyond the execution chamber was a daunting experience. Georgina stood by the door, shining the light along the passage, seeing that the execution chamber was at the end of a corridor, and that the corridor was a cul-de-sac, ending in a blank brick wall. She had not noticed that when they came in. Further along – to her right – was the condemned cell, which Chad had pointed out to her, and beyond that was a tiny shower room, and then a heavily barred door leading to the condemned man's own exercise yard. Could someone have got in through that door? But Georgina thought it did not look as if it had been opened for years. Beyond that again was the door leading out into the main part of the prison, through which they had come earlier.

There was no one in the passage. Georgina took a few cautious steps away from the execution chamber, holding the torch like a talisman, letting it play over the cobwebbed walls and the pock-marked floor. Nothing stirred. Had she after all imagined the footsteps?

'Hello? Is anyone here?'

It sounded absurd and clichéd in the extreme, but it also sounded terrifyingly eerie, because in the enclosed space her voice bounced off the walls, and swooped back at her. She went a bit further along, ready to dart back into the execution chamber and slam the door hard. Nothing moved anywhere, but Georgina was beginning to have the feeling that she was not on her own. She had the feeling someone was watching her through a chink or a crack. She could not decide how far to trust this feeling: it might just be nerves.

Here was the condemned cell – the door was lying on the ground just inside. Georgina remembered Phin making a good story of how they had pushed it open and how it had fallen off its hinges, nearly deafening everyone. She shone the torch inside, but the room was empty – unless you counted the thick layers of agony and despair that hung on the air. Dreadful. (And were the unseen eyes still watching her?)

The shower room was next, its door wide open. It was a grisly, concrete-floored compartment, not much wider than the corridor. Incredibly an antiquated shower trough was still in place, and pipes hung out of the walls like clusters of spiders' legs. Georgina thought the condemned cell had had some kind of basic loo behind a half screen, but they must presumably have brought the condemned prisoner in here to shower each day. Had he cared about that? If you were going to die, would you care whether you were bathed and shampooed? She shone the torch inside, but nothing moved.

She called out again, and again Calvary's thick shadows sent her own voice back at her.

Anyone here, anyone here, HERE, . . .

Or were the echoes playing a trick? Mightn't they be saying, *someone here . . .?*

She reached the end of the corridor, and stood for a moment by the oak door. Should she go back through it into Calvary's maze of corridors and cells? She thought it might be very easy to get lost out there. Even Chad Ingram, who had a map of the layout and who had been in here before, had hesitated at one of the intersections, clearly unsure whether to turn left or right. Perhaps she ought to open the oak door and call out once more before going back. The footsteps seemed to have gone – they might not have been footsteps at all, in fact. They might have been some peculiar echo – something to do with the plumbing – water dripping somewhere. Georgina did not actually think this was very likely, but at least nothing sinister seemed to be prowling around out here.

She reached for the door's handle, and turned it. It would not turn. Was it stuck? Georgina tried again, and then shone the torch onto the edges where the door met the wall. It was not stuck at all, it was locked – it was a simple old mechanism, and she could see the steel tongue was locked across. The key was nowhere to be seen. Was it on the other side of the door?

But Chad had definitely said he would leave this door unlocked because Georgina needed to be able to get outside the building to make a phone call in an emergency. That was why he had left her the spare key to the main outside door. But if he had left the door unlocked, who had locked it? Prickles of fear jabbed her mind, and with them suddenly came another memory, causing her to whip round and stare back down the corridor.

The bathroom door. When they came in here it had been closed. Georgina definitely remembered that; she remembered Chad pointing it out. And now it was standing wide open. Had Chad or one of the others opened it? Georgina could not think of any good reason why they would have done that.

Icy fear was scudding across her skin in waves. Someone's in here, she thought. Someone who's locked this door – and taken away the key – and someone who's pushed the bathroom door back to the wall so he could stand behind it to hide.

She shone the torch over the walls again. Had there been a movement from within the bathroom? If there really was someone in here, what should she do? Could she scoot back along the passage and get inside the execution chamber and slam the door? But what then? Could the door be locked from inside?

She was just making up her mind that at least she must get back to Jude, when the movement came again. A figure darted out of the tiny bathroom, ran past the condemned cell and into the execution chamber. The door slammed hard with a dreadful booming thud, and Georgina's earlier question was answered because in the enclosed space the sound of a lock being turned from inside was clear and unmistakable.

The owner of the footsteps had locked her into this corridor. And whoever he was, he was now inside the execution chamber with Jude.

CHAPTER THIRTY-ONE

Jude had waited in an agony of impatience for Georgina to come back and say everything was all right, that after all it had only been water dripping somewhere, or mice.

If he could have got back into the room he would have gone unhesitatingly out to see who might be prowling around, and be blowed to being blind – he thought he had never hated his blindness as much as he hated it at this minute. Not even those first anguished weeks compared with this – with being stuck in this place, fearing something had happened to Georgina, and not being able to get to her. Several layers down he was aware that his anguish for Georgina was far more than it would have been if it had been Drusilla or Phin or even Chad who was in danger, but there was no time to examine this feeling. In any case Georgina was probably firmly hooked up to some revoltingly healthy man who took her disgustingly for granted, and treated her abominably . . . and had his sight. Oh hell.

After a few moments he managed to locate the steps which were in a corner of the vault, and he felt his way up them, missing his footing once or twice and banging his head when he reached the top. But although he threw his whole weight into trying to raise the small trapdoor, and also tried using the walking stick to force it upwards, it was absolutely immoveable. Damn.

He retraced his steps, expecting to hear Georgina come back. But the minutes dragged on, and there was only the thick silence. From feeling worried, Jude now began to feel genuinely frightened. Chad had said he had checked this place but how far had he been able to do that?

From overhead, he heard a sudden yell of anger or pain or both – Georgina's voice! – and then running footsteps coming towards the execution chamber. The door was slammed and there was the sound of a key turning in the lock. Georgina? No, he could hear her voice from a long way away, shouting something. There was a second or two of relief at that, because for the moment she sounded all right. But the relief was instantly replaced by a new fear, because clearly the prowler was in the execution chamber. Even if Jude had not heard the man's slightly laboured breathing, he would have sensed his presence.

For a moment he had absolutely no idea what to do. Did the man even know he was down here? But no sooner had the thought formed than there was the rasping of machinery. Above him something seemed to shudder, and there was the sound of pulleys engaging. The gallows trap, thought Jude. My God, he's closing it! He's shutting me into this God-forsaken vault!

As the door locked back into place, he felt the darkness become stifling and menacing, and was aware again of the lonely agony of the prison. Calvary's ghosts pressed against him, holding out their dead hands, pushing their swollen discoloured faces at him . . .

Now you're down here with us, said these unseen faces. Now you've joined us and you can't get away. For a fleeting, shutter-flash second Jude saw in his mind the face he had seen the previous night. A narrow well-shaped skull, with thick just-greying hair, a sharp clear jawline that even the dislocation of the neck could not blur.

And then the inner image vanished, and he was back with the choking darkness, and the unknown prowler overhead. And Georgina trapped somewhere beyond the execution chamber.

Think, dammit, said Jude angrily to himself. You can't get out of here by brute strength, but you might get out by using your wits – it wouldn't be the first time you'd done that. So where's that famed sharpness that got you out of so many awkward places in the past?

There had to be another way out of this vault. There must have been some means of taking the executed prisoners away – taking them to a mortuary, perhaps, or an infirmary room. It was unlikely that the bodies had been carried up the stairs and through the smaller trap, because the stairs were too narrow and awkward. And it was even less likely that they would have been taken through the main part of the prison. So how had it been done, *how?*

Mentally he reached for the map he had made of the vault – eight feet deep, and rectangular in shape. Steps up to the trap behind him, in a corner. None of that any damn good. Jude began to tap around the walls with his stick, feeling for a break in the solid brickwork. There must be something, there must . . .

And there it was. A door. Set deeply into the brickwork, with a handle on one side. Jude did not give himself time to wonder if this door would be locked; he turned the handle straight away. It felt loose and it was unpleasantly rusty, but it moved and although the hinges groaned like a thousand souls in torment, the door opened outwards fairly easily. The accreted dust and dirt of years came away and a breath of foetid air gusted outwards.

For a moment panic engulfed him because anything could be beyond this door – the prowler might be crouching there, waiting to pounce. But if Jude could get near enough to a window or even an outer wall, he should be able to phone Chad. He hated having to call for help – he wanted to go rampaging through Calvary himself, find Georgina and then beat to a pulp the madman who had brought about this situation. As he felt his way cautiously forwards, he wondered briefly who the man was. Presumably he had a key. And hopefully the camcorder would have picked him up, although this would not be much comfort if Jude and Georgina were attacked and injured, and it would not be any help if the man spotted the camcorder and smashed it up.

Tapping around with the stick seemed to establish that beyond the door was a tunnel, brick lined, not very wide. It might lead anywhere or it might lead nowhere, but Jude thought there was a strong possibility that it led to the infirmary or perhaps some kind of morgue.

The ghosts were still with him as he went along – the hanged men who would have been carried along this tunnel. Had the man whose face he had seen been carried along here? Presumably he must have been. Presumably he had been a murderer, and he was buried in the prison's grounds.

Several times he misjudged distances and twice he walked into a jutting bit of wall. The tunnel curved which made it difficult to make any kind of mental map in his head. Every few paces he stopped to listen, but there was no sound of the intruder following him. He thought the man had stayed in the execution chamber.

The tunnel widened slightly, and Jude felt a faint brush of cooler air ahead of him – a door? A window? Worth trying to get a signal again? He was just reaching for the phone when he heard the sound he had hoped not to hear. The shudder of metal and timber as the trap was opened again. That could only mean one thing: the man was about to spring down into the vault and come after him.

Jude's every instinct screamed at him to whip round and confront whoever this was, and the familiar frustration tore through him again. *I can't see!*

He plunged on as quickly as he dared, feeling for Chad's number on the phone's keypad at the same time. Please let it ring out – please . . . but it was still dead.

The prowler was coming quietly, but Jude could hear him. He could sense the man approaching. He could not imagine what he wanted – he supposed he was a druggie high on something. But if he pounced, Jude would put up as good a fight as he could. He gripped the walking stick gratefully, and it was then that the cooler air seemed more definite and the stick made out the shape of a doorway and of a half-open door.

Then I really am out of the tunnel thought Jude, and moved forward again, trying to fix the position of the doorway on his mental map, keeping to a left-hand wall. After a few feet he encountered what seemed to be a deep old stone sink. Was it? Yes, his hands identified old-fashioned taps and pipes. Then surely this was far enough above ground to pick up a phone signal. Would there be time to reach Chad before the madman in the tunnel made a move? Even if he did not manage to speak, surely if Chad saw a call registering from Jude's number he would respond.

He was just reaching into his pocket for the phone when there was a rush of movement from within the tunnel, and he knew the person who had stalked the darkness was standing in front of him.

Vincent thought the plan was unrolling beautifully. It was not unrolling precisely as he had thought it would, but as long as he stopped the television people's activities and Georgina's delvings – and did not get caught in the process – the sequence of events did not matter.

It gave him a savage satisfaction to raise the trapdoor and shut the dark-haired man in. Vincent sensed his sudden panic. The next bit was interesting, because he wanted the man to find his way through the old mortuary tunnel, and come out into the burial yard. Would he do that? Vincent knelt on the edge of the trap, listening, hearing the tapping of the man's stick. Yes, he had worked out that there would have to be another way out, and he was trying to find it. Ah, there he went now!

Good! Vincent waited until he judged the man had got to the far end, to where the tunnel opened onto the mortuary, then raised the trap again, and sprang down into the vault. He switched on his torch, and padded very quietly along after his prey.

The man had reached the mortuary, exactly as he had hoped. Vincent waited, standing just inside the tunnel, wanting the man to move forward a little more so he could step out. His idea was to unbolt the outer door, and get the man into the burial yard. He hoped not to have to use violence, because he wanted everything to look like a genuine accident, but he would do so if necessary. Seen at closer quarters, the man was a little older than he had seemed in the King's Head: perhaps thirty-six or thirty-eight. When he half turned his head, as if listening for sounds from within the tunnel, Vincent saw he was not wearing dark glasses. Even in the dimness it was possible to see he had remarkably vivid blue eyes. Vincent found it disconcerting, because for a moment, he had thought the man could see him. Could he? Was this some kind of elaborate trick? No, it was all right, but he knew Vincent was there, Vincent could tell.

He was moving forward again, going in the direction of the door. Perhaps he could feel cooler air coming in from it. He had stopped, though – why had he done that?

Ah, of course! He had reached into his pocket and was holding a mobile phone. He was going to call for help, probably from Dr Ingram. So, violence it would have to be. Vincent sprang forward and before the man could react or put up any kind of defence, he had knocked the phone from his hand, sending it skittering across the floor into a dusty corner.

Among the preparations he had made before leaving his house was the fashioning of a makeshift cosh. This had been easy; he had filled an old sock with soft dry soil from the end of his garden. Plainly he would have to knock the man out before he could move to the next stage of his plan. He swung the cosh and brought it down on the man's head. He fell to his knees, then crumpled forward and lay still. Vincent bent over to make sure he was genuinely unconscious – yes, he was. Very good. The weapon wouldn't be found – the soil could be tipped away and the sock burned.

He unbolted the outer door of the mortuary – this was the only door that was bolted from inside – and propped it open. Cool night air filtered in, and he could see the shadowy mounds of the graves beyond.

Now for the strenuous part. Vincent considered his victim, seeing he was quite slimly built but that it was the slimness of whipcord strength rather than weakness. In the end, he simply grasped the edges of the man's coat and dragged him down to the burial yard outside. It was quite difficult but not as difficult as he had feared, although he had to pause a couple of times, and when he reached the lime store he was puffing like a grampus. He would have to watch that, it would not do to become out of condition. People would notice; they would say he was getting flabby.

He propped the man against the side of the row of outbuildings. Once he got him inside the lime store and wedged the door firmly closed, he would return for Georgina. His mind flew ahead, seeing how he would unlock the door to the execution suite, and how she would come out at once, and how he would be waiting for her. He would have to remain well hidden, of course, because if anything went wrong she must not be able to identify him afterwards. But it ought to be possible to knock her out in the darkness, and get her into the lime store as well. And then . . .

And then he would cover the drain with the supermarket carrier bag folded in his pocket and weight it in place with a stone. After he had done that he would knock away the rusting tap from the rainwater butt and flood the courtyard.

Tomorrow, when the news got round, people would be shocked to hear that someone of Dr Ingram's standing – actually C. R. Ingram who did all those television programmes and wrote all those books – had been so irresponsible. That he had allowed a blind man the run of Calvary, and that the man had blundered into the lime store along with Georgina Grey, and that both of them had been trapped in there, and . . .

And died? That remained to be seen, but when Vincent remembered how the small pieces of lime had reacted to water, he smiled.

He had brought the oilskin rain hat in his pocket, the thick gardening gloves and glasses, because whatever happened to these people, he was not risking any damage to himself, not he! He put these on, and then carefully opened the door. As it swung open the powdery lime, disturbed by the movement, stirred slightly. For a moment, against the blackness of the store's interior it seemed to writhe upwards into the blurred, shifting outline of a man – a man who was trying to hold out his arms but could not because his arms ended in stumps from where the quicklime had eaten his hands away.

'But it's only what a murderer deserves.'

Vincent shook his head to clear this macabre image and to dispel the odd little whisper in his mind. It was not at all like him to have these fantasies and he was perfectly accustomed to Calvary's atmosphere. The circumstances were bizarre, of course, so perhaps he was entitled to an attack of nerves.

He bent down to hook his hands under his victim's arms, and began to drag him inside.

CHAPTER THIRTY-TWO

September 1939

Walter Kane thought he could say with truth that he liked most people. He could usually find something to admire or enjoy or appreciate in everyone he met.

But he could not find anything to admire or enjoy or appreciate in Denzil McNulty. He had met him a couple of times because McNulty had acted as locum at Calvary when Walter was away. He had not been away much at all since coming here, but he had taken a short holiday the previous spring, and he had had one or two long weekends in London. He always returned with pleased anticipation of the work ahead and the men in his care.

He supposed McNulty was a good doctor, but he could not find any humanity or humour in the man. He certainly could not find any on the morning after Elizabeth Molland vanished from the dark road between Thornbeck and Kendal, when McNulty came up to

Calvary and requested to see Walter as soon as convenient.

Walter, thinking there might be a medical matter on which McNulty wanted to consult him, or even that McNulty was trying to lure him into the Caradoc Society's various activities, saw him at once.

'I should perhaps apologize for coming in when everything's in such turmoil,' said McNulty, taking the seat Walter indicated. 'A very shocking thing, this business with Elizabeth Molland.'

'Yes, it is.'

'It must be a great relief to you to know that at least she didn't have acute appendicitis.'

Walter had the sensation of something suddenly squeezing around his ribcage, but he said, 'That was not a definite diagnosis. But she was presenting with enough of the symptoms to make it imperative to have it investigated. It was a difficult situation but—'

Denzil McNulty said, 'But a patient with acute appendicitis could hardly have walked out of an ambulance and got into a car on the road between Thornbeck and Kendal almost unaided, could she, Dr Kane?'

'I think,' said Walter carefully, 'that you're under some kind of misapprehension, Dr McNulty. Or someone has been spreading spiteful lies.' Saul Ketch, he thought. I knew he was a sly greedy one, out to make trouble! 'The crash knocked me out for several minutes. I have absolutely no idea what happened or how she got away.'

He stood up, hoping McNulty would take this as dismissal but McNulty did not. He said, 'I'm not misinformed and I don't think there have been any lies.

I don't think you were knocked out at all.' He leaned forward. 'Dr Kane, let us not play these games. Somebody gave Elizabeth Molland some kind of emetic, and that somebody coached her in the symptoms of appendicitis. Probably it was a hefty measure of mustard in warm water – easily done without anyone noticing it. Especially if you happen to be the prison doctor. Or,' he said very softly, 'a distinguished visitor.'

Again, Walter experienced the sudden tight panic around his chest. Lewis. But he said, 'If you're thinking I arranged an escape for her—'

'I don't think you actually arranged it,' said McNulty. 'But I think you let someone else take advantage of the situation – perhaps you even guessed the situation was false.'

Walter said furiously, 'You'll take that back, McNulty.'

'Listen, I don't care who it was who fed the girl an emetic, but I do think the two of you were in it together.' He broke off and then said, 'You and Elizabeth's father.'

'That's nonsense. I've met Molland and he's the last person—'

'I'm talking about her real father, Dr Kane. Lewis Caradoc.' As Walter stared at him, he said, 'Did you really think I didn't know? I always knew what went on inside this prison, Walter. To a great extent, I still know. People tell me things. Useful things. Twenty-odd years ago Lewis Caradoc fathered a child onto that slut Belinda Skelton, and it was Caradoc who was the grey eminence behind Elizabeth's disappearance last night. He arranged for her to be spirited away, and he did it so well she hasn't been found'. He waited, but when Walter did not reply, said, 'And so, having laid our cards on the table, I think it's time to be open. I think we can be of use to one another, Dr Kane. Because for the sake of you and Lewis Caradoc, I think you'll want me to keep very quiet about all this.'

'I did nothing,' said Walter angrily.

'Let's hope the General Medical Council come to the same conclusion.'

'If you have some mad idea of blackmail,' said Walter, 'you can go to hell. Even if I were likely to submit to that, I haven't any money. I'm a bad choice for blackmail, McNulty.' But Lewis isn't.

'It isn't money I want,' said McNulty, and quite suddenly he seemed to change. Walter stared at him and saw the thin figure become sly. He did not precisely hunch his bony shoulders, but the impression of someone hugging a secret to his chest was strongly there.

'What then?'

'I want,' said McNulty, 'to conduct an experiment in the execution chamber. I've tried it before and it went wrong. That was in Lewis Caradoc's day.' He paused briefly and Walter, still trying to sort out the confusion in his mind, saw a spasm cross McNulty's face and saw that Denzil McNulty hated Sir Lewis. 'I've been waiting twenty years for another opportunity,' said McNulty. 'I'm a very patient man, you see, Dr Kane.'

'The execution chamber? But I couldn't possibly give my help in any kind of experiment in the last moment's of a man's life,' said Walter, staring at him.

'I think you will,' said McNulty, and smiled. 'I think when it comes to it, you'll give your consent.'

'I certainly will not! I don't even want to hear what

your experiment is, McNulty. Because whatever it is, I won't be part of it.'

'Oh, I think you will,' said McNulty. 'I shall talk to you again about that. I can't tell when – it may be a long time in the future or it may be quite soon. It depends when a condemned prisoner next comes here. But in the meantime, remember that the next man to be hanged at Calvary is mine.'

He went out, leaving Walter at the mercy of a tumult of emotions. Uppermost was that he was not going to give in to McNulty's bizarre experiment, whatever it turned out to be. If he had to, he would face the music over Elizabeth Molland. His conscience was not precisely clear – he had believed Elizabeth's symptoms, but he had made those phone calls to Lewis and Molland. 'I thought you should know,' he had said, and Lewis had said, 'I understand.' And in a very short while there had been the car on that dark road, and Walter had watched Elizabeth taken out of the ambulance by a tall man whose face he could not see.

As he went about his normal work, McNulty's words kept repeating in his mind, 'The next man to be hanged at Calvary is mine.' That was what McNulty had said, 'The next man to be hanged is mine.' I won't allow his experiment, whatever it is, he thought. Of course I won't. But would McNulty really report him to the General Medical Council? If there were to be an investigation he would almost certainly be cleared, but people would remember afterwards. Oh yes, Dr Kane, they would say, wasn't there something about him helping a murderer to escape from prison?

'The next man to be hanged is mine.'

415

Walter was to think – a long time later, when he could think clearly again – that neither he nor Denzil McNulty could possibly have foreseen that the next man to be hanged at Calvary would not be a man at all.

It would be a woman.

December 1939

'Violet Parsons,' said Edgar Higneth, facing Walter in his office in the bleak light of a freezing December morning. 'She's being sentenced tomorrow, and there's not much doubt about the verdict.'

Walter had been immersed in work – there had been an outbreak of influenza and a number of the men and several of the staff had gone down with it – but Higneth's words jerked him sickeningly back to the conversation with McNulty. The next man to be hanged, he had said. Would he care that it was a woman? What exactly did he want?

He asked Higneth for details about Violet Parsons. 'I must have missed the newspaper reports about this one, and with the influenza epidemic we've had here . . .'

'There's hardly been anything in the papers,' said Higneth. 'It's all war news, of course. A single murder gets a bit overshadowed by Hitler, and Parsons isn't a particularly interesting case from the point of view of the newspapers. Just a middle-aged woman who killed her husband.'

'She's been found guilty?' said Walter.

'Oh yes. The jury were out for only four hours. There is one curious feature of the case though. It didn't get much attention but apparently she used to hold seances with her husband in the twenties. Violette Partridge she was then.' He looked at the calendar he kept on his desk. 'If it is the death sentence,' he said, 'she'll be here by Friday. And – oh, my lord, this will be a nasty one. Counting the required three weeks exactly, execution would fall on Christmas Day.'

'Christmas dinner and the carol service,' said Walter expressionlessly, and Higneth shot him a quick look.

'They'll most likely make it just after Christmas,' he said. 'Boxing Day or the next one, I expect. But I'm thinking more of Calvary being snowed up and cut off, so that Mr Pierrepoint or one of his colleagues can't get here to carry out the sentence. Parsons might be penned up here, not knowing how long she's got to wait before we hang her.'

'That'll be inhumane,' said Walter. 'Mightn't they send her somewhere else for the execution?'

'They might. I'm telegraphing them to suggest that, in fact. They may insist, however. But I've pointed out that if she does come here her execution might have to be a makeshift affair. With snowstorms and blizzards forecast, it's possible that all the usual people won't be able to get here.'

Clara Caradoc thought there were times in life when you were extremely glad you had removed yourself from a situation and a group of people, especially when that situation – and those people – had turned into something very distasteful indeed.

Once she would have championed the lady she had known as Violette Partridge. She would have said, very earnestly, that poorest Vita had been shockingly treated

417

and that excuses must be found for her. That Man, Clara would have said in scathing reference to the perfidious Bartlam, had ruined Vita's life and deserved all he got.

But nobody deserved to be poisoned with rat-bane taken from the gardener's potting shed, not even Bartlam. Clara, faced with the undoubted fact that Vita had administered the poison and had stood gloatingly by while Bartlam writhed and suffered and finally expired, did not want to hear the woman's name ever again. She told Lewis it was a scandal and a disgrace, and she would not have thought it of Vita – indeed, of any woman.

'Poison so often *is* a woman's weapon, I'm afraid,' said Lewis, looking up from a report he was writing for some government department. Something to do with the incarceration of prisoners of war, it was, and the setting up of some kind of internment centres for them. Clara had not enquired into the details although, of course, it was very praiseworthy of Lewis to be contributing to the war effort and quite gratifying that the government had sought his assistance. Father had said so, only a week earlier.

Clara herself would naturally be doing what she could for her king and country in due time; it was being said there would actually be raids on English cities from the air, and that Red Cross centres would be set up to help treat the injured. This seemed scarcely possible, but Clara had already thought that her organizational skills would be very useful there. Mamma had done something similar in the Great War and Clara, in the months before Caspar was killed, had helped her.

'I went to the first day of the trial,' said Clara suddenly.

418

She had not known she was going to tell Lewis this, but the words were out before she realized it.

'Did you?' He looked up from his report, not shocked or annoyed, merely interested and prepared to discuss it if she wanted to. This was another of the things Clara's father admired about him; quiet concentration on whatever you said to him. That was what you noticed about Caradoc and even though he was older now – approaching his seventieth birthday, that quality had not diminished. It was a quality that for once Clara found extremely comforting.

'I was very plainly dressed,' she said. 'No one recognized me.'

'It wouldn't have mattered if anyone had. How much of the trial did you see? Did you form any opinion as to her innocence or guilt?'

'I tried to be completely impartial at the start,' said Clara. 'But the facts were quite overwhelming. Do you know, Lewis, when she made that second marriage – that bluff little man, rather common I always thought him—'

'Fairly well-off, of course.'

Clara ignored the trace of cynicism in Lewis's voice. 'She must have known perfectly well that Bartlam was still alive.'

'I wouldn't be surprised if she had known all along,' said Lewis.

'A bigamist,' said Clara, trying out the ugly word. 'That was what she was. Well, one can only thank God there were no children.'

'I've only read the briefest of details about the case,' said Lewis, 'but didn't the real husband – what was his name? Bartlam, was it? Didn't he turn up and try to blackmail her?'

'Yes, he did, which does not surprise me in the least. If there was any money to be made out of any situation, then Bartlam Partridge was the one to make it,' said Clara. 'A very untrustworthy person. There had been some very distasteful episodes over the years.' She frowned, and in a different voice said, 'But for Violette to feed him poison – Well, I see now that I was sadly mistaken in her, Lewis. A cruel and heartless woman and I have absolutely no sympathy for her at all.'

CHAPTER THIRTY-THREE

'There'll be absolutely no sympathy for this one at all,' said Edgar Higneth, reading the Home Office telegram to Walter, the telegram that confirmed Violet Parsons would be brought to Calvary Gaol, where the sentence of death would be carried out.

'A cruel and heartless woman,' he said. 'She married her second husband knowing full well Bartlam Partridge was still alive. And given Bartlam's apparent history, she should have known he'd use the fact to get money out of her. As a rule I dislike seeing any woman brought to the gallows, Walter, but in this case I can't find it in my heart to pity her.'

'D'you think she'll be a difficult prisoner?' said Walter, his mind going back just three months to another female prisoner who had not been in the least difficult, but who had turned his life upside-down. Where was she now, Elizabeth Molland? Would he ever dare ask Lewis about her? And had it in fact been

Lewis that night? You can't be sure, thought Walter, you really can't.

Higneth said, 'You can never tell who'll be difficult and who won't. Sometimes it's the quiet ones who give the most trouble at the end.'

'How old is Violet Parsons?'

'Fifty.' Higneth glanced back at the telegram. 'They say Mr Pierrepoint is being engaged for the twenty-seventh of December.'

'She will have to go through Christmas, then.'

'Yes, she will, but we'll try to keep the festivities as much removed from her as we can.'

Walter did not say the festivities at Calvary were fairly subdued anyway. There was morning service in the prison chapel, followed by a turkey dinner for the men. Small gifts were allowed from their immediate families, and there was a carol concert in the afternoon, given by one of the local church choirs. Walter would attend the service, but afterwards he had been invited to Christmas dinner with Sir Lewis and Lady Caradoc. There would be a party of about a dozen and probably charades and bridge during the afternoon. Dancing in the evening – probably in the big oak-floored hall. Lady Caradoc had graciously suggested they could play gramophone records for that. Walter was looking forward to it.

'I know I said I haven't got any sympathy for Violet Parsons,' said Higneth, 'and nor I have. But in common humanity, Walter, we'll have to do what we can to make it as easy as possible for her.'

Violet Parsons did not look like a woman who had stirred rat-bane into her husband's drink and then watched him die writhing in agony. Nor did she look like a woman who held seances and purported to talk to the spirits of the dead in return for money. She looked like a woman whose counterpart could be found in almost any English village. A devout church-goer, an indefatigable collector for charitable causes and a sitter on committees. When she was brought in, she was wearing a grey skirt and a fawn-coloured blouse with a coffee-coloured lace modesty vest. Her hair was arranged neatly, and the only faintly exotic note was a velvet cape which she wore over her shoulders, and a drift of rather cloying violet perfume.

Once in the condemned cell, she listened politely to Walter's careful explanation as to how he would hope to help her through the days ahead, and replied with perfect composure to his medical enquiries. No, she was not on medication of any kind, save the occasional soda mint for dyspepsia if she drank tea that was too strong. Yes, she would accept any sedative doses Dr Kane prepared for her. She had no illnesses or conditions he needed to know about. She had no allergies other than shellfish, which gave her a rash. Lobster was particularly trouble-some on that score, although she did not suppose lobster would be served to her here.

Asked what religion she practised, Violet Parsons said religion was a very individual matter, and she regarded herself as being on a higher spiritual plane than that symbolized by the singing of hymns or the holding of fêtes for rebuilding the church spire. She believed she was about to pass over to the Other Side where she would meet loved friends and dear ones who had Gone Before. She would be asking forgiveness of those she might have injured when she got to the Other Side, so there was not much point in the chaplain trying to forestall this by badgering her for confessions or admissions of sin. In the meantime, if they had to mark her down as anything, they might as well put Church of England. It was all one to her.

When Walter tentatively broached the matter of Christmas Day, Violet Parsons said, composedly, that she knew it was the custom to celebrate the birth of the Christian Prophet, although for herself she could not see how eating roast turkey and plum pudding did that. She would be agreeable to being served with her share of it if that was all the kitchens had to offer on the day, but would they remember not to include sage and onion stuffing and to put only a very few Brussels sprouts in the dish because they always provoked her dyspepsia. Thank you so much.

'In any other circumstances she'd be told very sharply that this isn't the Savoy,' said Edgar Higneth who was watching snow cover the whole of Torven, and worriedly tuning in to every available weather forecast on the wireless. But he authorized the order for plain turkey with potatoes, parsnips and a small helping of sprouts.

The following day Violet Parsons said she would prefer not to wear the prison garb if they did not mind, although if it was an inflexible requirement she supposed she could do so.

'Let her wear what she wants,' said Edgar Higneth, impatiently. 'Check everything for pins or sharp ends, and for strings or belts, of course. And take away shoe laces and stockings, unless they're those cotton affairs. Don't let her have silk stockings.'

'None of us can get silk stockings at the moment, sir,' said the wardress to whom this was addressed. 'She's brought lisle ones with her. There's a lot of stretch in them; I shouldn't think they could be used for any suicide bids.'

'Well, make sure.' Higneth, a confirmed bachelor, was not very well informed about ladies' under garments, although he had been known to admire a well-turned ankle and a rumour had once circulated that he had a weakness for chestnut hair. One of the younger wardresses had offered to prove this by dying her hair chestnut and trying to vamp him, but since the war you could not get chestnut hair dye any more than you could get silk stockings, and the wardress had then left to join the Wrens so the plan had to be shelved until the war should end. By which time nobody would care, because they would all be too busy celebrating the downfall of that evil man in Germany.

'All you have to do,' said Denzil McNulty, seated in Walter's surgery, 'is request an extra weighing of the prisoner – a very precise weighing – immediately before the execution. And then a second weighing within minutes of death.'

'And that will prove or disprove the existence of the soul?' said Walter, who had listened in disbelief to the details of McNulty's proposed experiment and the reasons for it.

'It could go a long way to proving it.'

'I don't care how long it goes, I won't do it. In any case, the second weighing would be impossible,' said Walter, glad to have found an unarguable reason for blocking McNulty's bizarre demand. 'You know that as well as I do,' he said. 'The body is always left for an hour before it's touched, and even then Pierrepoint will be there with his assistant.'

'But it's not looking as if Pierrepoint will manage to get here,' said McNulty. 'Hasn't Edgar Higneth already said this may have to be a makeshift affair. All you have to do, Walter, is order the first weighing. I'll see to the second one, providing you request my presence at the hanging. Since I know the lady that won't be thought so very odd. It'll look as if I'm there to comfort a friend in her last moments.'

Bloody hypocrite, thought Walter angrily. One day I'll see him hanged in that cell himself for this.

He said, 'I didn't know you knew Parsons.'

'Oh yes. Rather a curious thing, isn't it? She was something of a stalwart within the Caradoc Society. A very worthy member of the group. A great friend of Lady Caradoc, as a matter of fact.'

'I didn't know she was involved in the Caradoc Society,' said Walter, who had not taken much notice of the Caradoc Society, beyond assuming it had been Lady Caradoc who had instigated it and bestowed the name on it, rather than Sir Lewis. Lewis, in fact, never mentioned it.

'No matter,' said McNulty. 'Well? Is our little arrangement confirmed?'

'No,' said Walter. 'You'll have to do your worst over the Elizabeth Molland business. I daresay it will reflect very badly on me even though I had nothing to do with it, but I can't help that. Tell whoever you like.'

'Yes, it will reflect badly on you,' said McNulty. He

swung the absurdly affected eyeglass he wore, as if, thought Walter, it was a monstrous single eye on the end of a black twitching nerve. 'But have you thought who else it will reflect badly on, Walter? Elizabeth's father, remember?' And then, as Walter hesitated, he said, 'And talking of fathers.' He stopped and smiled.

There was something in that smile and in McNulty's tone that caused a tremor of apprehension to slide down Walter's spine. Nicholas, he thought. He knows about Nicholas, and he's going to use it against me in some way. Son of a traitor – something like that. It's a good weapon for him, as well – the whole country's gripped by anti-German fever. If the army medical corps got to hear about Nicholas they might refuse my request to join them and go out to France.

Denzil McNulty said, 'Nicholas O'Kane.'

Oh, be damned to you, thought Walter furiously. He said, 'Yes, Nicholas O'Kane was my father. You obviously know that. You also obviously know he was a traitor to his country and he was hanged in this prison in 1917. The debt was paid.'

'Was it?' said McNulty softly, leaning forward. 'Are you sure about that? Are you sure your father died?'

'Of course I'm sure. I know the date – my mother brought me to see him two days before the execution.'

'Supposing I were to tell you that the execution never took place,' said McNulty. 'That he escaped?'

'I shouldn't believe you,' said Walter after a moment. 'This is a trick. It's some twisty plan you've cooked up to make me give in to your blackmail.'

'It's no trick, I assure you. I was present that morning,' said McNulty. 'You can look up the records – you'll find it's perfectly true. Or you can ask Lewis Caradoc – he was there.'

'I certainly don't believe that.'

McNulty leaned forward, his pale eyes fixed on Walter. He said, 'Lewis Caradoc was the governor here. On that morning in 1917, he and I arranged for Nicholas O'Kane's escape. Your father went out of this prison, back into the world.'

Somehow Walter fought back to a semblance of composure, but when at last he managed to speak his voice sounded to him distant and a bit blurred.

'That's an extraordinary claim, Dr McNulty. But I don't normally listen to fantastical tittle-tattle.'

'It's fantastical all right, but it's certainly not tittle-tattle.' McNulty was watching him closely. 'Ask Lewis Caradoc if you don't believe me?'

'That's exactly what I shall do,' said Walter furiously. 'Now get out of my surgery.'

He sat in the familiar low-ceilinged room, and heard his own voice repeating Denzil McNulty's extraordinary claim, and waited to hear Lewis Caradoc say it was a complete fabrication, and that McNulty was a twisted liar.

Lewis said, 'Walter, I'm so sorry you had to find out.'

'It's true?' said Walter, staring at him.

'Yes, it's true. I should have foreseen McNulty couldn't be trusted – I should have found a way of telling you. But you and I didn't meet until so many years after-wards, and then it seemed better not to . . .' He frowned. 'Did McNulty tell you the details?'

'No.'

'Well, perhaps details don't matter so very much now. Your father was foolish and reckless as a young man, although it was always my opinion that in those years – I'm talking about the Great War now – he came under unfortunate influences. Because of it, he betrayed this country and sold secrets to Germany, and on that morning in 1917 by all the rules of man and God he deserved to be hanged. Young men died because of what your father did, Walter,' he said, and his voice lost some of its colour. Walter knew Lewis was remembering his own son, Cas. 'But Nick O'Kane believed in what he did,' said Lewis. 'I sat in the execution chamber of Calvary with him and listened to him talking and saw the passion in his eyes. It was the wrong passion – and I think he knew by then that it was wrong – but he had fought wholeheartedly for a cause he believed in. He had fought for his own country.'

'Ireland,' said Walter, half to himself.

'Yes.' The shadow was still in Lewis's eyes, and Walter thought: was it because of Cas that he helped my father? Did he see some kind of link between them? Two reckless young men, fighting a war – prepared to kill or be killed? He was not sure if he could ever ask Lewis about that, and he was not sure if Lewis would tell him.

From out of the tumbling confusion, he said, 'Is he still alive? Could I trace him?'

'He changed his identity after that night – name, religion, everything. He changed his entire way of life,' said Lewis. 'I don't think you should try to trace him.'

'Why not?' There's something else, thought Walter suddenly. There's something he hasn't told me – he's trying to decide whether to do so now – I can *feel* him struggling to decide. When Lewis spoke again, he was sure of it.

'I think you should let the past go,' said Lewis.

'No. I can't let it go. I need to find him – to understand why he did all those things. What is it you aren't telling me? For God's sake, Lewis.'

Lewis made a curious gesture as if bracing himself to lift a heavy weight or withstand a blow. He said, 'Walter, the name that Nick O'Kane took – the name he lived under for the rest of his life—' He stopped, and Walter suddenly knew what was coming. Oh God, no, he thought. Oh God, no, not that.

Lewis said, 'The name your father took was Neville Fremlin.'

Neville Fremlin. The name he took was Neville Fremlin, *Neville Fremlin*. The dreadful words drummed into Walter's brain over and over, and he felt as if all the breath had been driven from his body. The blood pounded in his head and there was a rushing sound in his ears and a sick darkness pressed down on him. I'm not going to bear this, he thought. I'm not going to be able to live the rest of my life knowing this.

But after a moment, he heard his voice say in a nearly ordinary tone, 'I don't think that can be right. I'd have recognized him. I spent a good deal of time with – with Neville Fremlin. I'd have realized.'

But he already knew Lewis had told him the truth. Everything was slotting together in his mind: the feeling he had experienced of knowing Fremlin, which he had put down to familiarity because of the publicity surrounding the trial – the instant liking he had had for

430

Fremlin – Oh God, more than liking! thought Walter wretchedly.

'How old were you in 1917?' Lewis was saying. 'Seven years old, wasn't it? And how many of those seven years of your life did you actually spend with your father? He was in Ireland for a lot of the time, wasn't he? You can't have spent more than a few weeks at a time with him, Walter. And twenty years later he was so different I doubt anyone would have recognized him. If I hadn't known the name, I'm not sure if I would have recognized him from the photographs in the newspapers.'

Walter pounced on this at once. 'How did you know about the name?'

'Because one of the things Nick O'Kane needed to establish his new identity was a passport. By 1920 passport regulations were a lot tighter than they had been before the Great War and a sponsor was required – someone of good professional standing. A prison governor, for instance. I sponsored Nick O'Kane's passport request,' said Lewis. 'He knew it was safe to ask me because I couldn't turn him in without giving away my own part in his escape. Equally, he couldn't turn me in without incriminating himself. Villains' pact.'

'Birth certificate,' said Walter, searching for flaws. 'He'd have needed a birth certificate – if not for the passport, surely at some time.'

'Yes, but your father was a very clever man, and he had lived and worked alongside people who knew how to forge things like that. You mustn't forget he had been a spy,' said Lewis gently. 'He'd know people who could provide such things without awkward questions being asked. And because of the Easter Rising of 1916 certain sections of the Irish people saw him as one of their minor heroes. He was one of the rebels who fought for Home Rule remember. He was on the steps of the post office building in Dublin when they proclaimed the Irish Republic.'

Walter's mind went back to those discussions in the condemned cell. He said slowly, 'A lot of what Fremlin said is suddenly clearer. About how he was glad I would be with him, and how one day I might understand.'

Lewis said thoughtfully, 'I wonder if he was thinking you might find out the truth some day. I wonder if he was trying to ask you to forgive him.'

'I might have forgiven him for what he did in 1917,' said Walter bitterly. 'I might just about have done that. But I can't forgive him for what he did later – of course I can't. All those women he killed. I can't feel anything other than repulsion for him. Sick disgust. It'd be a hell of a legacy to give any children I might have, wouldn't it? A grandfather who was a mass murderer.'

'Yes,' said Lewis, half to himself. 'I understand exactly how you feel. Your father and my daughter.'

When Walter finally returned to Calvary and his work, he found that the thing that stayed uppermost in his mind was not so much that his father had killed five women – although that was a black anguish in itself – but that he himself had watched his father hang. I walked with him into the death chamber on that last morning and saw it done, he thought. I listened to his heartbeat falter and then stop, and I pronounced him dead. And afterwards I helped cut his body down, and saw him thrown into that shallow grave, and his body covered with quicklime.

The images burned into his mind like acid, and he thought he would never be free of them. But with them was the knowledge that his father had kept the truth to himself. He might have used it to get my sympathy, thought Walter. He might so easily have done that – emotional blackmail to persuade me to help him escape, but he didn't. He remained as Neville Fremlin right to the end.

The days immediately prior to Christmas passed in a blur. He managed to carry out his various duties at Calvary, and wondered if he would ever feel anything again other than this sick despair. The influenza seemed to have blown itself out but there were minor ailments to deal with. A couple of the warders had to be treated for unmistakable hangovers and one of the younger wardresses confessed weepingly that she feared she was pregnant. Walter examined her and had to confirm her fears. He managed to persuade her to contact a cottage hospital just outside Lancaster where staff were particularly helpful to girls in this predicament, and could arrange adoptions. She clung to his hands, thanking him and said she had felt like chucking herself in the river, indeed she had, Dr Kane, but he had given her hope and after all, life went on, didn't it and you got through these things somehow?

Life went on ... But couldn't life as you knew it, end when you had been told something so appalling that your whole existence was drained of all colour and all meaning? Walter had gone along to Calvary's office by this time and had looked in the old files, giving the secretary the reason that he needed to check back on a particular treatment for an inmate at the end of the last war.

There was the entry for Nicholas O'Kane.

Hanged at eight o'clock in the morning of the 17th of November 1917. Buried in the precincts of Calvary Gaol.

What had they buried that day? Some kind of dummy corpse?

I don't think I'm ever going to be able to come to terms with this, thought Walter. My father killed those women – he murdered them for their money and their jewellery. And he exerted that Svengali spell over Elizabeth Molland – if I'd spent more time with him, he'd have exerted it over me as well.

And in the meantime, life went on, even when you felt as if you were dead inside.

He visited Violet Parsons diligently every day and tried without success to reach the woman's mind. He could not tell if she was resigned to what lay ahead of her, or if she was working out some deep and sly plan for cheating the sentence.

Edgar Higneth's prophecies about the weather were fulfilled. Snow began falling three days before Christmas Day, and on Christmas Eve a telegram was delivered by a boy who had spent an hour struggling up the hill from Thornbeck. The telegram said that Mr Pierrepoint would do his very best to keep his appointment on 27 December, but roads were already impassable and train points were frozen and it was not looking very hopeful. When Higneth tried to telephone the Home Office for advice the phone lines were dead.

Clara Caradoc's Christmas dinner party had been cancelled since hardly any of the guests could reach Thornbeck, but Lewis had sent a message – again by the telegram delivery boy – to say that if Walter could get to their house he would be most welcome to share their dinner. By that time Walter felt he could not bear the gaol's confines any longer. He attended morning service in the prison chapel, then wrapped himself up in thick scarves and mufflers and set out to walk across the fields. A stinging blizzard was blowing and he wondered dispiritedly if he would reach Sir Lewis's house, and then he wondered if, having reached it, he would be able to get back to Calvary. Then he wondered if he cared.

By the time he reached the old house he was soaked to the skin and shivering. He downed the large rum and blackcurrant that Lewis mixed for him, and the warm room with the crackling fire in the big hearth began to blur and seem unreal. He ate two mouthfuls of the excellent dinner Lady Caradoc's cook served, and then laid his knife and fork carefully down. The room was starting to spin; he thought he made an effort to fight it off, but it closed relentlessly around him. He tumbled into a blessed unconsciousness where nothing was required of him, and the only things he was aware of were voices saying he had a fever, and not to worry about anything at all, and everything was being taken care of.

'Everything's taken care of,' said Lewis Caradoc, seated on the window-seat in the guest bedroom of his house, smiling at Walter who was still lying in bed. 'I've told

Higneth you've picked up the tail-end of that wretched influenza outbreak – a perfectly acceptable statement. And everywhere else life's returning to normal – the telephone lines have been restored, and Higneth telephoned earlier to say Pierrepoint can't get over to Calvary, but the Home Office are sending one of his assistants. It's not ideal, but he's an experienced man and he'll manage very well. He's hoping to get to Thornbeck by Thursday – that would mean Violet Parsons' execution could take place on – oh, Lord, on New Year's Day. That's an irony, isn't it? The first day of the year and the first day of a new decade. I don't suppose the Parsons woman will care, though. I don't suppose she'll even notice the date.'

'What about a doctor?' said Walter. 'Because I think I could manage—'

'Walter, do stop worrying about Calvary,' said Lewis. 'You've been in bed for nearly four days – your temperature's been sky-high for most of those days, and you can't possible attend a hanging. Higneth will get hold of a locum – there are any number of GPs in the area he can call on.'

McNulty, thought Walter at once. He'll call on McNulty. But it's all right, because McNulty won't have any hold over Higneth, and his wretched experiment will never happen. He felt a deep relief at this knowledge. And by the time the next condemned man was brought to Calvary, he, Walter, would probably be hundreds of miles away – perhaps in France, helping to fight the war.

It was later that evening that he suddenly said to Lewis, 'I've been thinking about my father being with Elizabeth. Those months they seemed to have lived together.'

A spasm of pain crossed Lewis's face. 'I think about that as well,' he said, and then, almost eagerly, 'She was entirely under his influence, of course.'

'Yes,' said Walter, and thought: but was she? What was really under that doe-eyed helplessness of Elizabeth Molland? She may have lived with my father, but she was *virgo intacta*. Most people had assumed there was a sexual relationship between those two – Lewis would certainly have assumed it. He tried to remember what had been said about that aspect of the relationship during Elizabeth's trial, but could not.

He said, carefully, 'I wonder where she is now.'

'She could be anywhere,' said Lewis.

'She could, couldn't she? It depends on the driver of that car – he might have taken her anywhere. He got her into the car pretty quickly and drove off into the night, but I couldn't see what direction he took,' said Walter, watching Lewis closely.

There was no doubt about his reaction. He flinched, and then said, 'I didn't know you had actually seen the driver? Did you tell the police you had?'

'No.'

'Why not?'

'Because,' said Walter, looking at Lewis very directly, 'all I saw was a figure in a long coat and a deep-brimmed hat. Whoever it was, I couldn't have identified him.'

'Yes, I see. You're sure of that are you?'

'Quite sure. I shouldn't think,' said Walter, 'that it will ever be known who drove the car that night.'

CHAPTER THIRTY-FOUR

As Edgar Higneth went through the snow-lit corridors on New Year's Eve he found himself thinking that Calvary had never been so extremely quiet before an execution. Normally the place filled up with such anticipation and angry fear that it was very nearly possible to cut slices of it. But this was not the case today, and it seemed as if the execution of Violet Parsons would go almost unnoticed.

The snowbound conditions were in some measure to blame for the curious atmosphere. The spiteful blizzard that had raged across Torven on Christmas Eve and Christmas morning had completely shrouded Thornbeck; the neighbouring villages and market towns were covered in a thick white blanket and Calvary itself seemed to be at the core of this cold whiteness, although they were not quite cut off from the world any longer.

At least the assistant executioner had reached them, for which Higneth was deeply thankful. The man had arrived at the prison midway through the previous afternoon; Higneth thought him a bit young, but they did not have much choice in the matter. As Higneth had told the Home Office when finally the call got through to Calvary, they had nearly got to the stage of telling the prisoner they did not know when they could hang her. This would have been unbearable, especially as Higneth, during his years as governor, had striven to make all executions as humane as he possibly could.

A doctor had reached them as well, which was another thing to give thanks for. Higneth would have preferred Walter Kane to be in attendance – he would have preferred Walter Kane always to be in attendance – but Kane was still confined to bed with a bad go of this wretched influenza. Higneth was glad to think that he was at Sir Lewis's house, being properly looked after. Kane had rooms in Thornbeck, but he slept at Calvary more often than not. This worried Higneth at times because it was no life for a young man, but at least Walter was being ill in comfort. Lady Caradoc might be severe and a bit humourless (an odd wife for Sir Lewis, Higneth had often thought her), but she would make sure Walter was properly cared for.

So taking things all in all, Higneth had been glad when Denzil McNulty made his way up the slope and offered his services as attendant doctor at Violet Parsons' execution. He had heard of Dr Kane's illness, he said – a miserable thing, influenza – and so if they needed anyone to take Kane's place for this execution? Ah, they did. Then, he would be more than happy to attend. As it happened he knew the prisoner – Higneth had probably heard that, had he? – and it might help her a little to have a friend there with her at the end.

Higneth did not know McNulty very well and thought him a bit of an odd one – all that delving into psychic phenomena, and his involvement with the Caradoc Society – but he had been glad to have this particular problem solved, and to know that a properly experienced doctor would attend the hanging. When he expressed his concern about the hangman, McNulty said, 'I don't think you need worry. You and I will be present, and we're both old hands at this.' He paused, and then said, 'I believe there's no need for this fledgling hangman to be part of the cutting down of the body afterwards.'

'No?' said Higneth, looking up in surprise.

'I believe we can come to a far more beneficial arrangement.'

'Beneficial? Beneficial to whom?'

'Why, to both of us,' said Denzil McNulty. He leaned forward. 'A little matter of a packet of mustard that found its way into Elizabeth Molland's cell last September. I'm sure you wouldn't want your masters at the Home Office – or anyone else – to hear about that.'

Edgar Higneth had always had a weak spot in his make-up, and this weakness was for young ladies. Not in any distasteful way: the desires of the flesh had never particularly bothered him. He had never wanted to marry – he had certainly never found any lady with whom he would have wanted to share that kind of intimacy, either mental, physical or emotional. One or two congenial female friends, perhaps, whom one might invite to accompany one to the occasional formal function. His position as governor required attendance at these things, and it was acceptable and pleasant to have a lady on one's arm for the evening.

But he had always had a strong and secret wish for a daughter. A young, pretty little girl whom he could take about and whom he could be proud of. A daughter who would admire him and think him wonderful, and who, when she was older, would be tolerant and indulgent and affectionate. Occasionally he had amused himself by imagining how she would look, this mythical daughter. Small and fair and kitten-faced, thought Edgar Higneth, allowing himself the odd moment or two of daydream. Nicely mannered – he would have made sure of that – but fragile – needing to be protected. He had never expected to meet this mythical figure; he had been perfectly content with his occasional dream.

And then Elizabeth Molland came to Calvary to be hanged, and Elizabeth Molland was the embodiment of Edgar Higneth's dream.

At first he had not entirely taken in what Sir Lewis Caradoc had said that day – the day he had come to see the prisoner.

'I can't let her hang,' Lewis said, facing Higneth in the governor's office after his visit to Molland.

'She's been found guilty—'

'Higneth, she's my daughter.'

A daughter. The old dream had come uppermost in Higneth's mind at once. He stared at the older man, his mind in turmoil. Caradoc had not said, 'She's innocent and I can't let her hang.' He had said, 'She's my daughter and I can't let her hang.' Did the words matter?

Who had Elizabeth Molland's mother been? Higneth wondered briefly, but he did not see how he could ask such an impertinent question; he did not see it mattered in this situation.

'Well, Higneth? Will you help me?'

Edgar Higneth, solid upright citizen, upholder of law and order, and overseer of the health and security of convicted murderers, had struggled with his conscience. But at last, he said, 'I'm not sure. No, I can't. It's too much of a risk.'

'I understand. And we have never had this conversation – I can trust you for that, can't I?'

'Yes, but—' Sir Lewis was already opening door. 'No, wait.'

'Yes?'

'Tell me what it is you want me to do.'

'Very little. Simply give her this later today.' Lewis produced a small envelope containing yellow powder.

'What is it?'

'Ordinary dry mustard. Perfectly innocuous in a small quantity. But this is not a small quantity – it's a very large quantity and if it's stirred into warm water it should make her sick. She'll do the rest – she knows what to do – how to produce the signs of a fever and so on.'

He's worked something out with her, thought Higneth. Am I really going along with this?

Lewis was saying, 'Can you manage it? Perhaps offer to sit with the prisoner while the duty warders have their supper?'

It would be an unusual thing to do, but it would not be entirely out of pattern with a prisoner under the death sentence. Higneth knew this, and Lewis knew it as well.

'Is that all you want me to do?'

'Yes. Just do this, and then afterwards know absolutely nothing.'

Higneth had waited until the time for the warders' supper break, and then had found a task for the relief warder – an important letter that must catch the evening post, he said, and there was no one else free to take it down to the village. The prisoner? That was easily dealt with: he would sit with her himself for an hour. Had they served the evening drink to her yet? No? Then perhaps they would bring along two mugs.

It was a little unconventional, but Edgar Higneth was by this time known for his humane treatment of condemned prisoners. For him to elect to drink his own mid-evening mug of cocoa with Elizabeth Molland was not so very remarkable.

As he went into the execution suite he still had no idea if he was going to do this. If he did, how would the plan unfold? Clearly Sir Lewis intended Elizabeth to be ill – presumably to require hospital treatment. Then was Walter Kane part of it all? Higneth was inclined to think not, but he had better not make any assumptions.

Seated opposite Molland, he thought again how difficult it was to believe this fair frail creature could have killed anyone.

She seemed unaware that there might be a plan to free her. She thanked him for coming and the conversation turned to Neville Fremlin. The tears welled up in her eyes almost at once.

'I trusted him so much,' she said. 'He spun magic. Like

an enchanter in a story. He bound me with a spell. But it was a monstrous magic. He destroyed me.'

She said it so wistfully and Higneth thought: the words, the sentiments of an innocent child, surely. A guileless young girl, still half in childhood, still seeing magic in people. But as she had said, it had been a monstrous magic that had trapped her.

He thought he was still unsure what to do, but he realized the decision had already been made. Not saying anything, he handed over the envelope Lewis Caradoc had given him. She took it without speaking, but Higneth saw her eyes go to the small washbasin behind the screen. Warm water from the tap. The tin mug which had contained her cocoa. The warders would return soon, but she would find a way to mix the drink that would make her sick, and she would find a way to tamper with the thermometer so it would appear that she had a fever – perhaps she would manage to take a mouthful of hot water, or furtively put the thermometer itself in a mug of hot water. Whatever she did, it would set in motion Lewis Caradoc's plan to save his daughter from the gallows.

Edgar Higneth thought they had got away with it. He thought no one had known, or would ever know. Until, three months later, Dr McNulty sat in his office, and put forth the most preposterous request Higneth had ever heard.

'No,' he said. 'Certainly not. Good God man, even if I were to agree – the soul isn't a thing that can be measured!'

'That's what I intend to find out,' said McNulty. 'And

I think you will agree in the end. It's a small, very swift, procedure – it can't possibly make any difference to the prisoner – but it will contribute greatly to our knowledge.'

Higneth thought Denzil McNulty was probably more interested in contributing to his own reputation in the peculiar world of psychic investigation, but he did not say so. He tried to think how best to handle this.

'It is such a censorious world, isn't it?' McNulty said before he could speak. 'A prurient world, as well. If I were to tell people what I knew – what had been found in the condemned cell – What Saul Ketch saw the night Molland was taken—'

'What did he see?' The question came out too sharply, and McNulty smiled.

'Oh, merely the prisoner being taken from the ambulance to a car.'

'Then he should have said so at the time.'

'But it's as well for you he didn't, isn't it?' said McNulty, and Higneth was unable to tell if Ketch really had seen something that night and told McNulty about it, or if McNulty was making it up to lend weight to his polite threat.

McNulty said, 'If I were to tell what I know, no matter how strong your denials, there would be extremely unpleasant talk. People would wonder and speculate. You might not care about your own skin, Higneth, but Walter Kane's career would be irreparably damaged.'

'Dr Kane has nothing to do with any of this,' said Higneth at once.

'Hasn't he? Are you absolutely sure of that?'

This was the real difficulty; Higneth was not

absolutely sure. He thought he would probably have sacrificed Lewis Caradoc (what *had* Saul Ketch seen that night?), but he did not think he could risk sacrificing Walter. A treacherous little voice in his mind asked whether the small experiment McNulty was proposing could really matter to this woman, this Violet Parsons, who had sent an unwanted husband to a painful death? What could it matter to her that she was asked to undergo a brief, extra weighing procedure on the morning of her execution? The prisoners were weighed each day in any case for the executioner to calculate the precise drop needed.

Higneth knew perfectly well that this reasoning was akin to what Catholics called casuistry – finding acceptable reasons for an unacceptable or a sinful action – but it was a thought that gave him some small comfort. He looked at McNulty and saw the man was smiling and nodding, as if he had followed these thoughts with disturbing ease. Unpleasant little weasel. Higneth would make very sure the man was not employed at Calvary in any respect whatsoever after this. He would find a way to dismiss Saul Ketch as well, and be damned to the shortage of men!

But when McNulty said, 'Well? You'll do it?' Higneth heard his own voice say, quite calmly, 'Yes, I'll do it.'

When the grey morning of the first of January 1940 finally dawned, Edgar Higneth was glad to know that at least he had made the whole execution process so much swifter. There was no longer the almost ceremonious walk out of the condemned cell into the execution chamber: no longer the solemn intoning of the funeral service during the procession. Calvary was an old and stubborn building and its modernization had been difficult and costly, but Higneth had stuck to his guns and finally the changes had been made. Violet Parsons would barely have time to realize that she was being taken to the scaffold before the noose was round her neck, and the trap was being dropped.

When Higneth entered the condemned cell shortly before eight o'clock, McNulty eagerly in his wake, the chaplain waiting outside, he was relieved to see that Parsons seemed perfectly calm. She appeared grateful for McNulty's presence; she took his hand, and said she was glad to have a dear friend to help her to the Other Side. Higneth remembered the stories of how Parsons and the husband she had poisoned, had held seances in London during and immediately after the Great War. It had not been much mentioned in the trial, but he thought there had been a suggestion somewhere that the seances had been full of tricks and devices to cheat the vulnerable bereaved clients who attended. But fraudster or not, faced with death it certainly seemed Parsons' own belief was genuine. Higneth hoped it would help her through the final moments.

The two duty warders did not seem especially curious about the weighing machine which McNulty had told them to carry in. Probably they thought it was part of the new methods which Higneth had introduced. It was an unwieldy machine with an unusually large platform – Higneth wondered if McNulty had had it specially constructed – and horizontal brass rods with what looked like dozens of tiny squares attached to them, each one a different size, each one marked as being pounds or ounces. The ounces were divided into sections, so that it would be possible to take the minutest fraction of an ounce into consideration.

'I am using ounces troy, not ounces avoirdupois,' said McNulty seeing Higneth's look. 'Troy allows for a little more precision – four hundred and eighty grains to the ounce.'

Violet Parsons weighed fourteen stone, five pound, four ounces and two hundred grains. McNulty wrote this down, and Violet said, 'I am glad to know I am contributing to our work. You will write this up, of course.'

'I shall, and it shall always be known as the Parsons' Experiment,' said McNulty. 'You will live on in our work, my dear Vita. But in two or three minutes you will be with the loved ones we have so often spoken with.' He stepped back, nodding to the waiting warders to indicate that he had finished his work.

Mr Pierrepoint's assistant was as swift and efficient as could be wished. Violet Parsons accepted the hood, and submitted to the strapping of her hands and ankles; there was a bad moment when Higneth thought the executioner's hands were shaking, but he seemed to manage well enough, and they did not shake when he depressed the lever. Twenty seconds from the moment they had taken Parsons out of the condemned cell to the moment the trap dropped. Smooth and swift and clean.

To do McNulty credit, once he had heard the heart slow down and then stop, he behaved with complete detachment. He waved the assistant aside, and went down into the vault himself where he cut the body down. Higneth saw the warders had carried the machine down

– he supposed McNulty had asked them to do so straight after the execution. Despite himself, he felt a sudden anticipation. What would the findings be? Would anything be proved? *Could* anything be proved?

The executioner seemed uncertain as to his role, but McNulty called up to say they would send for him presently, and Higneth asked the warders to take the man to his office, to wait there. He thought the chaplain looked curiously at the open trap, but he, too, seemed to shrug, and went quietly out. Higneth stayed where he was. A part of him wanted to distance himself as much as possible from the entire business and he certainly did not believe in any part of McNulty's experiment. But a tiny part of him was strongly curious, and he wanted to see this out.

Violet Parsons' body lay a bit untidily on the weighing machine's large platform while McNulty moved back and forth, writing down figures, and making calculations. It seemed to take him a very long time. Higneth, standing almost forgotten on the edge of the gallows trap, thought surely there could be no real evidence of the soul's existence in all this? Dead weight was different to live weight anyway. And there were so many other factors that would cause a change of weight: the stretching of muscles – the neck could stretch by several inches. The loss of bodily fluids. Could McNulty allow for all that precisely enough to form a theory or make a judgement?

It seemed as if he could. At least, he seemed as if he thought he could. He suddenly looked up at Higneth, his thin sallow face framed in the open gallows trap. His eyes were glowing with an unnatural light, and he said,

'A detectable change in weight. The weight is less by twenty grains.'

You're mad, thought Higneth, staring at him. You're a man obsessed. This isn't proof of anything at all – certainly not of the soul existing.

But he said, rather coldly, 'I see. I am glad you found your experiment satisfactory. Thank you for attending in Dr Kane's place.' And turned on his heel and left. As he went along the passage of the execution suite, behind him he heard the door of the execution chamber being closed.

CHAPTER THIRTY-FIVE

After Georgina heard the door of the execution chamber being closed, she wasted several minutes and a great deal of energy trying to open it. Then she wasted even more minutes and even more energy trying to open the thick oak door leading out to the main part of Calvary. Neither would budge. Calvary's locks might be old, but they were solid and they held.

She heard the mechanism of the gallows trap being operated – it thrummed and shivered even through the closed door, and Georgina realized with horror that whoever it was who had locked her in here, had now shut Jude in the gallows vault. The thought of Jude helpless and trapped, was so appalling she almost forgot her own danger. She paced up and down the corridor, clutching the torch which might serve as a weapon, and began to examine systematically the entire suite to see if she could find some other way out.

The exercise yard seemed a reasonable possibility, but

the lock on its door was rusted so firmly into place that it would take hours to break it. What else? Was there a window in the shower room? There was not. Calvary had not been built in the days when bathrooms had to have either windows or efficient extractor fans, and probably this one had only been used when there was a prisoner here who was under sentence of death. That left the condemned cell.

The atmosphere in there was nearly as bad as the execution chamber, but Georgina shone the torch painstakingly around the walls and the floor. There was nothing, not even the smallest air vent through which a desperate prisoner might squeeze. She glanced at her watch and saw far too long a time had elapsed since she had been shut in here.

The sound of the gallows trap being operated again made her heart jump. Was the prowler going down into the vault to attack Jude? If so, why? Oh God, thought Georgina, how did I get myself stuck in this bloody condemned cell, with a maniac on the loose, and a gallows on the other side of this wall, and . . .

Her thoughts snapped onto a wholly new track. The gallows was on the other side of the wall. And although Calvary had been built in the grim old days when prisoners had to take that infamous grisly walk to the scaffold, hadn't most prisons later tried to make the process more humane? Hadn't they adapted things or rebuilt them so that a panel could slide open or a concealed door operate and there, just a few steps ahead, was the noose? Thirty seconds from condemned cell to death. Except that might not have happened here, because the two rooms were next door to one another so it might not have been thought worthwhile. Calvary was old and solid so it might have been a problem to make the alterations. But it might, it just might . . . And if she could at least get into the execution room . . .

Georgina shone the torch over the wall. Nothing. Just a smooth flat surface, battered by time, cracked with neglect. Where would a panel or a concealed door be? In the centre? No, because the point was to keep out of the prisoner's sightline. Nearer the corner, then? Think, Georgina, you're supposed to be the one who knows about the design of buildings and the layout of their interiors. Yes, but you don't get much call to twink up the interior of a prison used for housing murderers!

She set the torch down on the ground so it shone directly onto the wall, and began to run her hands slowly over the surface. It was a fairly disgusting process, because the wall was filthy and in places the plaster was crumbling away, but it had to be done. Jude was on the other side of the wall, and he was locked in there with some madman. I'm not going to find anything, thought Georgina, in panic. I really am stuck in here, and once the prowler's dealt with Jude he'll come back and deal with me.

With the framing of the thought her hands felt a change in the wall's surface, and her heart leapt with hope but also with fresh panic, because it might not be anything at all. But please let it be, please . . .

Under the accumulated layers of dirt and mould, the wall had a seam about a foot in from the end. A doorway? A panel? The seam only went about six feet up. Door height. She worked her way further along, and found a corresponding seam. The outline of a door. But how did it work? Supposing it had become stuck in place with the years?

She pushed against it, and felt it yield slightly, but no more than that. How about sliding it? Right to left? No, there was not enough room for it to slide along – it was too near the corner. Left to right then? Perhaps whoever had designed it had been left-handed.

This time there was no mistaking its movement. The whole section of the wall slid several inches to the right, and Georgina gave a little gasp of relief, and threw her entire weight into the task. Slowly, agonizingly, scraping and protesting after years of disuse, the panel moved along until a rectangle had opened up in the wall.

Georgina snatched up the torch, and stepped through.

The room was empty – unless you counted the un-mistakable presence of its past, which Georgina did not. She saw the red light of the camcorder was still showing, which presumably meant it was running.

The one door of the gallows trap was open as it had been when they came in. Was the prowler hiding down there? What about Jude? When she advanced to the edge of the open vault and shone the torch down, there was no sign of anyone. Georgina frowned and knelt down on the edge, trying to think. They had both been in here – she had certainly left Jude here and she had seen the unknown man dart along the passage and come in and lock the door. She got up to check the door. Yes, firmly locked. No key anywhere, which might mean all kinds of things.

This did not make sense. Either she had fallen into one of those old crime books where the centrepiece was a locked room, or . . .

There was another way out.

The vault. It had to be in the vault – there was nowhere else it could be. Without pausing to work this out any further, Georgina swung her legs over the edge of the open vault and, tucking the torch in the belt of her jeans, lowered herself cautiously down. Jude had said the drop was deeper than he thought, but he had managed it all right, and so . . .

But although she was prepared for the drop, she landed awkwardly, and a vicious pain tore through one ankle. She gasped, and half fell, her whole foot throbbing appallingly. She did not think it was broken, but it had certainly been a bad wrench. Could she put her weight on it sufficiently to get out of this place? She would have to.

If the atmosphere in the room above had been bad, this was a hundred times worse. It was like being at the bottom of a thick silty sea, but it was important to remember it was only a structure made of bricks, cement and timber, and that there were no such things as ghosts.

She shone the torch around, and almost at once the light fell on a door, partly ajar, with what looked like a brick-lined tunnel beyond it. Had Jude gone through that tunnel? He must have done. Georgina considered calling out, but she had no idea where the prowler might be; it might be better not to let him know she had found a way out of the execution suite. Moving as quietly as possible, she opened the door to its fullest extent and stepped through.

The torch cut through the blackness of the tunnel, showing up brick walls, encrusted with dirt, and draped with cobwebs. The floor felt dry and crunchy and, as

Georgina moved awkwardly through the darkness, cobwebs floated their grey fingers against her face.

The tunnel was hot and the air felt thick and stale, and as she went awkwardly along, trying not to put too much weight onto her injured foot, Georgina kept hearing sinister little rustling sounds. It was horridly easy to think these were footsteps – that someone was creeping along behind her, stopping when she stopped, dodging out of sight when she shone the torch back down the tunnel. It was nerves, nothing more, although she thought she was entitled to succumb to nerves in this situation. She went on, cursing her sprained ankle, trying not to imagine that hands were about to reach out of the darkness and grab her, but imagining it anyway. Strangler's hands – the ghost hands of all the murderers who had been brought along here. Had Neville Fremlin strangled any of his victims? It was no time to be thinking about Neville Fremlin, though. But supposing she suddenly saw that face Jude had described – a bulging-eyed throttled face, the neck swollen from the hangman's noose. Supposing it suddenly swam out of the darkness in front of her— Stop it, Georgina! Just get out of this bloody place, phone Chad and find Jude.

The tunnel was curving around to the left, and then to the right. Georgina stopped once, to strap her scarf around her ankle. She had to bind it over her shoe because her foot was so badly swollen if she took her shoe off she might not get it back on, but once done, it made walking a bit easier.

She was just hoping the tunnel did not lead to a locked door or a dead end, and that she would not come upon Jude's unconscious body, when there was a new sound.

Georgina stopped, and shone the torch back down the tunnel. Had it come from behind her – sounds were peculiar down here – or had it just been her foot dislodging a bit of rubble? She listened intently, but nothing seemed to move.

She had taken four more steps when the sound came again, and fear swept over her, because this time there was no doubt. Someone was in the tunnel behind her.

The only thing to do was keep going forwards as well as she could, and hope she reached the outside before the owner of the footsteps made his next move. Clearly he had unlocked the execution suite doors – including the door to the execution chamber itself – and clearly the first lot of sounds had been him lowering himself into the vault.

She moved as fast as she could, hoping against hope that when she reached the end of the tunnel there would be a way out. Her pursuer did not seem to be trying to catch her up – Georgina suddenly wondered if he was aware she had heard him. Or was he aware and was he simply enjoying playing a macabre cat and mouse game with her?

The tunnel ended abruptly – the torchlight picked out the outline of a door. Georgina did not give herself time to wonder if it would be locked, or what she would do if it was; she grabbed the handle and pushed. It was not locked. It swung open with a protesting groan of ancient hinges, and beyond it was a stone-floored room with a deep old sink in one corner, and several old-fashioned cupboards on the walls. Directly in line with the tunnel was a door that looked as if it led outside. There was a hefty bolt at the top and also at the bottom. Did that mean it would be unlocked – that all she had to do was draw the bolts? But would there be time to do all that before the owner of the footsteps emerged from the tunnel? She shone the torch quickly round the room. Jutting out from one wall was a long, waist-high struc-ture – not quite a table, but too wide for a workbench. There were grooves down the sides, and pipes protruded from the underside. Dissecting table, thought Georgina, staring at it. I'm in the mortuary, of course – they'd have to have a mortuary close to the gallows. But it'll have to be the door or nothing, because there's nowhere in here I can hide.

The bolts screeched when she drew them back, but the door opened at once, and cold night air came straight onto her face. It felt marvellous. Georgina saw she had come out in the courtyard of the burial ground – the courtyard she had found a few days earlier. Surely that meant she had only to go through the latched door and be outside? But what about Jude? There was still no sign of him. She reached for the phone, glancing back into the shadowy interior of the mortuary as she did so. Was the prowler still in the tunnel? Was he watching her? Georgina stepped out into the courtyard, and slammed the door of the mortuary – it would not stop the prowler because he would simply open it, but it might gain her a few extra minutes. She was just scrolling down to find Chad Ingram's number, when she heard her name called from somewhere to her right. Jude's voice? She pressed the Call button for Chad, having no idea if the high walls would still be cutting off the signal, and then looked about her. Nothing moved, and for a moment she thought her ears must have been playing tricks, because there was nowhere in the courtyard to hide anyone. So where was Jude? Georgina drew breath to call out, then paused because of alerting the prowler. It was then she saw the small inner courtyard leading off this one.

Her ankle had reached the stage of being so swollen she could no longer feel it, and when she tried to walk, it gave way and she fell sprawling to the ground. But now she could see the little row of ramshackle outbuildings within the inner courtyard. Was Jude in there?

Georgina managed to get to her feet, and by dint of hopping and slithering, got herself across to the out-buildings. There was a thick plank of timber wedged across one of the buildings acting like a massive wooden bolt.

'Jude?'

'Georgina? My God, I've never been so glad to hear you! Was it you who slammed that door just now? I hoped it was, so I yelled, and— Oh, never mind that – can you get me out of this place? I don't know what it is, but it's the most noxious place I've ever encountered.'

'There's a sort of bolt across the door,' said Georgina, taking hold of it. 'It's a bit stiff – in fact somebody's wedged it really tight. Are you all right?'

'Of course I'm not all right, I'm stuck in this bloody hell-hole, and when I get hold of the sick bastard who put me in here—'

'I've got the wedge out,' said Georgina. 'Here goes the bolt.'

She set the strip of wood down and had just taken the edge of the door to pull it open, when running footsteps came pounding across the courtyard behind her, and before she could do anything – before she could even turn to see who it was – she was pushed hard into the dreadful blackness, and the door was slammed.

She was dimly aware of Jude lunging for the door, but there was already the sound of the wooden wedge being put back in place, and the door held firm. Jude swore, and then grabbed her – Georgina had no idea if he found her by judgement or luck – but his arms came round her, and she clung to him, gasping with pain and shock.

'Are you all right? Georgina, are you all right?'

'Yes,' said Georgina, who had got her breath back by this time. 'I was locked in the execution suite, but I found the panel from the condemned cell – only I sprained my ankle jumping into the vault to find you.' She thought he would release her, but he did not.

'And came along that tunnel?' he said.

'Yes, only whoever locked the doors followed me, and he's just pushed me in here. I've tried to get a call out to Chad, but I don't know if the signal was strong enough, and it was only a few minutes ago anyway.' She was fishing the torch out of her pocket as she said this, and switching it on. 'We're in some kind of store,' she said, puzzled. 'It isn't very big – it's like an old-fashioned coalhouse. There are big chunks of rock everywhere.'

'Rock? What kind of rock? Stones?'

'I don't know what they are. Quite pale lumps of some crumbly substance – a bit chalky-looking. But nobody would store rocks, would they?'

'It could be lime,' said Jude slowly. 'Blocks of dry lime. In fact I can't think of anything else it could be.'

'Quicklime,' said Georgina, in horror, 'for the burials. Is that what you mean?'

'It'll be just ordinary lime,' he said, at once. 'I think you have to pour water on it to make it fizz up into quicklime. So we're perfectly safe, and in any case it'll be so old it can't possibly have kept its properties.'

He stopped, because they had both heard someone moving outside. Jude banged hard on the door and Georgina shouted, but there was no response. There was a loud crack that might have been anything, and then running footsteps.

'Your attacker I should think,' said Jude.

'Yes. It sounds as if he's running away, but—' She broke off and grabbed his arm.

'What? What is it?'

Georgina said, 'There's water coming in under the door.'

In the dimness of the store the water looked like black ink. It came in thick spider-leg rivulets, and it trickled across the ground.

'If it reaches the lime blocks,' began Georgina. 'Oh God, what will happen?'

'I don't know. But I can't believe it will be harmful after all these years,' said Jude. 'I really can't. But—'

'What?'

'Just in case there isn't an opportunity again,' he said and, pulling her against him, he kissed her hard.

'Oh, I do hope there is an opportunity,' said Georgina involuntarily, and saw him smile.

'You've given me an irresistible reason for getting us out of this,' he said. 'Don't worry, Georgina darling, we'll be all right.'

'Will we?'

'Of course. In fact—' He broke off, and tilted his

461

head, listening. 'In fact, that sounds like the cavalry now,' said Jude. 'I wonder what kept them?'

Only then did Georgina hear the sound of a car coming very fast up the hillside.

CHAPTER THIRTY-SIX

'What I can't work out,' said Drusilla, 'is how you were able to phone us for help, Jude. Didn't you say that when you were attacked the phone was knocked out of your hand.'

'I can't work that one out either,' said Chad. 'Or are you going to sell us some off the wall idea about sleight of hand or legerdemain?'

'Much simpler. The phone never was knocked out of my hand,' said Jude. 'It was in an inner pocket.'

'I still don't understand,' said Drusilla.

They were in the coffee room of the King's Head. Drusilla had fetched most of Georgina's things from Caradoc House and booked her into the one remaining room.

'You can't possibly climb all those stairs with that ankle,' she had said. 'In any case, you won't want to be on your own after tonight.'

Georgina, still battered and dazed, had given in. They

had all made statements to the police – they had been asked to call at the police station the following day to check their statements and sign them – and the police doctor had strapped up her ankle, which was starting to feel much less painful. The police, summoned by Chad, had made a thorough search of Calvary, and they had posted a couple of officers out there for the rest of the night.

'But of course,' said Jude, 'whoever made those bizarre attacks has long since gone. Probably miles away by now.'

For the moment Calvary and its mysterious darknesses had receded. For Georgina the world had shrunk to Thornbeck and this warm room, and to Chad, Drusilla and Phin. And Jude. He was sitting next to her, and although he was pale and dishevelled he did not appear in the least discomposed.

He was explaining about the phone. 'When I got out of that noisome tunnel, I stood for a moment, trying to make a mental image of where I was. I'd tried the phone once by then but there was still no signal so I'd put it back in my pocket. I was just thinking I'd try it again when I realized someone was standing in front of me.' He frowned. 'It was a bloody eerie sensation, I'll have you know. Whoever it was just stood there, and I had absolutely no idea who it was or what was going to happen. So I thought I'd help things along. I reasoned that if he thought I was going to make a phone call, he'd do something to stop me. So I pretended to do just that.'

'To make a call?'

'Yes.'

'You took a hell of a risk,' said Chad, angrily.

464

'I know. I was actually quite frightened, although I was more frightened for Georgina because I couldn't think how to reach her. But I thought if the prowler made an actual attack,' said Jude, 'I'd be able to put up a fight and bring the thing to a head. Then I'd get outside and phone you, Professor. But I was blowed if I was going to risk losing the phone in the process.'

He paused, and Phin said, 'Oh! You used the dictaphone!' And beamed with delight at having worked out what Jude had done.

'Yes,' said Jude and smiled. 'I used the dictaphone. I was fairly sure the room would be dark.'

'He might have had a torch,' said Drusilla.

'If he did, I don't think it was switched on,' said Jude. 'I'd have felt the light on my face. I'm sorry, I can't explain that, but there's a sensation when strong light's directed at me. Unmistakable.'

'Go on,' said Chad.

'The dictaphone is much the same size and shape as a modern cellphone. I thought if I kept it in the palm of my hand and appeared to be tapping out a number – Anyway, it did the trick. He did make a move. The trouble was that the move he made was to clump me on the head and drag me into the lime store and wedge the door tightly shut. Fortunately it wasn't a very hefty clump and I don't think I was out for more than a few minutes. When I came round, I still had the real phone, of course. There was a bad moment in there when I thought I still couldn't get a signal, and I had no idea where I was, other than it was somewhere quite small and there was a – a kind of stinging dryness in the air. But I did get a signal and I called Chad and told him to get out there faster than a cat escaping hell. Sorry, Georgina, there wasn't time to explain all that to you.'

'So *that's* how he got to us so quickly,' said Georgina. 'That's what I couldn't work out – I'd tried to get a call out a few minutes earlier – before I got pounced on as well. I didn't know if the call had registered, but I did know it would take at least fifteen minutes for Chad to get there. I'm extremely glad you got there when you did, Chad.'

'I'm extremely glad you got us out before the water reached the blocks of lime,' put in Jude.

'Could the water actually have activated it?' asked Phin worriedly. 'Do we know that yet?'

'It looked as if it was fizzing a bit,' said Chad. 'And the police doctor said it certainly wouldn't have done Jude and Georgina much good to be in there for any length of time. I've given the police the camcorder, by the way. We're hoping it picked up the figure who came into the execution chamber and closed the trapdoor on Jude.'

'It should have done,' said Jude.

'Yes, but it might not be clear enough to identify him. They've asked us to view it with them tomorrow, so we can talk them through what we were doing. Half past ten at the police station – OK everyone?'

'We've got to go to the station anyway to sign statements,' said Drusilla.

'Where does all this leave your programme, Professor?' said Jude. 'I don't suppose you bargained for sinister midnight prowlers or murderous tramps, or whoever was on the loose tonight.'

'Hardly,' said Chad. 'But I don't see why we can't stay with the original brief. Showing the experiment, and describing Jude's mind-image and so on. I suppose the permission to use Calvary might be withdrawn. Somebody somewhere might decide we shouldn't have been let in because it was dangerous in there, or something like that.'

'It'd be a pity if you had to abandon it,' said Jude.

'I'm hoping we won't. I thought we might collect the names of a few people hanged there, to tie in with that image you had, and make that the centrepiece. Georgina, could we use Walter's Execution Book? I mean, actually show it in close-up?'

'Yes, of course.'

'Thank you. I'd like to speculate on what kind of imprint some of the condemned prisoners might have left on Calvary – it would be good if we could track down a few details about one or two of them.'

'Such as Violet Parsons?' said Drusilla, smiling.

'Violet almost warrants a programme all to herself,' said Chad, thoughtfully.

'Oh God, start working out a new budget, Phin.' This was Drusilla.

'I'd love to, but you absolutely have to do the thing on Neville Fremlin as well,' said Phin eagerly. 'Couldn't we do two spin-offs of the original – one for Parsons, and one for Fremlin. That'd be really neat.'

'Phin and I have got out some figures for the Fremlin idea,' said Drusilla. 'And we're halfway through the draft of a really good proposal. Black and white shots of his shop in Knaresborough, and the newspaper reports from the trial. Phin's trying to trace the people who rented the shop after him.'

'It sounds like a pretty classy place,' put in Phin.

'Fremlin wouldn't have had a place that wasn't classy.'

Georgina, listening with interest to all this, found herself enjoying the enthusiasm they all had for their work, and the way they could suddenly plunge back into it, and put aside the drama of the night.

'If we do use the Execution Book,' Chad said, 'we'll give Walter a credit, of course, Georgina. And you. Has any of this got you any nearer to him?'

'No,' said Georgina. 'I keep thinking I'm going to find him – I mean, that I'll find out why he left that socking great legacy to the Caradoc Society and ignored his wife and daughter for the rest of his life. But every time I think I've found a clue it sort of slithers out of my grasp.'

'Keep at it, though,' said Chad. 'Because that's usually the exact point when the missing bit of jigsaw suddenly turns up. Is anyone having any more coffee? Or a drink? Because if not, I think I'm for bed.'

'So am I,' said Drusilla. 'I feel as if I've lived about a hundred years in the last twenty-four hours.'

'Georgina and I should be the ones saying that,' said Jude. He stood up. 'I'll walk Georgina to her room.'

'Shall I come with you and walk you back?' said Phin, and yelped as Drusilla trod on his foot.

'Oh, I don't think you need bother to do that,' said Jude vaguely. 'I daresay I'll find my own way.'

'I just wanted to make sure you're really all right,' he said, five minutes later in the tiny bedroom the King's Head had allotted Georgina. 'There hasn't been much chance to ask you, what with police and statements and all the rest of it.'

'I'm sort of all right,' said Georgina. 'At least, I'm not absolutely all right, but I will be.'

'That's what I thought.'

'How about you?'

'The same. I was frantic when I realized that madman had trapped me and was probably going after you next.' His hand came out to her, palm upwards, not fumbling, simply offering it to her if she wanted to take it. Georgina took it immediately.

'How will you get back to London?' said Jude. 'You won't be able to drive, will you?'

'Drusilla's going to drive my car with me as passenger. That will leave more room for you in Chad's car.'

'That's what I thought. How depressing.'

'Why is it depressing?'

'Because,' said Jude angrily, 'I ought to be able to scoop you up and put you in a fast car and drive you back to London myself!'

'There's no need to be so prickly about it,' said Georgina. 'There's no need to be chauvinistic about driving, either.'

'I've been called many things,' said Jude, 'but never a chauvinist. I can see I shall have to re-think my whole approach. There's no need to smile, I mean it.'

'How did you know I was smiling?'

'The atmosphere changes when you smile. I wish I knew what you looked like. Do you match your voice? Not everyone does.'

For a moment Georgina was thrown, and then without pausing to think about it, she took both his hands and brought them up to her face.

He understood at once. She thought he had probably

been taught this method of 'seeing' people when he was first blinded. She stood very still as his fingertips lightly traced the bones of her face. He had cool hands with sensitive fingers but his touch was entirely impersonal.

'Thank you,' said Jude at last, taking his hands away. 'I think I've got it quite well. The only thing I can't tell is the colouring.'

'Brown hair. Fairly light brown,' said Georgina. 'And grey eyes.'

'Real grey? That pure colour like silk?'

('Tap-water eyes,' David used to say.)

'I suppose so,' said Georgina.

'Good. They turn luminous if they're pleased or happy, those kind of eyes,' he said. 'You're not pretty, but I suspect you might be beautiful.'

('You aren't one of the real stunners, are you?' David had said. 'But you scrub up quite well.')

'It's not a modern face, I don't think,' went on Jude, 'but that's your good luck. You could hop on a time-travel machine and pass unchallenged in fourteenth-century Florence, or Czarist Russia.'

'Or a Victorian slum,' said Georgina. 'Thanks. I'll remember all that next time a time-travel machine comes along.'

'Why the slum?'

Georgina had a sudden ridiculous desire to say, Because it's where I might end up if the police can't track down David and my money. She said, 'No particular reason.'

Without warning, Jude said, 'Will you have dinner with me when we get back to London? Properly, I mean, not just a scrappy meal like we've had here. Or are you firmly hooked up to some nice man who's fiercely protective and jealous?'

'I'm not hooked up to anyone and I'd like to have dinner with you very much,' said Georgina.

'Would you really? Good. I'll leave you to your chaste couch for what's left of the night. Don't think about the ghosts too much. Except Walter. I think Walter might be rather a nice ghost.'

'So do I.'

He moved to the door, reaching for the frame with one hand and Georgina said, 'Can you get back to your room all right?'

'Turn right out of here, five paces along, left-hand dog-leg, second door on the right,' said Jude promptly. 'Sleep well.'

Vincent could not believe it. After all his planning and care – after the way he had adapted his original plan, going with the flow as people said – the whole thing had misfired!

It had all been working out so well although he had had a few anxious moments wondering if Georgina would find the panel in the condemned cell, but she had done it in the end. Clever, you see. A really intelligent, worthy opponent.

He had not hit the man very hard with the sandbag – just enough to stun him for five or ten minutes – and he had shut Georgina and the man in the lime store, as planned, and placed the plastic bag over the grid of the drain, weighting it with a stone. Then he had kicked away the corroded tap from the water butt. He had jumped well clear as the water gushed across the courtyard, but he had seen it was already running down to the door of the lime store. Exactly as he had wanted!

He was just making his way around the side of the building, when car headlights suddenly sliced through the darkness. For a dreadful moment Vincent thought he was about to be caught, but he was sufficiently quick-witted to dodge back into the deep shadows cast by the old walls and to stand there unseen. He didn't succumb to panic but his mind was in tumult. Chad Ingram was not due back here until two a.m. – Vincent had based his plan on that.

But it *was* Ingram. From where he stood, Vincent could see him in the driving seat with the American boy next to him. They stopped the car in front of the main door, and tumbled out. Dr Ingram said something and the American pointed, and then they set off around the side of the building. Vincent could hear them talking – he could hear the anxious breathless voice of the American boy saying that Georgina had mentioned a door in the wall at lunch.

It sounded as if Georgina had been out here on her own, the bitch! But did these two know Georgina and the man were trapped? How could they? Had a phone call been made? Vincent had himself knocked the man's phone out of his hands, and Georgina had been in the enclosed rooms of Calvary where phone signals were impossible – he was certain about this because it was one of the things he had tested over the years. But something had brought them racing out here. Black, bitter fury rose up in Vincent, because none of this should be happening. None of this had been intended. He waited until Dr Ingram and Phin were out of sight and earshot, and then went quickly down to his car and drove home. Once in the safety of his own house he poured a whisky and soda and sat drinking it, staring ahead of him for a very long time.

Mother would not have been pleased at the failure of his plan, although it was difficult to know how she could have done any better. Or was it? Wouldn't she have said Vincent had tried to be too clever? Luring people into an old store, and trying to slake ancient lime, she would have said, scathingly. Could he not have used some simpler method?

Ah, but the plan might not have failed completely. They might all be so alarmed by what had happened that they would abandon all these ideas of television programmes, and great-grandfathers. The Home Office or the Prisons Authority – or somebody – might forbid them to use Calvary as a subject in the film – yes, that was a promising line of thought. In fact, Vincent would make it his business to ensure the Home Office got to hear what had happened. Tomorrow, he would find out which government department to contact. There might be headings in Yellow Pages, or under local council phone numbers. And then, once the incident was general knowledge in Thornbeck – as it would soon be – he could write a letter. A concerned local resident, he would be, and the letter would be well written and efficient so people would take notice of it.

The one redeeming factor was that Vincent himself could not possibly be suspected of involvement in tonight's attacks. Georgina certainly had not seen him – even when he made that quick sprint out of the con-demned cell where he had been hiding behind the door –

nor when he had run across the courtyard to push her into the lime store. And the man was not able to see at all.

Georgina and Dr Ingram would report what had happened to the police, of course. Vincent thought he would have to be prepared for that. As a respected, responsible resident of the town he would be as shocked as everyone else when the news got around.

Most likely the attacks would be put down to a vagrant. As Vincent went up to bed, he felt safe in the certainty that no one had seen him.

CHAPTER THIRTY-SEVEN

'It's Vincent Meade,' said Georgina, staring in disbelief at the shadowy footage on the police monitor, and the figure frozen into immobility.

'She's right,' said Drusilla, leaning forward. 'It really is Vincent.'

'Are you sure?'

'Yes, I am,' said Georgina.

'I'm sure as well,' said Mr Huxley Small, who was apparently present in the dual capacities of police solicitor and managing agent of Calvary. 'Sergeant, don't you agree? You know Mr Meade, don't you?'

'Not really,' said the detective sergeant, who had been taking notes, and who was studying the screen closely. 'Not enough to positively identify him from that.'

'But why would Vincent be in Calvary?' demanded Georgina. 'Why would he close the gallows trap on Jude and – and shut us both in the lime store, and all the rest of it?'

'I don't know, Miss Grey. Let's have a look at the shot again.'

The young constable who was operating the camcorder, wound the film back a bit and they watched the man come into the execution chamber a second time.

'It's definitely Vincent Meade,' said Mr Small. 'I've known him for years, I couldn't mistake him.'

'But how would he have got in?' said Drusilla. 'We were so careful about locking up and so on.'

'We'll need to question him,' said the sergeant. 'But I'm not sure if this is enough for us to actually charge him with anything. All we've got is a shot of him inside Calvary Gaol, closing the gallows trap. That's peculiar behaviour, but it's not firm evidence of him shutting Mr Stratton and Miss Grey in the lime store. It's suggestive, but it's not proof positive, right, Mr Small?'

'Quite right.'

'Mr Stratton, you hadn't met Mr Meade, I think?'

'No,' said Jude. 'So I can't help you.'

'Miss Grey, was there anything about your attacker that would tie him to Mr Meade? Build – voice – body scent.'

'Nothing,' said Georgina. 'Whoever attacked me didn't speak and I only got a fleeting glimpse of a figure in the execution suite. The man I saw was the right sort of build for Vincent, though. But look here – this is all absurd. Vincent doesn't know Jude and he hardly knows me. He invited me here.'

'The Caradoc Society invited you here, Miss Grey,' said Mr Small. 'Vincent Meade merely wrote the letter in his capacity as secretary.' He frowned, and then said, 'I dislike gossip and in my profession it's strongly discouraged, of course. But I do feel a certain responsibility in this case.' He glanced at the sergeant, and then said, 'If you've finished with Miss Grey and the others?'

'Yes, for the moment.'

'Then,' said Mr Small, 'perhaps we might walk along to my office for a little more discussion. Miss Grey, are you able to manage that? It is only a few steps along the main street.'

'Yes, certainly.'

'Dr Ingram? Mr Stratton?'

'D'you want all of us?' said Chad.

'Yes, if you would.'

Georgina liked being in Mr Small's office again; she saw herself describing it to Jude afterwards, and Jude's appreciation of the blending of the Victorian era and the twenty-first century.

'None of this is your fault,' said Chad, as they were gestured to seats facing the large mahogany desk, behind which Mr Small looked even wispier.

'No, but I think you are owed some explanation.' He regarded them, and then said, 'Vincent Meade.'

'Yes?'

'If he is proved to have been your attacker, he will, of course, have to answer for the consequences. I make no excuse for violence of any kind. But I would like you to know that Vincent is a man with a very unfortunate childhood. His mother's name before her marriage was Elizabeth Molland. That doesn't convey anything to you?'

'No,' said Chad, having glanced at the others.

'I thought it probably wouldn't. It's a long time ago.

Elizabeth Molland was originally thought to have been one of Neville Fremlin's victims.'

'That's interesting,' said Drusilla, leaning forward eagerly. 'Mr Small, we've been researching Neville Fremlin a bit, along with the programme on Calvary.'

'Ah. Indeed? Well, Elizabeth vanished at the start of his killings,' said Mr Small. 'And she was known to have frequented his shop in Knaresborough, so it was a reasonable assumption. But the police didn't find a body, so there was always a question mark over what had happened to her. Fremlin would never talk, so they say. He went to the gallows without confessing to a single one of the murders with which he was charged.'

'I didn't know that,' said Drusilla.

'Very gentlemanly behaviour, according to all the accounts,' said Mr Small rather drily. 'The police tried very hard to get the truth about Elizabeth from him – in fact, Miss Grey, when he was in the condemned cell they asked your great-grandfather to talk to him about her.'

Georgina felt a sudden spiral of anticipation. Was this to be the link that would take her back to Walter? 'And – did he do so?'

'According to the reports, he did,' said Mr Small, 'but he couldn't get anything out of Fremlin any more than the police could. It was only after the hanging they found that far from being a victim, Elizabeth was alive and well. Moreover, she had acted as Neville Fremlin's accomplice.'

'His accomplice? That's a twist to the tale,' said Chad. 'And she was caught?'

'Yes, eventually. She was tried and taken to Calvary in 1939. It ought to have been something of a cause célèbre of course – Fremlin had been – but war had just been declared, and the newspapers were full of that.'

'But how does any of this explain Vincent getting into Calvary and attacking Jude and Georgina?' said Chad.

Phin, who had listened in respectful silence to everything so far, said eagerly, 'I can see how it might. Uh – excuse me, for butting in. But how about Vincent wanting to – um – protect Elizabeth's memory? To stop anyone knowing she'd been found guilty of murder – especially murder alongside Neville Fremlin, what with him being notorious and all?'

'I don't see how shutting Jude and Georgina in the lime store would stop people finding out about his mother,' objected Drusilla.

'Well, see, there are two ways it could go. One is that it could make it seem as if there were hobos or druggies up there. Two is that if nobody believed Jude and Georgina about being attacked and locked in, it would make us all look irresponsible. Careless. We'd seem like people who got shut up in dangerous parts of the building. Either way we'd probably be ordered off the premises.'

'That's very astute of you,' said Small, looking at Phin with approval.

'He is astute,' said Chad, and Phin was covered in such delighted confusion that he could not speak for a moment.

'And Vincent could have wanted to protect his mother's memory,' said Georgina. 'That's perfectly credible, you know.'

'What happened to her?' asked Drusilla. 'Because

obviously she was let out in the end, and married and had a son. Did they reprieve her or did she serve her sentence, or what?'

'She was not reprieved and she did not serve a sentence,' said Mr Small. 'She was condemned to death, but she escaped.'

'*Escaped?*'

'Yes. She was got out of Calvary just before the execution. I don't know the details of the escape itself, and I don't know if your great-grandfather was part of that escape, Miss Grey. But he was certainly Calvary's doctor at the time.'

'Then he might have helped Elizabeth to escape,' said Phin. 'That's possible, isn't it?'

'Especially if he thought she was innocent,' said Jude.

'Oh, she was not innocent,' said Mr Small at once.

'You can't know that,' said Chad.

'I do know it, Dr Ingram. I have it on very good authority.'

'Whose authority?' asked Jude, and Georgina glanced at him, because for the first time she had heard an incisive note in his voice and she remembered he was a journalist, used to interviewing all kinds of people, used to chipping away until the truth emerged.

'The authority of my own ears, Mr Stratton,' said Small. He paused, and then said, 'I don't think I'm betraying client confidentiality over this – the people concerned are all dead. But I don't think it's an exaggeration to say that no one who ever met Elizabeth Molland ever forgot her. I was still very young when I met her, and I have certainly never forgotten her.

'You knew her?' said Jude.

'I met her in 1958,' said Mr Small. 'I was in my early twenties – newly qualified. My father was unwell and looking to retire, so when Lewis Caradoc needed help, I was the one assigned to him.'

'Help?' said Jude.

'Legal help,' said Mr Small, 'with a prisoner who had been recently admitted to Holloway Prison.'

'Elizabeth Molland.'

'Yes.'

'Neville Fremlin's cat's paw,' said Jude thoughtfully. 'The sorcerer's apprentice.'

'Oh no,' said Mr Small at once. 'Elizabeth never played apprentice to anybody, and certainly not to Neville Fremlin. It was the other way round. But it was not until more than twenty years after Fremlin was hanged that the truth came out.'

August 1958

A great many years had passed since Lewis Caradoc had driven through that rain-swept night with Elizabeth in the car, but there were times when he could almost imagine it had been last week.

This, of course, was one of the tricks that extreme age played. Time altered its dimensions; it made the events of the past seem more vivid than what you had just had for lunch. Even so, he was fairly sure his mind was as sharp as it had ever been. He could still enjoy his books and his music, and he was interested in what went on in the world: sputniks and beatniks and atomic power, the new dance from America they called rock and roll. Lewis had a suspicion that if it had been around in his youth he might have considered it rather attractive and exciting. When you were approaching your ninth decade you no longer had the feelings you had in your youth, but he could still admire the brightly dressed modern girls with their flouncy skirts and the spiky heels that made their ankles look so very trim. But it was the last bastion of age to dislike modern fashions and tastes, so he usually agreed with his contemporaries that the music was discordant and the hairstyles outrageous.

There were not so many of his contemporaries left nowadays, of course, but there were enough. He was still invited to people's houses for lunches and sometimes for whole weekends. The weekends were becoming a bit tiring, although he always accepted the invitations and dressed as sprucely as ever for them. Over the last few years he had taken to wearing a small goatee beard; a number of people said it made him look rather donnish. Scholarly. Clara would have liked that. A pity she had not lived to see it. And Caspar would have been proud of his distinguished father.

If Caspar had lived, he would have been married with children – by now the children would probably have children of their own. I'd be a great-grandfather, thought Lewis rather wryly. It was sixty years since his son died in the mud and terror of the war to end all wars. It was twenty years since he had snatched his daughter away from Calvary, and got her onto the ferry from Holyhead to Ireland. It seemed wrong that Elizabeth, whom he had only known for those few hours, should be more vivid to him than Caspar was. Was that because he and Elizabeth had shared those frantic few hours as they made that desperate drive through the night, with

Lewis watching for roadblocks and constantly looking in the driving mirror for signs of pursuit?

When first he put her in the car, she had seemed unaware of what was happening. Lewis had expected this; he had known Walter would give her something for the pain he believed her to be suffering. They had driven for almost an hour before she roused, enough to take note of her surroundings and of Lewis himself.

'You're my rescuer,' she said. 'Thank you for getting me away from that place.'

It had stopped raining by then, and a watery moonlight shone into the car. It showed up the pure delicacy of her face – beautiful bones, thought Lewis – and he saw her eyes were filled with tears.

'We're not out the woods yet, I'm afraid,' he said gently.

'Aren't we? But the further we get, the safer we'll be, won't we? Where are you taking me?'

'To Holyhead to the ferry for Dún Laoghaire. You should be in Dublin this time tomorrow.'

'Safe?'

'I think so.'

'Shall I live there? I haven't any money.'

'I know that. I've brought money for you. It's in an envelope in the glove compartment.'

'How much money?'

The question struck an odd note, but Lewis said, 'Enough, I promise you. You'll probably have to buy Irish punts with it – you could do that in a bank. Can you manage that by yourself?' He had no idea how much she understood about currency and finance and travelling.

'Yes, of course I can manage that,' she said. 'I like the

idea of Ireland. Neville lived in Ireland for a time – he told me that. He made it sound so beautiful. You're giving me the chance to make a completely new life, aren't you, Lewis? You're being very kind to me. Why is that? Why are you risking so much for me, Lewis?'

Lewis . . . It was the first time she had used his name, and incredibly Lewis heard the caress in her voice – a caress that was so nearly sexual in quality that in other circumstances he would probably have felt a tug of physical desire. She did not know who he really was, of course – she had absolutely no idea he was her real father – so perhaps it was understandable she should use a little feminine charm on him. Innocent, he thought. She's so very innocent.

'Oh, old-fashioned gallantry,' he said, as lightly as he could. 'You're too young to die, and I think you were under Neville Fremlin's spell.'

'Mr Higneth thought that as well, didn't he?' she said. 'He was just as kind to me. He gave me the stuff you told me about – to make me sick.' She thought for a moment. 'That doctor – Dr Kane. Did he know all about this?'

'No.'

'Are you sure?'

'He didn't know anything,' said Lewis.

'I wouldn't be so sure,' she said, consideringly. 'He's very clever. Although he wasn't clever enough to know I was a virgin.'

The words struck a discordant note in the car. Lewis looked at her, but she was watching the road. 'Dr Kane got it all wrong about me,' she said. 'He was so surprised when he found out I hadn't been to bed with Neville Fremlin.'

'Hadn't you?' This was one of the most bizarre conversations Lewis had ever had. He concentrated on the dark ribbon of road unwinding in front of them.

'Oh no!' she said. 'I don't think I'll ever want to go to bed with anyone.'

'You'll think differently in a year or two,' said Lewis after a moment.

'Will I? I suppose I'd like a baby of my own some day.' Again she sent him the sidelong glance. 'You're thinking this is a strange conversation for us to be having, aren't you? I suppose it's because we're together like this. Danger brings people closer together, doesn't it?'

'Sometimes.' Had it brought her close to the man she had known as Neville Fremlin?

'It's so odd,' she said, 'but I feel that I can tell you all these things. About me. About Neville.'

Lewis thought: but I don't want to hear them. I don't want your confidences, Elizabeth – not when they concern Fremlin.

'I think,' she said, 'that Neville saw me as a – a goddess. That's what he said, anyway. So I don't think he ever even wanted to be in bed with me – you don't go to bed with goddesses, do you? He said I was the most perfect thing he had seen – like a china figure. And he used to read poetry to me, can you imagine that?'

'It's sometimes considered very romantic,' said Lewis. 'What kind of poetry?'

'Dull stuff. Something about not dying for flag nor king, but for a dream. Something about a dream that had been born in a cowshed or something and because of it Ireland had got to be free.'

So Nicholas had still had that dream, thought Lewis.

He never lost sight of that, not even at the end of his life.

'My papa would have said it was a lot of sloppy sentimentality,' said Elizabeth.

My papa. Lewis said carefully, 'Didn't he – your father – like poetry?'

'Oh no, he was always too busy making money and being on councils and things. I used to tease him about it.' She looked out of the window. 'Is that the road to Holyhead?'

'Yes.' Lewis swung the car left, and thanked whatever powers might be appropriate that so far they had been unchallenged. 'We're not far away now,' he said. 'The ferry leaves at six – I'll see you safely onto it, of course. We can have some breakfast somewhere beforehand, if you like.'

'Oh, yes, please. Do I let you know how I get on in Ireland?' she said. 'Do you want me to do that? To write to you or something?' And then, before Lewis could even start to sort out his emotions, she said, 'No, it would be better not. If I got into your life I'd be a great risk, wouldn't I?'

'Yes. But if you're ever in trouble,' said Lewis slowly, 'you must write to me at once.'

'Can I? That makes me feel very safe,' she said. 'Don't give me your address though. If I ever need you, I'll find you.'

Lewis slowed the car down, and turned to look at her properly. 'Do you think you ever will need me, Elizabeth?'

'I might,' she said, returning his steady regard. 'Yes, I might need you one day, Lewis.'

I might need you one day, Lewis.

But it had been nearly twenty years before she did need him.

The letter that startled him out of his uneventful days arrived on a summer morning, just after breakfast. The posts were inclined to be a bit relaxed in this small Cotswold village, because there were so many retired people living here, and the postal services either thought retired people did not need the immediacy of letters at the crack of dawn or that they could not cope with them until after breakfast. Lewis was drinking a second cup of coffee and filling in *The Times* crossword – it was one of his small vanities that he could still complete it inside his own time limit – when the letters dropped onto the mat; he went along to pick them up at once.

And there it was. Unfamiliar handwriting, but un-mistakably feminine. It could have been from anyone of a dozen people. Lewis opened it ahead of the others, curious to find out. It was dated three days earlier and the address was Holloway Gaol for Women.

My dear friend.

Do you remember many years ago saying that if ever I needed you, I should get in touch? That time has come. I do need you – I am in dreadful trouble, and feel you are the only person I can turn to.

If you could come to see me I should be for ever grateful. I am sure they will allow it – with you being who you are.

I am older and a little more worldly-wise now, and I think there was more than just gallantry in what you did that night in 1939. I do not ask questions, of course, but it is with that in mind that I ask for your help now.

If you have read the newspapers, you may have realized that lies are being told about me. Lies from jealous people, people who write newspapers and make up stories to sell their papers. The lies they are telling have nothing to do with the affair that bound us together so long ago. This is an ordeal of a newer date – it began barely three months ago.

In case you have not recognized the photographs in the papers, I should explain that my name is now Meade – I was briefly and unhappily married. I am on my own in the world, except for a very dear son who is just twenty.

I hope and pray to hear from you.

Your friend,
Elizabeth

There were tasks in life that could not be shirked. Lewis finished his coffee, tucked the letter in his pocket, and went in search of a train timetable.

CHAPTER THIRTY-EIGHT

May 1958

Saul Ketch had thought for some months that it was high time he retired. He was no longer a young man – he had not been a young man for many years – and when he looked back over his life, he resented having served the doctor for almost all that time.

He had done some bloody risky things for Dr McNulty, and what had he finally got for it all? Bloody servant's work, that was what he had got! Sodding kitchen work in the doctor's posh retirement house – the house he, Ketch, had helped buy. They both knew, didn't they, that without Ketch's little snippets of information – a juicy titbit here, a tag-end of spicy gossip there – Doctor bleeding McNulty would not have had the money he had now. He said it was all in order to further his work, as if chasing spooks was work! Ketch did not believe a word of it.

And then there was the travelling! Ketch would never

have thought he would have to make so many journeys! Following this one, spying on that one. He had, in fact, rather enjoyed the spying – one or two ladies, there'd been, and Ketch was never averse to peering through a window if a tart was undressing or getting tupped by somebody else's husband. Although wasn't it just like old mean-guts, to insist Ketch travelled third class on those jaunts, doling out money as sparingly as if he minted it himself.

You might have thought the doctor, being a man of advancing years (he must be seventy at the very least, dried-out old herring gut), would be slowing down by now, but not a bit of it. No sooner had he handed over the running of that unnatural Society of his, than they were off on a whole new series of ideas. Ketch was, on balance, inclined to be relieved they had done with the Caradoc Society. To his mind souls and suchlike were best left alone. He'd had an aunt, potty old gowk, she'd been, Ketch had never been able to make head nor tail of half she said. She reckoned to see things other folks did not, and she told how spirits used to come and knock on her door of nights. Ketch's family laughed raucously at this every time they heard it, and said the only things to knock on Aunt Nan's door were the bailiffs.

Ketch always joined in the laughing, but as a small child, Aunt Nan had once said to him he was one of the gallows folk, and she saw him standing under a scaffold. That was an eerie one, no matter how you looked at it!

The doctor was after the real gallows folk now; he was looking through the records of his years at Calvary, jabbing a bony finger at this page or that, saying as how they might put the screws on him, or him. Not so many people had ever come out of Calvary, of course – those that hadn't been there for life had been taken to the execution chamber – but there were a few. The doctor was going after those few: he said they might have married or have taken good jobs and wouldn't like it known they'd been inside the murderers' prison. A good weapon, this, the doctor said, cackling to himself as he sat over his fire of an evening. It gave Ketch the creeps to hear that cackling going on.

Anyway, the doctor had fastened on that whey-faced tart who had been got out of Calvary at the start of the war. Ketch had thought that one had already been sucked dry, but the doctor said, aha, that was where Ketch was wrong. You had to look at the thing from another angle, he said. You had to turn a situation upside-down – all right, arse about face if Ketch preferred the term – and see what you could make of it.

And what they could make of this, said Dr smart-dick McNulty in his annoying, you are stupid and I am clever voice, was something very good indeed.

What?

'What,' said McNulty, going jab-jab with his skinny finger, 'happened to Elizabeth Molland after Lewis Caradoc and Edgar Higneth got her away?'

Ketch did not know what had happened to her, but he did not say he did not much care.

McNulty said, 'I've been looking up records of marriage and suchlike. And it seems Elizabeth Molland is now Elizabeth Meade. You'd think she'd have discarded the Molland name, but not a bit of it, the brazen little cat. Or perhaps she had discarded it for everyday life but had to use it for the marriage. Anyway, there it was in the register, and if my information is right she's a respectable widow now. So we're going to find her, Ketch.'

When the doctor said, We're going to find her, what he really meant was that Ketch was going to find her. Ketch it was who had to go around the countryside, following up what the doctor called leads but what Ketch called a sodding nuisance.

He pointed out that Molland would recognize McNulty the minute she saw him, but McNulty said, very sharply, that she would not. They had never met, and during her time at Calvary Walter Kane had been the attending doctor, or did Ketch not remember? Had Ketch's wits gone a-begging again?

'Well, she'll recognize me,' said Ketch sullenly, and McNulty said, possibly, and to be on the safe side Ketch had better keep well back from this one.

Keeping well back did not, it appeared, prevent Ketch from having to do most of the legwork. But they found her, all right. Elizabeth Meade, recently moved to Southend-on-Sea – a snobby old place that was, as well! Ketch, plodding sulkily through the streets, calling at register offices and house agents to get an address, talking to neighbours and shopkeepers and vicars, hated Southend-on-Sea. He hated the way people looked down their noses and pretended not to know what you said to them, or said, Oh, you're from the *north*, as if it was another planet.

Even so, he found her. He did his long lost servant of the family act, which could be adapted to fit almost any situation, and he found her. He took the information back to the doctor: name, address, family just one child –

a son of eighteen or so. Bit of a namby-pamby one to Ketch's mind. Bit of a mollycoddle.

'Hm, interesting, that,' the doctor said. 'I can't quite see Elizabeth Molland mollycoddling anyone. But we will see. Ketch, I am going to Southend-on-Sea. I am going to take a house for the summer, and I am going to get as much as I can out of that murderous little harpy.'

It was easy. It was so easy, Ketch found himself gape-mouthed in astonishment.

The Meade female had changed quite a lot – she was older, of course, and she had become a boring respectable woman wearing fawn cardigans with permed hair and pearls. She belonged to a gardening club and she knitted pullovers for her son, and they went for neat little drives in a tidy, well-polished little car.

McNulty said, 'And this is the female who helped kill five women and then a couple more on her own account. God Almighty.' Then he said, briskly, that leopards did not change their spots and leopardesses changed them least of all, never mind the beige woollens, pleated skirts and the court shoes.

Meade did not know who McNulty was, of course, McNulty had been quite right about that. She seemed very pleased to be made a friend of, to go on little drives or to teashops for afternoon tea. She was very fond of afternoon tea, she said. A dying custom, wasn't it, more was the pity. Ketch, sweeping and cleaning the house McNulty had taken on the edge of the town, hiding in the kitchen when the Meade person came to Sunday lunch, wondered at times if they really had got the right woman, because it was difficult to square afternoon tea with mass murder. But he knew deep down it was the same woman. You had only to look at the hands. People thought Ketch was stupid and dull and did not notice things, but he noticed hands, and he noticed the Meade woman's hands. Like little claws, they were. Exactly as they had been all those years ago.

Afterwards, Ketch thought he ought to have foreseen what happened. Then he thought the doctor ought to have foreseen it, because this was Elizabeth Molland they were dealing with. Well, the doctor was dealing with her to be correct; Ketch would not have gone within a mile of the bitch, not even if she had been wearing the crown jewels or held out her hand and said, Come to bed.

She and the doctor had gone for a walk after lunch. That was perfectly normal. Ketch had not served the lunch, of course, and he had not cooked it, either. They had a female who came in for the cooking; she cooked lunch, left a ready to heat supper of some kind, and that was that. Today there was roast pork with apple sauce, and very nice too. Ketch had his in the kitchen. He did not care where he had it.

He followed them when they went off for their walk. This was what the doctor had told him to do. It was a nuisance to be pounding along on a hot day, but at least they did not walk very quickly. Whatever the Meade might have been in her younger days, now she belonged to the, I can't walk far, poor little me brigade. Load of balls to Ketch's mind; she was tough as snakeskin.

Still, he did as he was told and kept his distance, watching what happened. Was this the day the doctor was going to tell her who he was, and say, 'And so, my dear, unless you pay me what I ask, I shall have to tell people who you are and what happened twenty years ago?'

How much would he ask? How much would the murdering bitch pay to keep her secret quiet? Ketch wished he could hear the conversation. Meanwhile, he watched them.

There they went, climbing the cliff path together – the doctor would not like that very much. He would huff and puff like a stringy old grampus: his lungs were in a disgusting condition, Ketch heard him gobbing and spitting of a morning.

They were standing at the cliff top now, and the Meade was pointing out the waves of the sea, silly tart. She was waving her hands around, making stupid gestures. Ketch wondered if she might tip herself over the cliff edge, but she did not. What she did do was dislodge the stupid scarf she wore round her neck and squeak like a frightened virgin when the wind snatched it away from her. And then – he could not quite see how it was done – but one minute she was clawing the air for the scarf and the next she was clawing straight into the doctor's chest. Clawing at him? No, Christ Al-bloody-mighty, she was pushing him! The vicious bitch was pushing him over the cliff. Ketch began to run lumberingly forward.

He was too late, of course. The doctor went over the edge, in a spidery cartwheel of arms and legs, his mouth and his eyes round Os of sheer horror and disbelief, because this had not been how it was supposed to be – she was the prey and he, Denzil McNulty, was the hunter. Only the prey had rounded snarlingly on the hunter, and the hunter had gone smashing onto the rocks below.

And may God have mercy on his soul.

*

'I never knew the finer details of the McNulty murder,' said Mr Huxley Small, regarding his listeners. 'A London firm had dealt with the defence – I suspect Sir Lewis Caradoc engaged them and I suspect he paid their fees as well. He simply asked me to accompany him to see a remand prisoner in Holloway Gaol – perhaps he wanted a witness to the conversations, perhaps he simply wanted an objective observer. I never asked. The prisoner was Elizabeth Molland.'

'And so you met her?' said Chad.

'Oh yes. I first knew her as Meade, of course – Mrs Elizabeth Meade – but Sir Lewis told me she had been part of the infamous Fremlin trial in the thirties. They were hoping that would not come out, of course. Somehow it never did – probably because she had created such a complete new identity for herself.'

'But why did Sir Lewis get involved?' said Phin. 'Paying her attorney and all. I don't understand that.'

'He was involved already,' said Mr Small. 'He had helped Molland to escape from Calvary.'

'Lewis Caradoc helped her escape?'

'He did.'

'Why?'

'I think,' said Mr Small, 'that Elizabeth may have been a part of his past.'

'A mistress?' said Georgina. 'Or wouldn't the age difference be a bit too much?'

'A daughter?' said Jude. 'An illegitimate daughter?'

'That is one possibility,' said Mr Small guardedly.

'Did Elizabeth talk about Neville Fremlin while you were there?' asked Drusilla.

'Oh yes. Not on that first day – and not for a long

time. At that stage she still expected to be acquitted, so she was being discreet. Careful. And then, when she was found guilty she thought she would be able to appeal.'

'Was she finally hanged?' asked Chad.

'No, they sentenced her to twenty-five years in gaol,' said Small. 'It was only when she knew the appeal would not be allowed that she talked to us – to Lewis Caradoc and to me – about Neville Fremlin. She was astonishingly open. I recall,' he said, 'that afterwards Sir Lewis used a phrase I had not previously encountered. He said she was guilty of the murderer's vanity. He said it was something that all killers possessed.'

August 1958

Lewis Caradoc thought he had encountered the murderer's vanity in practically every man or woman he had seen hanged during his years in Calvary. But he had not expected to encounter it in his own daughter.

The years had altered her a great deal. The fair, fragile girl had become a ladylike, neatly dressed woman of forty. Even in the cell at Holloway Prison, Elizabeth Molland – now Elizabeth Meade – wore a cashmere twin-set with a pleated skirt, and good nylons. She had applied a little discreet make-up and her hair was immaculately arranged.

'I did think they would at least allow me a chance to appeal,' she said, having listened to the decision. 'But they are spiteful and jealous men, so perhaps I should not be surprised. I'm grateful to you, Sir Lewis, and to you, Mr Small for coming to tell me, though.'

It was Small who asked if there was anything they could get for her. 'Anything that would make life a little more comfortable?'

'Oh no, thank you. My boy will be able to bring me whatever I want. My life is over, of course. This place will be no life for me.' A quick gesture took in the bleak surroundings. 'All I really need are my memories to see me through the years in this place,' she said.

'Memories? Neville Fremlin?' Lewis had not known he was going to ask this, but she smiled at the words.

'I knew you would ask me that,' she said. 'Yes, Neville is one of the memories, of course. He was an opportunity that I saw and took when I was very young. I always did seize my opportunities – you knew that, didn't you, Lewis?'

Lewis . . . She knew quite well who he was by this time – Lewis had never told her but he was sure she had guessed – but she still used his name with that sudden soft purr.

'Is that all Fremlin was to you? Weren't you in love with him?' She'll say she was, he thought. And then I might be able to find some of what she did forgivable. (And justification for what I did that night, nearly twenty years ago?)

But she said, with incredulity, 'Of course I wasn't in love with him! How could I have been! I was twenty – he was nearly fifty!'

'Surely there was some degree of emotion, though? He forced you to do all those things. To help him kill all those women.'

She laughed. 'Oh, Lewis,' she said, 'let's stop pretend-ing. I don't need to pretend any longer really, do I?

You'll never be able to repeat this conversation, will you? We both know why.'

The memory of that rain-swept night forced its way to the surface again. Was she always this calculating? thought Lewis.

'And Mr Small is bound by professional secrecy – so you won't tell, will you, Mr Small? In any case, no one would believe you. So I can enjoy the luxury at last of telling someone that Neville Fremlin never forced me to do anything. It was the other way round. I was the one who killed them all and he was the one who tried to cover it up. I was the murderess,' said the lady in cashmere and pearls. 'And I enjoyed it very much.'

Lewis thought he must be mishearing or misunderstanding. Or she must be mad. Delusional. He said, 'Are you saying you were guilty all those years ago?'

'Of course I was guilty. I thought you knew that at the time. The court said I was guilty and they were quite right. I killed all those women.'

'But you did it under Fremlin's influence,' said Lewis. 'That was what everyone said. It was what most people believed.' Please let her say she was influenced by him, that she was mesmerized . . .

'Yes, I know it was what they all believed,' she said, smiling at him. 'Wasn't that fortunate for me?'

Lewis was unable to take his eyes from her. 'At the beginning, people thought Neville Fremlin had killed you. Your parents thought it.'

'I know. Well, I didn't know at the time, but I knew afterwards. I used to go into Neville's shop – I pretended it was to buy things, but really I knew he was fascinated by me, so I thought he might be a way of getting away from my parents.'

'Why did you want to get away from them?' It was so long since Huxley Small had spoken that his voice made Lewis jump.

'Because they were so dull,' said Elizabeth. 'Stuffy. They made my life so dull. There were rules and I had to keep them, and I found it boring. I was nineteen – twenty – and I wanted excitement. Of course,' she said, in the ladylike tones that were so bizarrely at odds with her words, 'of course, I have since learned better. But in those days . . . Anyway, I told Neville my parents thought I was visiting a cousin in Margate. I can't imagine why I said Margate, but for some reason it was the first place I thought of. So he thought it was safe to be together for a little while. You know, it is *so* good to tell someone all this,' she said again.

'Like the confessional of the Roman Catholic church,' observed Mr Small, and she turned to him smiling.

'Yes, of course. How clever of you to see that. Neville once said something very similar. It made me wonder if he might have followed the Catholic religion himself at some time in his life. Well, quite soon, I found that Neville hadn't got as much money as I thought, and I hadn't any money at all. That was dreadful – I wondered if I had made a mistake. I've always liked to have money.'

Memory unrolled again, and Lewis saw the younger Elizabeth's face look avidly at him when he said there was money for her to get to Ireland and begin afresh. In his mind he heard the younger voice, saying, 'How much money?'

It was Small who said, 'Money must always be honestly come by, however.'

'My money *was* honestly come by. I worked for it,' she said indignantly. 'When I realized Neville wasn't as rich as I thought, I worked out a plan to get money from somewhere else. From women – older women on their own. I had to go quite far afield to find them in case I was seen by people who knew me and I had to be particularly careful to avoid places where my parents might go, of course. But it wasn't so difficult. I got into conversation with women in teashops and on buses and things. I befriended them and I listened to them talking about their youth – how they had never married, or how their sweethearts were killed in the war. I mean the first war,' she said. 'Not this last one. It was very dreary listening to them, but I did it very well.'

She would have done it very well indeed, Lewis could see that. Those lonely women would have been pleased at the attention of such a pretty, well-mannered girl and they would have liked bringing out their sad memories to share with her. And then she had killed them. He said, 'But didn't Fremlin realize what you were doing?'

'Not until I told him.' She smiled at them, and again Lewis was aware of the murderer's vanity looking out of her eyes.

'I had five altogether,' she said. 'Five ladies I used to meet, all quite separately of course. All wealthy. I'd meet them for lunch or tea, or an afternoon concert. Eventually I suggested to them – still one at a time, you understand – that we took a boat trip on the River Nidd. I said there was a boathouse that hired boats and a man to row us. They all thought it was such a good idea – so nice of me to suggest such an outing. The boathouse had long since been closed up, but none of them knew that. It was a lonely place, that boathouse,' she said. 'And it was very dark and quiet inside.'

For a moment, the scene was dreadfully clear. Lewis could see the deserted boathouse, and he could smell the damp timbers and hear the soft lapping of the river. He could see Elizabeth – a much younger Elizabeth than now – crouching in the shadows, waiting for her victims. Or had she quite openly taken them inside?

'The boathouse was where you hid jewellery later on,' he said, his mind going back to that earlier trial.

'Yes, it was. There was a little cubbyhole near the door,' she said.

'And you killed all those women? Neville Fremlin's five victims?'

'I did,' she said. 'One by one. Quite close together, actually – in one case there was only a couple of days between, although by the time the police found the bodies in Beck's Forest, they were – well, it was no longer possible for the police to know exactly when any of them died.'

'No,' said Lewis, staring at her. 'No, that's something they never established.'

'They'd be able to know today, wouldn't they?' she said, as if considering an academic point. 'They have so many tests they make now.'

'How did you kill them?' said Lewis.

'The first two I strangled, using my silk scarf – I did it from behind and it took them by surprise. It was easier than I had expected, but they struggled a lot, so I stabbed the others through the base of the skull with a skewer.

Once each one was dead I took her keys and went to her house to take money and jewellery and so on.' She frowned, and Lewis saw she had almost forgotten her surroundings, and that her mind was back in the past. 'I managed to drag the bodies to the edge of the decking so that they'd be washed into the river,' she said. 'At least, that was what I meant to happen. The boathouse generally flooded in heavy rain so I thought all I had to do was wait for rain and everything would be washed away.'

'But it wasn't?' said Huxley Small.

'No. It didn't rain at all,' she said. 'Can you believe that in England! And the police were starting to be suspicious by then. Three of the ladies were regular customers at Neville's shop – that was how I met them – and the police were seeing that as a link. I began to panic. In the end I told Neville.'

'You told him what you had done?'

'Yes, I did. I cried a lot,' she said reminiscently. 'I said I had done a terrible thing – that I thought I must have been mad for a time – that I had been jealous of the women for having money when I had hardly any – I said all kinds of things on those lines. Then I asked him to help me and in the end he agreed. I knew he would; he would have done anything in the world for me.' There, again, was the soft complacency.

'He buried them for you?' said Lewis. 'In Becks Forest?'

'Yes. He made me take him to the boathouse – he said something about confronting the consequences of what I had done. I remember it was late afternoon – the days were already growing shorter and it was that half-light that plays tricks on your vision. We parked the car and walked along the river path. It was very quiet. I pushed open the door of the boathouse, and there they all were. Lying where I'd left them. Some of the faces were turned to the door as if watching for someone to come in and they were like things out of a nightmare by then – I've never forgotten how they looked. I remember there was waterlight from the river. It rippled over the walls, so that the dead faces looked as if they were moving.' She shuddered again, and then said, in a brisker voice, 'I don't think Neville believed me until then – he just stood in the doorway and his face was absolutely white. But he made me go away while he dealt with it all. I stayed at an hotel in York – I liked York,' she said. 'And Neville took the bodies out of the boathouse one at a time over the next couple of weeks. I think he had to take at least two of them back to his shop to get rid of their clothes and wedding rings – everything that might identify them. He left intervals between the trips in case anyone noticed him coming and going – he was clever like that, you know.'

'Yes,' said Lewis. 'Yes, I know he was.'

'Once he came out to York to tell me what he was doing. He talked to me for hours that night. He said he didn't believe I was really wicked, but people sometimes did bad things in their lives especially when they were very young. You got in the grip of a strange madness; he said when he was young he had been in the grip of madness for a time.'

O'Kane's traitorism, thought Lewis. Did she really never know who he was? But he thought she had not; he thought she had always been immensely self-centred.

'Neville said the important thing was to recognise that you had been wicked and mad, and do what you could to put it right,' said Elizabeth. 'Do good in the world if you could – sort of atonement. I told you I thought he was once Roman Catholic, didn't I? Oh, and he said never to make the mistake again and never to let the madness in again. So I cried some more and said I was sorry and I really did think I had been mad, and then I talked about entering a convent to – what do they call it? – to purge my soul of the sin. I thought he'd like that. But I think by then he knew the police were watching him,' said Elizabeth. 'He had sold the jewellery for me, you see. *I* couldn't go into horrid pawn shops to sell the stuff or into sleazy secondhand jewellers'. So Neville did it. And if there was money – actual cash – he put that in his bank. I didn't have a bank account. Females didn't in those days – at least girls of twenty didn't.'

'He kept the money and the jewellery?' asked Huxley Small.

'Not at first. He had some silly idea of trying to find the families of the dead women. I told him they hadn't had any family: that was why I picked them,' she said. 'Then he decided to give the money to charity, although I expect I'd have persuaded him to keep it if they hadn't arrested him. The police found the bank entries or deposits or whatever you call them. That was all very incriminating indeed.' She looked at them. 'Then they caught him burying the last of the bodies. Are you wondering why he took all the blame for me?' she said.

'I can just about accept that a mother might go to the gallows for a child, or even a brother for a beloved sister,' said Lewis slowly. 'But Fremlin only knew you for a few months.'

'It wasn't completely for me,' she said, and Lewis thought, so she's not quite as self-centred as I believed. 'Neville thought he deserved to die for whatever it was he did when he was young. I didn't really understand and I don't understand now. But I do remember that on the night before they arrested him, he sat up all night, talking to me. There had been lots of police questions and interviews by then, and he thought they would charge him and that he could end up being hanged. But he said it would be a – what did he call it? – a rough justice. I think it's a quotation or something,' said Elizabeth. 'He liked quoting things. He said he deserved to die because he had been responsible for the deaths of a lot of young men in the Great War. He had sold information to Germany or something, and because of it ships had been sunk. I said if he felt so guilty why didn't he just confess, but he said it was very complicated – there was somebody out in the world he wanted to protect. Personally,' she said, 'I thought he was being ridiculous. I still think so.'

Lewis said, 'Come back to the present. Tell me about Denzil McNulty?'

'There isn't much to tell. You know it all, don't you?'

'Why did you kill him?'

She looked at him as if he might be mad. 'He threatened to tell the world who I really was,' she said. 'To – what do they call it? – to blow my cover. My beautiful comfortable life that I had created over the years would have been in tatters. My boy's life would have been utterly ruined.'

'So that's why you killed McNulty. To stop him from talking.'

'Of course that's why I killed him,' said Elizabeth.

CHAPTER THIRTY-NINE

Vincent was surprised to answer a knock on his door just after lunch, and to find two policemen there. A detective sergeant, it seemed, and an ordinary constable. Might they come in and have a little word with him?

Once inside, the detective sergeant said a disturbance had taken place at Calvary the previous night. 'You'll have heard about it, I daresay? News travels in a small place like this, doesn't it?'

'Indeed I have heard about it, Sergeant. Dreadful, I thought it.' Vincent had in fact gone out and about quite early that morning, specifically to find out if the news had yet got round. He had bought groceries in the supermarket and a newspaper at the newsagents', and he had gone into the post office for stamps. By midday everyone was talking about what had happened, so he felt perfectly safe in admitting to knowing about it, and to asking how he could be of help.

'It seems,' said the detective sergeant, 'that Dr Ingram

and his assistants put a camcorder inside Calvary last night.'

'My goodness,' said Vincent, but an icy hand had closed around his stomach.

'We've watched the footage – Dr Ingram was very helpful in passing it over to us – and there's a figure on it that isn't part of his team. A man went into the execution chamber last night, and shut the gallows trap – we understand Mr Stratton was down there at the time, as part of the programme.'

'Mr Stratton?'

'Mr Jude Stratton.'

'I don't know him.'

'The thing is, Mr Meade,' said the sergeant, 'the figure on the film has been identified as being you.'

'How ridiculous,' said Vincent. 'Who made the identification?'

'Miss Georgina Grey and Mr Huxley Small. I daresay you know Mr Small acts as police solicitor in most cases, and he's seen the film. And so procedures being what they are, we have to check it all. Perhaps you could tell me where you were last night?'

Vincent decided the best approach to this was to adopt a slightly high-handed, bluffly tolerant tone. He said he had been quietly at home all evening. No, there was no one who could confirm that. No, no one had called or phoned. A rather quiet life he led, you see.

'Do you have a key to Calvary, sir?'

'Of course not,' said Vincent at once. 'And really, if you're going to take any notice of some half-baked film—' He gave another of the little laughs, inviting them to share the nonsense with him.

They did not share it. The constable made a note in a pocketbook, and the two men got up to take their leave. 'I daresay you won't be going anywhere for a few days, will you? We may want to talk to you again.'

'I am at your disposal,' said Vincent.

After they had gone he replayed the interview over in his mind. He was not inclined to be at all worried. There was nothing they could prove, and he had conducted himself extremely well.

'I wasn't very impressed by him,' said the detective sergeant as they walked back to Thornbeck's little police station. 'Were you?'

'He struck so many poses you couldn't tell which was real and which wasn't,' said the young PC.

'I wouldn't mind having another go at Vincent N. Meade,' said the sergeant. 'There's something wrong somewhere. I wouldn't mind getting a search warrant and seeing if we can find that key, as well. But I suppose he'll have chucked it into the nearest lake by the time we did that.'

'If he is guilty of something, we'll get him one day,' said the PC.

'Elizabeth died in Holloway Gaol,' said Huxley Small to his listeners.

'I don't think I can find it in my heart to feel sorry for her,' said Jude drily.

'No, indeed. Lewis Caradoc told me he spent the rest of his life regretting what he did on the night he got her out of Calvary. He felt he had – well, foisted a killer on society.'

'He really did fix for her to escape?' Phin was clearly finding this part difficult to believe.

'Of course he did,' said Jude. 'He thought she was Trilby to Neville Fremlin's Svengali. They all thought it. She fooled them all.'

'But in the end, she never really did get away with the first batch of murders,' said Chad thoughtfully. 'And so her son came to Thornbeck.'

'Yes. He was only in his early twenties then, but I recall him telling people his mother had known Thornbeck briefly as a girl,' said Mr Small. 'He said it was somewhere he could feel close to her.'

'The part of Thornbeck she had known was Calvary, of course,' said Georgina. 'And that was what he was trying to keep secret.'

'Yes. And he did keep it secret, you know. I only realized who he was – that he was Elizabeth's son – because I had met her,' said Small. 'And by the time I had made the connection, Vincent was already the Caradoc Society's secretary.'

'Difficult to dislodge,' said Jude.

'There was no good reason to dislodge him. Being the son of a killer was not sufficient a reason to demand his resignation. He was doing a fair enough job of the secretaryship.' Small paused and looked at Georgina. 'Miss Grey, Denzil McNulty tried to blackmail Elizabeth Meade, we know that for certain. It occurs to me that blackmailers seldom stop at one victim.'

Georgina looked at him blankly.

'Lewis Caradoc was the man behind Elizabeth's escape from Calvary in 1939,' said Small, 'but Walter Kane was the prison doctor at that time.'

'You think he might have been involved?'

'I don't know. But if so . . .'

'The Caradoc legacy,' said Georgina. 'That's what you mean, isn't it? You think Denzil McNulty found out something discreditable about Walter – perhaps that he had helped a murderess to escape – and so Walter had to pay him to keep quiet.'

'It would fit the case,' he said, and Georgina again had the tantalizing sensation of being within reach of the past but not being quite able to grasp it.

'McNulty, according to the reports, was a fanatic about his involvement in the Caradoc Society. It's my guess he would have stopped at nothing to further its aims.'

'Did you know him?' asked Chad.

'I met him briefly a couple of times. A thin sallow man he was, humourless and absolutely driven by his investigations into psychic phenomena. There was little else in his life, in fact.'

'I don't like the sound of him at all,' said Drusilla. 'And if he blackmailed Georgina's great-grandfather, I'm very glad he got his come-uppance at Elizabeth's hands.'

'When was the bequest made?' asked Chad. 'Georgina, I'm sorry if I'm going into your family's privacy.'

'There's nothing private about any of it,' said Georgina at once. 'It was 1940, wasn't it, Mr Small?'

'January 1940, Miss Grey. The wording was a bit ambiguous, but it's all perfectly legal.'

'Just before he left for the war,' said Georgina. 'I wonder if you're right about the blackmail, Mr Small. It wouldn't explain why he abandoned his wife and daughter, but—'

Huxley Small said, 'But your great-grandfather was never married. I thought you knew that.'

This was the last thing Georgina had expected. She stared at Small. 'Are you absolutely sure?'

'There are no absolutes in law, Miss Grey – at least not in that sense. We traced you through your grandmother, as you know. We just looked through the various registers for people with the name Kane who were born between 1940 and 1950. The internet,' said Small surprisingly, 'is extremely useful for this part of our work these days. Your grandmother was Caroline, born in 1941.'

'Yes.'

'She's listed as being the daughter of Walter Kane and of a Catherine Kerr. But we didn't find any marriage certificate for them, and the fact that the certificate only gives the mother's maiden name is significant,' said Small, 'although not conclusive, of course.'

'Walter and Catherine might have been married abroad,' said Jude, 'or under some arcane religion not recognized in English law. Georgina, are you sure you haven't got any papers of any kind for your grandmother?'

'No, nothing.' Georgina was beginning to wonder if she was related to Walter at all. She said, 'I don't know a great deal about any of them. My mother died when I was in my teens, but she talked once or twice about her mother – my grandmother.'

Chad said, 'Phin, this is one for you. See what you can find about Catherine Kerr and Caroline Kane, will you?'

But Phin had already started a new page in his notebook and was enthusiastically scribbling the names down.

If Catherine Kerr could be found, he would find her. Not through the dusty road of ancient files and mildewed church registers or cobwebby memories, but through the sharply modern route of computer screens and keyboards, and the spidery web of the internet.

January 1940

Walter sometimes thought that when he was able to look back on these months, it would be Elizabeth Molland he would remember most vividly.

This was curious, because although Elizabeth Molland ought to have been a secondary player in the drama surrounding his father – although Walter himself had only met her those few times – she remained strongly in his mind. He wondered if he would ever be able to ask Lewis Caradoc where he had taken his daughter that night.

The cold whiteness continued to enclose Thornbeck for most of January and when, towards the end of the month, Walter left Lewis's house and returned to Calvary, he saw that it enclosed Calvary as well.

But although he had recovered from the frighteningly abrupt fever and weakness, everything seemed unreal. He moved through the days like a mechanical toy, and all the while the knowledge that Nicholas O'Kane and Neville Fremlin were one and the same person drummed relentlessly in his mind. A traitor and then a murderer. Walter thought he had just about accepted the man who had sat in the condemned cell twenty years earlier, and who had talked about dying for a dream and whose eyes had burned with fervour and defiance, but he could not accept the urbane killer who had sat in that same cell a second time.

He was grateful when he was notified that he had been seconded to the army's medical corps; a rank of captain had been assigned him and he would be required to report for duty in the first week of February.

'I expected it, of course,' said Higneth, when Walter told him. 'You're not one to stay in this backwater when there's fighting going on.' He regarded Walter with a sort of sad resignation. 'I'd better see about getting a replacement for you, Walter, although I'd have to say whoever he is, he won't be as good.'

Walter said, hesitantly, 'You won't be considering McNulty, I don't suppose?'

'No!' It came out with startling violence.

Walter looked at him for a moment, but only said, 'Well, if I can help with choosing a replacement – perhaps interview applicants for you – I'd like to do so.'

'That would be very valuable indeed,' said Higneth with unmistakable sincerity.

'I'm glad you're not letting McNulty back in,' said Walter after a moment, and then wondered if he had stepped over a line, because Higneth's expression was suddenly angry. Was there something he was missing? Surely McNulty could not have worked his blackmail on Higneth? Surely Higneth had never done anything to lay himself open to McNulty?

But then Higneth said, in an ordinary voice, 'No, there's no possibility of McNulty coming back.'

As Walter left the office, he was aware of a slight lifting of his senses. I'm going to be free of McNulty, he thought, and I'm going to be able to shake off the memories of this place. I'll be hundreds of miles away – France to begin with, and then who knows where? – and the danger will be different danger. I'll find a way of severing the links and I'll forget about Nicholas O'Kane who cheated the gallows and then came back to them as a mass murderer.

But it seemed Nicholas's history was to deal him one last blow.

'So you're leaving Thornbeck, Dr Kane,' said Denzil McNulty.

'I am.' In the cold light of the January morning, McNulty looked sallower and thinner than ever. Walter thought he had the appearance of a man burning up with his own passions. 'I'm leaving for France in two weeks,' he said.

'So I hear. Then,' said McNulty, 'I dare say you will want to put your house in order before you go. To pay all debts, for instance.'

'Everything's in order and I have no debts,' said Walter shortly.

'My dear boy, it's a fortunate man who can say that with complete truth,' said McNulty. 'I'm sure, if you think back a little, you'll recall one debt that was never paid.'

'I owe nobody anything.' Walter felt a tightening of his stomach.

'No?' said McNulty. 'What about the payment to me? The payment for my silence about your part in the Molland girl's escape? You slid out of the original agreement very neatly, didn't you, but—'

'We never had an agreement,' said Walter angrily.

'Even if I hadn't been taken ill, I would never have allowed your inhuman experiment on Parsons! But you did it anyway, didn't you?'

'Edgar Higneth was a very useful ally,' said McNulty in an oily voice, and Walter thought: So there *was* something between them.

'I am writing a paper on the experiment,' said McNulty. 'I shall present it anonymously, of course, and neither Calvary's nor Violet Parsons' name will appear. But I think it will be known, in a discreet way, that I was the one behind it all.'

He's revelling in this, thought Walter. But he'll get his come-uppance one day. I just wish I could be the one to deliver it to him.

'You know, Walter,' said McNulty, 'I think the real crux of all this is your father. You don't care very much if the truth about Molland comes out. But you can't bear people to know your father was Nicholas O'Kane. And I can't say I blame you. It's something that might ruin you very thoroughly indeed, isn't it?'

The doctor who turned a blind eye to the escape of a convicted murderess. It was not something that could ever be proved, but it was indeed something that might stick very firmly. McNulty was right about that. He was also right when he said it was the truth about Walter's father that he really flinched from – although the irony was that McNulty did not know the full extent of that truth. But stir up the old stories about Nick O'Kane, and someone at some point might see a likeness between the two men. Lewis Caradoc had said Nicholas had made use of other people to create his new identity. Papers had been provided – a birth certificate, perhaps other things.

Some of those people might well still be alive – still in England. It could all come tumbling out, thought Walter, appalled. It really could. Oh God, what do I do?

McNulty sensed the hesitation, of course, and he pounced, not heavily or fumblingly, but with a precision that a part of Walter's mind could not help admiring. He said, 'They're both bad secrets to have, aren't they, Walter? Elizabeth Molland and Nicholas O'Kane. A man would want to distance himself from those two as much as possible. He'd want to break all the links leading back to them.'

A severing of the links, thought Walter. Remarkable he should use that phrase.

'I believe,' said McNulty, 'that when Nick O'Kane was sentenced to execution, he made sure his only son inherited his estate.'

Nicholas O'Kane's estate. The money that had come to Walter when he was twenty-one. The money his mother had seen as being drenched in her husband's treachery. 'I should see the drowned faces of all those young men you betrayed . . .' she had said that day, and Walter had never forgotten it.

The money was in the form of bonds and investments, and although it would have been quite an attractive sum in 1917, it was not so very large now. It had paid for Walter's medical training and it had bought that bouncy little car in which he had first come to Calvary. Other than that he had not touched it. He had wanted as little to do with it as possible.

The money was the last sad, shameful link to those twin evils, Nick O'Kane and Neville Fremlin, and Walter thought if it was the price he had to pay for Denzil

McNulty's silence, he would pay it and feel better for it.

He looked at McNulty very steadily, and said, 'Would a Deed of Gift meet the case?'

'It would.'

'To the Caradoc Society?'

'What else?'

What else, indeed, thought Walter. The man's a fanatic, but I suppose there's a symmetry about handing over Nick's money to him – to his Society. Lewis's Society. He could not decide if the fact that Lewis Caradoc's name headed the Society made any difference. Probably it did not.

He said to McNulty, 'It must be understood that there will never be anything more between us. This is a once and for all payment. You can threaten me until hell freezes but you won't get anything else – not money, not favours, not blind eyes turned to bizarre death experiments – nothing.'

'I understand.'

I'm severing the link for good, thought Walter, going about the unfamiliar process of transferring his father's money to the Caradoc Society. There's a symbolism in this. I'm repudiating everything about my father. He need never appear in my life or my thoughts or my memories again. And one day McNulty will get his come-uppance, I'll keep believing that.

Once in France, his whole energy devoted to the appalling injuries inflicted by war, Walter thought less and less about the past. He did not dare think about the future – he had no idea if he would live to see it, and he had no idea if the people he worked alongside – the other doctors, the chaplains and nurses – would see it either. He would have been sorry to see any of them killed – they were loyal hardworking comrades – but there were one or two he would have been devastated to lose. One or two. One. One in particular . . . She had grey eyes rimmed with black, and when she was moved by something they became very clear and shining.

'I have a vision,' he said to her. 'And it's of you and I having dinner in London on my next leave. A civilized dinner – a good restaurant. Good food and perfumed air and wine.'

'And candlelight,' she said, smiling, so that the grey eyes shone. 'I'd like candlelight.'

'I'll arrange the candlelight as well,' said Walter. 'I'll light up the whole of London with candles if you'd like it.'

'I don't need the whole of London,' she said. 'Just you, Walter.'

'We'll survive to eat that dinner, Catherine.'

'Oh yes.'

He was to think, a long time afterwards, that at least the image he had of Catherine to carry with him through the years after her death was the image she would have liked.

He had taken her to the Hungaria – Sir Lewis, appealed to for somewhere to eat in war-torn London where the food and service were still reliable, had re-commended it and had even known the head waiter. Walter was given a quiet corner table and attentive service. In the candlelight Catherine's eyes had had the clear glowing look of deep happiness.

They had talked and talked, because there might not

be time for them to talk in the future and because this was only a seventy-two hour leave for Walter who was being posted to North Africa. And then after dinner, because there might never be time in the future and there might not be a future for either of them, they had gone back to the flat Catherine shared with two other nurses, who were away, and there had been candlelight again, this time in the little bedroom overlooking a quiet London square.

'We're making memories,' she said to him in the rose and gold dawn, shortly before he left. 'They'll last a long time, these memories.'

The memories were made up of shining grey eyes and candlelight and wine ... of the scents and sounds of midnight filtering through a partly open bedroom window, with thin curtains moving slightly in a soft summer wind ...

It turned out that all Walter would have of Catherine would be those memories because a year later, when he was still in Tobruk, news had come that her Red Cross post in London had been bombed, and a letter came saying so sorry to report, so dreadfully sorry to tell him Catherine Kerr had been among those killed.

CHAPTER FORTY

Vincent had played and re-played the police interview, and he was confident they had accepted his word. In any case, he had nothing to be worried about. No one knew what he had done at Calvary that night.

No one knew, either, what he had done over forty years ago, on that afternoon in the bleak cell where they had taken Mother.

August 1958

She had submitted to the cruel jealousies and plots of the men in court – the men who had hated her and wanted her to be punished.

'I have had to suffer jealousy for most of my life,' she had said to him in the horrid grey room where they had kept her throughout the trial. 'And now, because a stupid old man tumbled off a cliff, I have to suffer this. He was an impostor, Vincent, you do know that, don't you? A man who had known me in my sad youth, that was who he was. A man who would have liked to have his revenge on me. Well, they shall not know about any of that, I can promise you. What happened to me all those years ago is nothing to do with anyone and I believe I have distanced myself from those years. I believe I can keep that sad part of my life closed. Remember, Vincent, if anyone asks you, that you know nothing about my girlhood. No matter what it costs, you must never know anything.'

Vincent had promised, but in fact he had been asked very little by the police and he had not been called to give evidence in court. If he had, he would have protested Mother's innocence. A friendship with the man they said she had killed, he would have said. An innocent friendship, embarked on out of the goodness of Mother's heart. She had a kindliness for old, lonely bachelors. Where was the harm? As Mother said to him, if the silly bumbling old fool must needs fall off the cliff it was nothing to do with her.

But the cold-eyed men in the court and the envious women on the jury had thought it was very much to do with Mother and they had said she must be put in prison.

Prison! Vincent had been horrified and filled with panic. Prison for the gentle unaware woman who had always wanted to surround herself with beautiful things – who had liked roses and porcelain figurines and silk dresses. Iron bars and locked doors and communal showers with concrete floors. Squalid lavatory arrangements in a cell shared by two or three women. Mother would never endure it. Vincent would never allow her to endure it.

No matter what it cost.

In the end she had to endure it for three months, which was the length of time it took for bewildering things such as visiting orders to be arranged, and arrangements to be made to travel to Holloway itself. Vincent managed to find rooms to rent in a narrow, mean, house fairly near the gaol. The house smelt of cooking and cigarette smoke and of the people who lived in the basement and who seemed to live on fiercely spicy curries. Vincent put up with it because Mother would be putting up with far worse than this.

He put all the things from the Southend house – the house they had shared – into storage, taking only his clothes and a few books and private papers. But there was one other thing he took, and that was the packet of digitalis tablets that had belonged to the Bournemouth major. They were quite old and they might not work, but they could be tried. If they did not work, Vincent would think of something else.

They did work. The entire plan worked very well.

Visiting took place in a big ugly room, where you had to sit opposite one another at a small table. Mother wore a shapeless apron, which enabled the warders to see she was not being given drugs by her visitor and sliding them into a pocket. Under the apron she wore her normal clothes: a cream silk blouse and a brown skirt. Vincent saw the jealous looks of the other women.

'Spiteful,' said Mother. 'They are a spiteful lot of women, Vincent. I expect you can see that for yourself.'

Vincent saw it very clearly. He saw, as well, how things were arranged on visiting days, and that cups of tea were available for the visitors, but that there was particular vigilance for those who drank them.

'Drugs,' said Mother, shuddering. 'That's what they watch for.'

But they did not particularly watch Vincent, and before the third visit he carefully crushed up the digitalis tablets. It was easier than he had dared hope to conceal the powder in his handkerchief and sprinkle it in the tea his mother drank. Vincent had said a cup of tea would be welcome after his journey here, and Mother agreed to have one as well, to be companionable.

'Dreadful tea,' she said. 'Always so strong. Quite bitter.'

The strong, bitter tea, had an almost immediate effect. She frowned, and then put a hand up to her throat as if it was suddenly difficult to breathe. Vincent glanced over his shoulder to see if they were being watched. Yes, the nearest of the warders had turned to see if anything was wrong.

Mother half rose from the table, clawing at the air. The colour drained from her face leaving it pinched and grey. She fell forward, gasping, and within four minutes she was dead.

There was an inquest, of course, but although the digitalis was found, an open verdict was recorded. It was fairly clear to Vincent, sitting haggard-faced in the public gallery, that the coroner thought it was a case of suicide, and that Mother had managed to come by the digitalis in some underhand way. It was also clear that there was pressure from higher up for the coroner not to record a verdict of suicide. Suicides in prisons were not liked; they meant internal investigations, possibly sackings, trouble and bad publicity. Far easier all round to let it be thought the prisoner had mistaken an ordinary dosage or had mixed up some innocent pills with that of another inmate. Sympathy was extended rather perfunctorily to the family of the deceased.

Vincent, thankfully leaving the sleazy rooms near the prison, making arrangements to get Mother's things out of storage and buy a nice little house of his own, was glad to know he had been able to release her. Four minutes was very quick. He would think of an appropriate inscription to go on her headstone. She would have wanted a suitable epitaph.

November 1958

'They've managed to hush it up very well,' said Lewis Caradoc to Walter. 'Just a small paragraph in the newspaper.'

Walter said slowly, 'And so the woman really responsible for all those murders – the woman who was your daughter and who caused my father to go down as one of the century's most cold-blooded killers – died ingloriously in a prison cell in Holloway Gaol.'

'She did. But the thing to remember above all the rest,' said Lewis, 'is that your father was innocent. He was *innocent*, Walter. He believed Elizabeth was worthy of a second chance, and he died in her place.'

'One day,' his father had said, 'you might understand

me a little better.' He wanted me to know, thought Walter. He hoped that one day I would find out.

He looked at Lewis. 'Was it for Elizabeth he died, or because of what he did in 1916? I think I might find myself grappling with that one for a long time.'

'I don't know the answer to that,' Lewis said. 'Perhaps he didn't know himself by then. But myself I think it was for 1916. Elizabeth said he talked about rough justice, and quoted the words of some Irish poet to her – she hadn't bothered to remember the words, but I know what that would have been and so do you.'

Walter said, half to himself,

'Know that we fools, now with the foolish dead
Died not for flag, nor king, nor emperor,
But for a dream, born in a herdsman's shed,
And for the secret scripture of the poor.'

'Yes, of course I know. He quoted it to me when I was very small. I think it was that kind of emotion that drove him.'

'He was a dreamer and a visionary,' said Lewis. 'Even though his dream was misguided and people died because of it. But later on he saw what he had done and he tried to make amends. Don't forget he studied pharmacy – he must have been in his thirties by then, Walter, and it couldn't have been an easy path to take. Maybe he saw it as carving out a new life and as a way of helping people. It's a branch of medicine, after all.'

'I told him I wanted to be a doctor,' said Walter. 'On that last day of his life – on what I thought was the last day.'

'It may have had something to do with his own decision. You'll never know that, but it's possible. It's something to hold on to. That and his innocence. You could perhaps mount some kind of campaign to get his name cleared.'

'Could I? But it would rake up so many things.' Walter did not say, And it would drag out all the facts about Elizabeth, but he knew they both thought it. He knew it was why Lewis and Huxley Small had agreed not to report the conversation they had held with her that day. She would be in prison for most of her life in any case, Lewis had said. 'If we requested a review of the sentence – presented the new evidence – they might change the twenty-five years to the death sentence. And I can't do it to her, Walter. She's a monster, but I still can't do it to her.'

Walter had understood this, and he said now, 'I want to let the past go and focus on the present.'

'Good. The house in Switzerland?'

'Yes, that's one of the things.'

'It looks a beautiful place, unless these photographs are a complete lie.'

'It is beautiful. I keep putting off signing all the papers and contracts, though. It just feels so far from everything.'

'It's as far as a three-hour flight,' said Lewis. 'Walter, if it's a question of money—'

'It's not,' Walter said at once. 'I'm very well paid by the Swiss clinics.'

'And you're doing very good work.'

'I like it. I didn't expect to end up doing this, but it came mostly out of that stint I did with MacIndoe immediately after the war. He's done such remarkable work, you know: patching up the bodies and faces of the airmen who were burned or smashed up. We use a lot of his techniques at the clinics. They're starting to call some of the procedures cosmetic surgery now,' said Walter, 'which makes it sound a bit shallow and vain, but we get a lot of burns victims and there are more people from car crashes now than ever. And deformities. Lewis, there are people with deformities or injuries who endure the most appalling lives. I had a lady last month who hadn't been out of the house for about ten years because of a huge birthmark on her cheek. We didn't entirely remove it, but we made it acceptable. She cried when she saw the result. Last week she wrote to tell me she had been to a restaurant for the first time in her life. It's so very satisfying to be able to help people like that.'

Lewis, listening with interest, said, 'You still have passion for your work.'

'Yes.'

'You look tired, though. It's not all work, I hope. What about the other kinds of passion?'

'I work most of the time, but I don't always live like a monk,' said Walter smiling. 'But there's never been anyone I've wanted to marry. Not since Catherine. I wish there had been time to marry her – even one of those scrambled wartime marriages.'

'I wish there had, as well. If I'd been at hand, I'd have done the scrambling for you.'

'It wouldn't have saved her from that wretched bomb,' said Walter. 'But it would have – this sounds stupidly romantical – it would have linked us for always. It would have linked us in the eyes of the world, as well. I don't care much about that kind of thing, but I'd like to have had things straight with her family. They wouldn't speak to me afterwards, you know. They wrote to tell me what had happened, but it was the barest details. I wrote to them a number of times, but they never replied. I'd have liked to share some of their memories. Things they would have known about her that I never did – her childhood and things like that.'

'Because sometimes,' said Lewis thoughtfully, 'one's own memories aren't quite enough, are they?'

Phin said, eagerly, 'I've found her.'

They were assembled in the Caradoc House flat. Chad and the others were preparing to leave the next day; Georgina, whose ankle was almost healed, had been helping Chad make notes from Walter's Execution Book.

Phin had run all the way up the stairs, carrying his laptop with him. He was festooned with notes and printouts, and his face was pink with delight and exertion.

'Who have you found?' said Georgina. 'Sit down. Drusilla's making coffee.'

Phin said he would have about ten litres of coffee, please, on account of he had been up all night, and was zonked. He did not look at all zonked, in fact he looked hugely delighted with the world.

He was given his coffee, and sat at the little gateleg table with Torven's dramatic purple slopes behind him, and assumed a scholarly air.

'I found Catherine Kerr,' he said, and Georgina felt as if a corner of the mystery had finally been peeled back, and that if only she could be careful and gentle, the whole picture might eventually be revealed.

'She died in 1942,' said Phin. 'See, a lot of authorities have websites now, with all the birth, marriage and death stuff listed. It took a bit of tracking down and I spent ages following up ones that turned out not to fit.' He looked at Georgina, pushing his glasses back onto his nose. 'I'm not absolutely one hundred percent copper-bottomed certain this is your great-grandmother,' he said. 'But it fits so well that I think it must be.'

'Yes. I see,' said Georgina. I'm being so cool and so controlled and objective, she thought, when really I know quite well this *is* my great-grandmother he's found. Walter's wife or girlfriend or whatever she was to him.

'Catherine was born in 1918 in London,' said Phin. 'And she died in 1942, again in London. The cause of death is given as "crush injuries to chest".'

'Bomb victim probably,' said Jude after a moment. 'It was the height of the air raids.'

'That's what I thought,' said Phin, pleased at this confirmation of his own idea. 'And her profession is given as nurse. That would go well with Walter, wouldn't it? I mean, he'd have met nurses in his work.'

'Yes, of course.'

'So then I went after her daughter,' said Phin. 'Caroline. That was a bit more difficult, because you had her as Caroline Kane, Georgina, later married to someone called Grey. But Mr Small had her as Caroline Kerr. So I looked for all three surnames. I found the birth registration in 1941 – Caroline Kerr – and I found the marriage to Alaric Grey in 1961. But I sort of wanted more. I wanted to link her with Walter. I thought you'd want that as well,' he said to Georgina. 'So I thought, well, what do people do in their lives. Specifically, what do they do if they might have a father living abroad.'

'The Swiss house Walter bought in the early fifties,' said Georgina. 'Oh God, yes, of course.'

'Yes. I'd got those notes from the boxes of stuff Mr Small gave you, so that meant I had the Lucerne connection. So I started on the airline companies,' said Phin. 'The lists of travellers from London to Lucerne any time after about 1951. There weren't so very many for that time – air flight was in its infancy, really.'

Georgina dug her fingernails into the palms of her hands. She glanced at Jude and saw he was listening intently to Phin, with the now-familiar tilt of his head. She thought she would have given a great deal to have been able to exchange a quick look with him and then realized, with a sudden spiral of pleasure, that she did not need to exchange a look; he knew exactly what she was feeling.

Phin said, 'A lady called Caroline Kerr is listed as travelling to Lucerne on 10 September 1960.' He looked at Georgina. 'I'm really only guessing now, but I think—'

'That it was the first time Walter met his daughter,' said Georgina.

July 1960

Sometimes memories aren't quite enough, Lewis Caradoc had said.

The letter came on a sun-drenched morning towards the end of a summer's day. At first Walter thought it must be some kind of sick joke, then he wondered if it was a very artful confidence trick and a request for money would be involved. You heard about such things: doctors were as good targets as the rest of the population, and Switzerland had long been known as a place for dodging the payment of tax or other dues. He read it again, more slowly, looking for flaws and inconsistencies. This time a cautious delight began to unfold deep inside him, because if only it were true . . .

I've only just discovered your existence, and I probably wouldn't have done so if I wasn't about to get married and had to ask my grandparents for a copy of my birth certificate. That was when they admitted you hadn't died in the war, as they had always led me to believe, and that as far as they knew you were still alive. This is the last address they had for you, so I do hope it reaches you.

The first thing I have to say is going to sound a bit absurd, and like something out of *East Lynne*, but I've also found out you didn't know about me. My mother, it seems, never told you in case you felt some obligation to marry her. My grandparents, in turn, never told me, because of the Shame.

But here we are, at the start of a new decade – the nineteen sixties – and nobody worries much about Shame any longer – I certainly don't. If you hate the idea of meeting I'll understand, but if not, and if you feel you could bear to see me, I'll be on the first available plane.

I should say that I don't think you would have regarded marrying my mother as an obligation at all. My grandparents filled me up with some very odd tales about you, but I don't believe more than about a tenth of them and I'd like to make up my own mind.

I won't send my love – not yet – but I'll hope very much to hear from you.

Caroline Kerr

PS I've enclosed a photograph of myself, so that you can see what you might have inherited.

The photograph, when Walter carefully unwrapped it from its extra layer of packaging, might have been taken twenty years earlier, on a sweet scented night in a London flat.

After a long time, he hunted out the sole photograph he had of Catherine and sat looking at it.

It's going to be all right, he said to the photograph. I'm going to meet her. I can even start to hope that Caroline's children – and her children in turn – get some good things from you: charm, a sense of humour, resilience.

And grey eyes that shone like polished silk when their owner was happy.

CHAPTER FORTY-ONE

September 1960

As Walter waited for Caroline on the seat at the end of his garden – his favourite spot in this house – his heart was beating so fast that if he had heard it in a patient through a stethoscope he would have been alarmed. I'm not ready for this, he thought. But when would I be ready? Catherine, why did you never tell me there was a child? Why did you never say so in any of your letters? Didn't you know you could have trusted me? Or was it your parents who persuaded you to act as you did?

He heard the sound of a car pulling up in the road, and his heart rate revved up even more. I don't know what to say to her, he thought. She's nineteen, that's all. Caroline . . . I like that name. I'm glad Catherine chose it. But she won't understand. She'll see me as some horrid old roué who seduced her mother and then vanished. What did they tell her about me, those disapproving grandparents who took her in when Catherine died?

But she wrote that letter to me, he thought. She said she would be on the first plane if I wanted, and although it isn't quite the first plane, it isn't far off. This is going to be dreadful. It's going to be awkward and false and she'll wish she hadn't come. I'll have to go up to the house now; they'll have let her in and shown her to the guest room, but I'll have to be there.

He did not move, though, and when he heard the quick light footsteps coming down the path towards him he stayed where he was. Incredulously, hardly daring to believe, he saw it was not going to be awful and it was not going to be false or wrong. She was not quite Catherine, but she was so near that Walter felt as if his dear dead love had reached out a hand and said, 'You see? *You* should have trusted *me*.'

Walter's daughter – Nick O'Kane's granddaughter – stopped and looked at him, and then said in a rush of emotion, 'It's all right, isn't it? I wasn't sure if it would be – all the way here, I was so nervous . . . I kept thinking it could go wrong . . . But it isn't going to go wrong at all, is it?'

'No,' said Walter. 'No, it isn't going to go wrong.' He held out his arms to her.

'I like to think those two did meet,' said Georgina to Jude, as they sat in the corner of the restaurant near Jude's flat. 'Caroline and Walter. Phin found so much information, and we got dates and things about it all, so it looks more than likely. She travelled to Lucerne in September 1960 – Walter died two months after that if Phin's dates are right.'

'I should think they are. I think he'd be very reliable about research.'

Georgina thought so as well. She was pleased that they all seemed to be staying in touch – Drusilla had asked if Georgina might be available as a freelance to consult about set dressing. The networks had their own people, she said, but quite often freelance designers were called in.

'When's Chad's programme due out?' she said, as the food was put in front of them.

'Spring next year, hopefully. It'll depend on the schedulers. I'm glad he went ahead with it – I was afraid at one point he might not,' said Jude. 'He got a bit more than he bargained for with this. Oh, and did you know they're trying to squeeze out a budget for the spin-off on Neville Fremlin. Phin and Drusilla are very keen to do that.'

'That would be good, wouldn't it? Will they be able to d'you think?'

'You can never tell. They might have to see how the Calvary thing is received. Unfortunately, in television it's nearly always down to the ratings.' He found the wine glass and drank, replacing it on the table with the familiar careful smooth movement. 'Georgina, getting back to Walter, it's deeply sad that he didn't see more of his daughter, but I'm thinking he was probably very happy to have met her.'

'If Phin's Caroline is the right one,' said Georgina, 'and I think she is, I might have the explanation I wanted.'

'About the money?'

'Yes.'

'You think McNulty really did blackmail him?'

'Yes, I do.'

'I think you're right. Because if Walter did help Elizabeth Molland – Meade – to get out of Calvary, it would have laid him wide open,' said Jude, thoughtfully. 'We'll probably never find out what kind of amount was involved or where the money came from—'

'Maybe it was an inheritance or something,' said Georgina. 'I'm only speculating, though.'

'Speculating's half the fun of research,' said Jude. 'So let's say that did happen. And for most of his life he thought he had no family – no one to leave money to. And then quite suddenly there was a daughter—'

'And he probably wanted to make a will in her favour – there was the house in Lucerne, wasn't there? – but he died before he did so. He might have died without any warning, as well, of course.'

'Or been too ill to even think about it.'

'Yes. I might be fitting the facts into a pattern I want,' said Georgina. 'But it seems credible to me.'

'It seems credible to me, as well,' said Jude.

'They've got a buyer for Caradoc House – did I tell you that? Some geological society who'll use it as their headquarters. Quite a good price, according to Huxley Small.'

'Shall you be disgustingly rich as a result?'

'No,' said Georgina and smiled. 'But a bit more solvent than I've been lately.'

'Enough to keep the design business going on your own?'

'I think so.' Georgina had not yet dared to look at this

possibility in detail, but she thought it was very hopeful. Especially if Drusilla had meant it about freelance television work.

'I'm glad,' said Jude. 'Will you come and see my flat quite soon and fling all kinds of dramatic colours around? Carpets and curtains and whatnot?'

'I'd love to. Lots of vivid emerald greens and peacock blues,' said Georgina.

'Good God, is that how you see me?'

'I think it's how you see yourself.'

'You're too perceptive for my comfort.'

The restaurant was small and attractive. Georgina had held Jude's arm as they went to their table, but from there he had simply said to the waiter, 'Would you read the menu out to me?' listened carefully, and appeared to have committed it to memory. When the wine was brought, he said, 'I'll have to leave it to you to pour it out; I'd better not risk sloshing it over the tablecloth. I'll bet it's white damask, isn't it? Yes, I thought as much. But we've got candlelight, haven't we?'

'Yes.'

'Don't smile like that – I know you're smiling because it's in your voice. I wanted candlelight for some reason I can't logically explain. I just like to think of you in that light. It's the grey eyes; I'm rather keen on grey eyes.'

'The candlelight's lovely,' said Georgina. 'And I've worn black to emphasize the grey eyes.'

'I like that as well,' he said. He held out his hand and Georgina took it.

December 1960

Walter thought that after all there were different kinds of happiness, and that this was a happiness he would never have expected.

After Caroline went back to England, he was aware of an almost overwhelming fatigue, but in a curious way it was a very restful fatigue, as if he had finally ceased to struggle with a task that had been almost more than he could bear. He had not yet got used to the knowledge that he had a daughter – that a part of Catherine lived on.

A daughter. Caroline. She was being married next spring to a man called Alaric Grey – he was something to do with the Slade, something to do with fabric design. Caroline had shown Walter a photograph of him, and Walter had seen that Alaric Grey was good-looking and had kind eyes and a generous mouth, and he had looked at Catherine's girl and thought: they will have such attractive children, these two. Will they have Catherine's beautiful grey eyes? Will I see them, I wonder?

He was still on leave from the clinic, although there was a list of patients waiting for his return. For the moment he could not focus his mind on them; he could only focus his mind on the past. That's an old man's habit, he thought sharply. You're barely fifty. You've got years ahead of you. Good years.

But he did not think he had so very many years. The menacing lurching within his heart had happened a number of times now; he supposed he would take the tests to see what was going on there, but he did not really need to take any tests. He thought he knew.

Not so many years left. Yes, there was the pain again. A vicious tightening around the chest. Unmistakable. Ah well.

Until it came again, it was good to sit in this well of deep happiness and of lassitude, and to think of the children that might be born in the future. Children who might have Catherine's grey eyes and who might hear about the notorious mass murderer, Neville Fremlin, but who would not know he was their ancestor. It did not really matter, not now. After all, what did ancestors matter?

CHAPTER FORTY-TWO

'I know ancestors don't matter, not really,' said Georgina, opening the door in Calvary's outer wall. 'And I know I'm being impossibly romantic. But I just feel it's a place that has a link to Walter. And it's something I want to do.'

'It's remarkable how different this place feels in the middle of the afternoon,' said Jude. 'I can tell it's sunless and a bit neglected, but I'll bet if you put a stone seat in and a couple of statues—'

'And an oriole window in the mortuary wall?' said Georgina.

'Don't laugh at me, you heartless wench. I was trying to conjure up an Oxford quadrangle.'

'Jude, it's a dank dismal graveyard, and I shouldn't think anyone comes here except Mr Small on his yearly inspection.'

'In that case why did you bring the laurel bushes?'

'Well, because I think there's just about enough light here for them to take,' said Georgina.

'That's not what I meant.'

'I know it isn't. I can't explain. I just feel I'd like to mark Neville Fremlin's grave. Just to show he's remembered.'

'To show he was innocent of all those murders – and that the only thing he was really guilty of was trying to cover up for Elizabeth?'

'Yes, that, as well.'

'The grave will make a good photograph for a book jacket,' observed Jude.

'Are you really going to write a book about him? About the whole Fremlin/Molland thing?'

'Yes, I am. It needs writing. I'd like to have it ready to coincide with Chad's programme – they're mounting quite a good publicity campaign on that, he says. Masses of trailers, and hopefully some of those viewers' choice teasers in the TV listings. But I don't think it'll be possible, not if I'm going to do the subject justice.'

'I'm glad about the book,' said Georgina. 'I think you'll do it well.'

'I hope so. It's odd, but I feel a – a sort of obligation to put the record straight for Fremlin.'

He paused, and Georgina said, very carefully, 'The image you saw in the execution chamber—'

She stopped, and Jude said, 'Say it.'

'You think it was Fremlin, don't you?'

'I don't know. It'd be a bit too neat, wouldn't it? The restless ghost haunting the place where he was wrongly killed – I'm not that much of a romantic, Georgina.'

But you'd like to think it was Fremlin, she thought. And you'd like to think your book will clear his name. I'd like to think it as well.

In a deliberately casual voice, she said, 'All this – the book, the TV programme – it'll all stir Vincent N. up a bit, won't it? Because it will mean the truth coming out about his mother.'

'I'll be very discreet about that,' said Jude, 'and so will Chad. It might be possible to keep her just as Molland, without bringing the Meade name in at all. But from the sound of it, Vincent's a very tough person – he was just about prepared to kill to keep his secrets, remember? That takes huge toughness. How are you getting on with the plants?'

'It's done,' said Georgina, setting down the small trowel. 'It looks quite good. I wish you could see it, Jude.'

'I wish I could as well. But I know it's there.'

'Shall we walk round the walls?' said Georgina standing up and depositing the trowel in her haversack. 'The car's around the front. But the sun's gorgeous, even though it is nearly December.'

'Yes, let's. D'you mind taking my arm? I left the stick in the car.'

'I don't mind at all.'

'To guide my steps,' he said. 'Is that a nuisance? Would it ever be a nuisance?'

'It might be at times,' said Georgina. 'I might lose my temper – you're not the only one who does that. But in a general sense, no it wouldn't be a nuisance at all.'

He drew her hand through his arm, and closed his free hand over it. 'I hate the fact that I shan't ever see you. But I can just about tolerate that if you can.'

'I can,' said Georgina.

'You're smiling again,' said Jude after a moment.

'Yes.'

'It's a very happy smile, isn't it?'

'Yes,' said Georgina. 'Yes, it's very happy indeed.'

Vincent had made a huge decision. He was going to leave Thornbeck, and he was going to do so quickly. He had not liked the sly questions of the police, and he had not liked the way people glanced sideways at him as he went about his day. Inquisitive. Even a bit jealous. The more he noticed it, the less he liked it.

Oddly, the prospect of leaving Thornbeck was not as daunting or as unhappy as it might once have been. Places ran their course for you in your life, he knew that from Mother. Thornbeck had run a very long course for him – the best part of forty years it had been – but he thought he had a good few years still ahead of him. He would make a niche for himself wherever he went. There would be all kinds of opportunities for an unattached gentleman, who was not rich but who had a modest private income left to him by his mother.

He had come to Thornbeck because of Mother, of course, but somehow she was no longer here. So he would sell his house and go somewhere he was quite unknown. He toyed pleasurably with all the things he might still do, and all the people he might still meet. He would look for somewhere peaceful, perhaps in the south of England this time. A small community was best; a nice village with a lively social life. He would look out the maps presently. And he would go quietly and without telling anyone, so people would be surprised and wonder what had happened.

'Vincent Meade,' they might say. 'Bit of a mystery man in the end. Always thought there were hidden depths there. Daresay we'll never find out what happened.' They might even say, 'Didn't the police try to trump up some kind of charge against him? Whatever the charge was, it was dropped. Shouldn't think anyone believed it. And that television chap seems to have got his knife into him as well – something to do with that programme about Calvary; bit of jealousy there, if you want my opinion . . . Interesting chap, though. My word, he'll be missed around here.'

The police had not precisely dropped the charges – they had left them on file, whatever that meant. But Vincent was not going to worry about it.

He was not going to worry about anything Dr Ingram and the rest might have turned up about Mother, either. He thought he could be pretty sure the programme on Calvary would not be made – not after the spanners he himself had put in the works! People becoming trapped in the lime store, and only being rescued by sheer good fortune! For a while he had been worried his plan had failed, but now he looked at things calmly, he could see he had very subtly put a stop to their activities.

Vincent was as sure as he could be that Calvary, with all its secrets, would be allowed to slip back into obscurity. And it was not very likely that Mother's name and her legend would surface in any other part of England; it was not as if people were going to be publicizing any of it or writing books or anything of that kind.

But it was not out of the question that someday,

somewhere in the future, Vincent would find himself confronted with Mother's ghost again. If so, he might find himself once again working out a plan to keep her memory sweet and good and untainted.

He would do so, of course. He had made that promise to her. He would do whatever it took.